SWEET REVENGE

The reckless and dashing nobleman was in love with the most glamorous young woman in London, elusive temptress Melia Melchester. When she spurned him for another man, Lord Brora craved only the joy of revenge.

Then chance showed him the way to humble Melia's arrogant heart and win her back again.

He would turn his typist into an enchanted Cinderella and flaunt her delicate beauty before all fashionable England — **as his fiancee!**

It was a flawless plot, destined to succeed miraculously . . . until the plotters fell into a **different kind of love-trap!**

Also in Pyramid Books
by
BARBARA CARTLAND

NO HEART
IS FREE

Barbara Cartland

"I have no peace, the quarry I,
A Hunter chases me,
Who can escape? No heart is free
From love . . ."

— *Eastern Poem*

 PYRAMID BOOKS   •   NEW YORK

NO HEART IS FREE

A PYRAMID BOOK

Pyramid edition published November 1972

Copyright © 1969 by Barbara Cartland

All Rights Reserved

ISBN 0-515-02845-2

Printed in the United States of America

Pyramid Books are published by Pyramid Communications, Inc.
Its trademarks, consisting of the word "Pyramid" and the portrayal
of a pyramid, are registered in the United States Patent Office.

Pyramid Communications, Inc., 919 Third Avenue,
New York, N. Y. 10022

CONDITIONS OF SALE

1

As Tally turned his car into Chesterfield Hill he saw
Melia going in at the door of No. 96. He noticed that she
was wearing the bright red coat and feather-trimmed
cap over which they had exchanged a few words a few
days earlier.

"Why do you want to dress yourself up like a post-
box?" Tally had demanded with less tact than usual.

Melia, who had been very pleased with her new winter outfit and was not inclined at the best of times to
stand criticism from Tally, had been annoyed.

"I have been much admired in it," she said, turning
round as she spoke to get a better view of herself in the
long, gilt-framed mirrors which decorated her mother's
large and usually overcrowded drawing-room.

"I don't doubt that," Tally had retorted. He knew
that Melia would be admired whatever she put on, for
she was at the moment the vogue and everything she did,
said or wore became the fashion overnight. Nevertheless, his dislike of the red get-up had persisted. It was
flamboyant! Somehow he felt that the colour was too
noisy and cheapened the beauty of Melia's much
photographed heart-shaped face and big dark eyes. But
he knew that the more he said the more he was likely to
antagonise Melia. She liked her own way, did Miss Melchester, and what was more, she was not going to stand
criticism from any of her young men, least of all from
the one on whom she had finally bestowed the favour of

her affections. "Love me, love my coat," Tally said to himself ruefully as he drove up the hill and drew up outside No. 96.

The door was shut—the big ponderous wrought-iron door outside which so many young men had kicked their heels despairingly waiting and longing for the elusive Melia. Tally switched off the engine of his car and had begun to unravel his long legs from among the controls when a voice at his side said:

"Buy a bunch of white heather, guv'nor; it'll bring you luck."

Tally turned to make an immediate gesture of refusal, caught sight of the face of the man who was bending down to offer him the heather, and smiled, even as the man ejaculated:

"Gor blimey, if it's not the Major! How are you, sir?"

"All right, thank you, Simpson," Tally said, getting out of the car, "but what are you doing?"

The man, a squarely-built, ugly looking fellow, dropped the piece of white heather into a tray full of similar pieces which he held under his left arm.

"I didn't know it was you, sir, or I shouldn't have spoken. I don't like you to see me doing this."

"I am sorry to see you doing it," Tally said. "Can't you get anything better?"

"Had a run of bad luck, sir," Simpson answered confidentially. Then, looking up into Tally's sympathetic eyes, he added with a sudden burst of honesty, "Well, it hasn't all been bad luck. I got a couple of jobs, but I didn't keep them."

Tally said nothing, but something in his bearing must have shown that he understood, so Simpson went on:

"You know what it is, sir, everything seems so tame after what we have been through. Bored, that's what I am! You know as well as I do we didn't want to drink when things were happening, but now it's different."

There was silence for a moment, before he added almost pleadingly:

"You understand, don't you, sir?"

"Yes, I understand," Tally replied, "but it is no use,

Simpson, those days have gone. We had a lot of fun, and we had hard times, too."

"We did an' all, but they was worth it," Simpson replied. "Do you remember that trip to Le Touquet, sir? Lor, I can see those Jerries' faces now when we walked into the Casino! And the time we smashed up that radar station? Coo, that was a night, that was! I can see you now dealing with three of them, and all three as dead as mutton by the time you had finished with them. Ah, those were the days!"

"Yes, I know, Simpson," Tally said, "but they are over and we have got to face it. We have got to settle down . . . all of us. It is not easy, I know that, but it is no use going to pieces. You never know, we might be needed again."

"Do you think we might, sir?" There was a sudden light in Simpson's face.

"Who knows? The world is unsettled enough; but if we are wanted, it will be the same story over again. We shall not want weaklings or those who have dissipated their strength."

Tally spoke deliberately, but he did not look at Simpson. He had opened his cigarette-case and was choosing a cigarette, but he knew the man had stiffened, his shoulders had gone back and his chin stuck out.

"You're right, sir, and I wouldn't have you leave me behind."

"Listen, Simpson, did you know I had started an advice bureau to help our chaps find the right sort of jobs?"

"No, sir, I hadn't heard anything about it."

"Well, I have. I tried to circulate you all, but some of you had left no address. Here's a card. Go along to 190 Dover Street tomorrow morning and tell Miss Ames, who is my secretary, that I sent you. She will find you a job that is worth doing, and then, Simpson . . . it is up to you."

The man drew himself up.

"I shan't let you down, sir, you know that."

"Yes, I know that. Good-bye, Simpson."

7

Tally held out his hand. The other man gripped it and there was something hard and resolute in the handshake, something, too, of the comradeship which had been more than a brotherhood all through the war. For the men who had served under him Tally had shown an affection which was not translatable into a language of peace. He smiled at Simpson. As he turned away, the man mechanically saluted, then turned and walked smartly down the street.

Tally watched him go. He remembered him well. A good lad, but somewhat of a scallywag with Irish blood in him. At times he had had to be restrained from almost imbecilic foolhardiness, but he had come through unscathed while wiser and better men had fallen. Tally sighed and chucked the cigarette he had just lighted into the gutter. It was a gesture as if he would discard his own thoughts of the past. What was the point of harping back? The war had been over for two years. Better forget it. The past was past. He must concern himself with the future.

He reached up, pressed the electric bell fiercely and impatiently. It was some moments before the door was opened slowly, almost it appeared reluctantly, by the grey-haired butler who had never, in Tally's experience at any rate, been known to smile.

"Good afternoon, Oakes," Tally said, and made as though to step into the house.

"Miss Amelia is not at home, m'lord."

"Oh yes, she is. I saw her come in a few minutes ago. You must have been having forty winks in the pantry or you would have heard her."

"I am sorry, m'lord, but Miss Amelia is not at home." Oakes' tone was so serious that Tally, who was pushing past him, stared at him in surprise.

"Good heavens, Oakes, I believe you mean it. Are you telling me in polite language that she is not at home to me?"

"If you like to put it that way, m'lord."

"Well, I'll be damned!"

Tally looked angry, then he laughed.

"What is it all about, Oakes? Come on, be human for once. Is she angry with me, or something?"

Oakes paused as if he were considering, and then in a tone which if not human was slightly less aloof, said in a low voice:

"As a matter of fact, m'lord, there's a letter for you. Miss Amelia informed me it was to be sent round to your Club over two hours ago, but I have not been able to obtain a messenger and no one in the house would oblige by taking it."

"A letter for me? Well, hand it over and let's see what it says."

From the depths of a pocket beneath his coat tails Oakes produced an envelope. It was large and blue and ornamented with Melia's large and distinctive handwriting.

"Now, what have I done?" Tally inquired as he took it.

"Perhaps it would be wiser, m'lord," Oakes suggested, "if you took it back to the Club and read it there."

"In other words, you want to get rid of me. Not on your life; I will read it here, and if I can give you an answer right away it will save me a postage stamp . . . or rather a telephone call."

Tally slit open the envelope with his finger and drew out two closely written sheets of paper. Then, regardless of Oakes' obvious discomfort, he leaned against the doorway and commenced to read.

At that moment the telephone bell began to ring.

"If you will forgive me, m'lord . . ." Oakes said.

"Run along and answer it," Tally replied, "and you can shut the door, I'm in a draught."

Obviously discomfited by Tally's persistence, Oakes, after hesitating a moment, finally did as he was bid and shut up the front door, leaving Tally inside, and hurried away to answer the telephone.

Tally read the first page, started on the second, and then with a sudden exclamation which was not unlike a roar of anger he threw his hat down on the chair and

9

went up the stairs two at a time. He flung open the door of a room leading off the first floor landing with a decision and speed which was reminiscent of the tactics he had used in the war. In fact, he entered the room with the suddenness and noise of a small typhoon.

Melia Melchester, who had been sitting on the sofa, started to her feet with an exclamation of surprise. There was no doubt indeed that she was a very pretty girl. She had taken off the red coat and feather cap which had annoyed Tally and was wearing a slim black dress which clung to her figure and showed to advantage the whiteness of her skin. Her dark hair was parted in the middle, and her eyebrows, as so many infatuated young men had told her, were like two delicate wings above the liquid beauty of her eyes.

"Tally!" she exclaimed. "How you startled me!"

Tally pushed the door behind him with a bang and walked across the room. He, too, was extraordinarily good-looking, with his lean brown face and wiry athlete's figure, but Melia was at this moment obviously too agitated to consider Tally's good looks. One white hand with its long red finger-nails rose as if to quell the tumult of her breasts, while with the other she supported herself against the back of a chair.

"I told Oakes to say I was not at home."

"Yes, I know," Tally replied, speaking for the first time, "but I want to know the meaning of this."

He held out her letter as he spoke, the blue paper rustling in his fingers.

"I thought I had explained myself very clearly," Melia replied.

"I want to know what it means," Tally repeated.

Melia took a deep breath and then, as if she were no longer frightened, she looked away from Tally and turned towards the fireplace.

"Tally dear," she said gently, "it is no use making a fuss. I am sorry, but I do not want to marry you."

"Why not?" Tally's question came out like an explosion.

"Because . . . well, because——"

"Because of what?" he asked imperatively.

"Well, there are lots of reasons, Tally dear, and it is no use your getting angry with me."

"Now look here, Melia . . ." Tally said, walking over to the fireplace and standing towering over her, "I have known you ever since you were a horrible squalling baby in a pram——"

"I was nothing of the sort," Melia said sharply.

"Yes, you were," Tally retorted, "and don't interrupt. What I was going to say was that I have never known you do anything unless you had a very good reason for it. If you want to break off our engagement, then you have got a reason for it and I want to know what it is."

"But why must I have a reason for everything?" Melia asked.

"Because you always have," Tally replied. "When I saw you the day before yesterday, you were perfectly happy to be engaged to me. What has happened in the meantime?"

"You thought . . . I was perfectly happy . . ." Melia corrected.

"What has happened in the meantime?" Tally persisted. "Who have you seen?"

Melia turned away.

"Come on, Melia, out with it!"

"Now listen, Tally, I don't think we should be happy if we married each other. I have explained that in the letter."

"You have explained nothing. You have drivelled a lot about our not getting on together, etc. None of which tells me anything. Damn it all, Melia, you know I love you."

Melia's expression softened for a moment.

"Yes, I think you do, Tally," she said, "but it is no use. I do not love you enough . . . not for marriage, anyway."

"Melia, it was only on Saturday that we were talking about putting the engagement in *The Times* and planning the actual date of the wedding. I had to go to the country yesterday to see my mother, otherwise I would have been with you. What did you do yesterday?"

Melia made a gesture of impatience, then suddenly clasped her hands together.

"Don't be difficult, Tally, please don't be difficult."

"I am not being difficult," Tally said sharply. "Really, Melia, you would try the patience of a saint. What I am trying to get at is what has changed your mind since Saturday?"

He tried to hold her gaze, but she moved from the fireplace over to the window. There she stood drumming her fingers on the pane and looking out on to the paved courtyard at the back of the house.

"It is no use, Tally, I won't discuss it," she said at length.

"You will," Tally said grimly. "You can't just chuck me over like that and not tell me the reason."

"I have told you, Tally, I don't want to marry you, and I would be grateful, yes, very grateful, if you would leave me alone. . . . I hope we shall always be friends."

Tally was just going to reply when the door was opened by Oakes.

"I beg your pardon, miss, but Mr. Danks is on the telephone from the House of Commons and would like to speak to you."

"Tell him Miss Amelia is out," Tally said sharply before Melia could reply.

"No, no, Oakes, don't say that," Melia said quickly; "tell Mr. Danks that . . . that . . . I will ring him up in a few minutes . . . I . . . I cannot speak now."

There was something in her hesitancy and the colour which suddenly came to her cheeks which roused Tally's suspicions. As Oakes shut the door, he wheeled round to her.

"What is all this? Good lord, Melia, you don't mean to say it's that chap Ernest Danks. You must be mad!"

"That's quite enough, Tally. Ernest is an extremely clever young man; in fact he will be, and at any moment too, the new Prime Minister."

Tally stared at her as if she had taken leave of her senses. He crumpled up her letter, which he still held in his hand, as if the action gave a relief to his feelings, and flung it across the room. Then he thrust his hands into his trouser pockets.

"So that's it," he said. "You're going to marry Ernest Danks. Well, I'll be damned!"

"Now, please, Tally, it's a secret for the moment. As you know, the Prime Minister is dying; it's only a question of hours. It would not be a moment for . . . for . . . Ernest and me——"

"I understand." Tally's voice now was very quiet. So quiet that Melia stared at him in surprise.

"I understand," he repeated. "I never believed that you really cared only for publicity. I thought there was something better in you than all that craving for notoriety, but apparently I was mistaken. Good-bye, Melia, and I hope you will be very happy with your Prime Minister."

Tally turned on his heel and went from the room. This time he did not slam the door but shut it gently behind him and went down the stairs one step at a time. He let himself out at the front door, got into his car and drove slowly away.

Men who had served with Tally in the war would have told Melia that in this mood Tally was at his most dangerous. Naturally buoyant and exuberant, when he was quiet and constrained it meant that he was angry and that he was planning how to avenge himself.

Tally drove round the park and as he went he thought of Ernest Danks—a man who had risen into political prominence in the last two years. He was clever, there was no doubt of that, but Tally, who had met him on several occasions, had thought him both self-opinionated and a social climber. Apart from the fact that it would be quite natural for him to be in love with Melia, it would be to his advantage to marry someone who could help him socially and from a financial point of view. Melia was rich; no one knew this better than

13

Tally whose estates marched side by side with her father's.

It had been suggested in their very cradles that he and Melia should get married. It was the obvious thing—two only children, two big land-owning famiies—only Tally the schoolboy had not been interested in girls. But Melia had grown up while he was at the war and he had come back to find her the acknowledged beauty of three seasons and the most sought-after young woman in London.

Tally had sauntered back into Melia's life with the conquering ease of an old friend and acknowledged suitor. To his surprise he found that Melia had very different ideas. In fact, she had shown him that he had no special place in her affections or her circle of admirers. This had put Tally on his mettle, for in the six years of war he had been trained to believe that nothing was unconquerable and that it was always possible to achieve victory through Commando tactics.

He concentrated on Melia as he had concentrated on planning a raid. He was just as successful. Melia surrendered and promised to marry him. Now that he had thought everything was arranged he had received a setback. He had in the last few weeks come to believe that Melia was really very fond of him. True, she was not a very demonstrative person, but Tally had asked her often enough and believed her when she said that she did love him. Now he felt not only disillusioned but foolish.

There had been no secret about their engagement. All their friends knew about it. It had only been a question of time before the proper arrangements could be made for their wedding.

Tally thought of the comments that would be made. "Poor old Tally," people would say. "But then, after all, a Prime Minister, a young one at that, is a better catch." He could see from Melia's point of view what a triumph it must be. It must be years since anyone married a Prime Minister. He could imagine the sensation it would cause. They would be married in Westminster Abbey.

14

The House of Commons would be there and the Lords. Perhaps even the King and Queen. How Melia would enjoy all that!

He thought of the avid interest she had taken in the references in the gossip columns to their own impending engagement.

"It is rumoured that the engagement will shortly be announced between the beautiful Miss Amelia Melchester, daughter of Sir Charles and Lady Melchester, and Lord Brora, whose brilliant exploits during the war . . ."

Melia had cut them all out and they had been pasted into her press-cutting books, big volumes bound in pale blue leather and embossed with gold. Well, Tally thought, she would have enough cuttings if she married Ernest Danks. He ground his gears in a sudden fury, turned his car and sped back through South Street towards Chesterfield Hill, then as he got there he changed his mind. Arguing with Melia was not going to do any good, he had got to think things over first; he had got to plan his attack, to work out a scheme.

He drove slowly, turned the corner and passed the house, but he would not stop. It was as he turned that he saw a taxi draw up at the door and Ernest Danks get out. He was a dark cadaverous-looking young man wearing the politician's inevitable black hat and carrying the inevitable dispatch case. He paid the taxi-driver and walked up the steps of No. 96. As he did so, the front door opened and Melia appeared. She had been waiting for him, Tally thought, and saw her hold out both her hands in welcome. It was that which both hurt and infuriated him, the gesture of Melia's white hands being held out to Ernest Danks.

He drove away, angrier than perhaps he had ever been in his life before.

"If the fellow were really attractive, I could forgive her," he told himself. "But if he were not going to be Prime Minister, she wouldn't look at him."

He knew that for the truth just as he knew that Melia

15

Melchester and Ernest Danks would have nothing in common save perhaps a consuming ambition to be in the public eye.

Tally drove his car across Berkeley Square, up Hay Hill and into Dover Street. He looked at his watch and saw it was after six o'clock. The office would be closed. No matter, he would go there for a moment and give himself time to think. He wanted to be alone. Several of his friends would, he knew, be waiting for him at White's. He had got to have some sort of story to tell them. He had got to collect his thoughts and his shattered pride.

His office was on the first floor. It was not a big place, but already it had served its purpose. Hundreds of men had come up those stairs despondently and gone down with a lilt in their bearing. A Commando was not always an easy man for whom to find a job. Being a tough guy in war did not always make an easy or pleasant employee in Civvy Street. But Tally knew how to talk to them and to get the best out of them now, just as he had got the best out of them when they had had to make an attack. There had been failures, of course, a few who were really unemployable, but for the rest it had merely been a case of finding a square hole for a square peg.

He had been lucky in having Miss Ames to help him. She relieved him of a great deal of responsibility and she had also had a lot of experience in the handling of men. Often when Tally failed to make a man amenable, to make him show the best side of himself to a prospective employer, Miss Ames succeeded. She had also an almost dog-like devotion for him personally and Tally was glad she was not going to be there at this moment. She would have seen that there was something wrong with him. He was, however, quite safe. Mary Ames left the office sharp every evening as the clock struck six. She had a train to catch to Peckham, where she looked after an invalid mother. Nothing short of an earthquake would persuade her to be late.

Deep in thought, Tally walked through the outer of-

16

fice. The typists' room was empty. Miss Ames' desk was covered with a sheet of newspaper. It was her usual procedure before leaving so that the cleaners in the morning should not untidy or disarrange her papers. There was a faint musty smell in the room of gas, paper, glue, of tea, indiarubber, and of the cheap Virginian cigarettes invariably smoked by the callers. Tally did not notice it. He was absorbed by his own problems; and kicking over a waste-paper basket as he passed and spilling its entire contents on the floor, he opened the door of the inner office which led to his own room.

It was only a small place, but he had it furnished more like a sitting-room than an office, with two big comfortable leather chairs in front of the fireplace and on the walls several sporting prints which he had brought up from his home in the country. His desk of polished mahogany was by the window. He seldom sat at it, but it was used by Miss Ames when he was out when someone wanted to talk particularly privately.

Tally entered the room and he was so sure of finding it empty that for a moment he was quite startled when at the sound of the door opening there was a convulsive movement from the desk. He stopped and stared, for raising her head from her arms, on which she had obviously been sobbing abandonedly, was a young girl. For a moment Tally did not recognise her, then he remembered that he had seen her before. One of the typists in the outer office had left to get married and Miss Ames had told him that she had engaged another. As he looked at the white tear-stained face staring at him in startled horror, her words came back to him, "She is very young, I am afraid, but girls are very hard to get these days and we must just hope that she will shape well." He had not paid much attention at the time as all such matters were left in Miss Ames' capable hands. Now he wondered if she had made a mistake.

The girl was hurriedly getting to her feet.

"I am terribly sorry," she faltered. "I came in here to bring some papers."

Her voice was very low and muffled from weeping.

"That's all right," Tally said. "I am afraid you are upset about something."

"I am sorry, terribly sorry . . . it was silly of me . . . I . . . I . . . did not expect anyone so late."

She arranged the papers on the desk and turned towards the door. She wiped her eyes with a ball of a handkerchief which Tally realised was already soaked with tears. There was something very young and pathetic about her. Instinctively, because he hated people to be unhappy, Tally attempted to be consoling.

"Look here," he said, "if something is really wrong, can't I help you?"

"No, thank you, and please forgive me for coming in here . . . It was stupid of me . . . but . . . I had a shock and——"

"I understand," Tally said soothingly. "Look here, sit down a moment. You look very white, you might faint."

"No, I am all right . . . really."

The girl was edging towards the door but Tally was alarmed by her pallor. He could see, too, that her hands were trembling.

"Don't go," he commanded. "I insist that you sit down. Now be a good girl and do what you are told. Don't argue! I have got something here that will make you feel better."

He went to the cupboard and opened it with a key which was always attached to his watch-chain. There were several bottles there. He always had a drink ready for the old friend who dropped in to see him and for the men who found it hard to talk without something to loosen their tongues. He scanned the bottles uncertainly. Whisky did not seem very suitable; then he remembered there was a bottle of brandy at the back of the cupboard. He pulled it out and put a little into a wineglass, adding a dash of soda.

"Drink this," he said.

"I couldn't, really I couldn't," the girl protested.

"You do as you are told."

Meekly she obeyed him. The spirit made her gasp for

a moment and then she drank it down as a child would drink medicine. Her eyes watered, but she smiled.

"Thank you, it is . . . rather drastic, isn't it?"

"Some people enjoy it."

"It is certainly warming, thank you so much."

She sat on the edge of the chair as if poised for flight.

"Now relax," Tally told her, and poured himself out a whisky-and-soda.

He shut the cupboard and sat down on the other chair.

"What is the matter?" he asked.

"I must go now," the girl said uncertainly.

"Why? Does time matter so very much—at the moment?"

She looked at him.

"No, you are right! I don't suppose it matters one way or another. I don't think anything matters."

There was a break in her voice.

"What has happened to upset you?" Tally asked kindly. She hesitated and he sensed that she was anxious to confide in someone. It wouldn't matter much who it was. Something had happened so overwhelmingly, so overpowering, that she felt afraid and lonely.

"I have . . . had a letter," she murmured at last.

"It usually is a letter," Tally said sympathetically.

"Oh, it is very kind of you to be interested, but it has . . . upset me. You see, it was from the man I thought I was going to marry and now . . . well . . . he doesn't want to marry me any more."

Tally stared at her.

"Why not?" he asked.

"He is going to marry someone else."

"I seem to have heard this story before," Tally said half to himself, and then quickly in case she should misunderstand him he added, "Go on, tell me more."

"It will sound silly to you, but I had planned everything . . . my whole life . . . round getting married. I had thought of it for a very long time . . . it seemed the only thing to do, the right thing . . . Oh, in fact, everything I wanted in the future. Now I do not know quite where I

19

am. I have got to start all over again. It is like being left alone in the middle of a desert. I don't know where to begin . . . or which way to go."

She clasped her hands together, the knuckles went white, and Tally could see she was fighting against a fresh outbreak of tears which threatened her self-control. He said nothing; after a moment she went on.

"I was so glad when I got this job here. It was better money than I had got anywhere else, but also Miss Ames seemed so kind and the work was so interesting. I wrote to the man I thought I was going to marry and told him all about it. His letter must have crossed with mine."

Her voice faltered and stopped.

"What is your name?" Tally asked.

"Jean . . . Jean MacLeod."

"You're Scottish?"

"Yes, I come from Glendale."

"Oh, do you? I know it quite well. It's not far from my own place in Scotland. My uncle used to have a beat on the salmon river. What made you come South?"

"Because I wanted to make enough money to have some decent clothes, to be married with something of my own. If I hadn't been so proud, I would have been married by now."

"Perhaps it will turn out for the best," Tally said, not because he thought so but merely because it was the conventional and almost mechanical thing to say. The words sounded ineffective to his own ears and he added, "But why doesn't he want to marry you?"

"He has found someone better," Jean MacLeod said. A sudden sob in her voice. "Someone more important. I know the girl. She meant to get him and she has succeeded. Well, they are welcome to each other. I wish I could show them that I didn't care. What I hate is their all being sorry for me, knowing that he has thrown me over for her. It means that I can never go back, never, with everyone commiserating with me that another girl has taken my man while I was away. You won't understand," she said suddenly. "It must all sound petty and silly to you, but I have lost not only the man I was going to marry but the whole of my past life as well."

"I do understand," Tally said, and something in the misery of Jean's voice stirred him. "I do understand; in fact, I am in the same position myself. I have just been chucked and for somebody more important."

"You don't mean that Miss Melchester . . ." Jean asked, wide-eyed.

Tally nodded.

"Yes, turned me down."

"Oh, but how awful! She is so pretty, so attractive."

"Yes, she is both those things."

His anger returned to him. Once more he saw Melia standing on the steps with her hands outstretched to Ernest Danks.

"But how could she?" Jean asked. "I don't understand it."

"I can," Tally replied grimly.

"Can't you do anything? Can't you persuade her?" Jean questioned. "At least you are here and you can see her. It isn't as if you were miles away, like me."

"I haven't thought what to do yet," Tally answered. "It has only just happened . . ."

"Oh, poor Lord Brora, and everyone knows about the engagement, don't they? What are you going to say to your friends?"

"It is just what I was wondering. Well, Miss MacLeod, we both seem to be in the same boat. Your young man has chucked you for someone more important, and my fiancée has done the same thing. I think the best thing we can do is to drown our sorrows together. What about another drink?"

"Oh, no, thank you, and . . . I must be going."

Tally turned towards the cupboard.

"No, don't go," he said. "You are the only person I feel I could talk to and I expect you feel the same about me. We are both in the same predicament. That at least gives us a bond in common, even though we haven't been formally introduced."

21

"I feel Miss Ames would be very shocked if she knew that you had found me here . . . crying on your desk."

"We won't tell her," Tally promised. "Now what are you going to have? There's whisky, gin or brandy."

"Might I just have a little soda water, please?"

"If that is what you really want; I personally am going to have a strong drink and drink damnation to all our enemies."

He poured some soda water into a glass and handed it to her.

"It's a poor way to drink to our revenge."

"I'm afraid that is something we shall never have," Jean said wistfully.

"Don't you be too sure," Tally replied. "We ought to be able to think of something."

"How could we?" Jean asked. "Oh, it's all right for you, but everyone at Glendale will be saying, 'Poor Jean'. How I loathe being pitied!"

There was a fierce note in her voice somewhat out of keeping with her frail appearance.

"And how I hate people saying 'Poor Tally'." Tally raised his glass. "Here's to our revenge."

And then suddenly an idea came to him.

"I have thought of something," he said.

"What?"

"Wait a minute, we have got to work this out carefully. You think that they will be saying 'Poor Jean'. I know that at any moment now my friends will be saying 'Poor Tally'. That is what we dislike?"

"Yes, of course, but . . ."

"Listen. There is one way we can turn the tables, one way we can stop their saying it."

"Yes, but how?" Jean asked in bewilderment. "What do you mean?"

"I mean," Tally went on slowly, putting his drink on the mantelpiece untouched and staring at her as though he saw not her but his plan gradually falling piece by piece into place, "I mean that people are always sorry for the one who has been forsaken, the one who has been chucked, but if we are quick enough we can get in first."

"I don't understand."

"Oh, yes you do! Can't you see it's the perfect plan, the perfect answer?"

"What is?"

"That we both of us get engaged first, before the others have time to announce their engagement."

"Engaged, but how? And who to?"

Tally looked at her, and smiled.

"It is so simple," he said, "to each other, of course."

2

Without waiting for Jean's reply, Tally jumped to his feet.

"This is tremendous," he exclaimed; "but it has got to be properly handled, and I know the very chap to do it, too."

He took up the telephone receiver and dialled a number while Jean struggled to find her voice. At last she stammered, "But . . . but . . . Lord Brora . . ."

"One minute," he replied. "Hullo, is that White's? Ask Captain Fairfax to come to the telephone."

He smiled at her with the receiver to his ear, and it struck her not for the first time how good-looking he was. When he came into the office the first day she had been at work there, she had thought he was the most attractive man she had ever seen. Now she felt that this must all be a dream. This absurd situation could not be real. With an effort her good Scottish common sense reasserted itself. She moved across the room and stood beside Tally at the desk.

"Listen, Lord Brora," she said quietly. "I know this is a joke, but I don't quite understand . . . please let me go now."

"Joke? It's no joke," Tally replied sharply, and then spoke into the receiver: "Oh, hullo, Gerald. No, I wasn't talking to you. Look here, I want you! Something important has happened and I want your help. Yes, at once! Action Stations, old boy!"

He laughed at something that was said and put down the receiver.

"He will be round in a few minutes," he remarked; then seeing Jean's troubled, anxious expression he added more kindly:

"Listen, leave this to me. We are both in a mess. We have both for a moment suffered a temporary, mind you, a very temporary defeat. Well, we are going to win. We are going to come out on top, whatever the betting is against us. Won't you trust me?"

He smiled at her again and suddenly Jean felt as if it were impossible for her to oppose him. She must just do what he wanted.

"But I don't understand . . ." she said uncertainly.

"Yes, you do," Tally said soothingly. "You are going to make that young man of yours look a fool. Now, when did you get the letter?"

Jean drew it from the pocket of her dress.

"It arrived by the six o'clock post," she answered. "I was just leaving; in fact, in another minute I should have gone. I stayed late because I promised Miss Ames that I would finish those letters for you to sign tomorrow morning."

"It's lucky you did," Tally said. "When was the letter written?"

Jean drew the sheets of paper from the envelope. Despite an almost superhuman effort she could not keep her hands from trembling or a sudden mistiness from dimming her eyes. Angus' handwriting stared up at her—*"Dear Jean."*

She had known something was wrong as soon as she had read those first words, so cold, so formal. She remembered the first time he had written to her. She had been so thrilled to see his writing. Ever since she had come South she had waited for the posts, waiting and longing to hear from him. The few words of affection he had written had meant so much. And now this—a cold dismissal of all the things she had planned, all that the future was to have meant for both of them. *"Dear*

26

Jean," she read again, and with an effort she remembered that Tally was waiting.

"He wrote this on Saturday morning," she said. "He must have posted it in Glendale about noon. He usually goes into the village on a Saturday for the things wanted for the farm at the week-end."

"So he is a farmer?"

Jean nodded.

"And you love him?"

"I suppose so!" She caught back a sob. "I thought it was so wonderful that he should want to marry me. You see, after my father died I had nothing. He was the minister in Glendale and I'm afraid he was never very practical. Anyway, when he died there were a lot of debts to be met and to pay them off everything had to be sold."

"What happened to you then?" Tally asked.

"I was only fifteen at the time," Jean replied, "and I went to live with an aunt, actually she was a great-aunt. She was very strict and not very kind. She made me work very hard in the house and garden and I had no friends of my own age. Then one day I met Angus."

Her face softened with remembrance. How could she explain to this strange young man what it had meant to her then? To speak with a man, to talk to someone kindly and human who seemed interested in her. It was impossible to describe the harshness of her life with her great-aunt. She was fed, she was clothed, she was given a roof over her head and there was nothing which could be described as real hardship or neglect. And yet it was a house of misery. Never for one moment was she allowed to forget her poverty or her orphan state. Never had she a possession which she was allowed to call her own nor, it seemed at times, even a thought or a feeling which was private or sacred from the prying eyes of her aunt or the sharpness of her tongue. Vaguely Jean sensed then what she was to know later—that there was a reason for the unceasing fault-finding and for her aunt's desire to crush her spirit until it was too broken or humble ever to rise again.

27

She had been crying when she first met Angus, and because she was so desperate in her unhappiness she had done a thing she had never done before. She had slipped out of the house when she should have been preparing the evening meal, had gone up on the moor behind the house to find some solace, some comfort in solitude. The sun was sinking and throwing strange lights on the moors and distant mountains, and as he came striding towards her, his hair burnished gold, his neck bare, he had seemed almost supernatural, an immortal from another sphere rather than a harassed farmer in search of some straying sheep.

They talked together only for a few minutes, but in those moments Jean had wakened to womanhood. She was no longer a child, cowed and browbeaten, but a young woman with something alive and virile stirring within her veins.

She had gone back to the house with a smile on her lips, knowing that she would meet him again. It had taken a year for them to get to know each other well, a year in which Jean ran innumerable risks of her aunt finding out that she had made his acquaintance. And in that year she had come to a new knowledge of herself and, she believed, a new knowledge of the world.

It was only when her aunt died that she discovered the reason for many things which had perplexed and surprised her during her childhood. She had learned, too, that with her aunt's death she was again penniless. The old lady had been living on an annuity. What she was free to bequeath she had left to the chapel. There was nothing for Jean except the knowledge that she was free. Free to marry Angus should he ask her.

He did ask her, and then some pride belonging to her Scottish forbears had made her prevaricate. She wanted a little time to breathe, time to purchase just a few things that she could call her own. Something within her revolted against the idea of going to Angus completely empty-handed; of asking him to pay for the very dress in which she would be married.

While working for her aunt she had taught herself
28

typewriting and also shorthand by a correspondence course. Her aunt had made her work hard at both, even as she had made her slave in the house, cooking and scrubbing, cleaning and mending.

"I shall make a good wife," Jean told herself. But she wanted more than that—a little of the beauty and glamour which she knew instinctively should be part of her youth. She wanted to be young, frivolous and gay, all the things she had never been allowed to be, and she wanted to go to Angus not as a poverty-stricken orphan but as a woman able to stand on her own feet and capable of earning money of her own.

Perhaps it had been an absurd idea, and yet it was deep-rooted in a pride that would not be denied; and so, despite Angus' pleadings and protestations, she had come South to London to get herself a job.

There had been plenty of folk in the strath to tell her she was a fool. Once her aunt was dead she learnt a good many things about Angus—that he was a catch of the neighbourhood; that all the girls had set their cap at him, one after the other. His was a fine farm, for his father had farmed it before him and his father before that. His family were well-off and Angus had had a good schooling. "Too good," some people had said, for he had "got a bit big for his boots" and was "after thinking himself the gentleman." There would have been nothing wrong in that, if he had not cold-shouldered many of the lads with whom he had grown up and tried to be friends only with those who owned the lodges and rented the moors for the season.

"I remember his mother," one old woman told Jean, "when she was proud to make the best butter of any farmer's wife up the strath, but Angus is not letting his wife work. Ye'll be a fine lady while others do the work for ye!"

"I'll be nothing of the sort," Jean laughed, but when she had tackled Angus on the subject she found that his ideas were very definite.

"There will be plenty to occupy your time," he said sharply, "without your doing a servant's work. Besides,

I'm not going to be tied to the farm. We will go down South and take a week or two in Edinburgh from time to time; in fact, we might even plan a trip abroad, who knows?"

Jean knew she ought to be thrilled and excited by such ambitious planning, but there was something self-conscious about the way he spoke, something that told her that his reason for all this was not that they should be amused, but something deeper and more complicated. She was intuitive enough not to press him at the time, but soon she learned what she wanted to know. She learned it with a sudden sinking of her heart when she saw Angus one day talking to some of the people who had come up for the season's fishing. He was laughing, joking with them, and they seemed pleased to see him. But there was something in Angus' attitude which made her feel slightly ashamed. There was only one word to describe it. She tried to put it from her mind even while it presented itself, but it persisted. He was "toadying" to them. Yes, toadying to people who he thought were of a better social standing than he was himself.

It was then for the first time that Jean compared Angus with her father and knew the difference. Before that moment Angus had been not only a man, young, virile, and in love with her, but an ideal, someone to be admired as well as adored. Now she saw him for what he was. A man young and virile it was true, but lacking that inner culture, that extra touch of breeding which she had taken so much for granted as part of her own inheritance. Fiercely she told herself she loved him the more because of it. Angrily she derided herself because she could see the difference between Angus, being too effusive, gesticulating a little awkwardly with his hands, and the men who stood listening to him, controlled, self-assured, and friendly without any obvious effort.

It was just before she left for the South, when her great-aunt's house had been emptied and put up for sale and she had moved into a small croft in the village to stay with old Annie who had once looked after her father at the manse, that she learned about Elizabeth.

"Do ye think ye are wise to leave, Miss Jean?" Annie had asked her.

"Wise, of course I'm wise. You know what I feel about it, Annie, and it won't be for long. I will make a little money, buy a few things and come back to dazzle you all."

"Don't leave it too long," Annie said ominously.

"What do you mean by that?" Jean asked.

"Yon Angus is a fine looking lad for all he knows it," Annie replied, "and there is another besides yourself that is always thinking of him."

"Who's that?" Jean asked.

"Mistress Elizabeth Ross, to be sure. She has to pass the farm every day when she is coming down to the village. Ye may be sure she makes the best of her opportunities."

"Nonsense, Annie," Jean laughed. "I know who you mean now. Why, she is older than Angus, and besides, Colonel Ross would not hear of his daughter marrying a farmer."

"When a woman is determined on something it is often the man as has to listen," Annie said enigmatically, and said no more, but her words stuck in Jean's mind. She had questioned Angus casually enough, nevertheless there was a little feeling of jealousy behind her questions, and she had known by the way he answered that he was pleased that Elizabeth Ross should be friendly.

"She has been very kind to me," he said, "and it is due to her that the old man has given me a day's shooting now and again when he is short of a gun. They are very nice people, Jean, the sort of people you and I will want to know when we are married."

Jean thought privately that Colonel Ross, who owned a large moor and spent only part of the year in the North, would have little time for an ordinary Scottish farmer and his wife. But she was already sensitive enough to Angus' weakness not to express her feelings.

31

Yet when she saw Elizabeth Ross in her car in the village next day she looked at her with curiosity. She was not good-looking, and there was something hard and determined in the sharp red line of her mouth.

Perhaps Jean was staring, anyway Elizabeth turned and looked straight at her. Was it her fancy or did the sharp mouth seem to tighten? Was there a look of antagonism in her eyes? Knowing she was a friend of Angus', Jean would have smiled, but abruptly Elizabeth turned her head away and starting her car drove off. Jean felt as if a cloud had passed across the sun. She felt depressed for no reason save that she knew that Elizabeth disliked her.

"She didn't know who I was!" Jean told herself soothingly, but she knew that was untrue. Glendale was too small a place for those who lived in and around it not to know everyone, if not indeed to speak to, at least by sight.

She went back to Annie's croft vaguely perturbed because she could not put her own feelings into words. She said nothing to Angus when he called next morning to take her to the station.

"I wish you weren't going," he said to her when they were waiting for the train, and Jean, treasuring his words in her heart, felt as if she must change her mind. It was not too late. She had only to say the word and Angus would put her small suitcase back into his car, drive her home to Annie and she could be married the following week. She felt the words were on the end of her tongue, and yet something prevented her from saying them. Something told her that she could not go empty-handed to the man she married.

Like a ghost from the past she could hear her great-aunt's sharp voice.

"If I hadn't taken you in, penniless and without means of support, you would be in an orphanage. What else would you have done if I hadn't fed and clothed you? The least you can do is to show your gratitude by working for your keep."

No, no, she would never put herself into that position again, never, never.

The train was signalled. Her eyes were misty with tears so that as the train came slowly into the station to carry her South, it seemed to come winged around with a thousand tiny rainbows. . . .

Angus' letter was still in her hands. Jean realised that her thoughts had led her away into the past and that Tally was still waiting for her to speak. His brows knit a little as if he concentrated intently on what she had to say.

"I am sorry," she stammered. "I was thinking for the moment . . . remembering."

"There is nothing to be sorry for. We have got to get down to immediate action. Now, does your young man say that he is going to announce his engagement?"

"No," Jean answered. "He merely says that Elizabeth Ross wants to . . . to marry him."

"Good," Tally said, ignoring the break in Jean's voice as she said the last few words. "What we have got to do is to announce your engagement before they get the chance to announce theirs."

"But it's absurd . . . impossible," Jean protested.

"Is it? Now listen to me. Do you mind your people being sorry for you; do you think they will be sorry for you if you announce your engagement to me before your young man has time to tell them that he is going to marry . . . what did you say her name was? . . . Elizabeth Ross?"

"No, of course not, but . . ."

"There are no buts," Tally said abruptly. "Now the point is this. We will send your friend a telegram, telling him that you are engaged and that a letter follows. You will pretend that you have not heard from him. Sit down and write to him tonight and date it yesterday. With any luck he won't be sharp enough to look at the postmark, and if he does he won't be certain that you have got his letter. After all, it might easily have arrived tomorrow morning, the posts being what they are."

33

"But what can I say in the telegram?" Jean asked.

"Oh, I will write that for you. Where's a piece of paper?"

Tally turned over one of the letters which Jean had typed for him to sign the following morning and started to write on the back of it. "What is his name and address?" he asked.

She told him and then waited in silence because she could think of nothing to say—her thoughts were chaotic and had no form or sequence.

"There, what do you think of this?" Tally exclaimed at last, and read aloud: *"Angus McTavish, Moor Farm, Glendale—Am announcing my engagement to Lord Brora. Deeply regret not being able to inform you of this sooner. Please forgive me. Letter follows. Jean.* I like the 'Please forgive me,' don't you?"

"But you can't send that!"

"Why not? If I know anything of the local post office, the whole village will know all about it long before your friend Angus gets the telegram. Whatever they may think or guess about his acquaintance with Elizabeth Ross, this will certainly take the wind out of their sails."

"Yes, that's true!" Jean said slowly.

At that moment there was a sound outside and the door opened.

"Hullo, Gerald," Tally called out, and a young man, fair and broad-shouldered, came into the room.

"What on earth are you doing in the office at this time of night, Tally?" he inquired.

"Plotting and planning," Tally replied cheerfully. "And we want your assistance, old man." He turned to Jean. "Let me introduce an old friend, Gerald Fairfax—Gerald, this is Miss MacLeod."

"How do you do?" Gerald said politely, throwing his hat down on the desk and seating himself in one of the armchairs. "Well, what's up, Tally?"

"I wish to announcement my engagement," Tally answered. "I want it done in a really sensational manner."

"Good heavens, you don't mean to say you have

34

dragged me round here just to tell me that," Gerald said disgustedly. "Why, Melia will have all the Press hounds in Europe sitting on her doorstep. There's no chance of anyone like me getting a new angle on it."

"I am not announcing my engagement to Amelia," Tally said quietly.

"What?" exclaimed Gerald, dropping his cigarette-case on the floor with a clatter as he sprang to his feet. "But, good lord, what do you mean? Not going to marry Melia?"

"I didn't say I wasn't going to marry her. I merely said I was not announcing my engagement to her. You must learn to be accurate, old boy." He turned to Jean. "Gerald is in the advertising business. Nice chaps, but they never get their facts right."

"What is all this about?" Gerald asked impatiently.

"Well, if you'll listen, I'll tell you. Miss MacLeod and I wish to announce our engagement to an astonished world."

Gerald's mouth shot open, then he closed it again. He looked across at Jean and it was quite obvious that he took notice of her for the first time since he entered the room.

"Well, I'll be damned," he said slowly.

"You are not being over-polite, old boy!"

"I'm sorry," Gerald said hastily, "but it really is a bit of a shock. I don't think I have met Miss MacLeod before, but she must forgive me."

"It's all right," Jean said quietly. "It's just about as much of a shock to me. You see . . ."

"You had better let me tell him," Tally said. "I suppose you will have to know the truth, but you are the only person who will. Cross your heart and swear to die if you tell a living soul what we tell you. Swear?"

"Of course I do. You had better tell me the whole story. You know you'll only get into a mess if you try to carry off too much on your own bat." And then to Jean aside: "I've known Tally since we were at Eton together. He always has been an impetuous sort of chap. I have to keep an eye on him."

"Stop talking and listen to me," said Tally. "What has happened is this. Melia has turned me down to marry Ernest Danks." Gerald whistled. "Yes, she thinks he is going to be the next Prime Minister. Is the old boy dead yet?"

"No, but the last bulletin issued this afternoon seemed to think that the doctors had given up hope."

Tally sighed. "Melia sees herself queening it in Downing Street and being married in Westminster Abbey and all that sort of thing . . ."

"Well, if she's made up her mind, nothing you can do will stop her," Gerald said.

"She's not married to him yet," Tally retorted ominously, "and I am going to teach her a lesson."

"I can see Melia appreciating that," Gerald remarked drily.

"And as things have worked out," Tally continued, ignoring him, "Miss MacLeod is in the same position. Her young man has chucked her and so we thought we would teach them both a lesson. That's where you come in."

"Me?" Gerald asked, ungrammatically.

"Yes, you! This has got to be sensational, old boy. Miss MacLeod wants to stagger the North, I the South. This has got to be bigger news than the Prime Minister's death and it's got to take the gilt completely off Melia's gingerbread. Do you get me?"

"I get you," Gerald said. "But are you certain you're wise, Tally? It all sounds a bit crazy to me."

"That's what I think," Jean interposed. "Please, Captain Fairfax, persuade him that we had better not do it."

"Now, Jean," Tally said reprovingly, "you are going back on what you promised me."

"Perhaps I am," Jean admitted, "but I am afraid that if I listen to you we shall find ourselves in a terrible mess."

"You leave that to me," Tally replied decisively. "I've been in messes before and far worse ones than this, haven't I, Gerald?"

"I don't know," Gerald answered, "but if you have

36

made up your mind I suppose it's no use trying to stop you, Tally."

"Well, how are we going to do it?"

"Do what?"

"Get into the headlines, you ass."

"I suppose we can make it interesting—'Famous Lord Brora, the leader of the Commandos . . .' and all that sort of thing?"

"No, no," Tally said emphatically. "Not that sort of thing. I want something really sensational, something that will make Melia's press-cutting books look like snippets from *Home Chat*."

"You mean a new angle on your romance, that sort of thing?"

"Good," Tally said derisively, "the brain's beginning to work at last. You're particularly slow today, old man."

"I'm sorry, Tally, but it's all rather a shock so far. Think I can have a drink?"

"Of course, help yourself, the cupboard's open."

"Thanks." Gerald got up and took out a bottle of whisky. "What about you, Miss MacLeod?"

"No, thank you. Lord Brora has already given me some brandy. I think that's why I'm agreeing to this crazy scheme."

"It certainly seems a bit mad," Gerald said, pouring himself out a whisky-and-soda. "Although, when I come to think of it, Tally's engagement to someone else is about the only thing that might bring Melia to her senses. She can't really want to marry this Danks man. I always thought he was terribly synthetic myself."

"That's exactly the right word for it," Tally affirmed. He turned and smiled at Jean. "I told you Gerald was clever; a little slow to get going, but when he starts . . ."

Jean smiled back and there was something about the badinage between the two men which made her feel young and carefree. There was indeed something about Tally which always created that atmosphere wherever he went. She had heard of him before she came to London in search of a job. But who hadn't? His exploits had always been front-page news and his personality had crept into the gossip columns to stay there.

There was practically no one who didn't know why Lord Brora, who had been christened George Sebastian Alexander, was called Tally. Jean had heard the reason several times from different people and had also read the story in one of the women's magazines. It made her smile as she thought of how Tally's father had been waiting while the hounds drew a covert when an old retainer had come riding after the hunt to tell him the good news that he had a son.

"Excuse me, m'lord," he had said, taking off his hat, "but I was to tell you that her ladyship has been delivered of a fine boy."

The other riders had crowded round with congratulations.

"Well, Arthur, what are you going to call him?" someone asked.

"Call him?" Lord Brora replied elatedly. "Why, he'll be called . . ." At that moment the fox broke cover and with a shout his lordship finished the sentence ". . . Tally-ho, gone away!"

The name had stuck all through Tally's childhood. At Eton his friends called him Tally, and he had gone from Oxford when war broke out with the name affixed to him as though it were a label. He joined the Commandos when they first started, and from that moment he became a personality which the English public learnt to love and admire. He was reckless, daring, and amazingly successful. The men called him "Lucky Tally". He lead them through the most amazing exploits and they swore the casualties were lighter because of his good fortune.

In the office Miss Ames had talked of Tally, and the men who came in for advice, help and jobs talked of him too.

Jean learnt that he was ruthless, yet the best friend any man could want in a tight corner; that he was impatient and yet nothing was too much trouble if someone appealed to his sympathy; that he was compassionate and yet in many ways extremely spoilt. Yes, she had heard all this and a lot more. Now for the first time she realised that all she had heard told her really little or nothing definite about the man facing her.

"Well, have you thought of something, Gerald?" she heard him say, and knew there was almost a command behind the seemingly casual words.

"Do you want a romantic story?" Gerald replied. "If so, we have got to have something sensational as to how you both met. You had better rescue Miss MacLeod from something. That is the sort of thing the public will expect from you, Tally. Do we set the building on fire or does she jump into the Thames?"

"Neither," Tally said quickly. "We don't want to be had up for arson and we don't want Miss MacLeod to die of pneumonia before the ring's on her finger."

"I know," Gerald exclaimed, turning to Jean. "Where do you live?"

"I've got rooms in Putney at the moment," she replied.

"Splendid. Well, you are walking across Putney Common late at night when you are set on by three toughs, you scream for help and Tally rescues you. You fall in love with each other at first sight and the engagement is announced immediately."

"Splendid," Tally said. "What happens to the toughs?"

"You would have to run after them," Gerald said, "but Miss MacLeod clung to you, begging you not to leave her alone."

"It's the most beautiful melodrama," Tally said; "and when did this take place?"

Gerald scratched his head.

"When are you going to announce your engagement?"

"At once!"

"That means that the *Express* and the *Mail* had better have it exclusive for the morning editions, and *The Times* will have it the following day. We ought to get some good pictures in the evening papers."

"What about my heroic episode as the knight to the rescue?"

"Oh, you'll just have to swear to it taking place. Better say it was last night. What were you both doing last night, by the way?"

"I went to bed early," Jean said.

"Anybody know that you didn't go out later?"

"I don't think so. I live in a boarding-house and we all have our own latch-keys."

"That's all right then. Where were you, Tally?"

Tally thought for a moment.

"I can't remember where I was. Oh yes, I do. You silly idiot, you were with me! Don't you remember? You came round after dinner and we sat talking until nearly midnight."

"Perfect, couldn't be better," Gerald said. "Well, that little drama took place at 9 o'clock last night and you spent to-day getting to know each other."

"No, no," Tally interrupted. "Jean's been here all day. She works in the office."

"I say, that's a bit of a snag," Gerald said. "Rather rules out the idea of meeting and falling in love with each other all in a flash."

"Another thing, too, it rather spoils the glamour," Tally said. "We don't want 'Typist weds Lord' sort of stuff in the *Daily Mirror*."

"No, of course not!" Gerald said. "Can you square your staff?"

Tally turned to Jean.

"Who have you seen since you've been here?" he asked.

"Only Miss Ames," Jean answered. "She told me there was another girl but she has been down with 'flu all the week. She is coming back tomorrow."

"Good! Miss Ames is as safe as a house. I'll telephone her tonight and tell her to keep her mouth shut until I see her tomorrow. Now you understand, we never met until last night, when you were taking a walk on Putney Common."

"But why was I taking a walk?" Jean asked.

40

"Now that's a sensible question," Tally said. "Why was she taking a walk, Gerald?"

"Going to post a letter to her friend in . . . Where do you live?"

"I live in Scotland," Jean replied.

"Perfect," Gerald approved. "Homesick for her native heath, stifled by the foggy air in London, she goes out into the dark night, etc., etc.! I say, I could almost write a novel on this."

"For goodness sake go and write some good copy for the papers," Tally expostulated.

"Right, it shall be done. By the way, be prepared for photographers and things tomorrow morning. I think Miss MacLeod had better not be photographed in Putney. It's a bit sordid. You had better fetch her early, Tally, and she can be done at your house in Berkeley Square. Is that mausoleum open?"

"I believe so," Tally replied. "Anyway there are a few old servants there and we can open up a couple of rooms. Let's make the photographs as gorgeous as we can; it will annoy Melia; she always wanted to give a ball in the Chinese drawing-room."

"Well, we can pose Miss MacLeod there."

"That's splendid," Tally approved.

Gerald, however, hesitated for a moment.

"You won't mind my mentioning it," he said to Jean, almost apologetically, "but have you got something very glamorous in which to be photographed?"

Jean's eyes widened.

"No, I'm afraid I haven't. In fact I've got very few clothes."

Gerald looked at Tally. They smiled at each other simultaneously.

"This is where Michael comes in!"

"Who's Michael?" Jean asked.

"Haven't you ever heard of Michael Sorrel?" Gerald inquired.

"Yes, of course I have," Jean replied, "the famous court dress-designer."

"Well, he worked for us," Gerald explained; "in fact

41

he did all our camouflage. We'll go along and see Michael right away."

Gerald got to his feet, but Jean turned to Tally.

"Please, Lord Brora, you must listen to me for a moment. We seem to be getting deeper and deeper into this and I can't allow you to buy me clothes. I don't think I can go on with it."

She felt Tally's hand go out and touch hers and then her fingers were in his warm, firm clasp.

"Listen, Jean, you said you would trust me. This is going to be an adventure for both of us. Don't be chicken-hearted before we have really started."

"I'm not really," Jean protested, "but . . ."

"As I said before, there are no buts," Tally said. "We will go and see Michael."

He smiled at her as he spoke. Their eyes met, and there was both a command and an appeal in his. For better or for worse Jean knew that she must follow him wherever it might lead her.

3

Driving through the streets in Tally's car with Gerald sitting behind, Jean tried to think, tried to realise that this was not just some mad escapade. She felt shy, apprehensive and afraid, yet at the same time there was something almost gay about the whole proceeding which seemed to give a lilt and a joyousness to all that was said and done.

More than once Jean forced herself to remember that she was unhappy, desperately unhappy, and that her whole future was at stake. But somehow for the moment Angus had ceased to have any reality save that of the dark shadow in the background. Tally's vital, vibrating personality monopolised all her attention. He thrust himself into prominence so that there was no room for anyone else even in her thoughts.

"I suppose Michael will be in?" Tally remarked to Gerald as he turned the car out of Berkeley Square.

"I hope so," Gerald replied; "if not, we shall have to ferret him out, wherever he may be."

The car drew up in front of the big, imposing-looking entrance of Michael Sorrel's shop. It was the best-known shop in the whole of the West End of London. Royalty, film stars, actresses, society beauties, in fact everyone who could afford to be really well-dressed had climbed the three big marble steps and gone in through the ornate portico to Michael Sorrel's showrooms. He was the most fabulous and the most glamorous dressmaker that the world had known for a quarter of a century, and his designs, drawn originally for the famous and the notorious, were copied by every shopgirl or factory girl in a greater or lesser degree.

Jean stared about her with interest as she was led into the great mirror-decorated hall off which the showrooms opened and through it into a large luxurious lift.

"Is Mr. Sorrel at home?" Gerald asked the liftman.

"I think so, sir. He went up to his flat when the shop closed."

"Good," Tally ejaculated.

The lift sped upwards until they reached the top floor of the building. Here another door was opened and Jean found herself in a warm, dimly-lit hall which smelt of some strange exotic Eastern fragrance. She only had time to take in that the lights were supported by huge carved figures of negro boys before she was ushered with Tally and Gerald into a big, low room, decorated entirely in white. Lying on the sofa in front of the fire was a young man. He was covered with a rug of white ermine backed with scarlet and by his side was a great bunch of white orchids flecked with scarlet spots.

"I am really too tired to see anyone, Carter," Jean heard him say in a languid voice as the manservant, who had preceded them, opened the door.

Tally went forward.

"You can't do that to an old friend, Michael. We want your help."

"Tally!" Michael Sorrel exclaimed, and throwing off the ermine rug he got to his feet. "I didn't know it was you, old boy! Come in, of course. It's only that I've had an exhausting day, absolutely exhausting."

Tally shook Michael by the hand.

"You remember Gerald, of course," he said, "and I want you to meet Miss MacLeod."

Jean held out her hand; Michael Sorrel took it in his. She had expected his grasp to be flabby and in keeping with his languid voice. Instead she found her hand was grasped firmly, the fingers somehow managing to be purposeful.

"We must have a drink," Michael said, turning to the manservant who was still waiting by the door. "Bring some cocktails, Carter—your special. Carter makes some marvellous cocktails," he explained. "And now I think of it, a cocktail is exactly what I need myself just now; I'm absolutely dead on my feet, as the old bodies downstairs say."

"Nonsense," Tally protested, "you know you are never really tired; it's all a pose, like this room."

"Why, don't you like it?" Michael asked, "I've just had it done up. Personally, I am delighted with it."

"Looks to me rather like the bridal suite on a luxury liner," Tally said unkindly.

Michael laughed, apparently quite unresentful of his criticism.

"You always are beastly about my flat," he said, "but as Gerald knows, it pays to advertise. It's what people expect me to like anyway."

"That's true enough," Tally said. "Do you remember all those gorgeous creatures you used to keep waiting downstairs when you were designing something for a raid? It makes me laugh to think of it. The telephone ringing because the Duchess of this or that or some film magnate wanted a special dress, money no object, and here we used to sit surrounded by camouflage nets and pots of paint trying things out to get the effect. Goodness, how we used to laugh!"

"It was fun, wasn't it?" Michael smiled. "And I often think of that ghastly night when you took me with you; made me come, although I was terrified. I shall never forget the chug-chug of that boat going across the Channel; I thought every German for miles could hear it! And that landing on the beach! I was simply paralysed."

"Nothing of the sort," Tally said. "You enjoyed it, you know you did."

"I was so thankful when it was over that I would have enjoyed anything," Michael retorted. "Ah, here's Carter with the cocktails. I hope you will enjoy it, Miss . . ."

He hesitated for Jean's name.

45

"MacLeod," Tally supplied. "Now, Michael, to business."

"At your service, my lord," Michael said and bowed mockingly; then, raising his glass, he added, "To the most glamorous person I have ever dressed."

Tally looked uncomfortable, for there was no mistaking the admiration and respect in Michael's voice.

"You are a fool," he said shortly, "but a clever fool and that is why we want your help. I'm engaged to be married."

Michael laughed, as unimpressed as Gerald had been.

"That isn't news, old boy. If you have come to see me about Melia's dress, she has been bothering me for weeks. She wants to be married in scarlet or something equally ridiculous. I have told her I won't allow it, and I won't."

"I am not engaged to Melia Melchester," Tally said, quietly.

There was no mistaking Michael's surprise.

"Not engaged to Melia! Don't be ridiculous, Tally! You must be."

"You are making it rather embarrassing for me, Michael; Miss MacLeod and I are announcing our engagement tomorrow."

For a moment Michael's expression showed his astonishment, and then suavely, with a poise which Jean envied, he recovered himself.

"My congratulations, Tally," he said, "and of course I wish you and Miss MacLeod every happiness."

"Thank you," Tally said, "and now, Michael, just listen to us for a moment. Miss MacLeod and I only met a very short time ago, but we want our engagement to be announced very quickly—as I've said, tomorrow. Now Gerald here is going to see to all that, but Miss MacLeod is in the unfortunate position of not being dressed for the part, so to speak. Her clothes are in the North where she has been living and we thought that you would be able to help us out." There was a pause and then as Michael said nothing, Tally added, "I am relying on you, Michael, as an old friend not to let me down."

The eyes of the two men met and it seemed to Jean as though something passed between them. She was not certain what was said wordlessly, but she knew that Michael Sorrel would not refuse Tally. He sighed and got to his feet, walking across the room to press the bell by the mantelpiece.

"You know I can't say 'No' to you, Tally," he said, then turned with his back to the fireplace and looked at Jean. She told herself that never had she been scrutinised so minutely and in such a penetrating manner. She felt herself flushing, but she knew that he regarded her not as a man might regard a woman, but as a craftsman regards the material with which he has to work.

Carter opened the door.

"See if Madame Marie is still downstairs," Michael Sorrel commanded, "and if she is, ask her to come here to me at once."

"Very good, sir."

Carter shut the door behind him.

"What exactly does Miss MacLeod want?" Michael asked.

"Everything," Tally replied briefly.

"And especially a dress to be photographed in tomorrow," Gerald interposed. "We want some photographs in the Chinese drawing-room at Berkeley Square. Tally wants those to be sensational, and you know what that means."

Michael nodded.

"It is difficult to know what type she is," he said, as if he were speaking of some lay figure which had no life or personality of its own. "Fair hair—with a touch of red in it—blue eyes . . . conventional, and yet . . ." He paused, and then in tones of horror, which would have amused Jean at any other time, he asked, "Where did you get that coat and skirt?"

"In . . . Scotland," Jean answered apologetically.

47

"I couldn't have believed it possible," Michael Sorrel remarked, "that anyone could murder a piece of tweed to that extent. However . . ."

He shrugged his shoulders while Jean felt the colour rise swiftly into her face. She felt that she ought to be angry or at least resentful, yet she knew what he said was only too true. She had been long enough in London to know that the coat and skirt of thick hard-wearing tweed bought for her three years ago by her great-aunt was both ill-fitting and ugly. But what could she do? She had no money as yet to buy another, and what she had saved out of her salary she had expended on shoes and stockings and on a neat, if not smart, hat. She knew what she must look like, sitting there badly dressed and tongue-tied in this beautiful, exotic room; and in that moment she wished she had never come, never met Tally, never embarked on this crazy adventure.

The door opened and a middle-aged woman wearing a smart grey dress came in.

"You wanted me, Mr. Sorrel?" she said.

"Yes, Marie, I want you very badly. You remember Lord Brora?"

"Of course," Madame Marie smiled. "How are you? It is nice to see you again."

"And I'm thrilled to see you, Marie," Tally replied. "I needn't ask how you are, you are looking splendid."

"We are all a little tired," Madame Marie said. "There is so much to do these days; you know what Mr. Sorrel is."

"He is never too busy to help an old friend, and that's what matters."

"Oh, Lord Brora, don't tell me you have come asking for something," Madame Marie cried reproachfully. "We know what your jobs are like and we haven't time for even a small one just now."

"Now don't faint, but I've brought you a very big one," Tally replied and laughed as Madame Marie put both her hands up to her face in pretended horror.

He introduced Jean, and the same scene which was becoming almost annoyingly familiar was enacted again.

48

Madame Marie was astonished to hear that it was not Miss Melchester whom Tally was to marry. She, too, Jean noted, was astounded that someone so badly dressed and insignificant should be engaged to anyone as famous and glamorous as Tally. But once the introductions were effected Michael gave his orders.

"Take Miss MacLeod downstairs, Marie," he said, "and get her into one of the foundation robes; then I can decide what we can do for her. We shall have to lend her a model or two to wear tomorrow, but, after that. . . ."

"Now, Mr. Sorrel," Madame Marie admonished, "don't forget that Her Serene Highness' dresses have to be finished this week, and there's all the gowns for that new show at Drury Lane. We have only just started them and we are nearly a fortnight behind with the ordinary routine work."

"It's no use, Marie," Michael said, "you know we can't refuse Lord Brora."

"No, I suppose we can't," Madame Marie answered gloomily, while Tally laughed.

"Will you come with me, Miss MacLeod?" she asked and Jean followed her obediently from the room, conscious as she went that the men must be looking at the tweed coat and skirt which had filled Michael Sorrel with so much horror.

The two women went down in the lift together; Jean was too shy to talk, but Madame Marie chattered unconcernedly.

"Fancy your being engaged to Lord Brora. I do admire him so. What wonderful things he did in the war! Of course, we saw a lot of him then. I expect he told you about all the camouflage work that was done here. It was strange to see our workroom girls decorating tin hats and making masks for men. But they were a splendid lot—Lord Brora's troops I mean. We got so fond of them, in fact, that we used to feel it a personal loss when any of the ones we knew were killed. And they just adored Lord Brora. You must feel very proud of him. Come along in here, Miss MacLeod."

She led Jean into a dressing-room.

"If you'll take your things off, I'll go and get a foundation gown for you."

She left the room, but for a moment Jean made no effort to undress. She stood staring at herself in the great mirrors which covered the walls, seeing herself from all angles as she had never had the opportunity of doing before in her life. She saw a white, strained face, a little too thin, but there was—although she did not know it—something very young and appealing in the soft mouth and tiny, sensitive nostrils. Her eyes were wide and dark, and with a sense of relief Jean told herself that excitement was not unbecoming. Then she glanced at her figure, at the thick and ungainly-cut coat with its unpadded shoulders and bagging pockets, at the skirt too full and too long. Yes, it was awful, she knew that, but how could she help it, and what alternative had there ever been? Almost angrily she took off her coat to reveal a flannel blouse, faded until its original colour was lost and only an indefinite dullness remained.

"It is all very well to be critical," she asked her reflection, "but do any of these people know what it is not to have a penny of one's own, to be utterly dependent on an old woman who hated youth and any form of female attraction?"

Often when she was a child Jean had thought that her aunt had deliberately chosen the most ugly and most unattractive garments for her to wear. When the old woman died she had learnt that the choice had not been unintentional.

She stripped off her coat and skirt, then stared at the ugly woollen underclothes she wore beneath them, washed until they had shrunk and hardened. They had never been attractive even when they were first bought. They had just been serviceable and Jean felt a sudden surging hatred for all the things that were hard-wearing and useful. She thought of the big white room upstairs, of those exquisite orchids faintly speckled as if with drops of blood. How lovely it all was! Tally had laughed, but to her it was the most beautiful place she had ever seen. The scent of Eastern perfume, the tinkling crystal chandeliers, the sofa with its great silken cushions and the ermine rug. Suppose one lived in a room like that, suppose one could possess anything half so beautiful. She pressed her hands suddenly to her eyes as if to shut out the reflection of herself. She remembered her aunt's parlour, dark and austere, with its heavy plush curtains and the linoleum-covered floor which she had polished daily until she could see the furniture reflected in its shining surface. She thought of her bedroom with its bare, white-washed walls and black iron bedstead, of the holland curtains and heavy, marble-topped washing-stand. How ugly it had all been, ugly and prisonlike!

"If only I could know something else, if only for a little while," Jean whispered to herself, and knew it was almost a prayer.

The door opened and Madame Marie came in.

"I think this will fit you, Miss MacLeod, but perhaps you had better put this on first."

She held out a garment of chiffon and lace, fragile and lovely. Jean had never touched anything so exquisite before. She stepped out of her woollen underclothes and into it. It was so transparent that she hardly dared to look at herself in the glass, but there was only a second or two before Madame Marie slipped over her head a long, white dress made of clinging silk. It was Grecian in style, cupping her breasts and leaving her shoulders and arms bare. It clung to her figure then swept down to the floor in lovely natural lines.

"This is what the girls always wear before Mr. Sorrel starts designing on them," Madame Marie explained. "It gives him an idea of their figures and what they will look best in."

Jean stared at herself. She had never realised that she had a figure before. Now she saw that she was very slim, with narrow hips and a tiny waist. Her shoulders were very white and her arms perfectly proportioned.

"I am not too bad," she thought encouragingly.

"I suppose . . . you couldn't loosen your hair a bit," Madame Marie said hesitantly, as if she thought Jean might think her suggestion an impertinence. "It is such a pretty colour, but you seem to have scraped it back so very severely."

Jean put up her hands and pulled out several hairpins.

"I have never had my hair cut," she explained.

She uncoiled the tight neat bun at the back of her neck, releasing thick strands of fair hair which fell on to her shoulders.

"Goodness!" Madame Marie exclaimed, "I had no idea you had as much hair as that. You must have done it up very tightly."

"Yes, I always have," Jean said briefly, not explaining that her aunt had made her do it that way.

She reached for her bag, and taking out a comb ran it through her hair.

"But it's lovely," Madame Marie enthused. "I can't think what you are thinking of to tuck it away like that."

"I couldn't think what else to do with it," Jean said shyly.

With the strokes of the comb her hair seemed full of electricity and danced out, glinting gold under the lights. It was not long and it lay on her shoulders, curling a little at the ends and falling in natural waves on either side of her face.

"It is really beautiful hair," Madame Marie said, and Jean knew that the admiration in her tones was sincere. She opened a drawer in the table beside the mirror. "Now look, Miss MacLeod, here's some eye-black. Just put a little on your eyelashes. I can see they are long, but they are too fair to show. You don't want to use much, just a little."

She held out a little red box with a brush. Jean took it gingerly.

"I'm afraid I don't know how to do it. You see, I have never tried to make up my face."

There was no disguising the astonishment on Madame Marie's face.

"Goodness me, wherever have you been all your life? Let me do it for you then. I will just get a spot of water to damp the brush." She was away only a minute and

52

when she came back she tinted Jean's eyelashes with an experienced hand. "There, that's much better. Now some lipstick; don't tell me you haven't got one?"

"I'm afraid not," Jean answered in a very small voice.

"Well, if they had told me that somebody existed in the world like you I wouldn't have believed them," Madame Marie said. "Not that I'm being rude, Miss MacLeod; you mustn't misunderstand me; but most of the girls today learn to make up in their prams. Wait a minute, I must get the exact colour for you. A sort of coral red would suit your skin. Yes, here's one." She took the lipstick from the drawer and touched Jean's lips with it. "I'm not going to suggest rouge, your skin's so lovely and white. . . . Just a touch of powder . . . this is the finest made. . . . Now look at yourself!"

Jean did as she was told. She stared at her reflection in the mirror and then took a deep breath. This couldn't be her, or could it? This girl in the very close-fitting, naked white dress with golden hair tumbling over her shoulders and big dark-fringed eyes above warm, red lips.

"I do look different, don't I," she said at last, and even her voice sounded strange to herself.

"Just wait and watch Mr. Sorrel's face when he sees you," Madame Marie said. "Come along and show him."

"But I can't go upstairs like this," Jean said, "I feel . . . I feel . . . naked."

Madame Marie laughed.

"You mustn't be shy of Mr. Sorrel."

"But Lord Brora's there," Jean said, and now there was a touch of panic in her voice.

"But you won't mind him," Madame Marie smiled. "Why, you are going to marry him."

"Yes, of course," Jean murmured, "but all the same . . . please, couldn't I have a cloak or something?"

Madame Marie stared at her as if she could hardly believe her ears, and then she disappeared for a moment to come back with a tiny white velvet cape edged with sable.

"Slip this on," she said, "at least it'll keep you from feeling cold."

There was a hint of laughter in her voice which silenced the other protests which Jean might have made far more effectively than any argument. Without saying anything more, she followed Madame Marie to the lift and they went up again to the top floor.

In the hall of the flat Jean took a deep breath. She was so shy that it was sheer agony to her to follow Madame Marie. She would have given anything at that moment for the floor to open and swallow her up, yet she forced herself forward, made herself enter the room where she knew the three men would be waiting. As always when she was afraid or upset she held her head high, striving to make herself seem taller than she was naturally, so that as she swept into the room in the long white dress she was indeed a very different person from the girl who, but twenty minutes earlier, had hurried out of it with her head thrust forward and her shoulders bent.

The men were grouped round the fire where she had left them. Michael was on the sofa, Tally and Gerald were both sitting in big white arm-chairs, their feet thrust out in front of them. As Jean entered, they got up slowly. Michael came forward.

"I'm sorry," he said, "I didn't know. . . ." Then he gave an exclamation, "Good God, it's Miss MacLeod . . . I didn't recognise you for a moment."

Madame Marie, who had been hiding behind the opened door, came in laughing.

"I thought you wouldn't. That's why I sent her in alone. Well, isn't this a transformation?"

Michael Sorrel stood back, his eyes narrowed, but Jean hardly noticed him. She was looking across the room at Tally, noting that he was staring at her too, but in a very different way.

"Now we can set to work," Michael said, almost triumphantly.

As in a haze Jean heard him giving instructions to Madame Marie. The dresses all had lovely names

54

—'Winged Arrow,' 'Golden Sunset,' 'Starlight,' 'Blue Moon' and 'Love-in-the-Mist.'

"Those will do for the moment," Michael Sorrel said at length. "And, Tally, if you can spare her for a moment or two tomorrow morning, I'll design her one or two original things which can be ready by the end of the week."

"But no, Mr. Sorrel they can't——" Madame Marie protested.

"At the end of the week," Michael repeated.

"And the dress for the photographs tomorrow?" Gerald asked.

"I'd forgotten that one. She must have 'Almond Blossom,' Madame Marie."

"But, Mr. Sorrel, you promised that exclusively to Her Serene Highness."

Michael Sorrel shrugged his shoulders.

"Miss MacLeod will look far more beautiful in it."

Jean started at his words. Could he have really meant them? For a moment she thought he was joking; then she saw he was quite serious. At last she found her voice and woke herself from the dream world in which she was drifting.

"Please, don't give me too many things," she said appealingly "just a dress to wear tomorrow will do. I don't want a lot, really!"

It was then Tally spoke for the first time, coming forward to stand beside her.

"Leave this to me," he said quietly. "You promised, you know, and besides you are going to look marvellous in them. Why don't you always wear your hair like that?"

She looked up at him. She had not realised until this moment how very tall he was or how very small and slight she was in comparison.

"But I couldn't leave it all loose like this," she answered simply.

"Why not?" Tally asked.

Michael Sorrel, who had appeared not to be listening to the conversation, broke in:

"But, of course, you must. I shall design a dress for your hair. It's perfect as it is."

"If Michael says that, you have got to obey," Tally said smiling.

"Must I?"

"Of course!"

He still stood looking down at her, and it seemed to her as though they stood alone. In the background she could hear Madame Marie's voice beseeching Michael Sorrel to remember their other commitments and Michael's quick, impatient answers. But for Jean she and Tally were alone looking at each other, meeting for the first time. . . .

Then the spell was broken as Gerald said from the fireplace:

"I think Miss MacLeod's going to prove extremely photogenic." He added nothing more, but Jean finished the sentence in her heart, 'and how it will annoy Melia.'

'That is what they're all thinking,' she told herself. 'They are not really interested in me! My hair, my figure, my clothes are of importance for one reason and one reason only, because they will annoy another girl.'

Suddenly little insignificant Jean MacLeod knew that she hated the beautiful Melia Melchester whom she had never seen.

4

Jean opened her eyes and realised that she must have
fallen asleep. They were still driving through the night
and now were right out in the open country. In the
moonlight she could see trees bare of their leaves, their
branches stretching heavenwards like some dark etching
by a master hand. She had a sudden glimpse of a farm,
its windows warm with golden light, and then the country opened out as they rode high on the Cotswold Hills,
the wind whistling round the car and making her glad of
the warm rugs which Tally had heaped upon her.

At the beginning of their journey he had talked a little, speaking of their plans, of Michael Sorrel and of
Gerald left behind in London to cope with the Press, but
after a while they had fallen into a comfortable silence.
The purr of the engine had been rhythmic in Jean's ears
until she fell asleep to dream she was back again at
Glendale and the moors were bathed in sunshine. It took
a moment now for her to remember where she was and
why. Then the strange, complicated events of the past
five hours came rushing back to her, tempestuous like a
floodtide.

Yes, it was true that she, Jean MacLeod, who this
morning had been an obscure, unknown little typist
travelling by Tube to the office where she worked, was
now dressed luxuriously in exquisite clothes by Michael
Sorrel, wrapped in fur-lined rugs and travelling in a
Rolls Royce beside a good-looking, famous young man

to whom her engagement would be announced tomorrow.

Even as she thought Jean looked up and the movement of her head caused Tally to turn and glance at her for a fleeting second.

"Had a nice sleep?" he asked.

"I am sorry," Jean apologised. "I feel ashamed for dropping off like that, but I suppose it is the warmth in here, and . . . of course . . . the excitement."

"Don't make any excuses," Tally said. "You must be tired; you had done a full day's work in the office before we started on . . . 'operation Brora'."

"It was not very hard work," Jean confessed. "I enjoyed it."

"Miss Ames said you were jolly good," Tally commented. "When I told her I was taking you away, she was quite upset at the thought of losing anyone so efficient."

Jean thought privately that if Miss Ames had been upset it was not because Tally was taking away a promising typist, but that a typist from the office should presume to be closely associated with him! Miss Ames' admiration of her employer was too obvious to escape the notice of anyone—even someone as unsophisticated as Jean—an admiration tinged with a respect which was almost reverent.

"What else did she say?" Jean asked curiously.

"She wished us every happiness," Tally said, and now there was a bitter note in his voice which she had not heard before.

"Was she . . . was she also very surprised that you weren't marrying Miss Melchester?"

"Surprised? Of course!" Tally replied. "That seems to be universal! But if you ask me, she was also relieved. Miss Ames never did like Melia. They were sweetly offensive to each other whenever they met."

Jean laughed.

"What a funny expression!"

"It describes their attitude exactly."

58

"Poor Miss Ames! She would do anything for you, Lord Brora."

"Tally," he corrected. "You must remember to call me by my Christian name."

"Yes, of course," Jean agreed, flushing a little at the rebuke; "but somehow it seems to be terribly familiar."

Tally smiled.

"We have got to begin to be that sometime; and, by the way, Jean, I thought you were splendid with Michael. It must have all been strange and even a little frightening, but at the same time you looked simply marvellous in his clothes."

"Oh, Lord Br . . . I mean Tally. . . . I wish I could say thank you for all the wonderful things you have given me. I've never even dreamt that I should have clothes like these."

Jean looked down as she spoke. She could see a little of the soft blue coat trimmed with beaver which she wore, and beneath it she could feel the warmth of a woollen dress that matched it. When she had been ready to leave the shop with Tally to go out to dinner, she had seen a stranger reflected in the glass. Never in her wildest imaginings had she thought that she could look not only so attractive but so utterly different from the girl who had worked so hard and so long in a house of misery and unhappiness. Too often the cracked, discoloured mirror which hung over the chest of drawers in her bedroom in her aunt's house had portrayed eyes swimming with tears and red with weeping, a face pinched and white with cold and unhappiness, and lips trembling as if in fear. Now the face that looked back at her was shining with a kind of inner light, and an excitement which showed itself in her bright eyes and her mouth, full and curved as if she must smile despite herself.

'I ought to be miserable about Angus,' she told herself severely; but the words meant nothing and she turned from the mirror to listen to Madame Marie's exclamations of admiration and watch the approval in Tally's eyes as she went across the hall to meet him.

It was Gerald who had thought that their original plan that Jean should return to her boarding house in Putney should be discarded, and Jean knew with a feeling of satisfaction that his decision was entirely due to her changed appearance.

"I don't think our story of an encounter with toughs on Putney Heath is romantic enough for Miss MacLeod," Gerald had said when Michael Sorrel and Madame Marie left the three of them alone in his sitting-room for a moment. Michael had gone to the model room at Madame Marie's insistence because she was afraid of what their regular customers would say if the shop was depleted much further for Jean's benefit.

"What do you suggest?" Tally asked.

"Well, I think that little rough and tumble had better take place in Hyde Park," Gerald said; "and when the papers wish to get in touch with Miss MacLeod tonight or tomorrow morning, it must be at some good address."

"What do you mean by good?" Tally asked sarcastically.

"You know exactly what I mean, Tally," Gerald replied patiently. "Let me suggest, in case it has escaped you, that Miss MacLeod requires a chaperon."

"A chaperon!" Tally exclaimed. "Good lord, I thought they went out of date years ago!"

"Not for very young and very nice girls," Gerald said with emphasis, and Jean would have thanked him if she had not been far too shy to utter a word.

"Yes, I see what you mean," Tally said reflectively, "but who the dickens can we get at this late hour?"

There was a pause in which Jean was suddenly aware that her heart was beating quickly. What was going to happen to her now? Somehow she was not so much afraid as excited.

Knowing Tally had become more and more of an adventure. Yes, a wonderful adventure.

"I know," Tally said suddenly, "of course, why didn't I think of it before?"

"What?" Gerald asked.

"It's your fault, my dear boy," Tally went on. "As an adviser you are not very good. In fact, to be honest, I am surprised at you, Gerald."

"Well, what have I forgotten now?" Gerald asked good humouredly.

"You are allowing me to announce my engagement without notifying the family. A tactless move and one which is likely to prejudice their feelings for my fiancée."

"Of course!" Gerald exclaimed. "You are right, old man."

"I know I am," said Tally. "We will have a little dinner, the three of us, and then I shall take Jean to my mother's."

"To Worcestershire?" Gerald asked.

"Yes, she's at home," Tally replied. "I will telephone her first so that she can prepare the fatted calf."

It was here that Jean's voice, small, low and apologetic, broke in on them.

"But please . . . please . . . before you make these decisions remember I could not possibly stay away. I have not got anything to wear . . . nothing at all suitable to take with me. I don't know what your mother would think of me."

"We will see to all that," Tally answered. "And, by the way, we had better pick up your things from your boarding house. We had better give them notice and pay the rent or they may think you have absconded or been kidnapped."

"Yes, of course," Jean murmured. At the same time all her first apprehensions returned to her. She had not anticipated being involved with Tally's relations.

What would his mother be like? she wondered. An autocratic dowager, annoyed because her precious son had become involved with an unknown young woman? She might even be suspected of being an adventuress. She shivered.

"Leave this to me," Tally had said, not once but a dozen times in their short acquaintance. She wished she could really leave everything to him and not be worried and distressed by her own emotions and anxieties.

Tally left the room and Jean looked across at Gerald. He smiled at her reassuringly.

"It is going to work out all right in the end."

"Do you think so?" Jean asked.

"I am sure of it!"

Jean sighed. Somehow, she had nothing to say to this, but she did wonder what the end might be. Was Gerald implying that Melia Melchester, who had broken her engagement with Tally, would change her mind and become re-engaged to him? Yes, of course, that must be what Gerald meant; then Tally would be happy and everything would be as it was except where she was concerned. For a moment she had a sense of blankness, then sharply she told herself that she was lucky to have even a momentary part in this unfolding drama.

"By the way," Gerald was saying. "Tally has given me your telegram. I will send it over the telephone at the first opportunity."

"Thank you," Jean said.

It was, of course, an important point in the plan of their campaign. She tried to imagine Angus' face when he opened it. What would he think? What would he feel? Would he be piqued to think that the girl whom he had discarded for someone of greater social importance had already discarded him for the same reason?

Jean felt very young and very inexperienced. What did she know about men or their feelings? Perhaps Angus' reactions would be quite different. She had been mistaken in thinking that he was really fond of her; perhaps she was mistaken in believing that he would mind whatever she did or said.

"Are you unhappy?" Gerald asked, looking at her intently.

"Not really! Only rather frightened of everything."

"I don't blame you," he said. "But now you must give me a few particulars about yourself—for the newspapers. What was your father's name?"

"The Reverend Evan MacLeod."

"He is dead?"

"Yes."

"And your mother?"

There was a moment's pause. Gerald glanced up from the note book in which he was writing. Jean's head was bent and he wondered if he had by his questions evoked sad memories. At last she spoke and her voice was very low and hesitant:

"My mother . . . is . . . dead."

Gerald was about to speak, perhaps to offer some sympathy; then he changed his mind. Perhaps it would be easier for her if he was strictly business-like.

"Your father was the . . . ?"

"Minister of Glendale, Sutherlandshire." Jean spoke quickly now as if she were glad to be able to answer this question.

Gerald looked at his notes.

"I think that is everything. Oh no, I must know your age. The more inquisitive newspapers are certain to ask it."

"I'm just nineteen."

Gerald wrote the number down and put the notebook and pencil into his pocket. Suddenly, Jean bent forward, her face tense, her fingers locked together as if she were agitated.

"Captain Fairfax, there is something I think I ought to——"

But what she was going to say he was never to know, for Tally came back into the room.

"I have fixed everything," he said gleefully to Jean. "Michael is lending you enough clothes for tonight. Tomorrow when we come back to London we will buy you everything you need. I have told the lift man to ring up and book us a table at Claridge's and we will go along there and get some dinner as soon as you are dressed. Hurry up, young woman, I am hungry."

"Am I to go downstairs to the dressing-room?" Jean asked.

Tally nodded.

"Yes, Madame Marie is waiting for you there. She is furious with me, so butter her up a bit."

"I will do my best," Jean answered, none too confidently. She hurried from the room wishing she felt more sure of herself and less like an unfledged bird.

Dinner at Claridge's had passed in a haze of unreality. She had never been inside a luxurious hotel before and the attentive waiters, the good food, and the glass of wine which Tally insisted on her drinking combined with the distant strains of soft music to make her feel as though she had suddenly been transported into a fairyland of which she had only glimpsed a brief reflection at the cinema.

After dinner Tally insisted on her sitting down and writing her letter to Angus, and then they got into the car and sped through the night to Putney. Gerald had suggested that he should deal with her landlady.

"Better not let her see you," Tally advised. "I don't believe she would recognise you as you look now; but if she did, she would think you had gone to the devil for a certainty! Besides, we don't want them to connect the quiet, well-behaved Miss MacLeod who stayed there with the smart, sophisticated Miss MacLeod whose engagement will be announced tomorrow morning."

"Perhaps it would be better if I changed my name," Jean said half seriously, feeling very unsophisticated indeed.

Tally shook his head.

"Let me give you a bit of advice, Jean. Never, never tell a lie unless you absolutely have to. The greatest art of deception is to tell the truth with maybe . . . one or two small reservations."

So Tally and Jean waited outside the boarding house in Putney and after about a quarter of an hour Gerald came out with all Jean's belongings in a small cheap suitcase.

"I gave the housemaid ten bob to pack your things and she was delighted," he said.

"I am sure she was," Jean smiled.

"She seemed a nice girl," Gerald went on. "Did she look after you well?"

"She didn't have much time to attend to the fourth floor back," Jean answered with a note of laughter in her voice. She felt it unlikely that either of these men would understand what life was like in a cheap, over-crowded boarding house where the landlady and one help did all the work.

"Now, have we finished?" Tally asked, starting up the car.

"I think so," Gerald replied. "You had better be pushing off for Worcestershire now. I'll find my way back to the West End. Don't worry about me."

Tally looked at the clock on the dashboard.

"It's just on nine o'clock," he said. "Perhaps you're right, Gerald. It will take us the best part of three hours. Sure you don't mind our leaving you?"

"Not a bit."

"Well, all right then. We'll be back tomorrow morning. Get busy with the Press."

"I will. Good night and good luck to you both."

Tally let in the clutch and Gerald waved his hat as they drove off.

As the car began to gather speed Jean asked:

"Won't your mother mind our arriving so late?"

"My mother won't think twelve o'clock late," he replied.

Jean wondered at his remark, but at the same time she was too shy to question him further. Now when they were alone, isolated in the warm darkness of the car, it seemed easier to talk to him. She asked shyly:

"Did your mother mind . . . when you told her? About me, I mean?"

"You mean about our being engaged?" Tally asked. "No, of course not!"

Jean hoped he would say more, but his eyes were on the road ahead of them and he seemed to have no further communication to make on the subject. They drove for some minutes in silence and then, because her curiosity forced her to speak, Jean inquired:

"Was your mother upset at your engagement to Miss Melchester being broken off?"

"Upset?" Tally queried. "No, I don't think so."

"Are you Lady Brora's only child?"

"Yes, I have no brothers or sisters and, incidentally, my mother is not Lady Brora. She married again after my father was killed. He had a bad accident out hunting. I was about twelve at the time. My mother's name now is Mrs. Melton, but my stepfather died of wounds after the fall of Singapore."

"How dreadful!" Jean cried sympathetically.

Tally nodded, but he said nothing more. They drove on in silence until once again Jean felt her head dropping. There was no getting away from the fact that she was tired. She told herself that it was more her mind than her body. So much had happened, and so quickly. . . . A lassitude crept over her. She thought again of the moment when she had opened Angus' letter, of the bitterness of her tears, of Tally coming unexpectedly into the office and his amazing proposition; of Michael Sorrel and of the clothes she was wearing and the clothes she was to have to wear tomorrow and perhaps the day after. The tunes played by the band at Claridge's kept repeating themselves as a background for her thoughts until her head slid sideways to rest against Tally's shoulder and she slept. . . .

She woke with a sudden jerk. The car had come to a standstill.

"We have arrived," Tally said. Jean opened her eyes and found Tally's arm round her shoulders supporting her.

"Wake up," he said, "we are home."

"Oh, dear, have I been asleep again?" she asked. "I am sorry."

A door opened and a sudden shaft of light shone out bathing them in a golden radiance as Tally helped her out of the car. Jean looked up at the huge house towering high above them. There were lights in many of the windows, and in the big porticoed doorway above a flight of wide stone steps stood a dignified, white-haired butler.

"Did you have a good run, m'lord?" he asked in a respectful voice.

"Pretty good, Barnet. It took us about three hours and five minutes. It's a bit over my record, but I drove carefully. I didn't want to frighten Miss MacLeod."

Tally turned towards Jean.

"Jean," he said, "I want you to meet Barnet. He has been with our family for fifty years and he has known all my misdemeanours ever since I was born."

"How do you do, Miss?" Barnet said as Jean shook him by the hand. "I'm pleased to welcome you to Greystones."

"Thank you," Jean replied, warmed and even a little comforted by his words.

"Goodness, it's cold," Tally said with a shiver. "It must be freezing, Barnet?"

"About six degrees, m'lord, when I looked at the thermometer just after dinner. Will you go into the drawing-room? There's a big fire there and madam is expecting you."

"Good! Come along, Jean," Tally commanded, and putting his hand under her arm he drew her up the steps and in through the front door.

The hall was big and lofty, panelled in oak with a great curving staircase. There were portraits in heavy gilt frames on the walls and tiger skins covered the polished floor. Jean wanted to look around her, but without pausing Tally led her to a door at the far end of the hall. He opened it and there was a sudden blaze of light and colour, the exotic fragrance of hot-house flowers and a buzz of conversation. The room was very large and crystal chandeliers hung from the ceiling. Round the fireplace there seemed to Jean to be a crowd of people, most of them sitting at small baize-covered tables playing cards. A tall woman in black velvet rose to greet them.

"Tally darling!" she exclaimed. "We wondered how soon you would get here."

"Hullo, Mother." Tally bent forward to kiss her cheek. "This is Jean."

"How do you do?" A soft hand touched Jean's for a moment. "Come by the fire. You must both be frightfully cold. There are sandwiches over there and some hot coffee. If you want anything more substantial Barnet will get it."

"I think sandwiches will be sufficient," Tally said. "We had dinner before we left."

They moved nearer the fireplace and now there was a chorus of welcome.

"Glad to see you, Tally. . . ."

"How are you, old boy?"

"What is this we hear . . . ?"

"Another engagement . . . ?"

"Really, Tally, you are incorrigible . . ."

It was difficult to separate the greetings or to connect the voices with their owners. Jean stood back until Tally dragged her forward and she shook hands with a dozen people. It was only when Tally had fetched her a sandwich and she had drunk a cup of steaming hot coffee that her nervousness permitted her to take in a few details of the people talking, laughing and chattering.

Tally's mother was astonishing; somehow she had expected someone old and elderly. Mrs. Melton looked absurdly young to be the mother of a grown-up son. She was very graceful, with a long neck and a face which could only be described as exquisite. There was, Jean thought, no other word for it. She had large dark eyes and her hair was cut quite short to form tiny grecian curls round her white forehead and at the back of her well-shaped head. She was not only beautiful but unusual.

'I should never get tired of looking at her,' Jean thought; 'she is the loveliest person I have ever seen.'

And yet, even as she admired Mrs. Melton she thought that hers was not a happy face; there was some-

68

thing restless and almost haunted about her wide eyes and something infinitely pathetic in the droop of her soft mouth. As they went on talking Jean realised that Mrs. Melton was not really interested in what they were saying. She was charming; she joined in the conversation, and yet it was as if only a superficial part of her was there and her attention and her thoughts were elsewhere.

'I am imagining things,' Jean thought, and yet the impression persisted.

After a while the guests who had been playing cards went back to their tables.

"We had better finish the rubber," they said; and Jean, Tally, and his mother were left alone by the fire.

Mrs. Melton stood with one white hand holding on to the marble mantelpiece, her head bent as she looked at the flames. Her frock flowed in long graceful lines to form a pool of deep shadow at her feet.

'She is lovely,' Jean thought again, and wondered of what she was thinking as she stared into the fire.

"Were you surprised when I telelphoned, Mother?" Tally asked, helping himself to yet another sandwich from the silver dish engraved with his crest—an eagle with outspread wings.

"Surprised?" Mrs. Melton asked vaguely. "Oh, about your coming down here. Of course, darling."

It was obvious that she was speaking merely conventionally and Jean could sympathise with Tally's impatience as he insisted:

"You understand that my engagement to Jean is being announced tomorrow?"

"So you said, darling. You don't want me to do anything about it, do you?"

"No, of course not," Tally replied. "I only thought you might be interested."

"But I am, Tally, really I am. And tomorrow, when she is rested, Jean must tell me all about herself."

She smiled at Jean, but when Jean would have eagerly smiled back, she looked away as if she had no interest in the response to her graciousness.

Tally looked at his watch.

"What about bed?" he inquired. "Have you got to wait up for all these people?"

"Oh, no, I expect they will go on playing for some time yet," Mrs. Melton replied. "I will take Jean up to her room. You won't have any more coffee?"

"No, thank you," Jean answered.

"Come along then," Mrs. Melton said. "Don't bother to say good night to anyone. They are all absorbed in their gambling."

She led the way from the room, walking quickly, the train of her dress slithering behind her over the soft carpet. Tally followed them into the hall.

"Sleep well. Ask for anything you want; and I will see you in the morning."

"Good night, Tally."

Jean was not certain if she should hold out her hand, but Tally did not seem to expect it so she smiled at him and turned away a little forlornly. She was afraid to leave him because he was her one link with her past self—an entity which seemed to her to be in the process of being quickly obliterated.

She was half-way up the stairs with Mrs. Melton before he spoke again.

"Good night, Jean."

She stopped for a moment, leaning over the thick oak banister. His head was thrown back. Against the dark panelling of the hall and the high carved fireplace with its leaping log fire he seemed a person of dignity and authority.

"Good night," Jean said uncertainly.

"God bless you," Tally replied, "and . . . thank you."

It was these words that she took with her to give her courage as she was shown into the big room, tapestry-hung, with a great four-poster bed. There was a fire in the grate and already her clothes had been unpacked. With a sudden sinking of her heart Jean realised that the housemaid had unpacked both suitcases, the one that Michael Sorrel had lent her and the one that Gerald had collected from her boarding house.

On the dressing-table with its high, triple mirrors were her pitiable toilet things—a comb with three teeth missing, a hairbrush of cheap varnished wood—and on the bed, laid out for to make her choice, were a nightgown of chiffon and ecru lace, exquisite in its detail and lovely in its sheer cobweb fragility, and beside it another nightgown of heavy cotton material ornamented only by two bone buttons at the neck and the stitches which she had put laboriously into it.

It seemed to Jean at that moment that her duplicity was revealed all too clearly. There were two Jeans—the pretentious one whom Michael Sorrel had created at Tally's insistence and the real Jean, plain, austere and serviceable. For the moment she thought of explaining everything to Mrs. Melton, of telling her the truth and revealing exactly why she was here. Despite her air of indifference and detachment there was something sympathetic in her manner which kept Jean from being afraid of her.

Should she speak? The words trembled on her lips. And then, before she could say anything, Mrs. Melton, having looked round the room as if to see that everything was in order, said:

"I do hope you will be comfortable, please ring if there is anything you want. Good night."

She turned towards the door without another word. It was almost as if she dreaded the exchange of any confidences or intimacy such as might be expected from the girl to whom her son was engaged.

"Good night," Mrs. Melton repeated and then the door closed behind her.

Jean stood for a moment looking after her. Then she turned her gaze once again towards those two nightgowns.

Had Mrs. Melton seen them? She must have! What could she have thought? To Jean they lay there accusingly—the true and the false!

5

Lady Melchester entered her daughter's room and crossing to the window flung back the curtains. Melia, who was asleep in the lace-covered bed, merely turned over and settled herself for further slumber.

"Melia!" Lady Melchester called sharply. "Wake up! I have got something to show you."

There was no response. Going to the bedside, Lady Melchester bent over and shook her daughter's shoulder.

"Wake up at once, Melia. This is important. Just look at the *Daily Express*."

At the words *Daily Express* Melia made a convulsive movement and sat up in bed. Her dark hair was pinned tightly to her head in neat curls and she wore a sleeping-cap of pale blue lace which matched her nightgown. Her nose was unpowdered and yet she contrived, even at that moment, to be amazingly pretty. She did not speak to her mother but instead yawned and held out her hand for the newspaper.

"Look!" Lady Melchester exclaimed dramatically. Melia glanced at the paragraph at which her mother's finger was pointing; then she clutched the newspaper convulsively with both hands.

"It can't be true," she gasped at length. "How dare Tally do this! How dare he!"

"I told you, Melia," Lady Melchester said wearily, "that you were making a mistake."

73

Melia raised her big dark eyes to her mother's face.

"You know what this means?" she said. "Everyone will say that Tally has chucked me! I can't bear it! How could he treat me like this? Oh, how could he!"

Mother and daughter stared at each other with something like despair.

Lady Melchester was an American. She herself had made what was termed a brilliant marriage in her first season in England. She had been presented at Court, and chaperoned by the American Ambassador's wife had gone to a State Ball at Buckingham Palace. There among the gilt and scarlet pomp and ceremony Sir Charles Melchester had fallen in love with her. That she was very rich had nothing to do with his interest, for he was a simple man who had never learned to scheme and was blissfully unaware for the whole of his life of the machinations of his wife and daughter.

Lady Melchester had been married for nearly ten years before she presented her husband with a child; and after Melia arrived she was content to rest on her laurels, making no effort to produce the much-longed-for heir. It was perhaps natural that Melia should be spoilt in her own home, but she also paid annual visits to her mother's relatives in America and there she learned that the world was made for women to walk on.

Across the Atlantic Melia acquired more than a knowledge of her own superiority. She learned to dress exquisitely, to be graceful, amusing and witty, and to have a sang-froid and a sophistication impossible to any of her British contemporaries. All the impressionable, pliant years of her adolescence were spent in America, for immediately war was declared Lady Melchester sent her precious daughter away to safety, and the welcoming arms of adoring relatives. Melia was a social figure in New York before her fifteenth birthday; her opinions were published as news; her post included film offers, requests for autographs, proposals of marriage and the fanatical eulogies of fans. It was not surprising that Melia had a somewhat inflated idea of her own importance in the scheme of things. History, geography, international events and national crises were of interest if directly or indirectly they affected her personally. Her success when she made her début in London was sensational. She captured the attention not only of the social world but also of the British public, who have always loved a beautiful girl and who were perfectly prepared to transfer some of their adoration from the better-known film stars to glamorous Miss Melia Melchester. The newspapers vied with each other in writing her up and photographing her at unusual angles, and the pictorial periodicals seldom went to press without including a photograph of her or a reference to the most notorious beauty of the time.

Melia's publicity soared like a rocket until there were few people in the British Isles and on the east coast of North America who had not heard of her. There had, of course, been numerous young men eager to seek her hand in marriage, but Tally had undoubtedly been the most distinguished and certainly the most attractive of them all. At first his assumption that they were intended for each other from birth annoyed Melia. She was used to flattery spread thickly and Tally's easy, familiar manner annoyed her until she set herself to teach him a lesson by making him fall in love with her. It had not been difficult.

During the war Tally had been far too busy to have time for women. There were various flirtations with which he wiled away his leaves, but in everything he did Tally was inclined to concentrate fiercely and to the exclusion of all else. The war had occupied him body and soul and he was therefore young in experience if not in years. When he first took it into his head to court Melia she found him direct, forceful and extremely obstinate. He did not respond as other men did to a slight coldness in her voice, to a gesture from her white hands or a quiver of her eyelashes, but she found as time progressed that Tally's masterfulness had a charm of its own. She rather enjoyed being browbeaten by him. For the first time in her life she had experienced a tiny thrill when he drew her possessively into his arms and kissed her, despite her efforts to evade him.

"No, Tally, no," she protested.

"Why not?" he asked. "I love you and I am going to marry you."

Melia had the feeling more than once that if she really abandoned herself to Tally's love-making she would experience a happiness she had never known. But the instinct to preserve herself from any feeling that was not thought out, calculated and schemed for kept her from surrendering herself. As it happened, she could not have evolved a method more calculated to keep Tally's interest. He had been trained in the hard school to conquer the unattainable and had learnt that the more difficult, the more elusive his objective, the more violent and cunning must be his assault on it. Tally put nearly as much thought and concentration into the winning of Melia as he had put into the achieving of his objectives in war-time. He was just as successful.

Melia at length promised graciously and in exactly the right setting to be his wife. She was an artist as regards herself. A band was playing in the distance a soft, seductive waltz and they had wandered away through the corridors of the great historic mansion where a dance was being held till they stood at the end of the long picture gallery. The moonlight was streaming through the uncurtained window at the far end. They seemed cut off from everything, alone with only the ghosts of the past.

Melia stood very still, one hand on the window-sill, the other raised to touch with the tips of her fingers the pearls which encircled her white neck. She was wearing of dress of soft, grey tulle relieved only by a huge bunch of crimson roses pinned between her breasts. She looked almost like a ghost herself save that there was a little pulse beating quickly in her throat. With a sudden, sweeping movement of her dark eyelashes she raised her head and looked up at Tally.

"You are lovely," he said hoarsely. "Say you will marry me, Melia?"

She hesitated for a moment and in a faint voice, so low that he could hardly catch what she said, she whispered:

"Yes, Tally, I will."

For a moment he could hardly believe his ears. She had refused him so often and for so long. Then he stepped forward and put his arms round her to draw her close to him. She gave a little cry and used both her hands to ward him off with surprising strength.

"My hair, Tally, my dress. Do be careful!"

"What does it matter?" he asked.

"It matters a lot. I don't want to go downstairs looking kissed and besides, our engagement is to be a secret for the moment. I don't want it announced until exactly the right moment."

"Now is the right moment for me!" Tally replied.

Melia laughed, and putting up her hand patted his cheek.

"Dear Tally. You mustn't be impatient."

He caught her hand and turning it over kissed the palm lingeringly.

"I love you, Melia, and you will drive me mad."

He was not certain what he loved most about her—her elusive grace, her exquisite features, or her voice which thrilled him even while she repulsed and scolded him. Yet even at that moment he found himself thinking how little he knew of the real Melia, of the heart that must beat somewhere in that exquisite body, of the brain which had worked behind that perfectly moulded forehead.

He didn't pretend to understand her and he chafed against keeping their engagement a secret.

"What are we waiting for?" he kept asking. "Let's get married and go to Switzerland for our honeymoon."

Melia pouted.

"I don't think I really want a winter wedding."

"Well, you are going to have one," Tally replied grimly. "If you think I am going to wait until next summer, you are very much mistaken."

But despite pleading, bullying and even threatening

Melia was adamant. She would announce her engagement when she was ready and not before. Her mother approved of the delay even while she was fond of Tally, having known him for many years.

"He is a dear boy and, of course, the title is a very old one. But at the same time, darling, I always visualised you as a duchess."

Melia made a little gesture of annoyance.

"And where is the duke?"

"That is the difficulty," Lady Melchester sighed. "All those beautiful eligible young men killed in the war! It was the same after the last one. Oh well, I believe the Brora diamonds are magnificent. Mrs. Melton has put most of them in the bank, but then she would."

"I will wear one of the tiaras to be married in," Melia said reflectively.

"I love diamonds and tulle," Lady Melchester agreed enthusiastically.

Melia had begun to prepare her trousseau, not actually ordering anything but asking for sketches and suggestions, and giving such very broad hints to the shops which she usually patronised that very soon there was no one in the whole of London who did not know of the impending engagement.

It was just when she had made up her mind to stop teasing Tally and give him a definite date for their marriage that Melia met Ernest Danks. She had gone to a charity ball, the tickets for which had cost her mother £5 each and which proved to be the usual, rather dreary evening in an overcrowded ballroom.

Melia had been on the point of leaving when a dowager, sitting at the same supper-table, had remarked to the man next her.

"I am surprised to see Ernest Danks here. He is a very serious young man, I am told, and should go far. My husband thinks he is likely to be the next Prime Minister."

"I think there is no doubt about that at all," was the reply.

Melia, vaguely interested, glanced at the man of

whom they were speaking. It appeared that he was looking at her at the same moment. Their eyes met, and though Melia looked away almost immediately she was well aware that he was both attracted and interested in her. She changed her mind about leaving the ball and within a few minutes she saw an elderly woman making her way through the dancers with Ernest Danks behind her.

"Oh, Miss Melchester," she said, "you won't remember me, but I am an old friend of your mother's. I want to introduce Mr. Danks, who tells me he has been longing to meet you for years. He has heard so much about you, of course, as we all have."

The elderly woman smiled and then slipped away, leaving Melia and Ernest Danks face to face.

"Will you dance with me?" he asked a little awkwardly.

Melia hesitated.

"I am with a party," she said conventionally and then added with a radiant smile, "but why not?"

She put her bag down on the table and ignoring the groans from the three young men sitting there who had been waiting for the favour of a dance, moved away in Ernest Danks' arms. It didn't take Melia long to find out a lot about him. He was a self-made man, but his youth and virility had made him outstanding in a rather dull and mediocre House of Commons. It was quite true that there was every possibility of his being Prime Minister. He had not only brilliance but popularity and there was no one else in the Government who could combine both those assets so successfully as Ernest Danks.

Despite such promises for the future Melia might not have been seriously interested had not the Prime Minister, who was well over 70, had a stroke in the Chamber. From the very first it was obvious that there was no hope of recovery, and Ernest Danks became overnight a figure of such potential importance that even Melia was impressed. It was then he had asked her to marry him.

"A week ago I would have hesitated," he said slightly

79

pompously. "I would have had so little to offer you; but even in a few hours things may be very different. Together you and I will create history from Downing Street."

It was a picture which was bound to appeal to Melia. She had lived for so long in the public eye that it seemed to her that nothing could be more fitting and sensational than that she should move from Mayfair to Westminster and embrace the dual crown of Queen of Society and social leader of the political world.

But now as she read the *Daily Express* and saw Tally's face looking back at her under the headlines, she felt as if he had destroyed with one blow so much that she worked for. It was one thing to throw over a good-looking, much talked about lord and another to be thrown over by him. Besides, the Prime Minister was not dead and until he was she had no intention of becoming officially engaged to Ernest Danks. Tally had stolen a march on her and combined with her anger at what she felt was an unwarrantable action on his part was another feeling—one of loss for him personally.

Tally had attracted Melia as she had never been attracted in her life before. Ernest Danks interested her, but she did not want him to kiss her. In fact, it always gave her a slight shock when he touched her hand with his short, square fingers. She had already made silent resolutions that as soon as she was married she would alter his clothes, the way he ate, the way he sat in a chair, and the manner in which he opened the door for her to pass through. Tally had never irritated her in such small ways, but now that he was engaged to someone else she felt a faint flickering in her heart not only of regret but of something extremely like jealousy. She read the headlines through again.

"COMMANDO HERO'S FIGHT IN HYDE PARK."
"LORD BRORA TO THE RESCUE."
"ENGAGED TO GIRL HE SAVED."

"Who is this girl?" she asked at last. "I have never heard of her."

"It doesn't say much about her," Lady Melchester replied.

"A parson's daughter. That doesn't seem very exciting."

"I wonder why they have not put in a photograph of her."

"Perhaps it is too unbecoming," Lady Melchester suggested cattily.

"Do you see what it says here?" Melia asked and read:

"When our correspondent telephoned Lord Brora at his home at Greystones, in Worcestershire, last night, Lord Brora confirmed his engagement and added: 'I am sorry my fiancée cannot speak to you. She has gone to bed.' Asked if he had known Miss MacLeod for a long time, Lord Brora replied. 'Long enough to know that we shall be very happy together.' He would give no indication of the probable date of his wedding."

Melia threw the paper down on the bed.

"Tally was with me at six o'clock," she said. "There is something behind all this."

"What did you say to him?" Lady Melchester said.

"I told you, Mother, what I said to him and that he was angry, very angry. He has done this just to annoy me, in which case he has succeeded. Give me my telephone book. It is over there on the writing-desk."

Lady Melchester got up from the bed.

"What are you going to do?" she asked.

"I am going to ring Tally and ask him what he means by it." She looked up the number in the crimson leather address book inscribed with her name in gold.

She picked up the receiver and gave the number. To cover her bare shoulders emerging from the lace and ribbons of her nightgown Lady Melchester fetched a cape of tiny coral ostrich feathers from the cupboard, and slipped it round her. It took a few moments for Melia to be connected to Greystones and while she waited she drummed with her fingers on the book by her side. Lady Melchester walked across the room, took a cigarette out of a silver box and lit it. She was nearly as perturbed as Melia. She had helped to a very great extent to build up the legend round her beautiful daughter. She was well aware that this morning's newspapers would be devoured by all their friends and that the comments on the news would be none too kind. Few people really enjoy the success of others, however much they may pretend to do so. Lady Melchester knew that Melia's triumphs had caused envy, malice and hatred among many girls of her own age.

At last the operator's voice told Melia she was through.

"I want to speak to Lord Brora."

"What name, please?"

"Miss Melchester."

"Hold on a moment, please."

She waited, squaring her shoulders a little as if to prepare herself for battle. She heard Tally come to the telephone.

"Hullo! Is that you, Melia?"

"Tally, how could you do such a thing?"

"Do what?"

"You know quite well what—I have just seen the newspapers."

"Anything of interest in them? We don't get them in this benighted hole until ten o'clock."

"You know perfectly well what they have got in them, Tally."

"My engagement to Jean?"

"What is the point of all this?"

"Point of what?"

"What are you doing. This ridiculous engagement. You know quite well that it is all made up."

"I assure you it is nothing of the sort, Melia."

"I hate you, Tally. I always thought you were cruel and beastly, but I never believed that you would treat me like this."

Melia's voice was almost hysterical.

"My dear girl, may I point out that you told me quite distinctly—in fact, I did have it in writing until I threw the letter down somewhere in your very charming sitting-room—that you had no further use for me and that you intended to marry the future Prime Minister."

"That was yesterday at six o'clock! How could you have got engaged between then and now?"

"Operational tactics, Melia."

"Tally, I hate you."

"So you have already told me."

"But I have got to see you. I have got to talk to you about this. You are to come up to London at once and see me."

"As a matter of fact we are coming up. Jean has a fitting with Michael and everyone is clamouring for photographs."

"I have got to see you,'" Melia repeated.

"I will ring you up when I arrive," Tally said airily. "But I am afraid I won't be able to get round until this afternoon. There is so much to do. Good-bye, Melia, and thank you for your congratulations."

He rang off before she could reply and stood for a moment looking at the telephone receiver with a smile on his lips. It was not a very kind smile, but there was a great deal of satisfaction in it. Then he walked back to the dining-room from where the butler had fetched him.

Jean came downstairs twenty minutes later and heard Tally's laugh ring out as he passed through the hall from the dining-room to the morning-room. Jean thought he sounded happy and carefree. She wondered if he was indeed as unhappy about Melia as he had led her to believe yesterday.

When she woke she had wondered whether she should get up or wait until she was called. She lay in the large bed, watching fingers of light coming between the high curtains veiling the windows. She felt like the Princess in the fairy story who slept on twenty-four mattresses and yet felt the pea beneath them. Her pea had been her conscience, which had kept her awake most of the night. Over and over again Jean had told herself that she was beholden to no one, that there was nothing wrong in entering into such an adventure, but some Puritan Scottish streak within her would not be satisfied.

"You are here under false pretences," it said accusingly, and even the softness of the chiffon nightgown enfolding her figure had failed to console her. When finally she had fallen into a fitful sleep she had dreamed that she was being scolded by her aunt for some misdemeanour, and when she awoke it was a relief to know that that at least was not true.

While she was wondering what to do, a maid came into the room, drew back the curtains and brought in her breakfast on a tray. Jean sat up and looked wide-eyed at the excellently cooked eggs, the wafer-thin toast in the silver rack, the curling pats of golden butter and the marmalade and jam in small cut-glass pots. The coffee was fragrant and delicious, and there were also a big juicy pear and a mother-of-pearl-handled knife and fork to eat it with. Jean thought of the breakfast she had eaten only yesterday in her boarding house, of the tablecloth stained from the previous night's supper, of the thick lumpy porridge, the minute portion of fried bread, the dark black tea in a cheap cracked cup, and the thick slices of bread on which she could spread a minute portion of margarine. How different this was!

She found herself eating slowly, savouring every mouthful; and as she ate, winter sunshine came in through the windows to light the room. Jean found that her curiosity could not wait. Before she drank her second cup of coffee she slipped from the bed to look out of the window.

In front of the house was a great lake and down to it sloped terraces and lawns. It was winter so that there were no flowers and the trees were bare, yet even so the landscape had a lovely, haunting beauty. The terraces were balustraded with stone mellow with age. The lake was grey and on the other side of it there was a small Grecian temple round which the trees clustered thickly. In the distance beyond the parkland Jean could see over the Vale of Evesham until far away on the horizon there was the barren beauty of the Malvern Hills. It was all so lovely that she stood entranced and not even the touch of snow on the top of Bredon Hill or the frost which silvered the lawns made her remember that her feet were bare and her body inadequately covered.

She was startled by a knock on the door. Because she was too surprised to reply, the maid entered.

"I'm sorry, Miss, I thought you said 'Come in!' " she apologised when she saw Jean at the window. "I came to say that your bath is ready and his lordship sent a message to say that the car will be round at nine-thirty."

"Thank you," Jean said.

"I will come back and pack, Miss, as soon as you are dressed, if you would not mind touching the bell."

"Thank you," Jean said again. As soon as the maid was gone, she made up her mind that she would pack her own things. She drank her coffee and went to her bath; then she dressed quickly and taking from the wardrobe the suitcase which Gerald had picked up in Putney, she began to fill it. She took from the elegantly-carved chest of drawers the ugly serviceable garments chosen by her aunt. There were two woollen jumpers, an odd skirt, an overall which her aunt had bought for her to wear when doing housework, some underclothes and three pairs of thick grey lisle stockings, which had been the only sort she possessed until she had earned her first week's salary. Jean remembered the thrill and her excitement when she went into a big Oxford Street store and purchased her first pair of silk stockings. "Mine, my very own!" she had said to herself as the girl wrapped them up for her and made out the bill.

Thinking of that moment and her pride in being able both to earn and spend her own money, she suddenly got to her feet. The suitcase with its worn, drab contents was a challenge.

"Why should I be ashamed?" she asked aloud. "Why should I be afraid of what the housemaid here has seen? Let them think what they like. If anyone asks me for an explanation I shall tell them the truth."

She was standing with her head thrown back a little

defiantly when a knock came to the door. It was the housemaid again.

"Excuse me, Miss, I thought perhaps you had forgotten to ring." She looked at the open suitcase. "Oh, but you shouldn't have started, Miss; I will pack everything and be in time for his lordship."

"Thank you," she said shyly. "Thank you very much." She hesitated a moment; then opening her bag which lay on the dressing-table, she took out two half-crowns. It was the first time she had ever tipped anyone. She flushed crimson as she pressed them into the girl's hand saying, "And thank you for looking after me."

"It has been a pleasure, Miss," the housemaid replied. "We all hope you will be terribly happy with his lordship. We all love him here."

Jean stammered some response, then slipped away downstairs. She walked slowly and very quietly because she wished to recover from her confusion, and she had nearly reached the hall when Tally turned in the doorway of the morning-room and saw her.

"Good morning, Jean. Are you ready to drive back to London?"

"Yes. My packing will be finished in a few minutes."

"Good. If we don't get back early, Gerald will be rampaging; and besides, you promised to look in at Michael's before luncheon."

"Yes, of course," Jean said.

She moved across the hall and stood by the fire, holding out her hands to the flames from two great logs.

"Had a good night?" Tally asked.

"Yes, thank you." It seemed rude to tell him that she had lain awake worrying. He seemed to be in unusually happy mood himself.

As if in answer to a question she had not asked, Tally said: "Yes, I have had good news."

"Who from?"

"Melia."

"Oh! What did she say? Did she telephone you?"

"Yes, she telephoned. She is very, very angry, and I

assure you that to get any violent emotion from Melia is as difficult as making Eros dance a hornpipe."

Jean did not know quite what to say to this, so she was silent, and after a moment Tally added: "I am going to see her this afternoon."

"Does that mean that she will ask you to be re-engaged to her?" Jean asked in a very small voice.

"Good lord, no!" Tally ejaculated. "This is only the beginning of the battle. At the moment Melia wants to scratch my eyes out. But we will wait and see!"

He gave a little chuckle as if of sheer joy, then he put an arm around Jean's shoulder and gave her a hug.

"You're being a perfect brick; I am awfully grateful."

Jean flushed a little at his action and was furious with herself for doing so. To change the conversation, she asked:

"Who is that?" and pointed to a large picture of a man sitting on a horse. His pink hunting-coat was in brilliant contrast with a wintry sky and in the background there was a great grey-stone mansion which Jean guessed was Greystones.

"That is my father," Tally replied. "And is exactly like him."

"He is very good looking," Jean said, and then realised that Tally was an exact replica of the portrait. She looked up at it again. "It must have been terrible for your mother when he was killed out hunting. Did they bring him back here?"

Tally nodded.

"I can remember it happening. He was riding a young mare which had a bad reputation. All the grooms were afraid of her, but my father was afraid of nothing. Nobody knows quite what happened, but the mare fell and rolled on him. He was terribly injured and hadn't got a chance of recovery. He died on the way home."

"How awful," Jean said. "I cannot bear to think of it."

Tally looked at her.

"By the way, that reminds me, my mother sent you

her love. She is afraid she cannot see you this morning. She has had a bad night."

"Oh, I am sorry," Jean said sympathetically.

Tally's tone was quite ordinary, but she felt there was something strange in his expression. Was she imagining it, she asked herself, or was there a tension, a sudden wariness about him, as if he anticipated surprise or inquiries? Was Mrs. Melton avoiding her? On the way back to London the question presented itself to her over and over again. She did not know why it mattered so much. After all, she told herself, it was quite likely that she might never see Tally's mother again; but she had admired her and, despite Mrs. Melton's vagueness, she had felt drawn towards her as if here was someone to whom she could talk, and with whom she could be completely natural. It was ridiculous, of course, just an absurd fantasy, and yet as they sped towards London Jean kept seeing that lovely face with its sad, haunted eyes and unhappy mouth.

The roads near London were crowded, and despite Tally's skilful driving, it was nearly one o'clock when they reached the West End.

"I told Parker to telephone Gerald," Tally explained, "and ask him to meet us at the Berkeley. You can go round to Michael's immediately after luncheon. He won't expect you to be punctual anyway."

Tally drew up the car in Berkeley Street, and as he helped Jean on to the pavement, several photographers encircled them.

"Just a moment, Lord Brora, please, we want to take you and Miss MacLeod together."

"That's right, and again, please."

"Will you walk up the street?"

"Smile, Miss MacLeod . . . that's fine."

"O.K."

"Thank you."

"Thank you very much, and good luck!"

Jean felt shy, but Tally laughed.

"This is Gerald's doing," he said. "He is a good showman!"

Jean said nothing, but now that they were back in London all her fears seemed to multiply themselves, so that it was almost with relief that she saw Gerald coming towards them, a sheaf of papers under his arm.

"You have seen the papers?" Gerald asked.

"No, of course we haven't," Tally replied. "We left before they arrived."

"Well, I've done you proud," Gerald said, sitting down on the sofa beside them. "Did you order me a cocktail?"

Tally nodded. He took up the *Daily Express* and handed the *Daily Mail* to Jean. He read the headlines in the first page and whistled.

"No wonder Melia was annoyed."

"You haven't seen the first edition of the evening papers," Gerald said. "The *Evening Standard* says it had been confidently expected that your engagement would be announced to a well-known society beauty."

Tally threw back his head and laughed.

"I am rather sorry for her," Jean said quietly.

Both men looked surprised.

"Why?" Tally inquired.

"She is only a girl, after all, and you are both trying to do her down."

Tally looked grim.

"Now, listen, Jean. You need not waste your sympathy on Melia. If anyone was born capable of looking after herself under all circumstances, it is Melia Melchester."

"But I thought you loved her?" Jean remarked gravely.

For a moment Tally looked nonplussed.

"I do," he said, "but that doesn't mean that I am blind to her faults. She has done a bit of calculating and I am doing some, too. We will see who wins. That is the position, and it is no use being soft-hearted at the very outset."

"No, of course not," Jean said, but she was not convinced.

After luncheon, Tally and Gerald took her to Michael
89

Sorrel's with instructions to hurry up and get her fitting over, as the photographers were waiting.

Madame Marie tried various models on her with a sour expression which told Jean all too clearly that these were gowns specially ordered for other customers. Finally, carrying in a box the precious 'Almond Blossom' dress she was to wear for the photographs, she hurried out of the shop to where the two men were waiting for her in the car.

"Madame Marie is very angry about this model," she told Tally, as she got into the front seat beside him.

"Let her be," Tally growled. "You are more important than all the princesses and duchesses whom Michael tries to make look glamorous."

"And succeeds," Jean added enthusiastically. "His dresses are so lovely. They make the ugliest person look wonderful. When I put on his clothes I felt exactly like Cinderella."

"Well, we must try and take you to a ball," Tally said goodhumouredly, and a moment later drew up outside a house in Berkeley Square. It was one of the very old houses in the Square, and outside on the railings were the iron extinguishers in which the linkmen used to put out their torches. Tally rapped loudly on a massive silver knocker, and the door was opened by a very old man.

"Good afternoon, m'lord."

"Here we are, Johnson," Tally said, and having introduced Jean to yet another old retainer, he led the way upstairs to where in a long, high-ceilinged drawing-room the photographers were waiting. It was a room of great beauty, but it had the dusty, musty atmosphere of a place which has not been lived in for a long time, and in one corner there was a large pile of dust sheets which had obviously been taken off the furniture. The walls were papered with an exquisite Chinese design of flowers and weird, exotic birds, and there were huge vases of delicate porcelain on ebony stands and gilt-framed mirrors which reflected and re-reflected themselves and the room. It was a fairy-tale setting, and Jean found only the photographer, busy with his cameras and arc lights, out of place.

"You can change along the passage," Tally said, and showed Jean to another big room, decorated in old rose damask and with a carved gold bedstead draped with rose-coloured hangings.

"What a lovely room!" Jean exclaimed.

"It's my mother's," Tally said. "But she never comes here now, and I am afraid it is rather cold in consequence."

Tally left her and Jean changed her dress, looking round while she did so. Although Mrs. Melton might not come to Berkeley Square, the room seemed ready for her occupation at any moment should she decide to do so. Her tortoiseshell brushes were laid out on the dressing-table, there were books and a miniature of Tally on the table beside the bed. There were cigarettes in a white onyx box by the fireplace and the Dresden china clock on the mantelpiece was going.

"It is a lovely room," Jean repeated aloud. Yet she felt there was a strange atmosphere about it. Was it of sadness or tension? She was not sure. It was then she saw that on the other side of the bed there was another photograph. It was in a silver frame, and despite the fact that she ought to be hurrying, Jean moved across the room to look at it.

It showed a striking-looking man with dark hair and a dark moustache. Obviously it was an enlarged snapshot, and it looked just as if he were about to speak, about to say something. In small, neat handwriting in the corner of the photograph was written: "To my darling wife, from Stephen."

That must be Mrs. Melton's second husband, Jean thought; and then, because she felt that she was prying, she quickly arranged her hair in the looking-glass and ran back to the drawing-room. The photographs took some time. She was posed against the vases, beside the gilt mirrors, in front of the ornate mantelpiece, and then standing alone in the centre of the floor under the glittering magnificence of the chandelier.

Finally the photographer said he had finished, and with a sigh of relief Jean excused herself and went back to the bedroom to change.

She entered the room, and it seemed to her that the photograph by the bedside commanded her attention.

"I wonder what he was going to say," Jean questioned. "Perhaps he still wants to say it."

The idea forced itself upon her, and she had the feeling strangely and insistently that there was something Stephen Melton wished to tell her. She knew now that the atmosphere in the room was his—she felt him there, was uneasily aware of his personality—almost, she thought, of his very presence. She chided her imagination, but although she turned her back to the photograph she was conscious all the time that it was there. It was an uncomfortable, uncanny feeling, and it was with relief that Jean put the 'Almond Blossom' dress back into its box and was ready to leave. At the doorway she looked back again. "I am quite sure he wants to say something," she thought.

Gerald was waiting for her alone downstairs.

"Where is Tally?" Jean inquired.

For a moment she fancied that Gerald looked embarrassed.

"He has gone round to see Melia," he said at length, "and we are to meet him at his flat for tea."

They walked out together into Berkeley Square.

"My instructions were," Gerald said, "that I was to take you shopping. What do you want to buy?"

"Lots of things," Jean replied, before she could consider the answer, and then added, "but I haven't got the money."

"Tally has plenty," Gerald said.

She looked up at him, having no idea how small and appealing she looked in the little feather cap which matched her blue tweed coat.

"Captain Fairfax, please answer me truthfully . . . Do

you think I ought to? . . . Let Tally pay, I mean." Her voice was very serious, and Gerald's was equally grave.

"I think it's quite all right to let him pay for necessities."

Jean smiled instantly.

"That's what I wanted to know," she said. "Just necessities. Such as a decent comb and hairbrush in case I have to go to Greystones again."

"Shall we go and get them?" Gerald asked. "Or shall we go to Tally's flat for a cup of tea first?"

"Tea first," Jean smiled. "I want to be certain before I buy anything that it is a necessity."

Gerald hailed a taxi and they got into it. As they drove off, Jean asked the question which had been hovering on her lips for some moments.

"Who is Stephen?" she said; and then, at Gerald's look of surprise, she explained, "There is a signed photograph of him in the bedroom where I changed."

"Oh, that's the Colonel . . . Tally's stepfather," he said. "But you must never, never mention him to Mrs. Melton."

6

"Why shouldn't one mention Colonel Melton to his wife?" Jean asked wonderingly.

Gerald looked ahead of him for a moment, as if he were choosing his words with care, and then he said:

"It is a rather complicated story, and I can't say that I know all the outs and ins of it. Apparently, Tally's mother had always been in love with Stephen Melton, even when she was very young, but he had no money, and when Lord Brora came along she was persuaded into marriage with him by her father and mother. I think, as a matter of fact, that she was very fond of her husband, and they were on the whole very happy; but the real love of her life was Stephen Melton, although she never saw him again until two years after she became a widow. He went East because he was broken-hearted at losing the girl he loved. He made a success of being a tea planter in Ceylon and then, because he found the climate did not agree with his health, he came back to England to find Margaret Brora free. I am told by people who knew them well that they were so ecstatically happy that they did not seem to belong to this world at all. Anyway, Stephen was a very decent chap and made Tally a very good stepfather. Then came this last war. Stephen Melton volunteered immediately, and it was inevitable, with his experience, that he should be sent East. He was in the Intelligence Service, and I understand that he did invaluable work until the Japs caught him at the fall of Singapore. He was wounded and I believe they treated him very badly until he died."

"How terrible," Jean whispered.

"It was terrible," Gerald went on, "and what was even worse was the effect of his death on Margaret Melton. She nearly went off her head, and the only thing she wanted was to die, too. She had waited so long, you see, for the man she loved; and another tragic thing was that all the letters he had written to her from Singapore, or at least the letters which she thought he must have written to her, were sunk in one of the ships returning to this country. It was all a ghastly tragedy, and I know Tally was distraught at one time to know how to deal with his mother."

"I think she is lovely," Jean said, "the loveliest person I have ever seen."

"Yes, Mrs. Melton is very beautiful," Gerald agreed, "but I always feel as if she is not really listening to what I am saying."

"I felt like that, too," Jean exclaimed. "Is she all right now?"

"Oh, she is all right in health," Gerald replied, "but I don't think she will ever get over her husband's death. She never mentions him, and Tally has told us that we are not to mention him, either. I believe that after his death, when she was so ill, the nurse had a difficult time to restrain her from killing herself."

"Poor Mrs. Melton."

"I am afraid we cannot do anything to help her," Gerald sighed, "and the only hope is that time heals everything."

"I wonder if it does really," Jean questioned. "I have the feeling that if one once loved someone as much as that, time would not count one way or another."

"What do you mean by that?" Gerald asked.

"It is only an idea," Jean replied shyly, "but I cannot help feeling that Mrs. Melton cannot be a very religious woman."

"Why? What on earth has that got to do with it?"

"Well, if she were, she would believe that she is going

to see Stephen again one day, and then they will be together for eternity."

"Do you believe in all that sort of thing?" Gerald asked.

"Of course," Jean answered. "Don't you?"

Gerald laughed rather awkwardly.

"Oh, I don't know. When we were in a tight corner in the war I used to pray, but I always felt rather ashamed of myself afterwards. You see, I usually forget my prayers when things are going right, so it seems rather unfair to expect God, if there is one, to pay attention to me just because I am in a hole."

Jean thought for a moment.

"Don't you think that God would be big-minded enough to understand that you felt like that?"

"Perhaps He would," Gerald said seriously. "I hadn't thought of that." Then he added: "I had forgotten you were a parson's daughter. I ought to have known you would have very strong opinions on these things."

"It is not because I am a parson's daughter," Jean answered. "As a matter of fact, I hated the God that my father was always talking about. He was a very merciless, frightening God, who was always looking out for faults in me and punishing me for them; but when my father was dead and I was alone, I discovered God for myself, and that is why I am quite certain that He is there."

The taxi stopped, and for a moment Gerald made no effort to get out. He turned to look at Jean and said quietly:

"You are a very surprising person, and when you talk to me like that I think that I, too, am certain that I believe in God."

"I am glad," Jean said impulsively.

Gerald raised his eyebrows.

"Why?"

"Because you will have something to help you, however unhappy you are, however difficult life may seem at any moment."

97

They sat looking at each other and then the taximan opened the door.

"Is this the place you wanted, Guv'nor?"

Tally's flat was at the top of a tall, old-fashioned mansion which had been modernised and converted. When they stepped out of the lift into the quaintly-shaped hall with its big oak chests and valuable old sporting prints, Jean found another fine setting and background for Tally.

The sitting-room was really lovely. The walls were lined with books; there were big comfortable armchairs, a sofa, and plenty of room for a man to move around. Gerald went to the window and looked out. They were high above the roof tops, but they could see in the distance a glimpse of the Thames, dull silver in the fading light of the afternoon.

"How lovely to be so high up," Jean exclaimed.

"You say that now," Gerald said, "but I think I have been more frightened in this room than anywhere else on earth. Tally used to plan many of his Commando raids here in the war. We used to sit round the table with bombs bursting over our heads and wonder whether the next one would take the roof off. Nothing would induce Tally to go to a shelter or to move his belongings elsewhere. 'I'm lucky,' he used to say. 'They won't touch me.' But some of us—I for one—were not so certain that we were born under a lucky star."

"He is lucky, isn't he?"

"Too lucky; that is why he is so spoilt."

"Oh, do you think he is?" Jean asked the question almost reproachfully.

Gerald nodded.

"He has always had everything his own way. He is rich, good-looking, famous, and all before his twenty-fifth birthday. What more could any man want?"

"He wants Miss Melchester," Jean said quietly.

"He thinks he does," Gerald corrected, "and perhaps as a matter of fact this will teach Tally a lesson, just as he is endeavouring to teach Melia one. Between ourselves, I think it will be jolly good for both of them. I am fond of them both, but that doesn't prevent me from knowing that they are both extremely spoilt."

Jean laughed.

"You sound rather like a severe schoolmaster."

Gerald laughed, too, and then he said:

"Do you know, this is the first time I have seen you laugh? You have always looked so frightened before. Will you be angry if I say it is an improvement?"

"No, I won't be angry," Jean said, "and thank you for the compliment."

She understood so well what Gerald meant. It was true that for the first time in his presence she felt at ease, unafraid and able to speak quite naturally. She wished she felt so sure and unafraid when she was with Tally. Gerald was a comfortable sort of person. She quite understood why Tally found him an invaluable friend. He was calm and quiet and good-tempered, and someone on whom one felt on sight that one could rely. Impulsively Jean said:

"I would like to thank you for being so kind to me, Captain Fairfax."

His eyebrows shot up again in an almost comical manner.

"Have I been kind?" he asked. "If I have, it has been very easy, and a pleasure."

"What nice things you say," Jean smiled; and for the first time Gerald saw that there was a little dimple in her left cheek.

"By the way," he said, "don't you think we might be a little less formal with each other? As Tally's fiancée you ought to be on Christian name terms with his best friend."

"I would like to call you Gerald."

"And I intend calling you Jean."

They laughed again, and while they were laughing the door burst open and Tally came into the room. They both turned quickly at his entrance, and it struck Jean how the moment Tally appeared the whole atmosphere sharpened and intensified. She was not sure if it was pleasant or not; all she knew was that when Tally was there the whole tempo seemed to rise and quicken.

"Oh, here you are," Tally said, and they could not be sure from the expression on his face how the interview with Melia had gone.

"Yes, here we are," Gerald replied. "Jean has been admiring the flat."

Tally walked across the room and put a log on the fire. It struck Jean that he was taking his time, as if he considered just how much or how little he would tell them of what had taken place with Melia. Then, having poked the fire, he lit a cigarette and stood with his back to the fireplace.

"You haven't inquired what has happened."

"We didn't like to," Gerald answered; "but do relieve our curiosity."

"I will," Tally replied. "Melia and I have had a hell of a row. She is very, very angry."

"I am not surprised," Gerald commented shortly.

"Do you know," Tally said reflectively, "I had no idea that Melia could be so worked up about anything." He was silent for a moment, and then unexpectedly he smiled. "She has got a temper."

"So I gather you have not kissed and made friends," Gerald remarked dryly.

"We have not," Tally answered. "As a matter of fact, Melia demanded that I break off my engagement immediately. I refused to do that, and she more or less turned me out of the house."

"Well, and where do we go from here?" Gerald asked.

"It is funny you should ask that question," Tally replied, "and I shall answer it literally. We are going somewhere, all three of us. We are going to Switzerland."

"To Switzerland?" Gerald echoed loudly, while Jean's response was only a murmur.

"Yes, to Switzerland," Tally repeated. "Mountains, snow and skis! I like the idea."

"But why Switzerland?"

"Don't be dense, old chap. Lady Melchester is taking Melia there so that she can forget this unfortunate little episode. The one person who is not going to forget it is Melia herself. But I can see the set-up. They want to escape the sympathy and condolence of their spiteful friends. But it isn't going to be as easy as all that. We are going, too. I didn't tell Melia that, of course."

Gerald scratched his head.

"Heaven knows where we shall all finish up in this madcap scheme of yours."

"I am not quite certain myself," Tally said, "but who cares? On with the dance and get to work, Gerald, old boy. You will have to get Jean a passport. Luckily old Briggs at the Passport Office was my Commanding Officer at the beginning of the war. He'll fix it for us quickly."

"How soon do you wish to leave?" Gerald inquired with mock servility.

"Well, I will give you until the day after tomorrow and not a moment longer. We'll fly, of course. Melia is going by train tomorrow morning. She loathes the air, poor Melia. It makes her sick."

"Listen, Tally," Gerald expostulated. "We can't just go like that—you and I and Jean. Think of the gossip! Jean will have to have a chaperon."

"Oh, bother the chaperon; must she?"

"Yes, of course she must. Really, Tally, you don't seem to have any sense at all."

"No, no, I expect you are right." Tally said good humouredly. "Well, who are we going to get?"

"Who, indeed?"

"I know. Mother will come if I ask her."

"Oh, but you cannot bother Mrs. Melton," Jean interposed.

"Why ever not?" Tally asked. "As a matter of fact it will do her good. Don't you think so, Gerald?"

"It might."

"It won't worry her one way or another where she is. I will telephone her now."

Tally picked up the receiver, but before he could dial the number Jean stopped him.

"Listen, Tally," she said in her soft voice, and going near to him put a hand on his arm. "Wouldn't you make things all right once and for all with Miss Melchester if you did what she wanted?"

"What do you mean?" Tally asked, the receiver still in his hand—its buzzing making a background to their conversation.

"I mean," Jean said with a desperate effort to explain herself, "that she has asked you to break off your engagement with me. If you did that, wouldn't she become engaged to you herself? Then you could be happy and get married quickly."

Tally smiled a little bitterly.

"If you heard the things dear Melia has just said to me, you would realise that I am the last person on earth that she would consider marrying at this moment. Besides, I gathered that Mr. Ernest Danks was even more in the foreground of the picture since my lapse from grace."

"Naturally she would say that sort of thing," Jean argued. "Any girl would, if she was jealous."

"If you think Melia is jealous of you, you are very much mistaken."

"Oh," Jean gave a little exclamation, as though his harshness had hurt her.

"I don't mean it like that," he apologised quickly. "It is just that I am such dirt beneath her feet that she would not demean herself by even speaking to me if she could help it, let alone have any feelings about me one way or another."

"But of course that is not true," Jean expostulated. "She would not be so angry if she did not mind."

Tally stared at her.

"My goodness, I didn't think of that."

"She is angry because she has lost you."

"She is angry because of her pride more than anything else."

Jean shook her head.

"Not so angry, and if you are clever and do what she wants I don't believe this Mr. Danks would count at all."

"I wonder if you are right," Tally said reflectively, knitting his eyebrows together, and then he added, "well, we shall have plenty of time to find out in Switzerland."

"If you go," Jean said, "you go alone. Don't take me with you. I am a woman and I think I know a little bit what a woman would feel in such circumstances. If she saw you alone and you were very nice to her, it might make everything all right again; but if I am there, it will only irritate and annoy her."

"You don't know Melia," Tally said with a sigh. "Does she, Gerald? Melia only wants what she can't get easily."

"Like you," Gerald said.

"Me? I am not like that."

"Of course you are," Gerald retorted. "Well, I will get the tickets for Switzerland. I need a holiday and, incidentally, I think I can get one of my newspapers to pay for it, which will be all to the good."

"Nonsense," Tally said. "You are coming with me as my guest. And that reminds me, I was going to telephone my mother."

He turned away and started to dial for 'Trunks.' Jean stood irresolute. She knew she had failed to convince him and yet in her heart of hearts she was sure that what she was trying to tell him was right. She realised that to convince Tally of anything against his will was as difficult as trying to move a mountain. Already he was through to Greystones and asking for Mrs. Melton. There was some delay while they fetched her.

"We will fly to Zürich," Tally said to Gerald while he waited, "and for heaven's sake get us on a decent airline. It is rotten weather for flying, anyway."

"Don't tell me you are frightened," Gerald said incredulously.

"No, but Jean might be," Tally replied, and Gerald, surprised at this consideration, looked at him question-

103

ingly for a moment until he saw that he was being quite sincere.

"Is that you, Mother?" Tally said into the telephone. "Look here, darling, do something for me, will you? I particularly want to go to Switzerland on Friday. If we cannot get on a plane, we will go Saturday morning, but I prefer it to be Friday. Will you come with us? Gerald's old-fashioned and won't allow us to go without a chaperon for Jean. . . . You will, that's wonderful! You always were the best mother in the world. . . . No, I am not flattering you, I am merely stating a fact. . . . Well, bless you, darling. You will come up tomorrow, won't you? . . . Yes, stay here, of course, I will light a fire in the spare room and kill the fatted calf. . . . What train? . . . . The 4.45. . . . I will meet you. . . . Good-bye, darling."

He put down the receiver. Gerald sighed.

"Oh, Tally, Tally, does any woman ever refuse you anything?"

"Not often," Tally answered smugly.

Gerald picked up a cushion from a chair on the other side of the fireplace and threw it at him.

"Well, that's all settled," Tally said with satisfaction, as he caught the cushion in mid-air and threw it back again. "Now what else is there to arrange?"

"Michael Sorrel," Gerald said.

"Well, there won't be time for many fittings," Tally ejaculated. "He will just have to lend Jean some more things until hers are ready."

"Can't I manage with what I have got?" Jean asked. "Think how angry Madame Marie will be."

"Do her good," Tally smiled. "But I will come round and charm her. What was it Gerald said? 'No woman can refuse me.' "

"You are getting unbearable," Gerald groaned. "By the way, we haven't bought Jean any of the things she wanted yet. I brought her here first for a cup of tea."

"Good, there is nothing I enjoy more than shopping for a pretty woman," Tally said. "You must wait for tea. What do you want first?"

104

"A brush and comb," Jean said shyly. Somehow the idea of Tally shopping with her made her feel more than usually shy. Her apprehension was certainly not without foundation, for although she protested he insisted on buying her a fitted dressing-case at Asprey's and then took her to Elizabeth Arden's and stocked it with all the right powder and cosmetics.

"Are you always so generous?" she asked despairingly as they got back into the car after Tally had bought her a large bottle of Chanel perfume and a dozen lace-edged handkerchiefs.

He looked down at her for a moment before he replied and then he answered her very seriously.

"No," he said, "I am not. To be honest I like giving you things. You look so pleased and I know that you need them. The last present I gave Melia cost me a hell of a lot of money and she hardly said thank you."

"Don't compare us," Jean said quickly.

"Why not?"

"It isn't fair to Miss Melchester. She is used to possessions. I have never had things like this before." There was a throb in her voice and Tally put his arm round her shoulders.

"You deserve everything I have given you and a great deal more. You are being jolly decent to me and I am grateful."

"I don't want to break in on this tender scene," Gerald said, and Jean wondered if there was a touch of sarcasm in his voice, "but I would like to point out to you, Tally, that you have not yet decided where Jean is to stay the night."

"Lord, what a fool I am," Tally exclaimed. "I never thought of that. Now, where can she go? If you think I am going to motor all the way back to Greystones you are very much mistaken. I have done enough motoring for one day."

There was a moment's silence, then Gerald asked:

"Thought of an alternative?"

"Can't she go to an hotel?" Tally inquired. "Somewhere highly respectable, of course, Browns for instance. I know my grandmother always used to stay there."

"Not without a chaperon," Gerald said sharply.

"Oh, lord!" Tally groaned. "Why aren't you a widow, Jean? Or a divorced woman? It would make life so much easier."

Jean laughed.

"I am sorry, but at the same time I think Gerald is being over particular. Let me go to some quiet, cheap place. Nobody would know who I am. I am not as important as all that."

"You are the famous Lord Brora's fiancée," Gerald said dramatically.

"Shut up, you ass," Tally exclaimed. "I shall get annoyed in a moment. There must be somewhere she can go."

"Well, if you cannot think of anywhere, I venture to suggest my sister's," Gerald said.

"But of course," Tally said enthusiastically. "Why the dickens didn't you say so before?"

"Thought it would do you good to think for a bit," Gerald retorted. "As a matter of fact I did mention it to Betty this morning."

"And yet you have kept me here puzzling just for the fun of it," Tally remarked. "Really, Gerald, for a friend you have an odd sense of humour."

Gerald merely smiled.

"Let us go and pick up Jean's suitcases from the Berkeley," he said. He bent forward from the back seat of the car and said to Jean: "Betty is not rich or grand but she is a dear, and I think you would be happy with her."

"I do hate to think I am being a nuisance to everyone," Jean said insistently.

"You are not," Gerald replied. "Betty would love to have you. Her husband is away. He is in the Navy, and she is often very lonely because I cannot be with her as much as I would like to. I promise you she will be very pleased to see you."

"Betty is a really nice girl," Tally approved. "I have
106

often thought I would like to have married her myself if I had had the chance."

"Nobody had a chance once she met John," Gerald laughed. "They are divinely happy; and by the way, Jean, she has got two children who rule the house, so don't expect peace, rest or quiet because you won't get it."

Jean smiled happily. She felt she was going to like Gerald's sister and that she would be like Gerald himself—a cosy person of whom one needn't be afraid.

"Shall we have tea first?" Tally asked, "or shall we go to Betty's now?"

"I told her we might turn up for tea," Gerald replied.

"He has arranged everything," Tally said resignedly to Jean. "He is only making all this song and dance to make himself seem more important."

They got into the car, piling in the purchases they had made in Bond Street and adding the suitcases they picked up at the Berkeley Hotel. Then Tally drove the car down Piccadilly and turning left at Hyde Park Corner negotiated some of the side streets round Belgrave Square until they stopped in a rather dingy road leading off Ebury Street. The houses were small and unpretentious, but when the front door was opened by Gerald's sister Jean knew that this was by far the happiest and nicest place to which Tally had taken her as yet. Betty was small, plump and fair. She was simply dressed in a flowered overall and her hair was untidy as if it had been ruffled by small fingers.

"Come in," she said. "I was beginning to despair of your ever turning up. The children have eaten nearly all the crumpets. We couldn't wait for you any longer."

"It is all Gerald's fault," Tally grumbled. "I will tell you about it while we eat what is left; and by the way, Betty, this is Jean."

"How are you?" Betty asked, holding out her hand to Jean and drawing her into the hall. "Why, you are cold. Shut the door, Gerald, and let's get to the fire. I am so glad you can come and stay with me," she said to Jean, and leading her through a door into the dining-room, she

107

added, "I'm afraid it is nursery tea. I hope you don't mind, but I cannot bear sticky fingers on the drawing-room covers."

The dining-room table was covered with a white cloth and despite obvious warnings that the children had eaten everything there seemed to be plenty of dishes stacked with sandwiches, cakes and scones. There were two children at the table. One, a sturdy little boy of about five, the other a pretty little girl of two. Both were wearing bibs and their mouths and fingers were sticky with jam.

"Don't attempt to touch them," Betty warned. "They are like the best type of glue, they stick to you and never come off."

"Uncle Gerald!" the children screamed with delight as they saw Gerald in the doorway and then added almost simultaneously, "and Uncle Tally!"

"Hullo, you horrors," Tally said. "I hear you have eaten all my tea. If that is true, I'm going to eat you up."

There were screams of pretended fright and it was with difficulty that Betty restrained them from getting down from their chairs and jumping about the room.

"Finish your tea," she admonished. "Don't excite them, Tally. You know they always behave like lunatics when you are here."

"Nonsense," Tally said. "I have a wonderful influence with children. It is just the same with animals. The wildest horse is tamed just by my experienced touch."

Betty laughed.

"Go on, you idiot, and take a crumpet quickly before Gerald eats the lot. They are a vice with him. I simply cannot balance the housekeeping accounts at the end of the week when he comes in to tea."

Jean, seating herself at the end of the table, listened to Betty and decided that she was the nicest person she had ever met in her life. Her mouth seemed to be permanently smiling and her eyes smiled at the same time. Her daughter was strikingly like her, an almost exact replica, while the boy resembled a large photograph on

108

the mantelpiece of a young man in naval uniform who Jean guessed was his father.

"Drink up your milk, Jim," Betty said to her son. "And, Lizzie, wipe your fingers on your bib."

"I'se going to sit on Uncle Tally's knee," Lizzie announced firmly, getting down.

"I'm sure he would much rather you didn't," Betty protested.

Tally laughed.

"Come along, Lizzie, you always were my best girl."

She trotted slowly round to him. Jim did not say anything for a few minutes but kept staring at Jean. Now he demanded of his mother:

"Who is she?" pointing to Jean with a fat forefinger.

"Don't point, Jim, it is not polite," Betty said. "That is Miss MacLeod."

"Mac . . ." Jim tried to repeat the word, and failed.

"Oh, perhaps he had better call you Auntie Jean," Betty said. "Do you mind?"

"I would love it," Jean answered.

"I warn you he is an incorrigible flirt," Gerald said. "I don't know what Betty will do with him when he grows up. He runs after every pretty girl in the neighbourhood."

"Don't you listen to your Uncle Gerald," Betty said, taking off Jim's bib. "Now say your grace."

"Thank-God-for-my-good-tea-can - I - get - down?" Jim said all in one breath. He moved round the table to Jean's side. "Are you coming to stay here with us?"

Jean nodded.

"Yes."

"I'se glad," he said with satisfaction, and while the others roared with laughter, Jean answered in a very quiet voice:

"So am I."

7

"And they all lived happily ever afterwards," Jean concluded.

Jim, sitting up in his small bed, clapped his hands together and Lizzie in her cot threw her fat legs encased in a flowered flannel sleeping-suit over her head with excitement.

"More, tell us more," Jim begged. "Please, please, Auntie Jean, tell us another story."

Lizzie rolled the right way up like a small, roly-poly pudding.

"More," she repeated. "More story."

"No more now, children," Betty said from the doorway. "I don't want to hurry you, Jean, but you promised to be ready for Tally at seven o'clock and you haven't even begun to unpack."

Jean looked at the blue enamel clock on the mantelpiece.

"Oh dear," she said, "I suppose I must go and change. To tell the truth I would much rather stay here."

"When you have got the chance of going out dancing?" Betty inquired. "What a strange girl you must be!"

Her tone was joking, but Jean answered her seriously.

"It is so seldom that I have the opportunity of being in a real home," she said.

Betty looked pleased.

"Does it seem like that to you?" she commented. "Sometimes I feel as if it is just a rubbish heap. I try to keep it nice, but it is a job doing everything single-handed and looking after the children, especially now that they can move about and leave a trail of untidiness wherever they go."

"I shouldn't mind anything they did," Jean said rapturously, looking at Jim in his striped pyjamas, his dark hair brushed back neatly, his cheeks pink and shining from his hot bath.

"They are sweet, aren't they?" Betty said, "although we ought not to say so in front of them. They are getting quite old enough to know that they can twist me round their little fingers. It is time John came back and injected a little discipline into the house. Not that he is anything but as weak as butter in their hands."

"Has he been away long?" Jean asked.

"Nearly a year," Betty answered, "and it seems like twenty. He is in the Far East. I am always frightened that the children will have forgotten all about him when he comes home. But you won't really forget Daddy, will you, Poppet?"

She let down the side of the cot and bent to tuck the bedclothes round Lizzie.

"Daddy!" Lizzie repeated dutifully.

"I remember Daddy," Jim said slowly. "He gave me my puffer-train."

"How lovely," Jean said. "Will you show it to me tomorrow?"

"It's broken," Jim said.

"Oh, dear, what a pity!"

"Jim very naughty and breaked it. Mummy was cross."

"Very cross," Betty said. "What do you think he did with it? Dropped it out of the window on to the pavement. It wrecked the train and missed an old lady's head by inches."

Jim looked at his mother out of the corner of his eye to see if she was really angry, and then, confident that she was not, said:

"I wish it had hit the silly old lady!"

112

Both Jean and Betty burst out laughing. They could not help it.

"You are a bad boy," Betty scolded. "Now cuddle down and I will tuck you in. You are both to go to sleep at once."

She kissed them good night, and Jean also bending over Jim felt his arms reach up behind her neck holding her tightly, his small warm mouth pressed against her cheek. When she left the nursery, there were tears in her eyes.

"I think you are the luckiest person in the world," she said as Betty followed her into the small bedroom next door.

"Because of the children?" Betty asked. "You wait until you see my John and then you will know that you are right and that I am the luckiest person in the world."

"How long have you been married?"

"Six years, and I have seen so little of him, but this is his last trip out East. When he comes home I think he is going to retire from the Navy and go into business. Oh, it will be wonderful to have him with me all the time."

There was an expression of radiance on her face which made Jean think to herself:

'Now I know what it is to be in love. I have never been in love, never.'

Slowly she began to unfasten the skilfully cut, blue woollen dress which bore the unmistakable stamp of Michael Sorrel's genius.

"What a lovely dress that is," Betty said. "I have been admiring it ever since you came here."

Jean said nothing for a moment and then as she looked at her reflection in the mirror she asked:

"Has your brother Gerald told you anything about me?"

"Nothing much," Betty confessed. "He rang me up this morning and asked if I had seen the newspapers. Of course I hadn't had time even to glance at one. Then he told me that you were engaged to Tally and asked if I would put you up here tonight. To tell the truth I was

113

rather frightened. I thought you might be like . . . well, like Melia Melchester . . . frightfully grand and sophisticated. But Gerald said you were a darling and incidentally, he was quite right,"

Jean flushed.

"Oh, thank you," she said. "I think that is the nicest thing I have ever had said to me." She hesitated for a moment and then she added: "It is not my secret so I cannot tell you all I would like to do about myself. But believe me when I tell you that this dress and all the other clothes I wear are very, very new to me, so please do not judge me by them. I am not smart and well-dressed really. I am just Jean MacLeod from the North, an awfully ordinary, unimportant person."

Jean spoke with a sudden tensity in her voice. She did not know why, but she was anxious for this nice young woman to like her. Betty jumped to her feet.

"Don't say any more," she begged. "I never judge people by their clothes. I expect it is because I am too frightened that people will judge me by mine. I did not look at your dress when I first saw you, but at your face. It is an awfully nice face, Jean. I knew we should be friends."

"I want a friend very, very badly," Jean whispered.

"Well, you've got one in me," Betty answered; then she added: "Don't think it impertinent of me, but don't be frightened of Tally. People talk an awful lot of nonsense about him. He is a terribly sweet person at heart; it is only that he has been spoilt by having so much—too much of everything which the world values—but I have always thought myself that he is singularly lacking in the things that make one happy."

"I wonder if you are right," Jean said reflectively. "It is difficult to tell. I cannot think of him as an ordinary person somehow."

"The children love him," Betty said quietly, "and that is a pretty big test, you know."

"Your children are so adorable," Jean answered. "I think they would be generous enough to like anyone."

"Don't you believe it; they have very strong likes and
114

dislikes." Betty paused, and then her eyes twinkled. "One person they don't like is Melia Melchester. The only time she came here to tea Jim regarded her with an unwinking stare for a long time and then at last he asked, in a very hostile voice, 'Who is that lady?' 'Hush Jim,' I said, 'she is a friend of Uncle Tally's.' 'Why?' Jim asked, and somehow or other there did not seem any adequate answer to that one."

Jean laughed for a moment and then she asked shyly: "Do you like her?"

"Not very much," Betty confessed. "I've tried to, tried very hard, for Tally's sake. He and Gerald are such great friends and he has always been so nice to me that I wanted to like his wife. I wanted to be friends with her, but I am afraid Melia and I have got very little in common. Melia thinks me dull, in which I am sure she is right; but I find her . . . well . . . almost unhuman. She is so glamorous and glittering, beautiful and unreal that I feel that I am watching her on a film and that at any moment the programme will come to an end and I shall go home in a bus to reality."

"Oh, Betty, you are funny," Jean laughed.

"It's the truth, and it may seem a bit premature to say so but I am terribly glad you are marrying Tally."

Jean would have replied impulsively, but she checked the words on her lips and turned away. She hated to lie to Betty, hated to let her believe that one day she would be Tally's wife. She wondered if, when the truth was known and she went back to obscurity, Betty would still be friendly; and she knew that it was almost disloyal to ask the question. Betty was a genuine, sincere person. If she liked people, she would like them for all time, whatever they did or whoever they were.

"Goodness, look at the time," Betty exclaimed suddenly. "Do hurry, Jean. Tally hates being kept waiting and he will say it is all my fault."

Jean did as she was bid, snatching the things out of her suitcase and changing into a dinner dress of soft green chiffon. It fell in long graceful lines and made her seem very slim and a little taller than she was actually.

The colour brought out the delicate tones of her skin and the faint natural flush of her cheeks. When she was ready, had done her hair carefully and just touched her eyelashes with mascara, as Madame Marie had shown her, she looked, if not beautiful, at least a very pretty and attractive girl. But as Jean regarded herself in the glass, she seemed to hear her great-aunt's sharp voice saying:

"Pull your hair back tightly from off your face. I won't have you running wild. There is bad blood in you, my girl, and don't you forget it."

Jean remembered how she had lain awake night after night wondering what her aunt meant; and now that she knew what was intended by that harsh condemnation, she was afraid for herself. For one wild moment she contemplated pulling her hair back, screwing it tightly into the nape of her neck and wiping the colour from her lips and the powder from her face; then some sensible logic within her mind told her it was not looks that counted, it was something deeper than that—personality and character—and if they were tainted, then the exterior did not matter one way or the other.

Very gently she raised her hand to the place on her cheek where Jim had kissed her. She felt again the small arms round her neck, and then she was praying with a passion of intensity:

"Oh, God, keep me pure and simple. Don't let me change. Let me keep decent within."

She had no further time to think, for even as the prayer ceased on her lips there was a cry from downstairs.

"Jean, are you ready? Tally is here."

She snatched up the short velvet coat trimmed with bands of sable which Michael Sorrel had designed to go over her dress and ran downstairs. Tally was standing in the hall. He was in evening dress and she thought he looked even more distinguished than usual.

"Oh, you do look lovely," Betty exclaimed admiringly before Tally could say anything. "Have a good

116

time. If you want anything when you come back, wake me up. Here is the latchkey."

She put it into Jean's hand.

"I wish you would come with us, Betty," Tally said.

"Don't be silly," Betty replied. "You know I cannot leave the children. Besides, you young things don't want an elderly married woman like me tagging along with you."

"When you talk about yourself being elderly, you make me feel a grandfather. As it is, I hardly know the difference between you and Lizzie."

"Idiot!" Betty exclaimed affectionately. "Now go along and enjoy yourselves."

"We intend to do that," Tally said. "Good-bye, Betty."

"Good night, Betty," Jean echoed, and ran across the wet pavement into Tally's car.

"Isn't Gerald coming?" she asked.

Tally nodded.

"Yes, but I promised we would pick him up at his flat. He telephoned that he had been delayed."

They were silent while Tally started the car; then as they drove off, he said:

"You will find some orchids on the seat beside you."

"Orchids!" Jean exclaimed. She picked up a white cardboard box, opened it and revealed two large, perfect, purple blooms. "Oh, how lovely! Thank you ever so much; I have never had orchids given me before."

"I thought you wouldn't have," Tally smiled. "And I'm glad to be able to give you them for the first time. Oughtn't you to wish or something?"

"I am always wishing," Jean said softly, "wishing that I shan't wake up too soon!"

"You are a refreshing person. I am looking forward to taking you out for the first time in London. I suppose you have never been to a night-club?"

"Of course not," Jean replied, "but ought we to?"

"Oh, there are one or two quite respectable ones."

"I do wish Betty could have come with us," Jean said

suddenly. "She is so sweet, and sometimes she must be lonely without her husband, even with those two angelic children to look after."

Tally turned round to glance at her for a moment.

"Do you really wish that or are you just saying it?" he asked.

"But of course I mean it," Jean answered in surprise. "I would have loved Betty to come. She has been so kind to me; and besides, it would have been grand to have had her with us this evening, wouldn't it?"

Tally was silent for a moment and then he said slowly and in rather a strange voice:

"I suppose we might have spent the evening at Betty's house if she couldn't leave the children."

"Oh, that would have been fun," Jean said enthusiastically. "Betty would have loved it, too."

"It is not too late to change our minds," Tally said, and again his voice was strange, almost as if he were choosing his words with care and calculating their effect.

"Could we?" Jean asked. "Oh, it would be wonderful. The only thing is, I am afraid she would not have enough food for all of us. I noticed when I was helping her to clear the tea that there was not very much in the larder."

"You helped her clear the tea, did you?" Tally asked.

"Of course," Jean replied. "It was awfully funny, she thought I was grand. I suppose my clothes impressed her. After you had gone, she said, 'Do you mind just going and sitting in the other room with the children while I clear away?' Then I said that I would like to help her. She looked surprised. It is funny what clothes do to one. She wouldn't have looked surprised yesterday."

"So you helped her?" Tally repeated..

"Naturally," Jean replied. "She tried to stop my washing-up and I didn't dare tell her how much washing-up I had done in my life; but I think she thought I was pretty competent."

Tally drew the car up outside a block of flats.

"This is where Gerald lives. Now, listen, I'll give you

118

your choice. We can either go on with the evening as I have planned it, pick up Gerald, dine at the Ritz, go into Ciro's to see the cabaret and finish up at Orchid Room, or we can go and get some food, take it back to Betty's and give her a surprise. It is entirely up to you."

He turned round in the driving seat and watched her face. There was a street lamp outside and they could see each other quite clearly. Jean did not hesitate.

"Oh, let us go back to Betty's," she said quietly. "I would love to give her a surprise. Don't think I am ungrateful and don't want to go to all those other places with you," she added insistently, "I do, but I would like even more to give Betty a happy evening."

Tally's face was expressionless for a moment; then he smiled.

"You are going to do exactly what you want to do," he said. "Wait here while I tell the porter to fetch Gerald."

"Of course," Jean answered.

Tally got out of the car and walked quickly into the big doorway of the flats. When he was gone, Jean sat wondering whether she had disappointed him in any way by deciding to spend the evening with Betty. Somehow she had the impression that for some strange reason of his own he was testing her when he gave her the choice. Perhaps she had been rude. After all, he had bought her these wonderful orchids and given her this exquisite dress. Would he feel his money was being wasted when she would not be seen in public with him? There was Melia to think about.

Tally came back and got into the car.

"I have sent up a message," he said. "I don't suppose Gerald will be a moment."

"While you have been away," Jean said, "I have been thinking about this evening and——."

"You have changed your mind?" Tally said, and there was a metallic note in his voice.

"It isn't that," Jean said. "It is just that I think you would rather go to the Ritz."

119

"It is all right, Jean," Tally said shortly. "I quite understand that you would prefer the Ritz."

"No, no, it is not that," Jean said quickly. "Please listen a moment."

He turned at her appeal. She thought there was something hard, almost hostile in his eyes.

"Please let me explain," she said. "You see, I thought when you gave me those lovely clothes and those orchids that you wanted to take me out so that we should be seen and Miss Melchester would hear about it. Well, she won't hear about them if no one sees me, so I feel that if we go to a restaurant I shall be——" Jean hesitated for a proper word——"well, repaying you a little for all the wonderful things you have given me."

She stammered as she spoke, for somehow Tally was disconcerting her. He looked so severe, so stern; and yet when she had finished speaking she wondered if she had imagined it all. The hostility had gone from his eyes, his severity relaxed.

"Is that really what you were thinking?" he asked.

"Yes, it is," Jean answered; "but I have explained myself very badly."

"We will go and have our evening with Betty," Tally said. "I think it is time you were off duty for a little while."

"Oh, thank you!" Jean said ecstatically.

Unexpectedly Tally reached out and put his hand over hers.

"I have never met anyone quite like you before," he said, and then quickly, before she could answer, he exclaimed, "Ah, there is Gerald. Get in, old boy."

"Sorry to be late, Tally. Hullo Jean," Gerald replied. He, like Tally, wearing a white tie and tails and sporting a red carnation in his button-hole.

"Our plans are changed," Tally said. "Jean and I have been having a heart to heart talk about Betty and we feel it is rather a lonely evening for her. What we are going to do is to go and see old Gustav, who, as you know, will do anything for me, get some really decent food out of him and a bottle of wine, and go back to

120

Betty's and have our dinner there. What do you think?"

"What does Jean think of that?" Gerald asked.

"As a matter of fact it is Jean's idea," Tally answered.

"Well, if you are quite certain that you don't want to make a sensational appearance at the Ritz," Gerald said.

"Jean thought of that," Tally replied. "I told her I thought it was time we all came off duty for a few hours. To tell you the honest truth I think I have had quite enough sensations for one day."

"And so say all of us," Gerald agreed fervently. "Drive on to Gustav's and don't forget that both Betty and I go for caviare in a big way."

It did not take them long to get what they wanted. Jean and Gerald waited in the car while Tally went in to see Gustav, at a small restaurant in Soho—waiters came hurrying out with covered dishes, and soon they were driving swiftly towards Betty's little home.

"I've got the latch-key," Jean said excitedly. "Do you think we can creep in very quietly and get everything ready downstairs and then call her? I expect she will be in her sitting-room, and if we are really quiet she won't hear us."

"You forget that Gerald and I were Commandos," Tally replied. "We taught ourselves to move as silently as Red Indians. You go ahead and open the door. We will leave the car just round the corner so that she won't hear it."

The plan worked splendidly. As Jean had anticipated, the ground floor of the house was in darkness and there was a light shining in the sitting-room windows on the first floor. They crept in. There was only one tense moment, when Gerald slipped in the dark passage with a bottle of champagne under his arm. But with an effort he recovered his balance and they carried everything into the dining-room.

Jean laid the table swiftly and switched on the electric fire. She had noticed two tall candles on the sideboard with red shades on them, and when they were lit they cast a warm glow over the polished table. Then, on

121

Tally's whispered instructions, they crept out again, closing the door quietly behind them, and slipping back into the side street they got into the car and drove with a flourish up to the front door.

"Don't use the key," Tally commanded. "Ring the bell."

Gerald did so, and a few seconds later Betty opened the door.

"Oh, it's you!" she exclaimed. "Have you forgotten something?"

"No," Tally answered, "but there has been a series of mishaps. The cold has broken the plumbing at the Ritz and we are unable to dine there. They were awfully sorry, but they could not provide us with a meal of any sort, so we thought the only thing to do was to come back and ask you to take pity on us."

"Of course," Betty smiled; and then her voice faltered, "Oh, darlings, I haven't a thing in the house to offer you. The butcher has been unusually mean this week and I could not get any fish today although I tried everywhere. Tally, how disappointing! I am afraid you will have to try elsewhere, and I would so have loved to give you a meal."

Tally took her arm.

"Didn't you know I was a magician?" he asked. "I have only to wave my wand and food appears automatically. Come this way, little woman. Shut your eyes while I cry 'Abra Cadabra.' "

He flung open the door of the dining-room. Betty stared, and then she clapped her hands.

"Oh, Tally, where did you get it all from? And how did you get it here?"

"Ha, ha," Tally said. "I told you it was magic. Now, will you or will you not feed us, young woman?"

"Feed you!" Betty exclaimed. "I am going to feed myself, but wait a minute. I will put some coffee on the stove. I can at least provide that, and if what I see there is a bottle of champagne we shall want some glasses."

"I couldn't find any," Jean said and put her hand up to her mouth.

"Now, there, you have given everything away," Tally exclaimed disgustedly. "Never trust a woman with a secret."

"I'm sorry," Jean said. But Betty smiled at her.

"Only a woman could have made the table look so attractive. Let us eat by candle light; it is much more romantic and exciting."

"And becoming," Gerald added. He had noticed that Jean, her eyes alight with excitement, her cheeks flushed, looked like a child at a party.

Betty inspected a big tin in the centre of the table.

"Caviare! My secret vice. Oh, Tally, you are an angel. And a whole cold chicken, Russian salad and a ham! I have never seen such a sumptuous meal. And what is on that plate over there?"

"Meringues," Tally added. "Gustav insisted on my bringing those. He murmured something about sweets to the sweet."

"So we have Gustav to thank for this. Gerald has often told me what a dear little man he is and how he used to cook for you after you took him prisoner in Italy."

"Trust Tally to capture the best cook in London," Gerald laughed.

"Is that what he is?" asked Jean, who had been listening to this conversation wide-eyed.

"There is more to the story than that," Tally said. "He was one of the Italians we sent over on our behalf to work among his own people; but we advanced too quickly, and among the prisoners my men took was found Gustav. We didn't dare to let anyone know that he was serving the British, so we kept him prisoner in the ordinary way and used him as a cook while we were on the job. When we came back to England, we brought him with us. His usefulness was over. You can only play that game once, the next time you get shot."

"Oh, I am thankful dear Gustav was not shot," Betty said. "Shall we start eating?"

"I'm starving," Tally said. "What about caviare to begin with?"

He ladled out big spoonfuls of it on to four plates,

then saw Jean looking at her portion intently. Under cover of Betty's cheerful chatter he asked in a low voice:

"Another wish?"

Jean smiled at him shyly and nodded. Gerald got up from the table and opened the bottle of champagne.

"Have a little wine with it," he suggested, and poured the golden liquid into their glasses. Jean looked a little doubtfully at hers.

"I don't know whether I ought to," she said. "You see . . . I have never drunk anything alcoholic except the brandy which Tally gave me yesterday."

"Tally gave you brandy yesterday?" Betty repeated. "What on earth for?"

"Oh, that's a long story," Tally said, "and we have not got time for it at the moment. I want to give you a toast. All take your glasses."

They lifted them obediently and looked at him, waiting.

"To Jean," Tally said surprisingly, "and may she be very happy."

8

Jean was never to forget her first sight of Switzerland. They ran into bad weather from the moment they crossed the Channel, and flew high above the clouds, seeing nothing of the country over which they were passing. At Zürich, where they landed, they drove in a blinding blizzard from the aerodrome to the railway station. During the rest of the journey to St. Moritz there was only the snow beating against frosted windows and later it grew dark. The train was late and did not get in to St. Moritz Station till 9.30, but they had dinner in the restaurant car and were interested, as they travelled higher and higher, to watch the increase in their altitude on the instrument at the end of the carriage.

It was not until Jean was shown to her bedroom in their hotel and she was alone that she was able to go to the window, pull back the starched white linen curtains and look out. It had stopped snowing and the moon had risen high over the tops of the mountains to shed its light, magical and unearthly in its beauty, over a world of snow and deep shadow. It was so lovely that Jean could only hold her breath, feeling as if she stood on the threshold of some fairyland more wonderful than anything she had imagined even in her most secret yearnings.

The tops of the mountains were silhouetted against the sky and seemed to reflect the moon so that they themselves shone luminous in the darkness; the great pine trees were silver with sparkling frost and below in the valley was a tiny village, its church spire pointing heavenwards as if in a gallant effort to emulate the peaks towering high above it.

"How wonderful!" Jean breathed aloud, and felt in that moment as if she herself were part of all that beauty, caught up ecstatically into the loveliness which was absolutely unearthly and spiritual. She was one with the Universe, no longer an individual battling alone without help or sustenance, but part of the great pattern of Creation. She felt the wonder of this knowledge possess her, bathing her in glory, linking her in a mystical communion with all that lived and breathed and had its being.

How long she stood there at the window she had no idea; she was roused by a knock at the door, and when she called out "Come in," her voice sounded even to herself strange and tremulous as her soul came from the heights back to the confines of the flesh.

Tally entered. He had taken off his heavy travelling coat and she thought how fresh and alert he looked after what had inevitably been a tiring journey.

"Are you all right?" he asked. "I came to see if your luggage had come up yet."

"I don't think so," Jean said, staring around her vaguely. Tally looked at her face.

"What have you been doing? Day-dreaming?"

Jean smiled.

"I have been looking out of the window. I don't think it is real."

"What isn't?" Tally asked; then glancing past her where the curtains were still drawn back, he understood. "It is lovely, isn't it? I was only a small boy the first time I came here, but I remember looking out and wondering why, when the world could be so attractive, mankind should build slums and start wars with which to torture and annihilate himself."

His tone was grave. It was the first time that Jean had heard him speak so seriously, and curiously she asked:

126

"Did you often think about such things when you were a boy?"

"I suppose I was a bit of a prig," Tally answered, "but at school I was an ardent reformer; I even planned that I would go into politics when I grew up."

"Why didn't you?" Jean asked, and added quickly, "That is a silly question. I was forgetting about the war; but there is plenty of time, isn't there?"

"Plenty," Tally said, and now his tone was no longer serious. "I might even rival Mr. Ernest Danks in his own field."

He was grinning, and Jean had the impression that he no longer wished to talk seriously; responsive to his mood, she smiled back.

"Why not? What is possible for him could not be impossible for you."

"A very nice flattering speech!" Tally approved, and then turned as there came a knock on the door and two porters entered carrying the luggage.

Tally sorted out the suitcases, sending those for his mother to the room next door and those for Gerald and himself further down the passage. He went away with the porters, and when he was gone Jean, after hesitating for a moment, crossed the room and knocked hesitantly on the door which separated her from Mrs. Melton's suite. It was a moment or two before her knock was answered, then she heard Mrs. Melton's voice saying sweetly, "Come in."

She opened the door.

"Can I help you?" she asked.

Mrs. Melton was sitting at the dressing-table. She had taken off the small brown hat trimmed with wings which she had worn for travelling and was combing her curls into place.

"Thank you, dear," she said, "but the chambermaid will unpack for me. She has been here for many years and I remember her well. Besides, there is not much to do until the rest of our luggage arrives."

Tally had arranged that his mother's maid and the

bulk of their luggage should come by train and they had brought with them by air only the minimum amount of necessities.

Mrs. Melton looked at her reflection in the glass, gave a little sigh and rose to her feet.

"Tally wants us to go down and have some coffee and after that I am going to bed."

"Do you think I ought to change?" Jean asked.

"Not into evening dress," Mrs. Melton replied. "But if I were you I should put on another frock. You will feel fresher and I don't suppose that you will be allowed to go to bed early, even if you want to."

"Thank you for telling me," Jean said, and added impulsively, "You won't mind if I ask you things like that, will you? You see, this is all so new and strange to me and I have no idea what is expected of me."

Mrs. Melton looked surprised, but she made no comment on Jean's statement save to say quietly:

"Of course, dear, ask me anything you want to know."

She said it charmingly and with a sweetness which was part of her charm. Yet Jean felt once again as if she were attending to her with only a small part of her mind, the rest being far away, unconcerned with this conversation or with anything that was happening around her.

She hurried back to her own room. As if just such an occasion had been anticipated, Madame Marie had told her to pack in her suitcase for the aeroplane a dress of deep blue velvet embroidered at the neck and wrists with coloured stones. It was an elaborate frock and Jean had wondered when she should wear it. Now it seemed to her the obvious dress to put on this evening.

She had a quick bath, wishing to linger in the warm, scented water, but afraid that she might keep the others waiting. Then she slipped on the velvet frock and as she touched her fair head with a comb she heard the electricity crackle and her hair flew out like a halo. It was as if the tempo were rising in herself. She felt excited and at the same time apprehensive. When passing through the hall and part of the lounge of the hotel to come upstairs to their bedrooms she had thought that this luxurious, expensive world was not only something new, something she had never known or anticipated in her whole life, but alien, perhaps an enemy of which she might be afraid. Now, because she was young and because the reflection in her mirror told her she was attractive, she felt a surge of pleasure creep over her whole body, tingling in her veins, pulsating in her throat. A moment earlier she had known a spiritual uplifting when her whole being yearned for and had been a part of the beauty of the night. Now what she felt was very different and yet it too was alive and vital, a surging forward, a longing and a desire which consumed her to the exclusion of all else.

She was ready! She picked up a handkerchief and put it in the flat velvet bag which matched her dress. "I do look nice," she told herself, and once again, because it was so difficult to escape from the comparison, she thought of herself only a few months ago climbing wearily up the long, linoleum-covered stairs in her aunt's house carrying a pail and a scrubbing brush. She remembered the bitter chill of the mornings when she scrubbed the doorstep and the chapped misery of her hands when she laid the fires and brought in the coals from the backyard. She remembered the nights when she had lain awake, cold and miserable, under the two thin blankets which her aunt considered sufficient bed covering. She thought of the days which had succeeded one another, first dull and drab in their unchanging monotony, and then suddenly, like a transformation scene, her secret engagement to Angus, London, and this.

She was altered and transformed; her whole life revolutionised by one wave of the magician's wand. "I'm happy," Jean whispered, and then some voice within herself asked, 'But is this happiness?'

She was not sure. It was still difficult to know what she did feel and what she did think. Always at the back of her mind was that warning voice. 'Be careful,' it told her. 'Remember; yes, remember.'

For a moment all the elation and happiness faded from Jean's face. It was not difficult to remember; it would be impossible to forget. The secret that she carried within her heart lay heavy upon her. Always it seemed to her that it stood beside her—a spectre from which there was no escape.

'Remember.' Yes, she would remember and must shape her life according to its warning. The thrill and excitement had vanished. She was alone, utterly alone with her own thoughts and with herself. For a moment she hesitated, then she moved swiftly across the room back to the window. The mountains were just as breathtakingly beautiful. She stood looking at them and gradually the tumult within herself died and a calmness and peace returned to her heart.

"Help me," she whispered. "Help me, God, to be . . . careful."

She turned from the window and went soberly across the room and knocked on Mrs. Melton's door. The expression on her face was one of peace. She had found comfort and in some degree reassurance.

Mrs. Melton was sitting in the arm-chair; her eyes were closed until the door opened, but Jean had the impression that she had not been resting but was tense, her mind active and concentrated in its suffering. It was obvious that to smile at Jean was an effort, but she achieved it.

"Are you ready? How quick you have been! I am afraid I have not hurried. I will just wash my hands and then we will go down together. I expect Tally will be waiting for us impatiently."

She went into the adjacent bathroom. Jean looked around her. Already the room had lost its impersonality. A dressing-gown of purple velvet lay on the bed and slippers to match, trimmed with marabou, on the rug. There were brushes and combs of mauve enamel on the dressing-table, a clothes-cover of finest lace thrown over the back of a chair, over all was the elusive fragrance of an expensive perfume, and by the bed was a pile of books, beside which stood a photograph.

130

Jean looked at the photograph and saw, as she expected, that it was of Stephen Melton. It was different from the one she had seen in Berkeley Square. This time it was a conventional portrait and gave her no strange feelings. He was good-looking, she noticed, and very attractive in a decidedly masculine manner. She thought, as she looked at the photograph, that she must have imagined all those queer sensations she had experienced while she was changing for the photographers in Berkeley Square. And yet, even while she told herself that she had been absurd, she doubted the argument of her own common sense. There had been something strange about her feelings that afternoon.

She wondered whether it would be tactless to ask Tally whether his mother and stepfather had spent a lot of time together at Berkeley Square.

Someone had once told her or she had read that walls are absorbent. That might be the explanation of her feelings about Stephen Melton's photograph. She had been in a sensitive, keyed-up state of mind and unusually receptive to atmosphere. It was easy to explain the whole experience away logically.

But somehow she was not satisfied. Something had happened in that pink and gold bedroom which could not be dismissed by a few words—something which could not be ascribable to excitement and unusual circumstances.

What was it then? And why should one photograph of Stephen Melton affect her so queerly, another leave her unmoved? She remembered certain episodes in her childhood when she had been what the Scots call 'fey'; but as she had grown older, there had been no more of them and she had almost forgotten that they had ever occurred.

As she was considering, Jean was staring at Stephen Melton's photograph by the bedside, and she had not realised that Mrs. Melton had come back into the room.

"I am ready at last," she said. "I am sorry to have kept you waiting, dear."

Her voice startled Jean, and she jumped uneasily. She

felt embarrassed, as if she had been caught prying into something which was not her concern. She moved away from the bedside, but was aware that Mrs. Melton knew what she had been doing. Mrs. Melton said nothing. She looked at Jean and then, very quietly, she walked across the room and turned the photograph face downwards on the table. For a second Jean was too astonished to do or say anything, while she felt the colour come surging in a crimson flood into her cheeks. Without thinking, she said the first thing which came into her mind.

"I am sorry. I was only looking at the photograph and thinking that the one in Berkeley Square was very different of him."

It was only as she spoke that she remembered Gerald's warning never to mention Stephen Melton to his wife. She would have given anything at that moment to have caught back the words, to have left them unsaid, but it was too late. They had been spoken and it seemed to her that they hung in the air, dark and ominous, like a thunderstorm which is about to break in all its violence. Mrs. Melton stood very still and then in a low, tortured voice, she asked:

"Which photograph do you mean? What are you talking about?"

It was too late now to retreat and Jean could only go on, feeling herself being sucked deeper and deeper into a whirlpool of her own making.

"There is a photograph . . . by your bed there," she stammered. "I hope you don't mind . . . but I changed in your room . . . Tally told me to . . . and . . . I . . . I noticed it . . ."

"Which photograph is it?" Mrs. Melton demanded peremptorily. It seemed as though she thrust aside Jean's explanations, striving to get to the crux of the matter and dispense with all that was unimportant.

"It is by your bed," Jean repeated. "It is just a head of Colonel Melton. He is looking straight into the camera."

Mrs. Melton gave a sigh. It was almost a groan.

"So that is where it is!" she exclaimed. "I've wanted it. I looked everywhere, but nobody would help me."

There was a moment's silence. Jean felt her heart beating quickly, so quickly and so violently that she was almost afraid Mrs. Melton would hear it; and then, even as the thought formulated itself, she knew that Mrs. Melton would hear and know nothing save those things on which she was deeply and wholly concentrated. She was standing in the centre of the room, her hands clenched together so that her knuckles showed white. Suddenly, she walked across to the bedside, picked up the photograph she had turned face downwards, and set it upright again. She stared down at it with a look of such utter despair and misery that it was with difficulty that Jean prevented herself from crying out; then with an obvious effort she turned:

"Thank you for telling me," she said. "I wanted that photograph so much. It is one of the few things I have left."

She spoke quite quietly and sensibly, and yet it seemed to Jean that there was the most bitter desolation in her tone and that she spoke as one who is abandoned, alone and without hope.

"Let us go down," Mrs. Melton said abruptly, and before Jean could say anything more she led the way from the room. Jean followed her, and as they walked in silence down the long, soft-carpeted passage, Jean was so desperately sorry for Tally's beautiful mother that she was very near to tears.

The men were waiting just inside the lounge, sitting comfortably on a big sofa with coffee and liqueurs on the table in front of them. Tally jumped to his feet at the sight of them.

"Here you are at last," he said. "I thought you must both have gone to bed, you have been so long."

"We thought we had been rather quick," Jean answered, making an effort to speak easily and calmly, because she felt as if she must protect the older woman until she had time to recover. Mrs. Melton sank down

133

on the sofa on the side from which Tally had risen, and stretched out her hand for a cup of coffee which Gerald passed to her.

"Won't you have a liqueur, Mrs. Melton?" he asked.

"Yes, please, I would like a brandy."

Tally glanced at his mother as if in surprise. He said nothing, merely drawing up a big arm-chair for Jean and seating himself at her side. Jean accepted a cup of coffee and refused a liqueur.

"I like that dress," Tally said, and as she looked up and smiled at him she saw that he glanced towards the end of the lounge which led into the dining-room. She knew then the reason both for his approval and for his impatience at their delay. He was expecting to see Melia, and the scene was set for her to be both astonished and discomfited by their appearance. Quite suddenly Jean felt angry with Tally. She had the feeling that there were more important things that he might be doing than chasing round the world after a girl who apparently did not wish to marry him. He was so clever, so handsome, and he had, too, a mother who was obviously desperately unhappy. Why worry over one young woman, however attractive, when the rest of the world was there for his taking? But even as Jean asked the question, even as she felt her impatience with Tally rise within her, she received the answer.

The door of the dining-room opened and Melia Melchester came into the lounge. There was no mistaking who she was. Jean did not need to be told by Tally's sudden tension, by Gerald's slow smile of recognition, or by Mrs. Melton's quiet comment.

"Isn't that Melia, Tally? I didn't know that we should see her here."

Mrs. Melton's question was superfluous, because it would have been impossible to mistake Melia for anyone else. She was outstandingly lovely, not to say amazingly beautiful. Her dress was of silver lace, the skirt falling in shimmering folds from the waist to the floor, and over her shoulders was a cape of emerald velvet bordered with silver fox. In her dark hair she had

pinned a green orchid, otherwise she wore no ornaments, and had no need for them. Her face was rather
pale, her lips very red, and her eyes, wide pools of
darkness, were looking around the room when she
caught sight of Tally.

It was like watching a play, Jean thought, and yet at
the same time playing a leading part in it. Everyone else
became only the audience and ceased to exist. Melia's
steps never faltered as she followed her mother. The
only sign she showed of any perturbation was when she
raised her arms to clasp her cape a little closer around
her, as if she felt a sudden chill. They drew nearer, Lady
Melchester still blissfully unaware of anything un-
toward, until suddenly she saw Mrs. Melton. She stared
at her and her gaze shifted to recognise Tally. She
hesitated and then took the bold course.

"Margaret!" she exclaimed. "What a supprise to see
you! And Tally, too! We have only just arrived."

"How are you, Sybil?" Mrs. Melton smiled. "We flew
over, and we also have just got here. Tally thought a
holiday in the sunshine would do us all good."

Lady Melchester gave Tally a glance which would
have annihilated a more sensitive young man, but Tally
was holding out his hand to Melia.

"How are you, Melia?" he asked.

She ignored his hand.

"Very tired, thank you, Tally. We had an exhausting
journey."

"I am sorry to hear that, and, by the way, I want you
to meet my fiancée. Jean, this is Melia Melchester, of
whom you have heard so much. Melia, this is Jean."

"How do you do?" Melia said to Jean, inclining her
head very slightly, as one might do to someone utterly
inferior.

"How do you do?" Jean said, feeling small, insignificant, and utterly commonplace.

At last she understood Tally's preoccupation, understood, too, the reason why he could not accept defeat
when it came to losing Melia Melchester. She was so
lovely, so exquisite, that Jean knew how hopeless it was
135

ever to try to be attractive or to command attention when she must be compared with one so polished, so finished in every possible manner. Even in her embarrassment at meeting Tally—and Jean felt it must be embarrassing—she managed to be in command of the situation. She had not expected to see him; he had anticipated seeing her; yet of the two Melia was the more composed and more unruffled.

Jean, sensing the anger passing between two young people, unexpressed in words, yet nevertheless vibrating on the atmosphere, felt uncomfortable and was grateful when Lady Melchester brought a welcome end to a situation which was almost intolerable.

"We must have our coffee," she said. "Come along, Melia."

"Won't you have it with us?" Tally invited, grinning a little at his sheer audacity.

Lady Melchester gave him an icy glance.

"No, thank you, Tally," she said, and swept away, Melia following behind her.

Tally and Gerald sat down together and for a moment there was silence—a silence, Jean felt, in which so many things were being left unsaid. Mrs. Melton looked bewildered.

"What is happening, Tally?" she asked. "Did you know Melia was going to be here?"

"Yes, Mother."

"Then why?" She wrinkled her forehead and made a little gesture with her hands. "I suppose I have been very stupid."

Tally reached across the table and touched her hand.

"No, darling," he said. "You are never that. It is my fault for not explaining things to you. But don't worry, everything is all right and going entirely according to plan."

"You are sure it is all right?" Mrs. Melton asked. She looked at Tally and then glanced a little doubtfully at Jean. It was so obvious that while she was quite at sea as to what was occurring, she remembered that there had

136

been a likelihood of an engagement between her son and Melia Melchester.

"It is all right, really," Tally repeated, pouring his mother out another cup of coffee, and as he said it Jean knew that he was making a mistake. This was not the way to treat Mrs. Melton, she thought, letting her remain completely absorbed in her own unhappiness instead of trying to divert her mind and arouse her interest in other things. Why, for instance, couldn't she know exactly what had happened between her son and Melia? It would do no harm, and it might serve to divert her thoughts from the past for at least a little while. On a sudden impulse Jean took action. She bent forward and said quietly:

"I don't think it is any secret, Mrs. Melton, that Tally has brought us here simply to annoy Miss Melchester."

She felt her face burn as she said the words. She felt Tally sitting beside her move in his chair, but she kept her eyes on Mrs. Melton, waiting for the reaction, perhaps even the awakening of a new interest of curiosity. But she was disappointed. Mrs. Melton stirred her cup of coffee and said absently.

"That sounds rather unkind and unlike you, Tally."

There was no real feeling in her voice, and Jean knew that her efforts to startle Tally's mother had failed. She sat back in her chair, her blood still throbbing from the effort she had made, and as she leant back she knew that Tally was looking at her. She forced herself to meet his eyes. To her surprise she saw that he was not angry. He had realised why she had spoken, and instead of being annoyed there was on his face an expression of comprehension and compassion. He understood. At that moment Jean liked Tally better than she had ever liked him before. He was not just a fierce, disruptive personality; he was also someone capable of tenderness, capable of seeing the other person's point of view.

She smiled at him shyly in apology, and he smiled back at her, then bent forward and patted the hand which lay upon her lap. It was a gesture of comfort and of reassurance. It was his way of telling her that he was

137

not cross, that he understood what she had done and why she had done it. Jean was grateful and felt a warm, responsive glow within her heart. Tally understood! Even the beauty and glory of Melia Melchester could not dim the happiness within her at the moment.

"Come and dance," Tally suggested. "Gerald, what about asking Melia for a dance?"

"Oh, lord," Gerald groaned, "you don't expect me to do that, do you? If there is one thing I dislike, it's putting my head into the lion's den."

"Yes, go and dance," Mrs. Melton said, finishing her coffee. "I am going to bed."

She got to her feet, kissed Tally, and held out her hand to Jean.

"Good night, dear."

"Good night, Mrs. Melton. If there is anything I can do, you will let me know, won't you?"

"Thank you, but I shan't want anything," Mrs. Melton replied, and her tone was final.

She smiled at Gerald and walked away. Tall and distinguished, she moved as though she never saw the people around her—waiters carrying trays of coffee and liqueurs, hotel porters hurrying with parcels and newspapers, pretty girls looking up at tall, sunburnt young men, old men and women absorbed in their newspapers or their knitting. She walked as if she were alone; and Jean, watching her, realised that Tally, too, was watching his mother.

"Well, what about this dance?" he asked.

"I am not a very good dancer," Jean replied.

"Are you certain of that?" Tally asked.

"No . . . not really," Jean answered. "But I am just afraid of disappointing you."

Tally looked down at her with an almost comical expression on his face.

"You know, that's the wrong answer."

"Why?"

"Because you ought to make me feel that I might disappoint you, not that you are afraid of ever disappointing me."

"But that wouldn't be true."

Tally laughed, a tender, rather sad little laugh.

"I am afraid for you, Jean," he said at last.

"Afraid?"

"Afraid that you will grow up and get spoilt, and most of all that you may get hurt. I wonder if you would have been happier if I had left you alone and not brought you into this madcap drama."

"Of course I shouldn't have been," Jean said hotly. "This is the most wonderful thing that has ever happened to me. You know that."

"I wonder," Tally said reflectively. He stood looking down at her for a moment. "Come and dance," he commanded, and led the way to the bar.

It was a big, low-ceilinged room, with an arched roof supported by wooden pillars from which concealed lighting cast a golden glow on the dancers; there were also a medieval fireplace and a long bar at which white-coated attendants dispensed every form of drink. At one end of the room was a band, and couples were already moving over the floor. Here was to be seen every form of costume. Women in full evening dress with diamonds and flowers in their hair; men in dinner-jackets; girls in their skiing clothes, who had not changed anything except their boots since the day's sport. Boys wearing windjammers with sheepskin-lined coats flung back carelessly from their shoulders; business men in neat, pin-striped lounge suits in which they would have seemed more at home at the office; and a number of people dressed in smart day clothes which blended evenly with the formality and informality of the others.

It was with a sense of relief that Jean realised that she could dance smoothly and comfortably with Tally. He was easy to follow and he chose no complicated or unusual steps. They glided round the room, and for the first time Jean realised how tall he was, for her head just reached to his shoulder.

"Why do you worry about your dancing?" he asked. "I think you are very good."

"I have done very little of it," Jean confessed. She did not like to tell him that the only times she had ever danced were when she was a child before her father died, and in the last few months, when Angus had on several occasions taken her to a local dance in the village.

"You are as light as a feather, which is half the battle," Tally said, and he drew her a little closer to him.

"Tomorrow," he went on, "you must have your first lesson in skiing. You have got good balance, so you ought to pick it up quickly."

"I hope I shall," Jean said. "I don't want to disgrace you."

She was speaking only half seriously, but Tally took her literally.

"You could never do that. I don't know anyone in the world who could play the part that you are doing, and do it so well."

She looked up into his face.

"I am terribly lucky, aren't I?"

"Why?" he asked.

"To be with you," Jean replied ingenuously.

For a moment it seemed to her that there was an expression of pain in Tally's eyes; then, just as he was about to say something, he looked across the room and his fingers tightened on her hand. She followed his glance and saw that Melia was coming on to the dance floor followed by Gerald.

The band changed from a foxtrot into a waltz. Gerald put his arm round Melia and they began to dance. Her dress, with its full skirt, swung out, her arm rested on his shoulder. She was like some lovely bird floating around the room. Jean tripped, missed a step, and apologised.

"I am so sorry."

"Come and sit down."

Tally's tone was harsh. Meekly Jean went with him to a small table at which were two chairs. They sat down, and there was something dark and ominous in the expression on Tally's face. She wondered how she could help him. She felt that she must do something decisive to bring Melia back to him. She could at last begin to understand the misery and unhappiness he must be ex-

140

periencing. This exquisite girl had been his and he had lost her. Jean tried to visualise more fully his unhappiness and sense of loss, but she told herself she had no real criterion by which to judge. She knew now in absolute certainty that she had never loved Angus. All she had felt for him was the call of youth, the desire to be loved, and the urge to escape from the misery and monotony of her aunt's household. Tally was so different. He had so much of all that was attractive, pleasant, and beautiful. But he wanted more. He wanted Melia, and somehow, by some means, Melia, too, must want him.

Jean glanced at Tally and saw that he was staring at Melia and Gerald dancing together, and his eyes were stern. There was also something she could not fathom in his expression. She felt an overwhelming desire to help him. 'I must make things come right for him,' she told herself. 'I must. I must.'

9

Tally stood high on the mountainside, the sun blinding him dazzlingly when he raised his dark glasses. He was alone and yet did not feel lonely. There was something exhilarating in the great peaks towering above him, in the feel of the snow beneath his feet, and the harshness of the wind which, blowing across the glacier, was icy despite the warmth of the sun.

It was a wonderful world, Tally thought, leaning on his ski-sticks. He felt free and untrammelled, and he thought how long it was since he had felt just this sense of being on top of the world, both mentally and physically. It was seven years since he had stood here last, seven years in which he had grown much older; years in which he had been forced to develop rapidly, to assume great responsibilities, and to make decisions which involved the lives of hundreds of other people. Strange years, yet full ones, and he knew that he would not put the clock back. He had gained much during the passing of time—friendship, companionship, and also a knowledge of himself and his own strength. He had lost much—those he had loved, years when he might have played and known only the pleasant things of life, instead of death and destruction, pain and horror; but still some of it had been worth while.

Yes, he was older in years and old in experience, yet he asked himself if he had indeed really grown up. What did he want of the future?

He looked down the mountain where a tiny village nestled at the foot of the run. Smoke was coming from

143

the chimneys of the houses, and he could see children tobogganing on the slope which ran down to the village. Was that what he wanted, a home and children, the security of being anchored in one place, knowing that if he uprooted himself from a certain spot he must uproot several other lives at the same time?

He looked back on his own childhood. How happy he had been at Greystones! Though an only child, he had never missed companionship. There had been plenty of visitors of his own age to play with, but they were not fundamentally important. There had been much interest and excitement without people; horses, dogs, a farm where he was allowed to run wild, the shooting and fishing when he grew older, and always the guiding hand and the understanding of his father.

He had adored his mother, but in a very different way. She had always been a person apart, someone very beautiful who had come to his bed at night, kissed him, and held him close, and told him that she loved him. He had turned to her when he was unhappy; he had clung to her when he went away to school; but she did not fill his life as his father did, although at times he fancied that she turned to him for something that he could not give her. It was only later, when he saw her radiantly and ecstatically happy in her marriage with Stephen Melton, that he understood what she had wanted, and what she had missed during those years when he had been so completely absorbed in his father and his home. Then, although he was pleased that his mother had at last found complete happiness, at the same time he wished for her sake that she could have found it earlier during the years of his childhood. He had never been jealous of her absorption in Stephen Melton, even though at times his heart ached to think that his father, who had been so wonderful to him, should not have known this particular sort of happiness, this glory which seemed to radiate from his mother and Stephen whenever they were together, until it became like a shining light which enveloped them to the exclusion of all else.

If this is love, Tally thought many times, I hope one
144

day I shall feel the same; and yet he found himself dreaming not so much of women, but of the time when he would have a son of his own and could share Greystones with him, as he had shared it with his father. He wanted to take his son out riding, to show him where the trout lay in the shallow streams which fed the lake, to walk over the meadows with him in the lambing season, to introduce him to the tenant farmers, and hear him make his first speech at a rent-audit dinner.

There are so many things which to a boy are thrilling moments never to be forgotten; his first shot with a gun, to be in at the kill out fox-hunting, stalking his first stag, the joy of sailing a small boat; and Tally could remember so vividly his satisfaction the first time he dared to dive off the old grey stone bridge at the end of the lake at Greystones into the depths of the cool, green water beneath. Yes, those were the things that he wanted to show and to share with his son.

As he grew older women had, of course, begun to play a part in Tally's life, but he had never felt serious about any of them. At the back of his thoughts was vaguely the idea that he would one day marry Melia. He remembered his father saying casually:

"The Melchester estate orginally belonged to Greystones. One of our ancestors sold it, I think, to pay a gambling debt, and we were never sensible or rich enough to buy it back again. It is a pity, for when I reach the boundary I always feel resentful of the thought that I can go no farther."

Tally never forgot the remark, and ever since he was old enough to understand, he could remember his nurses and governesses exclaiming:

"Don't they make a pretty pair. Oh well, perhaps one day . . ."

Now, thinking of Melia from the top of a mountain, Tally wondered what it was which made him love her. For the first time since he had set himself out to capture her, he tried to imagine her at Greystones. Somehow, Melia did not fit in with the mellow peace of the old house. It was easier to think of her in Berkeley Square,

145

giving big parties in the Chinese drawing-room, sleeping in the rose and gold bedroom which had been his mother's, and sitting at the head of the big carved refectory table in the dining-room, which on important occasions would be laden with gold plate. Yes, those were the appropriate settings for Melia; ones in which it was easy to visualise her exquisite beauty.

Well, time would see her there, Tally thought. He did not really believe that Melia would ever marry Ernest Danks. It was hard enough to imagine Melia married to anyone, let alone to a man with whom she had nothing in common. If it came to that, they hardly spoke the same language. What did Ernest Danks know of Melia, her interests, and her friends? What did he know of her feelings, her emotions, her ambitions, and her secret desires? Tally stopped. An astounding question had suddenly presented itself to him—did he himself know Melia any better? What were her ambitions, besides love of publicity? Who were her real friends in that chattering, superficial crowd of acquaintances with whom she filled her days and nights?

Even as Tally asked himself the question he laughed. He was getting absurdly serious. Melia was the most beautiful creature he had ever seen in his life; surely it would be enough to know that one could go through life loving her, possessing her, knowing that she bore one's name? And yet, would it? asked a cold voice of logic that was as icy and as chill as the wind. Tally pulled his dark glasses over his eyes and set off down the run.

An hour later he came skiing down the roadway to the hotel just as Melia was stepping out of a horse-drawn sleigh which had brought her up from St. Moritz. She smiled at Tally. Tally lifted his glasses. She was certainly looking lovely; her face was framed in fur, and she wore a scarlet skiing suit beneath a fur coat.

"What have you been doing, Melia? Shopping?"
Melia nodded.
"Just a few things Mother and I forgot."
She turned to go into the hotel, but Tally stopped her.

146

"Come and watch the skating with me," he said. "I want to talk to you."

She hesitated for only a moment, then gave her parcels to one of the porters.

"I can't stay long," she said. "It will be getting cold as soon as the sun goes down."

Tally kicked off his skis, gave them to an attendant, and taking Melia's arm led her along a small, tree-bordered path which led down to the skating rink. There was a flight of steps which they must negotiate before they reached the terraces set with seats. As they walked down them, Melia nearly slipped, and only the fact that Tally's arm was linked in hers kept her from falling.

"Steady," Tally said warningly, and then, as she turned her face to him, he asked: "You have not told me yet if you are glad to see me out here."

"No, I am not," Melia replied. "Why ask silly questions?"

"Are you still angry with me?"

"Furious. I didn't want to make a scene last night in front of your mother, but I do think you are behaving badly, Tally. I know you have only come here to annoy me. There is nothing I can do about it, as you well know. If I am rude to you and your fiancée, people will say it is pique; but I shall get even with you, sooner or later."

There was a tone of suppressed vehemence in her voice.

Tally looked at her in astonishment.

"I will tell you one thing, Melia. I have at last stirred you to some emotion. I used to think you hadn't a feeling in the whole of your body."

"If you felt like that," Melia said acidly, "it's surprising that you wanted to marry me."

"Want," Tally corrected. "No reason to put it in the past tense."

"Then why," Melia asked, in a note of triumph, "are you engaged to Miss MacLeod?"

Tally saw that he had fallen into a trap, but it was typical of him that he was not disconcerted. He laughed.

147

"Good for you, Melia. You have got some brains tucked away somewhere, after all. But I admit nothing. Jean is a very attractive, very sweet girl—no one could be surprised at my wanting to marry her. What are you going to do about it?"

"I won't even discuss such things with you under the present circumstances," Melia replied. "If you were to break off this ridiculous engagement and go back to London, then when I came home we could———."

She hesitated.

"We could do what?" Tally prompted.

"Discuss the matter."

They had reached the bottom of the steps by now and Tally suddenly turned Melia round to face him, putting both hands on her shoulders.

"Listen, Melia. Do you mean that?"

"Of course I do."

"Very well, then," Tally went on. "Look me straight in the eyes and swear to me on the Bible or anything that you hold sacred that you are not really going to marry Ernest Danks. If you will promise me that, in all seriousness, I might consider doing what you want me to do."

Melia hesitated. Her eyes met his, and then she looked away.

"Really, Tally," she began, after a moment. "I don't think it is for you to make conditions."

Tally's hands dropped from her shoulders, and he laughed a harsh, bitter laugh.

"So you were only cheating me, after all? Trying to get me to agree to what you want, while you still intend, when the moment is propitious, to announce your engagement to Ernest Danks. Thank you for nothing, Melia. I shall continue to enjoy my engagement to Jean MacLeod."

Melia realised that she had lost her opportunity.

"Take care the engagement doesn't cost you too much," she said bitterly. "Girls of that sort have an unpleasant habit of blackmailing people."

With this parting shot she turned and walked away

148

from Tally, leaving him standing in the path looking after her. Melia did not go to the ice-rink; she went into the hotel through another door and upstairs to her bedroom. Her mother was sitting writing letters in the adjoining room, but she did not join her. Instead, she sat down on the chair drumming her fingers angrily on the arm and staring at her own reflection in the big mirror on the other side of the room. What was she to do about Tally? The present position was intolerable. Here they were, all cooped up in the same hotel, the place filling up with their friends from England, who would all watch this unfolding drama with an unremitting interest and a certain amount of cattiness. Retreat would be undignified. At the same time, to watch Tally flaunting his engagement while hers could not be announced was infuriating to say the very least of it.

Melia pulled off her gloves and looked down at the ringless third finger on her left hand. She would have given much at the moment to have seen it adorned with a big solitaire diamond and to know that she could go downstairs and brandish it in Tally's face. She thought over their conversation and wished she had had the courage to tell him a direct lie, but somehow it was hard to lie to Tally. He had not pretended to be in love with Jean MacLeod.

'He loves me still,' Melia thought, with a little smile of satisfaction, and then an idea came to her. She jumped to her feet, walked towards the writing-desk, pulling her fur-bordered cap from her head and running her fingers through her dark curls.

Yes, Tally still loved her. She had a new plan of campaign, and her lips were parted in the suspicion of a smile. At last she sat down and, opening a box which contained her own special notepaper, she took out a sheet and wrote hastily.

Forgive me, Tally. It makes me miserable when we quarrel. Come and have a drink about six o'clock, and let us forgive each other.

Melia

She read it through and then slipped it into an envelope and telephoned for a messenger.

The note was brought to Tally in the lounge a few minutes later. He was sitting on the sofa talking to Jean and Gerald. Jean was wearing the skiing clothes which Mrs. Melton had helped her choose early that morning in St. Moritz. They were not as elaborate as Melia's, but the blue windjammer was extremely becoming and matched her mittens and peaked cap of wool that she wore over her fair hair.

"How did you get on?" Tally asked.

"Not very well," Jean confessed. "I had no idea that anything could be so difficult! The instructor kept saying, 'Bend your knees, ladies, please'; but as soon as I tried to do as he asked, I fell down. I think I am black and blue all over. I shall never, never, learn to ski."

Tally laughed.

"You always feel like that at first. In a few days you will be shooting down from the top of the mountain and finding it as easy as walking."

"I hope you are right," Jean answered, "but I rather suspect that I shall be so stiff tomorrow that it will need a crane to move me about anywhere."

"Where is mother?" Tally asked Gerald.

"She watched the skating for a little this afternoon, and then she went upstairs to lie down. I don't think she slept very well last night."

"I have an idea that something upset her," Tally said. "She never came here with Stephen, did she?"

Gerald shook his head.

"Not that I know of."

"Then it couldn't have been that. I thought something might have reminded her of him. Perhaps I am mistaken."

Jean felt guilty. It must be her fault that Mrs. Melton had not slept well. She had spoken of Colonel Melton and those few words might have brought back a host of memories and a renewed sense of loss. She half thought of confessing to Tally what she had done, but changed her mind and said nothing.

It was at that moment that the note arrived from Melia. The porter offered it to Tally on a tray. Tally looked at the envelope in surprise, then opened it and read the few lines it contained. For a moment he looked pleased and then, as if his instinct warned him that things were not as simple as they appeared, he read the note again.

"All right, no answer," he said sharply to the porter, and, turning to the others, he said, "Melia wants us all to have drinks with her at six o'clock."

Neither Jean nor Gerald said anything, and Tally lay back in his chair frowning. There was something grim and yet vaguely pathetic in his expression. He was well aware that Melia had not intended the others to be included in her invitation, and he thought it would be amusing to watch her face when he arrived with the whole party. He was not deceived by the pleasantness of her note. Melia had some new plan to get her own way—she was not particularly scrupulous as to what methods she used, and she would use sentiment and friendliness as weapons without hesitation if they would give her what she wanted.

"I think I will go and have a bath," Tally said, getting to his feet.

"I must change, too," Jean said, and then added shyly: "You don't want me to come with you at six o'clock?"

"But of course," Tally replied. "Why ever not? Besides, engaged people do go about together, you know."

He smiled at Jean as he said it, and it took some of the sarcasm from his words. She knew that he was upset, knew something unpleasant had occurred, but had no idea what it was. He walked away before she could reply, and when he was gone she, too, got to her feet.

"I will go and change," she said to Gerald.

"Come back here when you are ready," he said, "and we will have a cup of tea. I know I need one. One's first day on skis is always extremely tiring."

"Thank you," Jean said gratefully.

151

She walked across the lounge and went up in the lift to her own room. As she changed, she found herself worrying about Tally. The joy and exhilaration she had known earlier in the day as she stood in the sunshine and stared at the sun-covered landscape was forgotten now, because of the cloud that had passed over Tally's face after he had read Melia's note. 'We should be so happy if she were not here,' Jean thought, and then laughed to herself. If it were not for Melia she would still be working in Tally's office in Dover Street, and would not be putting on a Michael Sorrel dress over her shining hair. How complicated it all was! 'I ought to hate Melia Melchester . . . I think I do hate her . . . and yet I have so much for which to be grateful to her.' she told her reflection in the mirror.

Jean finished dressing, tidied her room, and was ready to go downstairs. It was then the idea came to her that she should speak to Melia Melchester. She shrank away from the idea, wished that it had never presented itself, and yet insistently it was there. Once again she saw the expression on Tally's face, heard the sharp note in his voice. 'Perhaps if I talk to her, she will be kind to him,' Jean thought, and in case her courage should fail her, she hurried down to the next floor, running down the staircase instead of using the lift. She knew the number of Melia's room, for she had come up in the lift with Lady Melchester that morning, and heard her give instructions to the liftman. Lady Melchester had acknowledged her presence by a frigid little nod, and Jean had been humbly grateful not to be entirely ignored.

As she walked along the wide corridor, her heart sinking lower and lower, she wondered whether she was doing the right or the wrong thing. But she knew that Tally's happiness mattered far more than her own feelings. She wanted everything to come right for him. 'Was she sure of that?' her heart asked her. 'Yes quite, quite sure!' she forced herself to reply.

She knocked on the door of number 206. For a moment there was no answer, and with a sense of relief Jean thought that she was not there. She could go away.

She had tried and Fate had been against her. No one could do more. Then she heard Melia's voice:

"Come in."

Jean entered a big sitting-room with the windows opening on to a balcony. There were vases of expensive hothouse flowers on every table and Melia, still in her scarlet skiing suit, was sitting on the sofa reading a letter. She looked up as Jean entered, and there was no mistaking the surprise in her expression.

"Miss MacLeod!" she exclaimed.

"Could I speak to you a moment?" Jean asked.

"Of course. Come in."

She made no effort to get up. She put down the letter that she held in her hand, a letter of many pages, closely written in a small, spidery handwriting on House of Commons paper.

"Won't you sit down?" she suggested, and indicated a small upright chair near where she was sitting.

Jean crossed the room. Now that she was here she felt suddenly panic-stricken. She sat down, interlocking her fingers together, and was lost as to how to begin.

"You wanted to see me?" Melia prompted at length.

Jean nodded.

"It's about Tally," she said, and then quickly, lest she should be afraid to say the words, "He is unhappy. I thought you could help him."

"I could help him?" Melia queried. "And what can I do about it?"

She was obviously quite unembarrassed, even slightly amused by this conversation, while Jean stammered and twisted her fingers. She envied Melia her calmness and the way she was in complete command of the situation.

"I thought if we talked about things we could perhaps . . . you would perhaps . . . understand."

"I am afraid I understand only too well," Melia said. "I told Tally that I didn't want to marry him, and to annoy me he got engaged to you. I am sorry if I am being too frank, Miss MacLeod, but that is the truth, isn't it?"

Jean nodded.

"I told Tally just a short while ago," Melia went on,

153

"it was a disgraceful way to behave, and I have no intention of reconsidering anything I have said or done until he stops this ridiculous engagement and goes back to London."

"Oh, you have told Tally that?" Jean whispered. The interview was not going as she expected.

"Yes, I told him that for a second time," Melia replied.

"And if he does what you want?" Jean asked, "if . . . our . . . our engagement is broken off . . . would you become engaged to him yourself?"

Melia got to her feet.

"I don't think, Miss MacLeod, you have the right to ask me such a question. Until Tally behaves properly and decently to me I should not consider him in any way. At the moment his actions are merely offensive . . . he has tried to hurt me . . . to make me a laughing stock."

"Miss Melchester, he loves you, you know that?"

"Do I?" Melia asked. "If he does, he has a funny way of showing it."

"I would so much like him to be happy," Jean said, "if I could help him in any way . . . I would."

"The best way you can help," Melia said sharply, "is by not being here. At the moment, to put it bluntly, you are complicating matters a great deal. Surely you can see that?"

Melia walked to the window and looked out. The sun was sinking. It was reflected by a glorious pink light on the tops of the mountains. The valley was in shadow, and in a very short time darkness would fall. Melia's profile against the sky was exquisite, yet there was something hard about the sharp line of her mouth and her square-set jaw.

"I am sorry," Jean said, and she also got to her feet. She could do no good by staying, she realised that.

Melia turned round.

"Who are you?" she asked abruptly. "How did Tally meet you?" She waited a moment and then, as Jean did not answer, but merely looked helpless and uncomfortable, she went on, "I suppose you won't tell me, but if you take my advice you will go back to where you belong. At the same time I should make him pay you well for . . . your services."

Jean might be shy, but there was a Scottish pride in her which would prevent her from being insulted without retaliation.

"I think that was a very unnecessary remark, Miss Melchester," she said quietly. "I came to see you because I wanted to help Lord Brora to find happiness. He has been very kind to me, but it is not, and never has been, a question of payment in money."

"No?" Melia asked, and then a sneer twisted her lovely mouth, "I suppose you have done all this for love."

Jean threw back her head and looked at her squarely between the eyes.

"Yes, I think that is the right word. I have done it for love."

She turned and walked from the room, closing the door quietly behind her. Then, only then, did she realise what she had done. She ran up the stairs, along the corridor and into her own room. There she stood for a moment quivering, her hands raised to her cheeks. Melia had insulted her. Melia had been hard, bitter, and rude. None of that mattered. What mattered was that quite unwittingly her words had revealed the truth.

Jean knew now that she loved Tally. Loved him overwhelmingly and with every fibre of her being. She had wanted to help him—wanted him to find happiness because she loved him. It was a love such as she had not only never known before, but had never realised was possible in its ecstasy and overwhelming tenderness—a feeling which she could not yet define, even to herself. She had known Tally such a short time, and yet into those few days had been packed so much experience that she knew time did not count. This was life. This fullness, this warmth within her. There was nothing possessive, nothing greedy in her feelings for Tally. For the moment it was a selfless emotion, and she was

155

grateful for having known him, for having the opportunity to wish that he might find happiness, not daring in her humbleness to ask that it should be anything personal.

She moved across the room. Perhaps that first night when she had gazed out on the beauty of the valley and known a spiritual ecstasy it had been love which had shown her how wonderful the world could be. A little of that ecstasy had remained with her ever since, giving a glowing wonder and inner meaning to everything she thought, said, or did. Now she understood that it had been the dawning of love within her. Now she could say in all truth that she was content with the knowledge that Tally was there, in the same world as she was, breathing the same air. She thought now she had loved him from the first second of their meeting; loved him when she had first trusted him, when she had known that she must do what he wished, however crazy, however strange it might seem.

Jean bent forward and rested her head against the window. Both double windows were closed, and yet she could feel the frosty air seeping in from without—icy cold, chilling her cheeks and breasts.

"Oh, Tally," she whispered to herself, and thought absurdly that if it gave him any satisfaction she would walk out into the cold night and die on the mountain.

Now that she had learned the reason for her feelings, the explanation of the tumult within her, she wondered why she had been so blind as not to realise the truth earlier.

The light beyond the mountains had faded; soon it would be dark. There was just a finger of gold on Piz Nair, the very topmost peak. Now that, too, was going. It was gone.

"My life will be in darkness when Tally leaves me," Jean whispered, and was suddenly panic-stricken. What would she do? She had had no thought of herself up till this moment, only of him. Now she thought of her life without him, and experienced a loneliness she had never known, not even in her hours of darkest misery in

156

Scotland. 'Then I had nothing,' she thought; 'now I have so much . . . but for how long?'

Tally's happiness was the thing that counted. Tally wanted Melia; and although she had bungled and mismanaged the interview of a few minutes ago, Jean believed that she could somehow help him to gain his heart's desire. She must not think of herself, but only of him. She was very still for a moment; then, realising that she was cold, she moved from the window and switched on the light.

She looked round the bedroom as though she saw it for the first time. The comfortable bed, the big looking-glasses, the fine rugs covering the polished floor were all evidence of a luxury she had never known previously. She looked at her personal belongings—Tally's gifts, scattered around. A dressing-gown on the chair, the brushes on the dressing-table, a bag lying on the chest of drawers, all were from Tally, everything she touched must remind her of him. And to him she was only the means to an end, a weapon he could use in his battle for another woman.

Jean put up her hands to her eyes. For a moment she was tempted . . . tempted to forget everything but her own need of Tally. 'Suppose,' came the whisper in her heart, 'I tried to capture him for myself? Suppose I showed him that I could really love him?'

Then she pushed the idea away from her. To begin with it was laughable. Who would look at her who had once loved Melia? She knew too that she would never stoop to such things. Tally had asked her help and she would not fail him. "I have got to be straight; I have got to be honourable," she said aloud. And raising her chin high, she went downstairs.

To her relief Gerald was sitting alone on the sofa where she had left him.

"At last," he exclaimed. "You have been a week of Sundays and I am simply dying for my tea."

"I hoped you wouldn't wait for me," Jean said. "I am sorry. Why didn't you start?"

"Always the perfect gentleman," Gerald grinned.

157

She sat down and he beckoned the waiter.

"What will you have?" he asked. "Rolls and butter and one of those luscious-looking cakes?"

"I am going to be expensive and say yes," Jean replied. "I am terribly hungry."

"So am I," Gerald agreed, and gave the order.

The lounge was full and more people were pouring in from the outer hall.

Tea was a fashionable hour when outside visitors appeared from the village, to eat the rich cakes and listen to the band.

"You are looking very smart," Gerald said appreciatively as Jean stared around her.

"Thank you."

She was making an effort to speak naturally and easily, and yet she knew that every nerve in her body was tense as she waited for Tally. She wanted to see him again, and yet she was half afraid. This new secret within herself, this knowledge of her love made her apprehensive and yet exultant.

Tea was brought, but she could not force herself to eat.

"You're not overtired?" Gerald asked anxiously. "Perhaps you have done too much; people often do out here, the air is so exhilarating."

"I'm quite all right," Jean said quickly. "I'm just not hungry, after all."

It was then that she saw Tally coming slowly across the lounge. He came near to the table and with a sinking of her heart Jean saw that he was frowning and that his eyes were dark with anger. He came up to them, pulled up a chair to the other side of the table and sat down. Then he looked across at Jean and said in a low, furious voice:

"What the devil do you mean by going to see Melia?"

10

Margaret Melton lay in bed with her arms behind her head, her thoughts making patterns in the darkness. She was tired but she knew that it would be hopeless for her to try to sleep and a long time ago she had given up attempting to woo slumber by unnatural means.

After Stephen's death, when her unhappiness brought her perilously near to losing her mind altogether, the doctor had prescribed sleeping draughts and she had taken them greedily, longing for a few hours' escape from her aching misery; but she found that while they gave her a merciful oblivion for a short space of time, the agony she experienced on regaining consciousness was not worth the relief. The unnatural depression they brought in their train merely intensified her suffering to such a pitch that it became in very truth unbearable. And so, as time went on, she gave up both the doctors' prescriptions and the doctors themselves, knowing that no physician could cure her illness which was of the heart and not the body.

Lying in the soft, comfortable bed, which should have brought her rest and relaxation, she tossed wearily from side to side, now switching on the bedside light to take up a book, only to discard it as she realised after a few pages that she was not concentrating on what she read; now looking at the luminous face of her travelling clock; now getting out of bed to walk across to the dressing-table in search of a handkerchief and to stand there with the drawer open, wondering what she had wanted.

There was nothing unusual in all this; it was Margaret Melton's nightly manner of passing the hours of darkness. At length her restlessness seemed to pass and she allowed her thoughts to come crowding in upon her —thoughts so vivid that they were in themselves almost dreams for she saw them pictured colourfully in her mind as she re-lived the past.

She saw Stephen as she first knew him, when he had come at her brother's invitation to stay at their home in the country. They were very poor, for her father had retired from active service in the Army and had only his pension to support himself and a growing family; but it did not matter, for they were very happy.

Looking back, it seemed to Margaret Melton that her childhood had been one of sunshine and of laughter. There were cooking and cleaning for her to do, for the one general servant they could afford was usually untrained and scatterbrained; but she had never minded the work so long as, having done it, she could escape into the countryside to climb Bredon Hill to the ruined Folly which stood like a sentinel on its summit; to go down to the Avon and watch the anglers compete for a prize which, whoever the winner, they would all celebrate in the small village pub at sunset; to run, redcheeked, after the hounds; or to tramp miles with the beagles. These were joys which needed no expenditure of money and which meant ecstatic hours of happiness in the companionship either of the country folk she knew and loved or of her beloved brother when he was at home.

Donald had known from the very first that she and Stephen would like each other.

"It was the reason I asked him," he said, boyishly proud that his friend and his sister should hit it off so well together. That was during the first holiday which Stephen Melton spent with them, and after that there were many of them.

Margaret was six years younger than he and yet always she seemed his equal in years and experience, just as Donald, who was also considerably her senior, found her the perfect comrade and companion.

It was hard now, looking back, to know at what particular moment she became consciously aware of Stephen as a young man. At first he was just another Donald, someone she liked, someone with whom she was utterly content to ramble over the countryside, to talk until the fire died low in the hearth or to sit in silence, knowing there was no need for words.

Perhaps it was the spring which told her that she was growing older and that she was desirable in Stephen's eyes. She remembered becoming aware for the first time in her life of the inadequacy of her clothes. There had never been any money to buy new things; they had to scrimp and save and very nearly starve that Donald might go to Oxford. At times Margaret would know that things were particularly desperate, when her father would walk about scowling and her mother would be near to tears. Usually after this yet another piece of furniture would disappear from the drawing-room—the silver had gone many years earlier, and her mother's jewellery—now it was a chest of drawers, a bureau-bookcase or a rather attractive chair.

Though they all knew that eventually nothing would be left to sell, they never mentioned the fact, believing that by some miracle what remained would be saved and they would be able to keep intact their home and their shabby gentility.

It was Margaret who saved them, of course— Margaret who moved from the small, down-at-heel house in the village to Greystones. But before this happened she had found and lost Stephen.

She found him one hot summer's day when they sat together on the summit of Bredon Hill. The valley lay below them, green and beautiful; the river, silver and slow-moving between its reed-bordered banks, seemed to shimmer hazily in the heat; and the dusty roads which wound between black and white cottages with thatched roofs were quiet and empty.

There was a feeling of breathlessness and silence

161

everywhere, a sense of tense anticipation, and Margaret felt within herself a surging restlessness, a yearning desire for something to happen. She lay back on the short, dry grass and stared up at the grey-stoned Folly towering high above them.

"How foolish to build such a thing!" she said, speaking more to herself than to Stephen.

He followed the direction of her eyes and replied:

"I don't know. Don't we all do foolish things at times?"

"Do we?" Margaret asked, talking for the sake of talking rather than inviting controversy.

"Yes, all of us," Stephen answered; "and if we are not foolish with stone, we are foolish with our emotions."

Margaret rolled over on the grass and sat up. There was something in Stephen's voice which told her that he was unusually serious.

"What is your particular foolishness?"

Stephen did not answer for a moment and then, with his eyes half shut, he said quietly.

"Falling in love with you, I suppose."

Margaret was never to forget that moment. She could still recapture the feeling which shot through her, half pain, half joy. She had been in love with him since the spring, loved him so that he filled her whole life; but she had never even dared to hope that he felt for her anything more than the affection which had been hers since she was a child.

For a moment she could hardly believe that she had heard him right, he had spoken so quietly, so casually; and then the sunlight bathing the valley and enveloping them had become almost too glorious to be borne. It seeped into her consciousness, consuming her with its brilliance, dazzling her with its wonder. She was part of it, part of a world so rich, so beautiful; but she had no words, no expression of any sort by which she could relieve the intensity of her feelings. Stephen sat up.

"I must go away and find myself a job."

"Why?"

Margaret whispered the word.

162

"So that we can get married."

That was all. That was their betrothal. He had not touched her, not even looked at her. But she was utterly content; she wanted nothing more. She would perhaps have felt it unnecessary if he had made any further expression of his feelings. They belonged. They had found each other. It was only later, when Stephen had gone, when she had lain night after night sick with crying, heavy-hearted and miserable, that she regretted that she had never known the touch of his lips, the feel of his arms around her.

"You have got to be sensible, dear," her mother had said, trying to be kind and sympathetic in her own rather undemonstrative manner.

Margaret had tried to be sensible. She had tried to understand the arguments which had been repeated to her over and over again. They were both too young. There was no money, not a penny except what Stephen could make. He had no influence, no family to help him. It was impossible for them to consider marriage for years. Under those circumstances an engagement was out of the question. There was not even to be an understanding between them.

Margaret would have resisted, would have fought for her happiness, would have known that all logic was ridiculous if her father and mother had not persuaded Stephen that he must behave decently.

"They are right," he said to Margaret at last. "I have got to think of you. You are so young. How can you possibly know your own mind at seventeen?"

He was only repeating parrot-like what they had told him, but because he loved her he was ready to do what was required of him. He went away. He did not even leave an address. Frantically she tried to write to him only to have the letters returned endorsed 'Gone away.' It seemed to her that those two words were written on her heart. Stephen had gone away; she had lost him!

It was three years later, when she had no idea whether Stephen was alive or dead, that she became engaged to Lord Brora. She liked him; she even grew in the years they were married to love him very dearly. He was a very charming and very lovable man; but she was never *in love* with him, and deep in her heart there was a secret shrine set apart for the memory of Stephen.

Looking back, she could never regret to any great degree the years she spent at Greystones as Lady Brora. She had been happy and had been able to give happiness to those around her. Her husband adored her and they were linked together in the joy of having a son. It was wonderful, too, to know that her father and mother were well off. The house in the village was repaired, the drawing-room was filled again with beautiful things; there was silver once more on the dining-room sideboard. Her father would potter about on the estate; he enjoyed the shooting parties in the winter; her mother was less thin and the expression of worry had left her face. It was a consolation for Margaret to know that she could give her every comfort in her later years; that she could afford to send her abroad to escape the severity of the English winter, and that the expensively efficient nurses who ministered to her in the last years of her life could be paid for without anxiety.

"Yes," Margaret thought very often, "I was happy then at Greystones."

It was only when Bredon Hill was purple against the deepening sky or in the spring when the first daffodils were yellow against the summit that she felt empty and lonely; then a wild restlessness would take possession of her and she must go walking alone through the woods and parkland, walking until she was almost too tired to think.

She never went to the Folly. Often as a child Tally would ask her:

"What is that funny little castle on the hill, Mummy?"

"It is a Folly, darling. A tower built many years ago by a mad old man."

"Does anyone live there, Mummy?"

"No darling." But even as she answered him she knew it was untrue. Part of her lived there; a young,

164

ecstatically happy part, knowing for the first time the wonder and glory of a world which held love.

The years passed by slowly and it seemed to her uneventfully. Then had come the tragedy and the shock of her husband's death while out hunting. She mourned him with a genuine sorrow. It was lonely without him in the great house which now she must care for because it was her son's heritage.

Then one day a casual acquaintance remarked:

"I hear Stephen Melton is back in this country. You used to know him, didn't you?"

Margaret felt as if someone had suddenly turned on all the lights in the room. She experienced a sudden pain within her so violent that for a moment she thought it was a physical one. Yet she managed to answer the question conventionally, thankful that years of control had taught her not to betray her feelings in public.

But when she was alone she knew she was trembling with excitement; the pulse beating quickly in her throat. Stephen was alive! He had come home! What could that mean? She went to bed that night expecting to dream of him, instead she slept as peacefully as a child.

She awoke in the very early morning. The pale dawn was creeping up a translucent sky. The great house was still asleep, not even the housemaids had risen to pull back the blinds and curtains. Margaret knew what she must do. She dressed swiftly and slipping down the cool, dark corridors, let herself out by a side door to the rose garden.

She walked swiftly, avoiding the road to the village and taking the twisting pathway through the woods which led her on to the uplands and beyond that to the foot of the hill. She was a little breathless when she reached the top. By now the sun was growing warm, although not warm enough to dispel the heavy dew of the night. It lay glittering on the grass, each drop iridescent as a rainbow. The Folly was just the same, old and grey, and perhaps a little more dilapidated than it had been eighteen years earlier; but it stood there, pointing a moral which perhaps no one had been able to translate; and there beside it, bare-headed in the sunshine, Stephen was waiting for her!

She went to him swiftly, with a certainty which needed no thought, no consideration. He put out his arms and held her close. For one moment they looked into each other's eyes, one long moment in which all things were said and unsaid; a long moment in which the years between vanished and were gone for ever. She had a second in which to breathe his name, a second in which her eyes, dazzled both by the sun and the glittering grass, were also blinded by tears; and then his lips were on hers and they were linked together by a flame which consumed them both, joined by a passion so fierce, so compelling, that for the first time in her life Margaret was afraid of her own emotions.

"Darling!" she said at last, "oh, my darling, is it really you?"

He held her so strongly and so possessively that she could hardly breathe.

"I have waited so long," he said hoarsely. "I only heard two months ago that you were free. I came home at once. I have got a little money, Margaret. Enough, at any rate; and now you can be mine, mine as you always were intended to be."

His lips sought hers again and she surrendered herself utterly, knowing, as she had always known, that she and Stephen were a part of each other and could never be divided.

They were married by special licence forty-eight hours later. There were many things to be decided, many things to be planned, but everything was so utterly unimportant beside their need for each other that all else must wait, even as they had waited for this consummation of their love.

Are there any words for real happiness? Margaret could remember the succeeding years only as a series of emotions. She vibrated to Stephen as an instrument can vibrate to the hand of a master musician. She adored him and he adored her. They would lie awake at night, their arms around each other, talking quietly of themselves, trying to fill in the gaps of the years when they had been parted, trying to make up for the youth they had both lost.

When Stephen said he had 'a little money' he made an understatement. He had done well in the East; as he said himself, he had had nothing else to live for, so he had worked hard. He had sold out his business at the top of the market and had come home with a comfortable fortune.

At first he wanted to take Margaret away from Greystones and give her a home of his own choosing; then he had understood that her obligation must be towards her son and that it would be wrong to separate Tally from the house and grounds that he would inherit on coming of age. Stephen therefore insisted on paying over a considerable sum every year to the estate; but because between him and Margaret there could be no shadow, especially one so vulgar and unnecessary as that of money, the transaction was forgotten and they lived complete in their happiness, not particular where they were as long as they were together.

Margaret wondered sometimes whether any woman could have had a more satisfying lover. Stephen was virile and passionate; but more than that he was tender and understanding. To be loved by him was to know the fulfilment of everything real and wonderful in life; to love him was to find a man great in little things as in big—a very perfect gentle knight.

Margaret had always been a beautiful woman, but her love for Stephen made her beauty so radiant that she could, if she had wished, have been one of the most talked-of beauties of the period. Needless to say she was not interested in society. She was content to be at Greystones, helping Stephen to run the estate, watching him instruct Tally in farming, organising the fêtes, sports and youth rallies—a task which the County and village demanded of her—finding in everything perfection because of her consuming, overwhelming love for the man whose name she so proudly bore.

She did not forget her first husband. Often it occurred to her that, had he known, he would have understood and have been glad that she was so happy. He had loved her, and love, if it is real love, is unselfish and has an understanding above pettiness and jealousy or the greed of possession.

It seemed to Margaret in those years that she would never grow old. She and Stephen had missed their youth, but they found it again together. They were young not only in their passion, but in their joy of little things, in their laughter, which seemed to come welling up within them like a clear and crystal spring. There were moments when he would lift her high in his arms as if she were still the mere slip of a girl he had known at seventeen.

"Tell me you love me," he would demand.

Sometimes just for the joy of making him compel her she would refuse to answer him. Then he would threaten her unmercifully until, laughing, she would finally capitulate and fling her arms around his neck.

"I love you, Stephen. I adore you, my darling."

Looking back, Margaret sometimes wondered when she first had a sense of urgency, when first she had known subconsciously that the sands were running out. It was difficult to realise now that at the time it had seemed nothing more than an intuitive desire to be with Stephen every possible moment. Sometimes at night she would wake him so that they could talk, feeling that she could not wait until tomorrow to say what she had to say. If he was away from her for only a few hours, she found herself listening for the sound of his voice or his step in the hall. If he were late, she would grow anxious and apprehensive; fears and stupid, distorted imaginings would beset her. But when at last he returned she would rebuke herself for being so idiotic. Why should she be so afraid, and of what?

Despite the Munich crisis the declaration of war in 1939 came as a shock and a surprise. Margaret had been so utterly content in her happiness that she

168

believed until the last moment that some miracle would save the world. Even then she did not realise the full potentialities of what would happen until Stephen, grim and for once inarticulate, told her that he must volunteer to go East. Then she cried out, pleading with him, begging him not to leave her.

"You are too old," she said. "There are jobs at home that you can do. Besides, the estate is a large one. You are a farmer now. Farmers are wanted; food is just as vital in war-time as munitions."

But even while she pleaded with him she had known that words would be hopeless to sway Stephen or divert him from what he believed was the right and honourable course. He knew the East, had lived out there for so long, and in war his knowledge of the people and their dialects would be of inestimable value.

There had fortunately been months of waiting; months when he was sent from one part of the country to another, being trained and training others. They were for Margaret months both of anxiety and of perfect happiness—when she and Stephen were together. Then at last he was gone.

He went very unexpectedly; just when they had been told that there was no likelihood of his going for another three months. A seat became available on an aeroplane; a commanding officer of importance asked for Stephen to go out on his staff, and he had left almost before Margaret had time to realise it. When the Japs came into the war a fortnight later she had two letters from Stephen, neither of them much more than scribbled messages written as he journeyed first to Malaya and then to Singapore. After that—silence.

In his last letter he said that he was sending her by the following mail a long letter to which he had been adding daily. It was a diary, yet in it, too, he had said many things which he had never had time to say when he was at home. That letter never reached her. First there was only the utterly devastating news that Singapore had fallen, then she learnt that Stephen was wounded and months later that he had died—tortured by the Japanese who believed that with his knowledge of the East he was keeping secrets from them.

She could not think of his agony without feeling the pain and horror of it grip her until she would cry out in the darkness. Had he thought of her? she wondered, and she knew the answer. Perhaps those thoughts had sustained him, perhaps they had brought some comfort and added courage to his tortured and racked body.

The nights following her knowledge of Stephen's death were little hells from which there was no escape. It was not only a desperate misery which consumed her; there was something even deeper, something which presented itself in a question repeating itself insistently over and over again—"Shall I ever see him again?"

As a child she had been brought up in the easy, rather lazy Protestantism of her father and mother. Conventionally they had gone to church on Sunday, conventionally they had been friendly with the Vicarage and had subscribed, however difficult it was for them to do so, to the Sunday School treat and the choir boys' outing.

Religion had meant little to Margaret, although there had been a moment, just before she was confirmed, when she thought that she had discovered something new, something alive within herself which would answer all her questions and all her as yet hardly formed desires. But the moment passed. The Confirmation, held in February when she was suffering from a bad cold in the head, had been little more than an empty ceremony from which no spirit of flame entered into her and no mighty wind swept away her doubts and irresolutions.

At first after losing Stephen in the summer when she was seventeen she had tried to pray; but she had found there were no adequate words for her sense of loneliness and loss. Once she went alone into the little village church, crept into one of the worn oak pews and tried to contact the God who knew all and understood all. But she failed.

As Lady Brora she had, of course, kept up conventionality. She had occupied the family pew every Sunday. She had been married by the Bishop of the Diocese, who also christened Tally and who paid a visit to Greystones at least once a year. There were subscriptions to the church, to charities and institutions; in fact, her obligations to religion increased, but the benefit she personally received from it remained unchanged.

At her first husband's funeral she listened to the words of the burial service and wondered why it meant so little to her. When the coffin had been lowered into the grave and she stepped forward to drop on it a bunch of lilies she wondered if that truly was the end. She could not feel convinced that there was a life after death.

She had never as a child learned to speak of such things. Her mother's ill-health had made death an embarrassing subject in the household. They had all avoided it tactfully so that in time Margaret found it difficult to speak of her thoughts and feelings about such things even to those she loved best. And she and Stephen had been so concerned with living that the subject had never presented itself save once, and then Stephen had said:

"I am afraid I have got a complacent regard for death. It is living that counts. People worry too much about what happens after."

"What do you think does happen?" Margaret asked shyly, forcing herself to conquer what was an almost repugnance to discuss the subject.

Stephen shrugged his shoulders and then reached out both his hands to her.

"Why worry, Margaret? We have got so much to do before we die."

They had not spoken of the subject again; but to Margaret, desolate at the news of Stephen's death, that short conversation had an immense signification. Stephen had not, she felt, believed in an after-life, and she had no reason to believe in it—therefore she would never find him again.

It was this which haunted her during the long nights; the idea of utter finality, that even in dying she would not be united with him. She would think of his body rotted and decomposed, the body she had loved and held, the body that had possessed hers. Was that all there was to it? Where was Stephen's mind? Where was his brain? His courage? His sense of humour and even his unfailing tenderness? Gone too? Rotted and decomposed with his flesh?

Sometimes Margaret had risen to bang her fists against the wall and cry out:

"Answer me!"

But always there was silence. She read the Bible seriously for the first time in her life, but it seemed to her that its teaching was meaningless. Some people might take comfort from it but to her the Gospels were only words; words which held no substantial lesson for her personally.

She searched the libraries for books; books on spiritualism, books of comfort and guidance written by eminent clerics, books of stange experiences; but always they failed beside the simple question: "If there is an after-life, why doesn't Stephen come to me?"

She could not believe that he would not seek to console her or at least to let her know that he was there. She could not believe that her unhappiness, her misery, could mean so little to him that, while others could contact those they had known on earth, he apparently was making no effort to do so. She would wait in the darkness, asking only for a revelation, for the touch of his hand, the sound of his voice, perhaps only the unmistakable feeling that he was there. She would lie tense and still; and then, when nothing happened, a bitter weeping would consume her until, racked beyond endurance, she would sink into an utterly exhausted sleep.

They had never gone to Switzerland together; they had talked of it, but somehow Christmas at home had seemed infinitely more attractive. A Christmas tree in the great hall at Greystones; a children's party for Tally, and other parties for the tenants and employees on the estate, one for old people, who received a pound of tea and five hundredweight of coal apiece as their Christmas present; another for the school children with

172

oranges, bags of sweets and Father Christmas in person bringing special presents for each child.

There was a real spirit of goodwill at these parties, and in them religion ceased to be merely a conventional habit; they reflected a true love of humanity and a warm comradeship; they expressed a Christianity that was indeed alive, forceful and pervading, and not just a matter of Sunday observance, subscriptions and pious platitudes on tombs. Here was something understandable, genuine, and stirring.

At Christmas, when they sat round the big log fire in the evening, Stephen would invariably say:

"We are getting a regular Darby and Joan, Margaret. Let me kiss you under the mistletoe before I forget how to do it."

What fun it had been! And Tally's holidays from school had passed so swiftly that there was no time to go to Switzerland.

"We are happy here," Margaret would say apologetically if the question of going away arose, and Stephen would agree. Yet he would have loved St. Moritz, she thought now.

When first he had gone overseas, she found herself thinking, "Oh, I must tell Stephen that!" and had written down every little incident, every amusing word or sentence spoken to her during the day. When she knew he was killed, it had been difficult to stop. She still wanted to tell him things so much that often to relieve her feelings she had written him letters—long, rambling, incoherent letters, written behind the locked door of her bedroom to a man who was dead and who would never read them.

Yes, Stephen would have liked Switzerland. She had come here in the past when Tally was a little boy when the doctors had said it would be good for the catarrh from which he suffered for several years. He had become a first-class skier and had loved the feeling of speeding over the snow, the wind on his face, knowing the freedom and exhilaration which comes from won-

173

derful untainted air and the towering beauty of the mountains.

Tally was glad to be back there again now. To Margaret the loveliness of the scene had brought an almost intolerable regret that Stephen had not seen it.

"We ought to have come here together," she told herself, and added, "Perhaps if I went up the mountain I might get in touch with him. Maybe it is easier for them to come to you in a rarified atmosphere."

But even as she formulated the words there came the utterly devastating question: Is he there to come?

"Oh, Stephen, Stephen!" she called voicelessly in the darkness, and strained her ears as she had strained them for years, knowing hopelessly in her heart that there would be no answer.

There came a sound! She held her breath and heard it again. Then she knew only too well that the sound was familiar and of this world. It was someone sobbing. She was so used to hearing it that for a moment she imagined it was herself until she realised that the sound was not within her own room, but coming faintly through the dividing door.

Margaret Melton sat up and switched on her light. It was two o'clock. She listened. Yes, there was still the sound of bitter weeping. It must be Jean, the girl to whom Tally was engaged. Margaret wondered what she should do. She personally liked to be alone with her sorrow; she resented an intrusion of any sort, especially sympathy. Perhaps Jean felt the same way. Then she remembered the difference in their ages. Jean was young, little more than a child.

Slowly she got out of bed, put on her velvet dressing-gown, and slipped her feet into her slippers. The sounds had ceased now and for a moment she hesitated.

She tried to think back to what had occurred during the evening. She remembered that Tally had gone out to dinner unexpectedly. He had sent her a message saying he had been asked by some friends to dine with them at another hotel. Jean had seemed quiet and rather subdued at dinner. She had thought perhaps it was because

174

of Tally's absence. Gerald had been as always charming and considerate, and she had noticed nothing very unusual; but then, she chided herself, she had been absorbed with her own thoughts, and paid very little attention to the young girl whom she was chaperoning. But something was obviously wrong. The sound of weeping broke out afresh.

Margaret Melton opened the communicating door. Jean's room was in darkness, but in the shaft of light she could see the girl lying on the bed, her face buried in the pillows.

"Is anything the matter, Jean?" Margaret asked softly.

Jean raised her face, and in the light from the door Margaret could see that it was pale and tear-stained. Then she saw that the girl was still in evening dress, the folds of the green chiffon falling over the bed and on to the floor.

"What is the matter, dear?" Margaret repeated. "Can't I help?"

"I am sorry," Jean stammered. "Sorry, if you heard me . . . I . . . I am . . . so terribly unhappy."

"I can see you are," Margaret Melton said. "Please tell me about it."

"I have done . . . something dreadful," Jean whispered.

11

Margaret Melton switched on the bedside lamp. Then, as Jean turned away her head to hide the tears on her cheeks, she walked across the room and closed the communicating door.

"Now," she said gently, "we can talk."

Jean made an effort to get off the bed, but Margaret stopped her.

"Stay where you are, dear," she commanded, "and if I were you I would put the eiderdown over your legs. It is easy to catch a cold in this climate, despite all the central heating in the hotel."

Jean did as the older woman suggested, arranging the folds of her dress with an almost pathetic effort to keep them from creasing before she leant back against the pillows with a little sigh.

"This is all wrong," she said weakly. "You ought to lie down, not me."

"I'm going to sit here," Margaret answered soothingly, pulling up a big arm-chair and arranging it by the bedside.

Jean put up her hands to her face, wiped away the last remaining tears, and pushed back the tumbled hair from her forehead with an air of utter weariness.

"I am so ashamed of myself for disturbing you like this. I . . . I thought no one could hear me."

"You are not to apologise," Margaret said. "As I am always awake at this hour, anyway, you are not disturbing me in the slightest; and if you talk about things being wrong, I can assure you it is very wrong for someone as young and pretty as yourself to be so unhappy."

Jean gave her a tremulous smile.

"You are much too kind to me."

"I have a feeling that I ought to have been very much kinder," Margaret answered. "But I am afraid I do not notice what is going on around me."

"I can understand that," Jean said simply.

"Can you?" Margaret asked. "I sometimes wonder to myself whether anyone can understand; but people are very sweet to me, particularly my son."

Jean made a little sound that was half an exclamation and half a groan, Margaret bent forward and touched her hand.

"Tell me, dear," she said, "is it Tally who has made you so unhappy?"

Jean nodded.

"It was entirely my fault," she said, as if in his defence. "I interfered; tried to do things my own way without consulting him and of course it was stupid of me. I see that now, but I cannot bear him to be angry with me."

"Suppose you tell me everything from the beginning," Margaret suggested.

Jean looked doubtful.

"Do you think I ought to? It is Tally's secret." Then she added, "But I don't suppose it matters. I have made such a mess of everything."

For a moment it looked as if her tears were going to flow afresh, but with an effort she continued:

"I would like . . . to tell you the whole story if you are certain it is—"

"I will take the responsibility," Margaret interrupted. "If you don't tell me, I shall ask Tally. He will tell me. He has always told me everything that I have wanted to know ever since he was a child. But I would like to hear your version first; besides, this seems rather a good opportunity, doesn't it?"

She put her hand into her dressing-gown pocket and brought out her cigarette-case.

"I am going to smoke while we talk," she said. "You don't mind that, do you? And now the rest of the night is before us, so let us take things calmly and easily."

There was something soothing and comforting in the way she spoke, and Jean remembered how on the very first night she had met Tally's mother she had thought that here was someone whom she could trust, someone in whom she could confide.

Haltingly at first, stammering a little over her words, she began the story of her momentous meeting with Tally, of the decision he had made, and how she had been swept into agreeing to his plans because the termination of her own love affair was in many ways identical with his.

"Do you love this man?" Margaret Melton asked, when Jean spoke of Angus.

Jean shook her head.

"I thought I did for a time," she replied, "and it seems strange to say it, but now in a week I feel so immeasurably older, so much more experienced, not only in judging other people, but in understanding myself. I have known so very few men; in fact, so few people altogether that I was, I can say it now, a simple fool in many ways. Angus made love to me, and it was not the man himself that attracted me or the things he said, but the idea of being loved; more than that, the idea of being wanted and of being important to anyone. It was such a change after the long years of being scolded and disliked by my great-aunt. It was like seeing the sun for the first time after being shut up in an underground cellar or cave. That anyone thought me nice was in itself a miracle. I had been told for so long and so often that I was ugly, bad and horrible."

"Why should your aunt have thought that?" Margaret Melton asked curiously; and then, as Jean hesitated, she added quickly: "Don't let me stop your story. That question can wait for another time; go on with what you are telling me."

Jean told her how Tally had taken her to Michael Sorrel, how by rearranging her hair and by taking trouble over her face she had acquired what she never known she possessed, an attraction.

"It is all so wonderful," she said; "I could not believe it was me. Can you imagine, Mrs. Melton, what it was like to go down to Greystones, to stay in a house like yours, to wake up in that big luxurious bed, to be waited on, to know that overnight, as it were, I had entered a new world, a world which had only existed before in my dreams—and not very clearly in them?"

"I suppose it is difficult for me to imagine the difference," Margaret Melton smiled; "but surely you had a happy home with your father?"

"Y . . . Yes . . ." Jean answered doubtfully, "but my father was not an easy man to live with . . . and we were very, very poor. He was proud of his ancestry, but that didn't in any way increase his stipend. The Manse was very shabby, the carpets threadbare, and we often had scanty meals because we simply could not afford to pay for the food we needed."

"Hadn't you any relations?" Margaret asked.

"No near ones, except my great-aunt. There are lots of distant cousins, of course, but why should they worry about me? I gathered, too, that there were reasons why my father did not wish to communicate with them; anyway, I never saw any of them."

"Poor child!" Margaret exclaimed.

"I was not unhappy until he died," Jean said quickly. "He always seemed very fond of me. He was not a demonstrative man, and he was entirely wrapped up in his parish, but I was content. I could even say I had a happy childhood until I had to go and live with my great-aunt."

For a moment there was an expression of pain in her eyes, and her mouth tightened as if in memory of those first months of despair and homesickness when she had wished with all the fervour of emotional adolescence that she could die.

180

"It is over now," Margaret Melton said gently. "Go on with your story."

So Jean continued, telling her what she knew of Tally's first meeting with Melia after their engagement was announced, the decision that they should come to Switzerland and the night she had spent with Betty and her children.

"Sometimes," Jean said, "for instance that night when we dined with Betty in her little dining-room, Tally seemed carefree, quite unconcerned about the future; and then at other times I have known that he was perturbed, perhaps terribly unhappy, and I felt that I would do anything to help him. Which was why—" she paused for a moment and took a deep breath—"which was why I went to see Miss Melchester this evening."

Margaret raised her eyebrows.

"You went to see her?"

Jean nodded.

"That is why Tally is so angry with me. He says that I have ruined everything, and upset his own ideas as to how to deal with Melia Melchester. He is furious, too, because Miss Melchester told him that she had been unkind, almost rude, to me. Tally felt that that was an insult levelled at him; I cannot understand why; anyway, he is angry. He told me off very crossly and then, as you know, he went out to dinner. I waited up until he came back so that I could have a word with him, but he would not talk to me. He just said quietly, 'I don't think there is any point in discussing the subject,' and with that he went away and left me. I know that I have failed him . . . and that he never wants . . . to see me again."

There was no checking her tears now. They ran down her cheeks, and suddenly with a convulsive movement Jean turned her head and hid it in her pillow. Margaret Melton bent forward and stumped out a half-burnt cigarette in the ash-tray by the bed.

"Listen, dear," she said. "Things won't seem so black in the morning. I promise you that."

"They will," Jean said in a muffled voice, "because I

181

realise that I must go home. The awful thing is . . ." and here her voice was almost incoherent, ". . . I haven't got any money for my ticket. I shall have to ask Tally for it."

"You need do nothing of the sort," Margaret Melton said, almost sharply. "If you want to go home, I will give you the money; but personally I do not think it is necessary, and Tally will not want it."

"But of course he will," Jean whispered. "Don't you understand? My usefulness has come to an end. I thought of that even while I was trying to make things right for him. I know it was inevitable that this . . . should all come to an end sometime . . . but . . . I don't want us to part . . . angrily."

Margaret smiled.

"You are much too young," she said, "and quite the wrong person to be involved in all this intrigue. It is typical of Tally's impulsiveness. When one knows him well, one just laughs at his escapades and expects them to be revolutionary, but at the same time he ought to be careful whom he involves. It is easy to get hurt, and that is not so amusing."

"Yes, very easy," Jean murmured.

"You love him, don't you?" Margaret Melton asked.

Jean looked at her wide-eyed for a moment, and then told the truth quite simply.

"Yes, I love him," she said. "But you must not blame him for that. I could not help falling in love with him. He made it quite clear to me from the very beginning that he loved Miss Melchester, and he has never at any time or in any way said or done anything that was not just the kindness of a friend or a brother, but . . ." Jean faltered for a moment, ". . . he is so attractive, so wonderful!"

"I think he is, too," Margaret said, "even though he is my son; but I am sorry, dear, that you should be hurt or made unhappy by him."

"You won't tell him that . . . that I love him?"

"No, of course not; but at the same time I feel that he has a certain responsibility to you, and I know that when he comes to his senses he won't want you to go rushing home. You came out here for a holiday, and a holiday you shall have."

"Oh, please, don't make him keep me here," Jean pleaded passionately. "I could not bear to be a burden or a hindrance to him, and I cannot help feeling that, despite all Miss Melchester said, if she gets her own way and the engagement is broken off, she may go back to him, may promise to marry him."

Margaret Melton opened her cigarette-case.

"I am not certain," she said very slowly, "whether I want my son to marry Melia."

"Oh, but you must," Jean said. "She is so lovely."

"Will that make her a good wife for Tally? You know, Jean, I have been very remiss. I have been so absorbed in my own unhappiness that I had forgotten that Tally was only on the threshold of his life, when it is very easy to make mistakes. I ought to help him, ought to guide him, as his father would have done if he had been alive."

"I think Tally would be happier if you did."

"For his sake, or for mine?" Margaret asked dryly.

"Both," Jean answered. "Will you be angry if I am very frank and say that I think Tally ought to tell you many more things than he does? I think he ought to confide in you, to try and make you interested in all that is going on around you; and I think, too, that he often is lonely. I don't know why I say that, I just have that impression. Please don't think I am impertinent because I am saying this."

"I don't, my dear. You have very decided impressions of people and things, haven't you?"

"Sometimes," Jean admitted, thinking of Stephen Melton's photograph in the bedroom at Berkeley Square.

There was silence for a moment, and then unexpectedly Margaret Melton asked:

"What did you mean yesterday when you said that the photograph of my husband I have here was so very different from the other one you had seen?"

Jean did not answer for a moment, wondering what to say, what words to choose for an answer; and after a second or so Margaret Melton asked:

"You did mean something definite by that remark, didn't you? There was something in the tone of your voice that imprinted it on my mind."

Still Jean hesitated. Could any good come of her telling Mrs. Melton of her strange feelings on that day in Berkeley Square? Besides, how could she put it into words? At last she stammered rather lamely:

"The photograph I saw in London was so vivid, I wondered who it was. It was impossible not to notice it and to feel that the man, whoever he might be, was someone outstanding."

"Stephen was outstanding," Margaret Melton said, and there was a tender smile round the corners of her mouth. "One could never, never forget him,"

"You must be so glad about that," Jean said. "It must be terrible for people who love someone very much to find that, as the years go by, their friends and others have forgotten the person whom they remember so vividly or that he has become only a vague, shadowy remembrance who is seldom spoken about."

Margaret looked thoughtful.

"I never thought of it like that. People never speak to me about him."

"Isn't that rather a pity?"

"Yes, and it is wrong. I see that now," Margaret replied. "I am letting them forget him. To me he will always be vivid, but to them he will begin to fade and become nothing more than a ghost of the past. Oh, Jean, that is important. I must not let things happen like that. I must talk about Stephen. I must keep him alive in other people's thoughts as well as in my own."

Jean had the impulse to say: "But he is alive, didn't you know?"—and then she felt that her words would be meaningless, that she could not substantiate them; and yet in that moment she was certain in her own mind with the utmost conviction, such as she had never before experienced, that Stephen Melton had survived the grave.

184

She could almost feel his personality, know that he was near; yet even while she groped for reassurance, she had begun, in the frailty of human understanding, to doubt her own conviction. She felt very young and immature. She had dared so much in speaking to Mrs. Melton of the husband she had loved so passionately; she would risk nothing more at the moment.

Almost as if she knew the subject was closed, Margaret got to her feet.

"I am not going to keep you up any longer," she said, "especially talking about myself. You are to go to sleep and in the morning I shall settle all your problems. Don't worry, and you are not to cry another tear."

Jean threw back the eiderdown and slipped off the bed.

"I will try not to, and thank you for being so kind."

She stood looking up at Margaret Melton, who was a head taller than she was, and then Margaret did a surprising thing. She bent forward and kissed Jean tenderly.

"Good night, my dear," she said. "I have often wished I could have had a daughter."

The door closed behind her and Jean was left with a feeling of warmth and comfort. She undressed quickly. As she crept into bed, she whispered to herself:

"I wish I had told her everything; yes, everything."

Margaret Melton did not go to bed. She walked about her own room for a short while, smoking and thinking; and then at last, as if she came to a sudden decision, she went along the passage to where her son was sleeping. She knocked on the door, but there was no reply. She turned the handle softly. The room was in darkness, and she groped along the wall for the light switch. She found several, turned one, and the room was illuminated by a small lamp on a writing table.

Tally was in bed and asleep. He was lying with one hand behind his head, the other thrown sideways. The bedclothes only half covered him, and the big feather eiderdown was flung on the floor. Margaret Melton stood looking down at him. In sleep he looked very young and very vulnerable. The lines which were characteristic of his quick, impulsive nature, had vanished when he was relaxed, and he lay there breathing quietly, as if he had not a care in the whole world.

Margaret thought of the nights when she had stood like this at the end of his bed when he was a little boy; thought of once when he was ill, and she had got up more than a dozen times during the night to go in to him to see whether the fever had broken. How anxious she had been! How wrought with fear and anxiety! Now she asked herself if that illness had been any worse for him than being hurt by love and made unhappy by troubles of the heart. She, who had suffered so much from love, had forgotten that other people, even her own son, could suffer, too.

She moved forward impulsively, and going to the side of the bed she put out her hand and touched his shoulder. His eyes opened, every muscle instantly tense, as if he were ready for action.

"It is all right, darling," she said. "It is only me."

"Hullo Mother. Anything wrong?"

Margaret shook her head.

"Not really, but I want to talk to you. Do you mind my wakening you up?"

"Of course not. I like it," he said, pulling himself up higher against the pillows. "Make yourself comfortable. I was dreaming of Greystones. I am glad you woke me up."

"Wasn't it a pleasant dream?"

"No, horrible. It is a nightmare I get sometimes; that I go back and find the house empty and desolate, no one living there, the garden neglected, and the trees cut down in the park."

"What a horrible dream!"

"I suppose it may happen one day, taxes and death duties being what they are; and when it does happen, I shall break my heart."

"I know you will," Margaret said. "I don't want to frighten you, Tally, but we have got to cut expenditure some way, and soon."

186

"I know," Tally answered. "I have been spending money like a drunken sailor, haven't I?"

"No, you have just been having a little fling now the war is over. I anticipated that and, as you know, your lawyers made arrangements to meet it; but the holiday is nearly over, Tally, and I think that something will have to go, either a part of the estate or perhaps the house in Berkeley Square."

"I couldn't care less if that was sold tomorrow."

Margaret raised her eyebrows.

"But when this was discussed six months ago, you said you refused to sell."

"So I did. That was because Melia liked it. She always imagined herself queening it there. The house was built for entertaining."

"Do you think Melia would be content with Greystones?"

Tally shrugged his shoulders.

"The question hardly arises at the moment."

"Doesn't it?"

Margaret Melton asked the question, and then said:

"Tally, I have got a confession to make. Perhaps it is not so much a confession as an apology. I have been terribly selfish."

"Good gracious, Mother! What do you mean?"

"Ever since Stephen died I have been a little crazy, I think, at times very crazy. I have shut myself away from you all, would not let you come near me—you know what I mean—and taken no interest in anything except my own unhappiness. Now at last I understand I am hurting not only you but also the memory of Stephen."

Tally sat up in bed and reaching out his arms pulled his mother towards him.

"Darling, I don't like to hear you talk like this. You have been wonderful to me always, you know that, and Stephen was the luckiest man who ever lived because you loved him, but it is true that you have not let us come near you. What has made you suddenly see it?"

"Jean has made me see it," Margaret said briefly, and watched the expression on his face.

"Jean?" he said incredulously.

"Yes, Jean," Margaret repeated, "and Tally, aren't you being rather harsh with that child? She is only a child, you know."

Tally raised his eyebrows.

"Has she been telling tales out of school?"

"She has been sobbing her heart out and packing her bags ready to leave tomorrow morning provided she has the money for her ticket."

"Oh, lord!"

Tally looked ashamed, then he said ruefully:

"I am sorry, Mother. I did not mean to upset the girl. She just annoyed me because she played right into Melia's hands. You know how I hate my plans of campaign being upset?"

"Yes, I know that," Margaret said; "but what you forget, darling, is that your plans, however clever they may be, usually mean that someone is hurt or wounded—and not always the enemy."

Tally smiled at her simile and said quickly:

"That is true enough, and I am sorry. I was rather a beast to Jean and she has been jolly sporting about the whole thing. There are not many girls who would have done what she did."

"There are not many girls who would have been able to carry it off. Have you thought of that?" Margaret Melton asked.

"No, I suppose not," Tally said reflectively. "It is funny, Mother, you know, I had no idea how attractive Jean could be until Michael dressed her up. I suppose she has told you the whole story?"

"Most of it, I think."

"It was a good idea, wasn't it?" Tally asked enthusiastically. "I would have given anything to see Melia's face when she opened the newspapers the morning our engagement was announced."

Margaret hesitated for a moment and then she said quietly:

"You know, Tally, if you love somebody very much the last thing you want to do is to hurt them. You would rather that they found happiness with someone else even if it meant your own loss, your own misery."

Tally looked at his mother.

"Is that true?" he asked.

"Yes, darling. I would have died to save Stephen unhappiness at any time in his life."

"But, Mother, you must see that that was an exception. When I used to see Stephen and you together, I used to think to myself, 'I hope that I shall love someone in the same way, that I shall be so wonderfully happy, so completely content.' But it doesn't happen, not to the ordinary chap like me. I want Melia, and if she would marry me we should get along all right."

Margaret Melton gave a little cry.

"Tally, Tally, that is not love! It is not even the beginning of it. Melia is a very beautiful person, but do you want to be with her all your life? Do you feel the world is empty and dark if she is not there beside you? Do you want to look after her if she is ill? Would you be content, if you had no money, to live in a tiny cottage with her; to work at the most menial tasks and know them no hardship because they were done for her? If she was ugly, diseased and crippled, would you love her just as much? Would you know that it was not her beauty that mattered but the real Melia inside? the part of her that belongs to you, a part indivisible?"

Margaret Melton spoke passionately so that her words seemed to vibrate in the air. There were tears in her eyes and both her hands went out to clasp her son's. Tally was silent.

"If you don't feel like that," Margaret went on, "and if Melia does not feel like that for you, then, Tally, do not marry her. One day you will find the right person, a person who means all those things to you and . . . it might be too late."

Tally bent forward to kiss his mother's cheek.

"I wish we had talked like this a very long time ago."

"I wish we had, too," Margaret said. "That is where I have been so wrong, Tally dear. Stephen would have disapproved of me. He always thought that living up to one's responsibilities was so very important. Do you remember the trouble he took over the estate? There was no detail too small for him to attend to. He was so anxious that Greystones should be just as fine a place as when your father was alive."

"You and father were happy together?" Tally said hesitatingly, and his mother saw instinctively where his thoughts were leading.

"Your father loved me as Stephen did," she said simply. "I was everything in his life, the one person he had ever wanted, the one person, I think, with whom he would have been completely happy. I did not love him as I love Stephen; but that was not his fault, and I don't think he ever knew, not for one moment, that he was missing anything. He was not a very introspective person and he was so completely content with what he had that to him life was perfect. I remember him once saying: 'If someone granted me a wish, I should ask only for what I have got. I cannot think of anything I could possibly want more.' But you and I are different, Tally. There is always a horizon to which we must go forward, must reach out with our arms. Even as a little boy you were not quiet and content. You were happy, tremendously happy with a zest for enjoyment, but always you were looking for more, believing that tomorrow would bring something a little better, perhaps a little more exciting. That is the way we are made, you and I, and nothing we can say or do can alter it. Because I know this, I can only say to you that you will never be content with second best; you have got to find the real thing, find it, recognise it, and know that the imitations which have gone before are only shams and not worthy of your consideration.

Tally was very still.

"Thank you, Mother," he said at last, and then with an engaging smile which made him seem suddenly very young, he added: "I don't believe I am as grown up as I think I am."

Margaret bent forward.

"You're not, darling. You are very young in some
190

ways. Just the little boy who used to look lost and bewildered the day he had to go back to school. But he would never admit it, never cry even one tear, however miserable he was."

Tally gave a great sigh.

"Let us go back to Greystones," he said. "I mean it!"

"Just as soon as you like," Margaret answered; "but first of all we have got to tidy up the pieces, haven't we? We cannot leave all these loose ends of your plans lying about."

"Do you mean Melia?" Tally asked with a grin.

"I was really thinking of Jean."

"Yes of course. Well, we will take her with us, and then I will find her a job, a really good one."

"All right, dear. Only be kind, won't you? Try not to be harsh with her. She is rather different from any of the young women you have known before. She is very sensitive."

Tally laughed.

"Mother, I think that is the first catty thing I have ever heard you say about my friends."

"Then I am afraid it is true of many of them. But Jean is different."

"Yes, I know she is," Tally answered. "I am sorry I was unkind to her tonight. I will be very nice tomorrow to make up."

Margaret Melton hesitated for a moment as if she would say something, and then she thought better of it.

"You had better go to sleep," she said. "And you can make plans in the morning. Are you doing anything special tomorrow?"

"Gerald and I are going for a long run," Tally answered. "He is getting fat, the old boy, and I have told him a little mountaineering will soon take it off him. We shall be back, of course, by tea-time. If I don't see you in the morning, look after Jean for me."

"I will," Margaret answered.

"I will have a word with her before I leave," Tally said. "And Mother, if you get a chance, find out what sort of things she would like to do in the future. She was working in my office, but somehow I think she is worthy of a better job than that, don't you?"

"I am sure of it," Margaret Melton said quietly.

She bent forward and kissed her son.

"Good night, darling, and go to sleep."

He put up his arms as he had done when a little boy and held her close.

"Good night, darling. I am so glad you came and talked to me tonight. It is just like old times. I feel somehow as if a lot of clouds have rolled away."

"They have," Margaret said gently. "The night is nearly over."

She glanced at the clock by his bedside as she spoke and Tally was not certain whether she spoke literally or figuratively. She paused at the door and switched out the light.

"Good night, darling," she said again.

"Good night, Mother, and thank you for understanding about everything."

"It was Jean who made me do that," she answered and the door closed behind her.

12

Jean came up the road from St. Moritz in a sleigh. The horses had red plumes nodding on their harness and the bells jingled with every movement, playing, it seemed to Jean, a little tune so gay, so joyous that she felt her own heart beating in unison.

She was happy . . . happy! Tally had come to her room quite early that morning and knocked at the door.

"Can I come in?" he asked.

She was startled at the sound of his voice, but she was already dressed for she had made up her mind to breakfast early so that she could see Mrs. Melton as soon as she was awake and decide whether or not she should leave for England.

Surprisingly she had slept well and when she awoke the misery of the night before had dispersed so that although she was apprehensive and not a little afraid of what the day would bring forth, her unhappiness was not so intense or as agonising as it might have been. At the sound of Tally's voice she felt a slow flush suffusing her cheeks and hesitatingly, almost inaudibly, she whispered:

"Come in!"

Tally put his head round the door.

"May I?" he asked. "I am sorry to disturb you, but Gerald and I are leaving in a few minutes."

"Come in!" Jean repeated.

"Oh, you are dressed," Tally exclaimed, "so it is quite respectable."

He smiled and Jean felt her heart turn over. He looked so very different from the scowling, angry man who had taken her to task the evening before. He came into the room looking very tall and slim in his grey skiing outfit. Round his neck there was a blue scarf which seemed to echo the almost steely blue of his eyes, and in his hands he held his gloves and a peaked cap with protecting ear-flaps.

Jean stood very still in the centre of the room. She was trembling, but she prayed that Tally would not notice her agitation. She waited and it seemed to her that he looked her over appraisingly before he said:

"I have come to apologise, you know."

Again he smiled at her disarmingly.

"Why?"

Jean was surprised that her voice was audible and quite composed.

"You know why," Tally replied. "I'm sorry, Jean. I was a beast. My mother has given me a good talking to about it and I feel as ashamed as I used to do when I pulled the little girls' hair at children's parties. It always was a temptation to make them cry."

"I don't want you to apologise," Jean said quietly. "It was my fault for being so stupid."

Tally laughed.

"Don't be magnanimous," he said. "I am a brute and I know it. Say you will forgive me, otherwise I shan't enjoy myself today, and I have been looking forward to getting right away from everyone, right up on top of the world."

He held out his hand and though Jean would have liked to resist him she found that instinctively her own hand crept out and into his.

"I really am sorry," Tally said seriously and with a gesture that had nothing theatrical in it he raised her fingers to his lips.

"Bless you. Look after my mother; she likes you a lot

194

and that is one of the best things that could happen. We will talk when I come back."

He turned towards the door, waved his hand and was gone.

For quite a long time Jean stood where he had left her. The world was shining again, golden and full of joy. Tally had forgiven her. Her desperate plans for running away, for returning to England need not be put into operation—at least for the moment.

At length she crossed to the dressing-table, sat down and stared at her reflection in the mirror. She could never get used to the change in her own appearance, but she knew even as she looked at herself that there was no comparison between her face and Melia's. She was pretty! It would have been dishonest not to admit the fact now when her eyes were shining and there was a flush in either cheek and her red lips were parted so that she looked very attractive. But Melia was beautiful, really beautiful; Jean did not intend to deceive herself. Tally would never look at her in love and desire, never want to hold her close to his heart. But she could have his friendship, could for a little while at least know that he was near, hear his voice and see those keen eyes light up with amusement. She must be content with that, must make herself content with it. It was greedy to ask for more.

She was happy, terribly happy, she told herself, and for the moment she could live in the present and forget the future. All too soon the fears which had beset her last night must become realities. She would go away; Tally's path and hers would diverge and she would be alone again. Alone, but not the same! She could never be the same after what had happened. She remembered reading once that experience is cheap at any price. She must be prepared to believe that; she did believe it. This experience was rich and satisfying; she must make it satisfy her through the long years when she would know that Tally was happy with someone else and that she was to him only a pleasant memory.

Jean jumped to her feet. She felt energetic and vital; she wanted to run, jump and sing; she wanted to be good enough on skis to go jumping down the mountain as if there were wings on her feet. She wanted to feel the untrammelled delight of propelling herself over the snow by her own volition.

She concentrated harder that morning on learning to ski than she had ever concentrated on anything in her whole life, and she felt well rewarded when the instructor said:

"You are much better, lady. You can go up to the second class tomorrow."

She had hurried back to the hotel to tell Mrs. Melton. Margaret congratulated her and then asked her if she would go down to St. Moritz and have a prescription made up at the chemist's.

"You had better take a sleigh," she suggested. "I will tell the porter to get you one."

"It will be cheaper to go in the bus," Jean replied.

Margaret Melton smiled.

"I always think being economical and doing things cheaply spoils a holiday. At home I am often so careful over small items that Tally accuses me of being stingy, but when I am on holiday I like to do things well however expensive they may be. I will tell the concierge to get you a sleigh and I know you will enjoy the drive."

"I wish you would come with me," Jean said.

"I would like to," Margaret Melton replied, "but unfortunately I have got a lot of letters to write; dull ones, all about the estate and repairs that have got to be done to the house. If I don't do them this morning they will never get done. By the way, I very nearly forgot. There is a letter for you."

"For me?" Jean exclaimed.

Margaret nodded.

"Yes, it was sent up to my room by mistake. I am so sorry."

She held out the letter. Jean looked at it and saw it was from Angus. Gerald had left instructions at her boarding house in Putney that any letters addressed to

196

her should be forwarded to Tally's office. This had been re-directed again by Miss Ames. Jean recognised the writing.

She took the letter and put it together with the prescription Margaret Melton handed her into her bag.

"Oh, and you will want some money too," Margaret said. "You will find a one hundred franc note lying on the dressing table. There it is."

"Thank you," Jean said.

"And while we are talking of money," Margaret went on, "I want you to let me give you some while you are here. I am rather horrified that my son, who seems to have thought of most things, including an elaborate trousseau, should have forgotten that no one, especially a woman, feels happy with an empty purse."

"Oh, please stop," Jean interrupted, "you are making me feel awful. I ought not to have told you that I haven't any money. You and Tally have done so much for me, I simply could not take another thing from either of you. It is only that I had not very much in hand when I started this . . . this adventure."

"You are not to explain," Margaret Melton said, "nor am I going to have any argument. After all, if I were in the same position I should want someone to help me. I am going to give you twenty-five pounds in Swiss francs. If you have any left you can change it when you get back to England. One day when you feel very rich you can pay me back, but I warn you that if you do I shall feel very hurt and disappointed. In the ordinary way and if I were an ordinary person I expect I should have given Tally's fiancée an expensive present as soon as his engagement was announced. If I had done that, you would have had to accept it; but this is a present not for Tally's fiancée but for a girl I like very much and who, I hope, likes me."

It was impossible to resist Margaret's charm or the sweetness in her voice.

"Oh, thank you, thank you," Jean said, "but I wish I could do something for you."

"You have done a lot for me," Margaret Melton

answered quietly, "but we will talk about that later. Run along now, dear, or you will be late for luncheon."

Jean did as she was told and as Margaret had predicted she enjoyed the drive into St. Moritz. She saw the great frozen lake as the sleigh took her slowly down the hill; the little wooden chalets, the great hotels and the ice-rinks where men and girls in bright coloured jerseys were moving rhythmically to the music of a radiogram. In the town she loved the little shops filled with delicious food, glittering watches or smart boots and shoes.

She did not have to wait long for Margaret's prescription at the chemist's, and then she slipped across the road to spend some of her present on a big bunch of flowers. It was the most expensive gift that Jean had ever given anyone in the whole of her life, but it gave her a peculiar satisfaction and she thought for the first time how splendid it was to be the giver rather than the recipient. It was only then, as the sleigh turned to take her back to the hotel, that she drew Angus' letter from her pocket and opened it.

She had waited deliberately, forcing down her impatience to read what he had written, so that her consideration for Margaret and the instructions she had been given should take first place. Now she drew out the letter from the envelope. It was very short:

Dear Jean,
I was extremely surprised at your news and by the newspapers which reached me at the same time as your telegram. I can only hope that you will be happy. Elizabeth and I will be married next month.
Yours,

Angus.

Jean read it through once and then again, and then suddenly she laughed. It was a laugh of sheer happiness, a laugh of freedom. She tore the letter across and then across again and threw the pieces out of the back of the

198

sleigh so that they fled away on the wind to lie forlornly on the snow-covered road.

She was happy, yes, utterly happy, because Angus no longer meant anything to her. She had not even a pang of regret in her heart; in fact, if she was honest, it was almost difficult to remember him at all. Had she really cared even superficially for him? Had she really contemplated marrying someone whom it was so easy to forget in so short a time?

"How young I was, how utterly foolish!" Jean whispered to herself and knew that it was true. So much had happened in so short a space of time and Angus had slipped away into the past unregretted, practically forgotten. Quite sincerely Jean hoped he would be happy. There was no doubt that he would make Elizabeth a good husband, his snobbery would keep him faithful and attentive; the question was whether Miss Ross would make him a good wife. Whatever the future held for them it was no business of hers. She was free! Free of Angus; free of that ugly, unhappy life that she had lived at her great-aunt's. It was all gone, and the thing that mattered at the moment was Tally's forgiveness and the touch of Tally's mouth against her fingers.

She could still feel the pressure of his lips. She found herself suddenly breathless at the thought. How she loved him! How difficult it was going to be not to let him know even for a moment that her whole being leapt at his approach! Jean threw back her head. The sun was warm on her face, the peaks of the mountains were sharp cut against the blue sky. She wanted to fling out her arms to the whole world and hold it close, to pour out the love that was within her, a love so great and so consuming that she felt that without it she would be as nothing.

It was almost a shock when she had reached the hotel; the drive had been so swift because she had been absorbed in her own thoughts. She threw back the shaggy fur rug and was helped to the ground by the hotel porter.

"Six francs, please, lady," the driver asked, and she gave him ten because she was so absurdly happy.

"Thank you, thank you," he bowed. "Good fortune and good happiness."

As she went through the swing doors of the hotel and up to Margaret's room, she felt that his good wishes were an omen. The sun was pouring in at the windows which were wide open and Margaret was sitting in a low chair, looking out into the valley.

"You are back very quickly," she said in surprise, glancing at her watch as Jean entered. "Five minutes to one," she exclaimed, "oh, my dear, how awful, and I have not written one of my letters. I had no idea that time could go so quickly."

"Does it matter?" Jean questioned shyly. "It is such a wonderful day that one wants only to be in the sunshine. The letters can wait. The sun may not be here tomorrow."

"That is common sense," Margaret Melton murmured. "Well, let us go down to luncheon, you must be hungry."

"I believe I am," Jean confessed. "I will put my coat in my bedroom. I won't be a moment."

She hurried away and returned to find Margaret standing on the balcony.

"You have made me feel you are right," she said, as Jean joined her. "I feel the sun cannot wait but other things can. We will go for a drive this afternoon. Would you like that?"

"I would love it," Jean said.

"We might even go up to Corvelia which is the highest club in the world. It is many years since I have been there, but I expect that they will recall that I was once a member."

"Do we go up in the funicular?" Jean asked.

Margaret nodded.

"Oh, I would like that," Jean said eagerly. "I want to do everything and see everything that is possible. I may never come here again and I shall have all the more to remember."

Margaret looked at her tenderly.

"What a funny child you are," she said; "but it is the right philosophy to have. Live every moment of your life fully and then you will not have so much to regret when you come to the lean years."

There was a deep sadness in her voice, and hurriedly, to take her thoughts from herself, Jean said:

"Let us go down to luncheon quickly so that we shall have more of the afternoon before the sun goes down."

"Very well," Margaret agreed, smiling at her enthusiasm.

They went down to the sun-bathed dining-room.

"Only two for luncheon today," Margaret said to the waiter as they took their seats at a table in the window.

The waiter brought a trolley piled with hor d'oeuvres with which they were to begin their meal. Every plate was a colourful masterpiece in itself and Jean found it difficult to choose which she would have among all the delicious dishes.

She started to eat and Margaret picked up a card which had been placed on the table. It was a printed notice and reading it she said:

"I see we are to have a treat tonight. Patience Plowden is to sing. Have you ever heard of her?"

Jean dropped her fork with a clatter.

"Patience who?" she asked.

"Patience Plowden," Margaret repeated and added hastily, "Why, what is the matter, dear? Do you feel ill?"

"I am all right," Jean muttered.

She had turned very pale and the room seemed to sway dizzily around her.

"You must be faint," Margaret said. "Would you like to go out?"

"No, no, I am all right really," Jean answered. "Could I have a drink of water?"

Margaret signalled to the waiter who brought it. Jean sipped her glass quickly and after a moment the colour came back into her cheeks, but Margaret noticed that her hand was trembling.

"Try to eat something," she said quietly, "and then tell me what has upset you."

"I . . . don't know . . . how to begin," Jean stammered.

"Let me help you," Margaret said. "It is something about Patience Plowden, isn't it?"

"Yes."

Jean took another sip from her glass.

"You know her?" Margaret asked.

"She is my mother," Jean said.

Margaret was silent for a moment, then she said:

"Don't tell me any more if you would rather not."

"But I would like to," Jean said.

"And I would like to hear," Margaret said, "but to please me you must try and eat something."

Jean made a valiant effort and after a few mouthfuls which she felt would choke her her tension relaxed and she found it easier both to eat and to speak.

"I suppose there could be no mistake about the name," Jean asked at length.

"I should hardly think so," Margaret said. "Patience Plowden is a very famous person."

"Is she?"

"But of course! She was one of our greatest singers before the war and then when war came she was in France. She could not get out of the country and she had to go underground. You know what I mean, of course?"

"Do you mean the Maquis and that sort of thing?"

"Yes, she became part of the underground movement. I believe she was wonderful in all she did; but they caught her at last and she was tortured and put into a concentration camp. Luckily it was not long before the end of the war and she was released with the Allied invasion, but her health was affected and she came to Switzerland under doctor's orders. As far as I know she has sung nowhere since and I imagine she is only appearing tonight because I see it is a gala evening in aid of the hospital for tubercular children at Davos."

Jean had listened wide-eyed to Margaret's story. Now she gasped:

"But I had no idea she was like that, you see——"

"Suppose you tell me what you know," Margaret suggested quietly.

"I am afraid it is very little," Jean replied. "I don't remember my mother at all. She ran away and left me when I was four years old. I thought she was dead; in fact I had taken it for granted that she must have died, especially as my father would never speak of her. Then when I went to live with my great-aunt she was always making veiled references to my bad blood. I could not understand why, until gradually I came to the conclusion that my mother must have done something awful. I had no idea what and I could only imagine the most ghastly things. When my aunt died, I found a letter and some newspaper cuttings. The letter was written to my father. It must have been amongst his papers and my aunt had removed it from the Manse. It was not a long letter; it merely said that she—my mother—was so utterly unhappy with him that she could bear it no longer; that she had a chance to go on the stage and she was going to accept it. She accused my father of never having loved her and said that she could not live any longer without love. I—I presumed from that that she had run away with someone else."

"She did not say so?" Margaret asked.

Jean shook her head.

"No, but I think my aunt must have thought so from the many things she said to me."

"And the newspaper cuttings?"

"There were only two of them. One showed a picture of my mother. I recognised it, of course, from the snapshots that had been taken when I was a child, and underneath was written: *'Miss Patience Plowden has a part in an Operetta opening at Leeds next Thursday.'* The other was a reference to a touring company who had appeared at Bradford and mentioned her as being 'among those in a distinguished cast.'"

"That must have been long before she made her name," Margaret said.

"I suppose so," Jean replied, "they were undated."

"So you have been imagining terrible things about your mother?" Margaret asked.

"I am afraid so. You see I had nothing to go on except my aunt's almost continual references to what might happen to me one day. I quite understand that the stage would seem terrible to her, apart from the fact that she would never forgive my mother for running away."

"I think it was rather cruel of her to leave you."

Jean sighed.

"The atmosphere at the Manse was often very grim."

"Then you can be sympathetic and perhaps a little understanding?" Margaret suggested.

"Much more than I would have been three weeks ago," Jean confessed. "Then I did not know what this life was like; then I had not known that people like you and Tally could be so nice."

"You would like to meet your mother?"

"Oh, no!" Jean spoke quickly and then hesitated. "Perhaps, I don't know. I should like to see her first."

"Suppose we finish our luncheon, and then I have got a suggestion to make to you."

"What is it?"

"Let us eat first."

Neither of the women were hungry and in a very short time they rose from the table and passed out into the lounge. Margaret led the way to a sofa in a quiet corner of the room.

"We will have coffee here," she said.

There were various people sitting about. Some had lunched early; some were having a cocktail before they went into the dining-room. There were family parties with young children in bright skiing suits, their cheeks rosy with the sun and exercise. There were elderly people too, and among them was a woman sitting by herself in a big arm-chair. There was a cup of coffee in front of her and she was smoking a cigarette in a long, black holder.

She was very thin and her dark hair was streaked with grey, but there was something extremely distinctive about her. She was beautifully dressed in simple clothes

204

which bore the unmistakable stamp of a Parisian dressmaker, and on one of her long fingers glittered a huge diamond which caught the rays of sunshine streaming through the window and reflected them dazzlingly as she moved.

Margaret Melton watched her for a moment or two, then she spoke softly:

"Jean, do you see that woman over there?"

"Which one?" Jean asked.

"That one alone by the fireplace."

"Yes."

"That is Patience Plowden!"

Jean started and her fingers holding her coffee cup gripped it almost convulsively. She was silent for a moment and then at last she said:

"She looks ill."

"She has been very ill. I know so much about her because the chambermaid who has been looking after me here—you remember the one I told you about who was here many years ago—knows your mother well. In fact, she often works for her at her chalet higher up the mountain. But your mother often stays here—mostly when she comes to St. Moritz for treatment or to shop. The servants all adore her, I gather, and look forward to her visits. I'm sure she is a very lovable person. As a matter of fact I knew her many years ago."

"You knew her?"

Jean turned her eyes to Mrs. Melton.

"Not very well. It was when Tally's father was alive. He and I were in Paris for a short time and we met Patience Plowden at the Embassy. She was singing there one night and very wonderful she was. She was young and extremely attractive in those days and it was at the very height of her success. It is sad to see her now, so thin, so emaciated after all she has been through; and yet, who knows? She may have found it worth while."

Margaret Melton waited for a moment and then she added softly: "Wouldn't you like to meet her?"

Jean hesitated.

"I don't know, I don't know. I cannot decide."

"Don't you think you are being rather a coward?" Margaret Melton asked.

Her voice was very gentle.

"Yes, perhaps I am," Jean answered.

Margaret went on: "Wouldn't it be better to annihilate once and for all the unkind things you have had to listen to and to bury all the bitterness which may be lingering in your heart?"

"Very well then."

Jean's voice was very low and yet she lifted her head courageously. Margaret Melton rose to her feet.

"Come along, my dear, and I promise you you won't regret it."

She led the way across the lounge. Patience Plowden looked up at her approach.

"I wonder if you remember me, Miss Plowden?" Margaret began.

"But, of course! It is Lady Brora, isn't it? Of course I remember you! That night at the Embassy! It is so long ago, but what fun we all had. Come and sit down; we must talk of the past. I have lost many things, but not my memory, thank God!"

Patience Plowden held out her hand with its glittering ring to Margaret and as they clasped hands Margaret turned to draw Patience Plowden's attention to Jean. Patience Plowden followed the direction of her eyes.

"Oh," she said smiling, "and this . . . ?"

"This," Margaret interrupted, "is a friend I particularly want to introduce to you. Her name is Jean MacLeod."

13

There was a moment's silence and then Patience Plowden repeated uncertainly.

"Jean MacLeod from . . . ?"

". . . from Glendale," Jean said in a voice which sounded strange even to herself.

Again there was a silence fraught with meaning, and then at last Patience Plowden with a gesture infinitely expressive and appealing said:

"Oh, my dear . . . and you know who I am?"

Jean nodded. It was impossible to force a sound from between her lips.

Margaret would have turned away, but Jean's hand stretched out convulsively and took hers, holding on to her frantically as a child might have done. She turned to her reassuringly, a tender smile curving the corners of her mouth.

"Shall we sit down, Miss Plowden?" she asked gently. "I know this must be a shock for both of you."

She put her arm round Jean as she spoke and pressed the girl into an arm-chair, for she sensed that she had lost for the moment the power to move and to act. Then the three of them sat looking at each other. It was Margaret who broke the silence.

"This is the sort of dramatic moment," she said, "that people write about so easily in books but which in real life is full of embarrassment."

Patience Plowden shot her a grateful glance.

"You are right, my dear; it is embarrassing to meet one's daughter after . . . now how long is it? . . . fifteen years?"

Margaret saw that Jean was very white and knew from the tension of her fingers that the child was fighting for self-control.

"As you say," she said talking to gain time, "fifteen years is a long time and from what Jean has told me she was expecting someone very different from you."

"I wonder what you did expect," Patience Plowden said to Jean with a twist on her lips. "I can imagine the things you must have heard about me at Glendale."

"I never heard about you, that was just the trouble!" Jean said, and the words seemed to burst from her.

"No? They didn't talk about me then?"

"Never! Never! I thought you were dead!"

"Perhaps it was better so. I had to be dead to you."

"Why?" Jean asked. "Why? You don't understand what it has been like these long years."

Very gently Margaret placed Jean's hand, which she was still holding, in her lap and then she said quietly:

"I am going to leave you two to talk together. I think, Jean, you ought to tell your mother everything; all that you have told me about your childhood. She should know . . . after all, it is her right."

Patience Plowden looked up with a whimsical expression on her face.

"Haven't I lost that right?" she said, "I have been a very bad mother to Jean, as you well know."

"That is for you to decide," Margaret said; "but I think it wise at all times that we should know the truth, for only when we know it completely and entirely can we give judgment. I will leave you now."

She moved away across the lounge. For a moment Jean was too overwhelmed with shyness and the emotions which beset her to speak, and then, as Patience Plowden sat looking at her, also apparently unable to articulate, she said:

"Do you mind meeting me again?"

"Mind! Of course not! You won't believe me, my

dear, but I have thought of you very often. I know it sounds easy to say that when I appeared so unconcerned about what happened to you, but believe me I had no alternative. Having left your father, I knew without asking the question that he would never let me see you or have anything to do with your up-bringing."

"I am sure that is true," Jean said reflectively, "and before I tell you about . . . that up-bringing . . . would you . . . could you . . . tell me a little bit about yourself? Why you left Glendale? Why, until Aunt Maggie died, I was given to understand that you were dead?"

"So Maggie is dead, is she?" Patience Plowden said reflectively. "A bitter, tyrannical woman! If it had not been for her I might never have left your father."

"I lived with her after he died," Jean said simply.

It was then she began to speak, began to pour out all the misery and unhappiness of her childhood. She had told the story before to Margaret, but not in the same detail or with the same sense of abandonment which was hers now. Here was somebody who not only could understand but had shared the same environment, had known her great-aunt and who was in part instrumental for her having lived in that house of severity and wretchedness. Jean had wanted to hear her mother's story first, but like an avalanche which sweeps away everything else before it the story of her own sufferings, her own hurts and injuries came pouring from her headlong.

As she talked, she felt in some measure as though the mere fact of her unhappiness being brought to the surface washed away much that had scarred and crippled her. Patience Plowden bent forward as she listened, her hands clasped together, her eyes fixed on her daughter, the lines on her own face deep-etched.

"Oh, my child," she murmured more than once; but she made no effort to interrupt or to quell the tempest. Only when she came to the end of her story, when she reached the point where her aunt died and she had decided to come south to London, did Jean's voice falter

209

and die away and as if the effort had been too much for her she put up her hands to her face.

She was unconscious of her surroundings. While she talked, people moved in and out of the lounge, the waitress had brought coffee, the page-boys hurried by with messages, but she and her mother might have been alone on a desert island. It was a meeting of two people, strangers from a superficial point of view, but linked together by something deep and fundamental, something untouched by the restrictions of circumstance.

At last Jean's narrative ended and Patience Plowden made a sudden gesture as if she would take Jean's hands in hers; then she changed her mind and sat back in her chair. There were tears in her eyes and a tremor in her voice as she said:

"Before I make any comment on what you have told me, little Jean, I want to tell you my own story. You have told me yours; only by an exchange of confidences and by utter frankness can we ever understand each other.

"I met your father when I was eighteen. I lived in Devonshire and all my family were Devonshire folk, but despite that we had foreign blood in us going back to the time of the Huguenots; perhaps that was why in the past ten years France has seemed to be my native land. Anyway, shall we say that by temperament I had more affinity with the French than with the British? I was impulsive, gay and perhaps somewhat frivolous.

"Opposite calls to opposite; we have heard it often enough; and when your father came to stay in the village for three weeks one autumn, we met and I found him extremely attractive. He was staying on holiday with some relations of his whom I had known since I was a little girl and with whom my folk were on terms of close friendship, so we very quickly got to know him and entertained him.

"Can you imagine how unexpected it was to find a man like your father—tall, good-looking, severe and what I would now call dour? But in those days his reticence, his reserve and his almost Puritanical outlook seemed to me wildly exciting. I had never met anyone quite like him. He attracted me just as I attracted him, and within a fortnight of his arrival in our village we were engaged to be married.

"My family begged me to consider, to think things over; but, of course, impulsively I insisted on being married at once and went back with your father to Glendale. I cannot begin to describe to you what my life there was like. Now, when I am older and more experienced in people, I still find your father's attitude hard to understand. He loved me, I think, in his own way, but at the same time he felt that such indulgence on his part was a weakness and he resented me even while he desired me.

"He set himself to discipline all the youth and gaiety out of me. Life at the Manse was of such intolerable harshness to someone like myself who had always been happy, who had always known kindness and understanding, that even now the memory of it is tinged with horror. Not once, but a dozen times a day, I would cry bitterly because your father took me to task for something I did not understand, but which I now realise was the warmth I evoked unwittingly within himself. I became to him a temptress; something wrong which he had not the strength to refuse but had to punish himself and me for every indulgence.

"You can imagine that after a year or so of this my spirit was nearly broken. Had I been older and wiser, I dare say I would have tackled things in a very different way; but as it was, I wept miserably and had occasional bursts of rebellion when I would defy your father and in consequence bring down further retribution upon my defenceless head. I was far away from home; I had no money to return; and even if I had, my pride would not have let me admit to my family that I had made a mistake in marrying the man I loved.

"I had been married for four years before I learned I was to have a baby; excited and thrilled, I believed that this might be a solution to everything and that your father might find a new tenderness and understanding for me in his pleasure at having a child. It was true that

211

while you were on the way things were easier, but after you were born a new factor presented itself in our lives—your great-aunt Maggie.

"She had a tremendous influence over your father; she was his one living relation with whom he had any contact, and she lived, as you know, only a short way up the strath so that she was a continual, if unwelcome, visitor at the Manse. She interfered in the parish and she interfered both in your father's life and in mine. I disliked her, she hated me, and after you were born our relationship took a turn for the worse.

"She made up her mind that you at least must be saved from the softness and frivolity which she thought were an intrinsic part of my nature. She was always complaining to your father that I spoilt you; she was always telling him tales of some stupidity or lack of discipline on my part which she averred would ruin you. She played up to the hardest and most austere part of his character; she even bullied him a little; and she waged an inexhaustible war against me.

"At the moment of my darkest despair something new and exciting came into my life. I had been suffering all the winter from a very bad throat and finally it got so bad that the local doctor insisted that I should go to Inverness and consult a specialist. There were grumbles and protests from your father and your great-aunt, but finally they allowed me to go. The specialist saw me, he examined my throat, and when he did so he exclaimed:

" 'I have never seen such vocal chords! You sing?'

" 'Not often,' I confessed.

" 'But you want to?'

" 'When I am happy.'

" 'But that is not often?' he hazarded sharply.

"I smiled, but said nothing. I was too proud to admit to any outsider that most of my days were spent in utter misery. Finally he took me to another room, went to a piano and struck a chord.

" 'Sing!' he commanded.

"I did as I was told, feeling shy and a little uncertain. He made me sing a scale; then he took some music from

212

the piano stool and choosing a popular and well-known song, which every errand boy had been whistling for months, he told me to sing that.

"I stammered my way through it, feeling that he was a little mad, but anxious to do as I was directed. Finally he took his hands from the piano and wheeling round to face me, said:

" 'I believe, young woman, that you would have a very wonderful voice if it were properly trained.'

" 'Well, that is one thing which never will happen,' I said.

" 'Why not?' he questioned.

" 'I am the minister's wife at Glendale,' I said, 'and the only time I am supposed to sing is in the kirk.'

" 'Supposed?' he echoed. 'What has that got to do with it? Surely you know your Bible well enough to know that it is wrong to hide your talents in a napkin. And I promise you, Mrs. MacLeod, that this is not an ordinary talent.'

"He stood for a moment as if in thought, then he said:

" 'Come back next week. I will give you something to clear up the soreness, but don't think you are so well that you have not got to see me again. Do you promise?'

"I promised. In fact, between ourselves I was only too eager to go back to him. Alone in the garden at the Manse and when I was out on the hills I sang to myself. My voice sounded good. My throat was better and there was no doubt even to my inexperienced ear that there was a richness and resilience about the sounds I could make which compared favourably with those who sang in the local choir or the singers I had heard at concerts and at theatres before I married.

"I went to Inverness the following week, not without a struggle, for your Aunt Maggie took up the attitude that I was pandering to my own weakness and that if I went on like that I should become a chronic invalid. I was shown into the specialist's room and found that he was not alone. With him was an elderly man with keen, perceptive eyes and one of the most intelligent faces I have ever seen in my life. He, my dear, was the reason why I ran away."

Jean stiffened a little and Patience Plowden smiled.

"Yes, I see you are thinking just what everyone else thought. But I assure you that Carlos was not my lover, only my master. I loved him because he was a genius, because he was the kindest, biggest-hearted man I have ever met in my life. I loved him and he loved me until he died, but it was a love far beyond the usual earthly emotion which people call love. It was the love of one artist for another, the love of a great man for an undeveloped, ignorant girl in whom he saw great possibilities.

"Looking back, I see how childish the letter was that I wrote to your father. I think I said in it that I could not live without love."

"Yes, you did," Jean murmured.

Patience Plowden looked at her.

"So you have read it?"

"Yes; that was the letter I found in my aunt's house, the one I told you about."

"I might have guessed what construction they would put on it; but I give you my word that I was innocent and stupid enough to be surprised when I received your father's reply denouncing me as a scarlet woman and telling me that I had broken every commandment as well as breaking up my life with him.

"Oh, Jean, if it had not been so serious it would have been funny. How can I tell you the joy of being free, the joy of being with people who understood, the joy of looking ahead . . . ? But I had left you behind. Don't think I did not remember that, but I believed—again it appears stupidly—that as you were one of them they would treat you well. I was the outsider, the foreigner, the alien in their midst. You were of their blood. Now for the first time I realise that I ought to have taken you with me."

"If only you had!" Jean said.

Her mother gave a little sigh and looked down at the great twinkling diamond on her left hand.

"It might not have been a success," she said. "I have

lived a strange life and a full one; I regret nothing that I have done, but at the same time it would not have been a life for a child . . ."

"At least I should have had you," Jean said.

"We should have had each other," Patience Plowden said simply; "but, who knows? Perhaps we were meant to develop along different lines so that we should find ourselves now, both, we hope, better people because of the suffering we have endured."

She put out her hand.

"Will you forgive me, little Jean?"

"Of course, Mother."

Jean put her hand into hers and the two women looked at each other. It was Patience Plowden who looked away first because she was blinded by her tears.

"And now," she said at last, "you will find happiness with Margaret Brora's charming son."

Jean hesitated. She had not recounted that part of her story which concerned Tally. Instinctively she played for time, trying to make up her mind whether or not she should tell her mother the truth.

"She is not Lady Brora any more," she said evasively. "She is Mrs. Melton, but her second husband was killed after the Japanese took Singapore."

"Poor thing! What a tragedy for her!" Patience Plowden exclaimed. "I lost so many friends in the war. So many people I loved."

"Mrs. Melton told me that you had done wonderful work in France."

"I did what I could," her mother corrected. "It was not much, but every little helped."

"And you are better now?" Jean asked.

Patience Plowden smiled.

"I will tell the truth as you are my daughter. I shall never be better. I shall linger here in the sunshine for a few years, maybe half a dozen, and then I shall die."

Jean gave an exclamation of horror.

"Oh, that can't be true!"

"Do you think I mind?" Patience Plowden asked. "My dear, the war taught me many things. Best of all it

215

taught me the unimportance of this world. This is only the shadow, the substance lies behind it. Jean, dear, I will tell you something more. When I die I shall meet someone I love very dearly. It is not Carlos, but I shall meet him, too, and I shall be glad because there is something between us which can never die, which is eternal. But there is another man and I am impatient to see him . . . so don't be sorry for me. In the meantime I have many friends here. There are residents in St. Moritz, you know, besides the hotel visitors who come and go like pretty butterflies but who leave no real impression behind them."

"But you are too young to die," Jean protested.

"Is one ever too young or too old to want real happiness?" Patience asked. Then she put back her head and laughed. "How serious I sound. Seven years ago I would not have talked to you like this. Before the war I was a much sought-after person, but not always a very nice person. I had got to the top of the tree, you see, and everyone wanted me to sing for them and everyone wanted to know me.

"I was too busy for the things that mattered. The war came and my career vanished into smoke. Then I began to make proper use of my voice. I sang to the boys who were going out to fight . . . and to die for freedom. I sang in the hospitals to men who were blind, to men who would never walk or use their arms again, and after that I sang to keep up the courage of those who must work underground because they walked in fear of their very shadow. Finally, I sang in my concentration camp. Sometimes, when we were so hungry that women would gnaw their fingers for nourishment, my singing would help a little. It passed the time and it made them forget, if only for a few seconds. Yes, Jean, I learned in those years why I had been given a voice. I learned, too, to know myself."

"You are wonderful!" Jean exclaimed.

"I like to hear you say so," Patience answered, "but I assure you that there were dozens of people with me who were far more wonderful than I was, and at times I was weak and stupid and frivolous just as your great-aunt had always stated."

"Oh, Mother, of course she would have disapproved!"

Jean was laughing now through her tears and Patience Plowden was laughing with her.

"My dear, I am so glad to have found you," Patience said softly. "We must thank dear Mrs. Melton for introducing us and while you are still here we must see a lot of each other."

"I shall hear you sing tonight," Jean said brightly.

"You will hear me sing," Patience Plowden repeated, "but my voice will never again be what it was. However, we need money for the hospital. You must come and see the children, many of them are friends of mine and once a week I sing to them."

They went on talking until finally the lounge filled again and it was tea-time. Only when Jean looked up to find Margaret Melton standing beside her did she realise how quickly time had passed.

"May I join you both for tea?" Margaret asked.

Jean jumped up to offer her her chair and pull up another for herself.

"But, of course," Patience Plowden said. "It is just what I would like. I will have a cup of tea and then I must go and lie down. If my doctor sees me, I shall be in disgrace for I am supposed to rest every afternoon."

"This afternoon has been an exception," Margaret Melton said, "and you have a very good excuse."

"A very good excuse," Patience Plowden echoed, and she took Jean's hand in hers. "Little Jean has been telling me how kind you have been to her. I am grateful though it is not for me, a stranger, to thank anyone for being kind to my daughter."

"It is difficult not to be kind to her," Margaret Melton said simply, and Patience Plowden nodded as though she understood what Margaret was trying to convey.

They had tea and talked a little, then Margaret looked at her watch.

."It is half-past-five, Tally ought to have been back by now."

"And it is dark," Jean said, "so they must really have been back some time. Do you think he is looking for you upstairs?"

"Ask the concierge to ring the rooms," Margaret said, "and if they are there, tell them to come down and join us for tea. I would like your mother to meet Tally before she has to rest."

"And I would be thrilled to meet him," Patience Plowden said.

Jean jumped up and went to the desk and asked the concierge to telephone upstairs. There was no answer, however, either from Tally's room or from Gerald's.

"His lordship should be in by now," the concierge said. "I will send a porter down to the ski-room to find out if he has returned."

"Oh, would you?" Jean said gratefully. "Mrs. Melton is rather anxious."

"Perhaps he has stopped at one of the other hotels for tea," the concierge suggested soothingly; but Jean was not reassured. She felt that Tally, after a long run, would have wanted to get home. He would wish to change and also it was unlike him not to realise that his mother would be anxious. The porter returned from the ski-room to say that neither Lord Brora nor Captain Fairfax had come back. By now it was a quarter of six.

"Something must have happened," Jean exclaimed. "What can we do?"

The concierge picked up the telephone.

"I will speak to the guides' office," he said. "Someone may have seen them as they came down the mountain."

But all inquiries proved to be fruitless, and while Jean was still waiting Margaret came to join her.

"Your mother has gone upstairs to rest," she said. "Is there any news of Tally?"

She spoke quietly, but Jean knew what anxiety lay behind her question.

She shook her head.

"But surely . . . there can't have been an accident?"

"The guides know which route his lordship took," the porter replied. "If he and Captain Fairfax are not back in a short while, a search party will go out to look for them."

"A search party?" Jean said with a little gasp.

"We will wait in the lounge," Margaret said, linking her arm with Jean's, and they walked slowly back to their quiet corner.

"Does that mean that there has been an accident?" Jean asked.

"Because they will send out a search party?" Margaret asked. "Oh no! It is no use jumping to conclusions. Tally or Gerald may have broken a ski or merely got held up. Folk who go on a long run here always leave a notice with the guides of their intended route and the time they expect to be back. It is a safeguard, you see, against things going wrong. Such a lot of things can happen."

She spoke calmly with a courage she was far from feeling, but Jean felt sick and afraid. The mountains which had seemed so beautiful in the sunlight were now shrouded in darkness. She knew it was bitterly cold with a keen wind blowing down from the glaciers, and she shrank from imaginative pictures of Tally battling against the elements or lying broken and injured in a deep crevasse.

The two women sat in silence, each deep in her own thoughts. They looked up to see a porter approaching them. Jean's heart leapt. Perhaps this was news, good news.

"A search party is leaving now, Madam," the porter said in a low voice to Margaret.

"I would like to see them before they go," Margaret said, getting to her feet.

"May I come too?" Jean asked.

She saw now that for all her calm self-control Margaret Melton was desperately pale and her eyes were dark as if in fear.

They went down to the ski-room. Three of the guides were there putting on their skis, checking their first-aid

219

equipment and getting ready a hand-propelled sleigh on which an injured person could be brought down from the mountains. There was little to say. Margaret spoke to them in their own language, holding out her hand to each man, and wishing him good luck and God-speed. Jean could only stand in the background sending out a wordless prayer that they would find Tally soon and bring him home safely to them. It was agony to have to go upstairs to their bedrooms and wait.

Jean sensed that Margaret wanted to be alone. She went into her own room and shut the door. She could not rest, could only walk up and down the floor clenching her hands together, wishing with her whole heart and soul that she could have gone with the men, could do something real and helpful in this emergency. She had not known it was so hard to feel helpless and unwanted.

Up and down the floor she walked, knowing with every step she took how much Tally meant to her. Every second of the day it seemed to her that her feeling for him deepened, and now even her sense of hopelessness had gone. She loved him beyond argument with herself, beyond logical common sense. She could only surrender herself to her own feelings; she could only let her love for him possess her utterly so that it radiated out from her now in a ceaseless prayer for his safety.

"Don't let him be hurt, God. Let him come back safe and sound. I ask nothing more than that. I will go away. I will be content just to see him again, just to hear his voice, if only he is safe and unhurt."

It was bargaining with God, but somehow it was inevitable when one was so desperate. Soon she was past even praying coherently. She could only raise her whole being in prayer—a worldless invocation to the Spirit 'above all and in all.'

It was eight o'clock before Margaret opened the communicating door.

"We must go down to dinner," she said, "and don't forget that you are to hear your mother sing."

"I have not changed. I don't want any dinner." Jean said quickly.

Margaret stopped her words with a gesture.

"We must not anticipate the worst," she said gently. "No news is always good news. Let us change. We shall feel better if we are in fresh clothes, then we will go down and try to eat some dinner. Tally is a very experienced skier and we should not allow ourselves to get panicked into anticipating what may never occur."

"I am sorry," Jean said humbly.

Margaret moved across the room and put her arms round the girl.

"Listen, dear," she said. "I know what you are feeling. I have been through this very often in my life, but you have got to ride yourself with a tight rein, got to learn not to show what you are feeling. It does no good and may only hinder you from doing the right thing at the right moment. If the men come back safe and sound, they will only be annoyed with us for being so silly. If anything has gone wrong, we shall need all our courage and our strength to deal with it."

"How wise you are!" Jean said, clinging to her.

Margaret sighed, but her expression was very tender.

"Have you forgotten already that I very seldom practise what I preach. I am the worst example of a woman who knows what is right and does what is wrong."

"You are not! You could not be!" Jean said loyally, and Margaret laughed.

"Go and put on your prettiest dress," she said, "and be ready to applaud when Tally tells you what an exciting adventure he has been having and how ridiculous it was of us to have been anxious even for one moment."

Jean hurried to do as she was told. Margaret's maid, Rose, had arrived that morning with the rest of her luggage and already the things were unpacked and hung out in the wardrobe.

She chose a dress of pale blue lace. It did something to her eyes and skin, making her appear very fair, slender and fragile. When she was ready, she went to Margaret's room and watched Rose fastening her into a dress of black chiffon.

221

"Are all your dresses black?" Jean asked without thinking.

"Most of them," Margaret replied, and Jean understood that she had not felt like wearing bright colours while she was mourning Stephen.

"Now we are ready," Margaret said at length, picking up a cape of white ermine and putting it over her arm. "Have I got everything, Rose?"

"Everything, Madam, and I have prepared his lordship's bed with hot bottles just in case he . . . he wishes to go to bed."

All three women understood what Rose left tactfully unsaid, but Margaret made no remark. She turned and led the way into the passage.

Jean felt as if food would choke her, but nevertheless she made a pretence of eating some of the delicious dinner that was served to them. They were later than most of the other diners and when they came back into the lounge they saw that everyone was filing into the big ballroom where Patience Plowden was to sing.

"We cannot go in," Jean said. "I don't think I could bear it."

Margaret turned to look at her.

"I have found out that your mother is to sing early in the evening. We will ask the head waiter to give us a little table on the balcony so that we can be near the door and can slip out if anyone wants us. As soon as your mother's singing is finished, we can leave anyway."

"That will be splendid," Jean said, but even then she shrank from the crowds laughing and chattering in the ballroom, from the young men twirling their partners to the sparkling music, and from the general atmosphere of gaiety. She felt as though a deep shadow lay across her heart almost suffocating her so that every moment was of agonised anticipation. How soon would they know? How soon would they hear? Would it be the best or the worst?

Almost in a dream she followed Margaret into the ballroom. Everything was arranged. The head waiter led them to a table overlooking the dance floor. It was near the door and yet they were in a position of advantage. They seated themselves and Margaret ordered half a bottle of champagne.

"Dutch courage, my dear," she said, and tried to smile, but Jean saw that her lips were trembling.

The dance came to an end and the leader of the band stepped forward.

"Mesdames et Messieurs . . ." he began, and announced in French that Patience Plowden would appear.

The lights in the ballroom were switched off and only the footlights were left as Patience Plowden walked on to the small stage amidst a great burst of applause. She looked far younger, Jean thought, than she had in daylight, and her dress of black tulle glittered with silver sequins. There were diamonds in her hair and round her neck and she looked glamorous and unreal, so that it was hard to remember that this was the woman whose story she had learned that afternoon or who as a young girl had cried bitterly in the shabby little Manse at Glendale because her husband was stern and severe with her.

Then she began to sing. Jean had been ready to force herself to attend, to take her mind off Tally, to concentrate for a few moments at least on her mother. No effort was necessary. Great liquid notes of music came soaring from her mother's white throat and seemed to catch hold of something within Jean's heart; to make her vibrate emotionally; to lift her from the confines of her own fears and imagining to a world of light and understanding.

For the first time she realised that music is the language of all peoples. She was not even certain in what language the song was written, she only knew that it spoke to her of all those things which mattered most; that it opened for her new horizons to which she could only throw out her arms yearningly.

The song ended and for a moment there was silence —a silence of utter appreciation—and then the applause broke forth, wave upon wave, until Patience held up her hand and sang again. Now her song was one of

223

spring, of joy and laughter, an exquisite whimsical little poem of youth and happiness.

Again Jean was drawn out of herself and something in her mother's voice seemed to capture her spirit. One more song followed, a song which had been popular enough before the war and which brought back memories to many of the older people there. Jean saw that Margaret's eyes were full of tears.

The whole performance had not taken more than ten minutes, yet Jean felt that it had taught her much. Then her mother bowed to the audience and was gone. They sought to have her back, applauding and shouting "Encore, Encore!" until the master of ceremonies stepped forward to say that Miss Plowden regretted that under her doctor's orders she might sing no more.

Then the dance music began again and Margaret and Jean went out into the lounge. They went to the desk.

"Any news, Fritz?"

The concierge shook his head.

"I am afraid not, Madam."

Just as they turned away the revolving door at the end of the hall opened and a porter came in. He spoke to the concierge in German, but Margaret understood what he said.

"A guide has come back, you say?" she questioned.

"Yes, Madam." The porter answered in English so that Jean understood. "He has come on ahead so that the doctor may be waiting when they get down."

"The doctor!" Jean exclaimed. "Then he is hurt? How badly?"

"One minute," Margaret said. "Who is injured?"

"The guide is just coming, Madam. He is taking off his skis."

The door revolved again and one of the guides, a thick, stocky young man with a cheerful smile and red cheeks, whom Jean had noticed earlier in the evening, came into the hall. As he walked forward he pulled off his gloves and blew on his fingers as though they were frozen with cold.

Jean would have run forward to meet him, but

Margaret stood still waiting until he came up to the desk.

"There has been an accident?" she asked in her quiet, low voice.

"Yes, Madam."

"Is it serious?"

"No, Madam. Only a broken leg. Berletti has set it. The gentleman will be all right."

"Nothing worse?"

"No, Madam."

"But which gentleman is it?" Jean asked.

She could contain the question no longer.

The guide turned to her.

"A fair gentleman, Miss. The . . ." He sought for the word . . . "the stouter of the two."

"It's Gerald!"

Jean breathed the name in relief.

"Poor Gerald!" Margaret exclaimed. "But a broken leg is not a too serious matter. You will get a doctor, Fritz?"

"I am telephoning for one now," the concierge replied.

"You will get the surgeon from the clinic?" Margaret asked. "He is much the best man in St. Moritz."

"Yes, Madam."

"How long will they be?" Jean asked the guide.

"Five to ten minutes, Miss," he replied. "I came very quickly; they cannot come so fast with the sleigh."

The quarter of an hour which they finally waited seemed longer. Jean knew that it would have seemed immeasurably longer had it been Tally who was hurt instead of Gerald. When finally the guides carrying Gerald with Tally walking beside them came into the hall it was with the greatest effort that she did not run forward to cry out her gladness. She made herself walk slowly behind Margaret.

"Hullo, Mother," Tally smiled; "I am sorry you should have been worried."

"It is all right now we know what has happened," Margaret said. "Poor Gerald! Is it very bad?"

225

"It was pretty bad at the time," Gerald answered, "but Tally looked after me and I can't thank him enough."

The guides, helped by the porters, moved forward and took Gerald up in the lift. He smiled at Jean as he passed, but she saw that he was very pale.

"Have you got a doctor?" Tally asked as soon as Gerald was out of earshot.

"Yes," Margaret said. "He should be here any moment now."

"We have had the dickens of a time," Tally said. "Gerald fell just as we were coming over the top on the last part of the run. It was bitterly cold up there and no protection from the wind whatsoever. I did what I could for him, but I did not like to leave him. I am afraid he got pretty chilled before the rescue party arrived. However, 'all's well that ends well' and thank God we are back."

"Thank God!" Margaret repeated.

"Of course you have been worrying your silly head?" Tally said fondly.

"Of course!" Margaret answered.

Tally looked at Jean for the first time.

"Have you looked after her?" he asked.

"I have done my best," she answered, feeling hypocritical as she said it, knowing that Margaret had done the looking after.

"Good for you," Tally said, "and now that the doctor will see to Gerald I could do with a drink. I am pretty cold myself, I can tell you."

"Have a stiff whisky and then come upstairs; you must have a hot bath at once," Margaret said.

But even as she turned Fritz came to the desk with a cable.

"There's a cable just arrived for Captain Fairfax."

"I had better open it," Tally said. "Gerald won't want to be worried at the moment."

He opened the cable, read it, and gave a long, low whistle.

"This complicates things."

"What is the matter?" Margaret asked.

He read it out: *"Lizzie very ill. Please return and help me with Jim. Betty.* What are we going to do now?" he asked.

There was only an infinitesimal pause before Jean said quietly:

"I will go back and help Betty."

14

"Come along, Jim," Jean coaxed for the hundredth time.

It was difficult to get the small boy to hurry himself. Hyde Park was full of absorbing interest—ducks, birds, dogs and other babies held his attention—and Jean, who believed that walking was good for him, had at times literally to propel him along, otherwise they would have remained stationary in the same spot for hours on end. She enjoyed her walks with Jim and, despite the cold weather and the frost in the air, they would manage to get home with their cheeks glowing and with a feeling of well-being, even if at times it was combined with physical tiredness.

It was extraordinary, Jean thought, how quickly she got through the work of the little house. What had once been drudgery at her aunt's was now a joy and delight because she wanted to clean, liked to cook, wash and tidy. It gave her a sort of inner satisfaction, a real pleasure, to see the shining results of her labours or to hear Jim say, "More, please Auntie Jean," as he passed his plate for a second helping.

She had arrived back from Switzerland to be greeted with open arms by Betty.

"You are an angel to come. I am absolutely desperate. Lizzie is in hospital and screaming the place down for me, and I can't find anybody to look after Jim except an old charwoman I sometimes employ, and as she is deaf and rather disagreeable I am frightened out of my life every time I leave him."

There was a suspicion of tears in her eyes, and a choke in her voice which told Jean all too clearly that her nerves were strained to breaking-point.

"Don't worry," she said. "I will look after Jim. I shall love it, and you can go and stay as long as they will let you in the hospital with Lizzie."

"That is what I hoped you would say," Betty replied, in a tone of fervent thankfulness. "The moment I got Tally's wire saying that you were coming, I felt things would be all right. I cabled Gerald because I was desperate. He wouldn't be much use, but he would have been better than nobody! But having you is just perfect!"

It would have been hard for Jean not to feel a glow of inner satisfaction at being so fervently welcomed; but at the moment there had been no time for thought, except to ask a few questions about the running of the house, and to hurry Betty off to the hospital. Lizzie had acute appendicitis with complications, and Betty had every reason to be desperately anxious about her.

At the same time Jim was certainly not a person one could leave on his own. Five minutes after Betty had left the house, Jean found him in the bathroom sailing his boats with both taps full on. He had, of course, already soaked himself to the skin, and Jean had to change him, which he not unnaturally resented.

"I'se all right," he said stoutly.

"Of course you are," Jean replied soothingly, "but you might get a cold, and then you would give me one. You wouldn't like me to go round the house sneezing all the time, would you?"

Jim looked up at her seriously.

"Would it make your nose red?" he asked.

"Yes, very," Jean answered.

"That would be a pity," he commented, and Jean laughed at the compliment.

It took her a day or two to find out where everything was; and here Jim was a help, for he was an intelligent,

230

quick-brained little boy, and often his help, even in remembering what local shops Betty patronised, was of great assistance.

Jean would take him shopping with her in the morning, and there was always a tussle whether he should walk or go in his push-chair, and only by promising him a bus ride to the Park in the afternoon could she persuade him that two long walks a day were too much for his fat legs.

They got along splendidly together; in fact, after a day or two Betty was declaring that she was quite jealous of Jim's affection for Jean. But they saw very little of her, and when she did come back from the hospital, she looked pale and hollow-eyed, and Jean learned that Lizzie was insisting on her mother's attention, both day and night.

"Nothing matters as long as my baby gets well," Betty said wearily, when Jean commented on her look of fatigue and the fact that she had lost a lot of weight. "It has been touch and go, Jean. I always knew I loved my children, but I don't think any of us realise how much they mean to us until the moment comes when we might lose them."

"Isn't that true of everything in life?" Jean asked.

Betty looked at her quickly but made no comment. Jean suspected that Betty guessed that there was something strange and not quite usual about her engagement to Tally. But she offered no confidence, and Betty never asked inquisitive questions. One afternoon, when Betty had escaped from the hospital for a few hours, and Jean had insisted on her lying on the sofa with her feet up, Betty said:

"You are a born mother, Jean. You mother me almost as tenderly as you do Jim; and by the way, you have been wonderful, you know that."

"Nonsense," Jean answered. "You know I love doing what I can for you and Jim, who, incidentally, is the nicest person in the whole world."

"He is awfully like his father in many ways, and by the way I have had a letter from John this morning. He

231

has only just got my cable telling him about Lizzie. I have come to the conclusion that the only consolation for being really desperately worried is the comfort of knowing that someone else is worrying as much as you are."

"She is better, though, isn't she?" Jean asked.

"We are very nearly out of the wood," Betty answered, "but we dare not say so yet in case we may be counting our chickens . . . Oh, Jean, I am so tired."

"Go to sleep," Jean commanded. "I am going to take Jim into the Park, and you are not to move until I get back and tell you that tea is ready."

"I don't think I ever want to move again," Betty said, in a voice heavy with sleep, and Jean tiptoed from the room and hurried Jim out of the house, unless he would make a noise.

They were earlier than usual, and having got a bus which took them straight to Hyde Park Corner, they had walked some distance before it was three o'clock. Jim was beginning to get tired. Jean looked at her watch.

"I don't want to take you home yet," she said, "in case you wake your mummy."

"Why does Mummy sleep in the day-time?" Jim asked. "I sleep at night."

"Mummy has been awake at night looking after Lizzie," Jean told him.

"Poor Lizzie," Jim said in a soft voice. "Lizzie very ill. She has got pains in her tummy."

"Yes, poor Lizzie," Jean agreed. "But she will be better soon and come back and play with you."

Jim digested this for a moment, and then he said:

"I will give her my new ball."

Jean smiled.

"You are a nice, generous person, Jim. The girl you marry is going to be very lucky."

This was beyond Jim's comprehension, and anyway his attention was caught by a dachshund puppy, and he ran after it for quite a little way before Jean caught up with him. When finally she overtook him, he pointed to an empty seat:

"Jim sit down," he said. "I'se tired."

"It is too cold," Jean answered. "We have got to keep moving or you will turn into a little block of ice."

"Let's go home in a bus," Jim suggested next.

Jean was tempted by the tone of his voice, but remembering Betty sleeping peacefully, she hardened her heart.

"No, Jim," she said, "we cannot do that." Then suddenly an inspiration came to her. "I know what we will do," she said. "I have got an idea."

"What is it?" Jim asked.

Jean's ideas, of which he had had considerable experience by this time, were usually good ones.

"We are going to see a house," she said. "A house which belongs to your Uncle Tally."

"Go in a bus?" Jim asked.

"No, in a taxi," Jean replied, taking Jim's hand as she walked into Park Lane and signalled to a passing taxi.

When it had deposited them outside the big front door in Berkeley Square, she felt a moment's apprehension, but firmly she forced herself forward. She had thought on several occasions that she would like to visit the house in Berkeley Square again; she wanted to go back into Margaret's bedroom and see if Stephen Melton's photograph had the same strange effect on her as it had had the first time she saw it. Hardly formulated, even to herself, was the idea that she was slightly clairvoyant at that moment.

Many years ago, when she had been a child, there had been occasions when she seemed to have second sight, but they had not happened as she grew older, though in her unhappiness she longed for such moments, if only to convince herself that there was something better and happier than the miserable life she was forced to live with her aunt. But it had seemed to her that the power of 'seeing', as the country folk called it, had left her. Only now, looking back on her strange and unaccountable feeling in Berkeley Square, she was sure that there was some reason for what she had experienced.

"I believe Stephen Melton wanted to give me a

message," Jean told herself, and thought that if only she could translate such a message into words it might bring immeasurable comfort to his wife.

She felt shy and a little embarrassed when she rang the bell, wondering hastily what she should say to the old butler when he opened the door. Things were made easy for her, because the man recognised her, and seemed to take it for granted that she should come to the house.

"I hope his lordship is well, Miss?" he murmured, opening the door invitingly.

"Very well, thank you," Jean answered, "but Captain Fairfax has broken his leg. This is his nephew, whom I am looking after at the moment."

"I am sorry to hear that about the Captain. Very sorry. Would you like a cup of tea, Miss, now you are here? It would not take me a moment to get you one."

"No, thank you," Jean answered, "though it is very kind of you to think of it. We have got to be home for tea."

She stood a little irresolutely in the hall, wondering how she could say that she wanted to go upstairs to Mrs. Melton's bedroom, but the old butler made it easy for her.

"I expect the young gentleman would like to see the electric trains in the games room? His lordship had them set up there when he was a schoolboy, and they are still in working order."

"I want to see the trains!" Jim said eagerly.

"You come along with me then," the butler smiled.

"Would you mind looking after him for a moment?" Jean asked. "There is something I want to get upstairs."

"That's all right, Miss," was the reply. "You will find us at the end of the corridor. In the room looking on to the garden."

"I won't be long," Jean promised and ran up the stairs two steps at a time.

Outside the bedroom door she paused. The house was very quiet. There was the close smell of rooms unlived

234

in, and an atmosphere of age and emptiness which made Jean feel as if she crept into another period of time.

Slowly she turned the handle. The door opened silently, and now she was in the room with every sense attuned for what she wished to hear. The curtains were drawn so that the room was a misty grey. It took her a moment before she could see the outline of the big gilt bed and the faintly shimmering light reflected by the looking-glasses on the dressing-table.

She stared across the room to where she knew Stephen's photograph was and then she stood very still, trying to contact him, trying to make herself fluid and receptive. She was unable to see the photograph but suddenly Stephen's face was before her eyes, clearly, vividly.

She waited, and then it seemed as if a voice within herself and yet from without cried:

"Look at my photograph!"

It was not what she expected and yet the instinctive voice was too strong to be disobeyed. She moved across the room, felt rather than saw the photograph beside the bed and taking it up went with it towards the window. Even as she moved she felt disappointed. She had expected something more, what she was not quite sure. This was in itself nothing she could repeat to Margaret Melton, nothing which could give her comfort.

She reached the window, drew aside the curtain, and looked down at Stephen Melton's face, his eyes looking straight into hers.

"Well," she said out loud, "what is it you want to tell me?"

Again it seemed to her that a voice said:

"The photograph! The photograph!"

She looked in perplexity at the photograph. She knew beyond all argument that the voice was not her own imagination and yet what could it mean? Stephen Melton's face was there and it stirred her strangely even as it had done before. That was all.

She stood looking at the photograph. Did it mean that

235

he wanted her to give it to his wife? She felt that it was impossible for her to presume such an action. She could feel the silver frame cold beneath her fingers and yet something warm and intensely living was trying to get through to her, trying to tell her something which it was imperative for her to know.

"The photograph! The photograph!"

What did it mean? She turned the frame over and then on an impulse, because she felt that perhaps the glass over the face was acting as some unaccountable barrier, she undid the back of the frame. It was held tightly by two clips; she slipped them on one side, raised the back—and understood!

There, pressed close against the back of the photograph, was a letter. Even as she took it in her hands Jean felt an overwhelming sense of relief which was not entirely her own. Stephen also was relieved that he had got through.

She drew out the envelope; it was sealed, and written on it was:

"To be opened by my wife in the event of my death."

Jean held it in her hand, then turned over the frame and looked down at Stephen Melton's photograph.

"So that's what you wanted to tell me," she said. "I only hope that it will help her to be happy again."

Did she imagine it or did somebody say quite clearly: "It will!"

She put the photograph back on the bedside table, drew the curtains across the window and slipped the letter into her handbag. Then she went downstairs to find Jim wild with excitement as an electric train, complete with its carriages, ran round the tracks, through tunnels and past tiny stations.

It was only later that evening when Betty had gone back to the hospital and Jim was asleep in bed that Jean realised the difficulty she would have in explaining to Mrs. Melton how she had found the letter, and why. She sat down at Betty's writing-table in the drawing-room and took up her pen.

"Dear Mrs. Melton," she started, and then sat staring

into space, wondering how she could put into words the strange feeling she had experienced that afternoon.

She tried for a long time, but still the words would not come, still she could not explain it clearly. She had never been good at expressing herself on paper and now it seemed almost impossible to convey in ordinary, stilted language how she had followed the intuition which had been hers over a month ago.

It was no use, she decided at last. She could not write to Margaret Melton. Finally she lifted the telephone receiver and inquired how much it would cost to put a call through to St. Moritz. It was expensive, but she had enough money left from the £25 which Margaret had given her. It would be embarrassing to tell Mrs. Melton what had occurred, but it would be far easier than writing it down in black and white.

There was some delay on the line and it was an hour later before the bell rang and she was told to hold on. A few moments and she heard Margaret's voice:

"Hullo! Margaret Melton speaking."

"Oh, Mrs. Melton, it is Jean here."

"Hullo, my dear. I thought it might be you when they said there was a call from London. Is everything all right?"

"Yes, quite all right. Lizzie is better."

"Thank goodness she is all right. I did not say anything to Gerald in case you were going to give us bad news. But he will be delighted. He also is better, in fact we hope to get him home by air in another week."

"That will be wonderful," Jean said.

There was a moment's pause and then she added:

"I telephoned you about something which it was too difficult to write."

"Yes, dear?"

Margaret's voice was soothing and calm. Hesitatingly, stammering over her words, explaining herself badly, Jean told how she had gone to Berkeley Square that afternoon to recapture the feeling that she had experienced before, and how she was certain that Stephen Melton's photograph had something to say to her.

237

There was silence at the other end. Margaret made no comment until at last Jean faltered:

"There was a letter at the back of the photograph and I have got it here for you."

She heard a long drawn sigh and an exclamation which was almost a cry of pain, then Margaret whispered:

"A letter . . . addressed to me?"

"Yes, it is addressed to you."

"Oh, my dear . . . and you will send it to me at once?"

"Tomorrow!"

"By air mail?"

"Yes, of course, by air mail."

There was a moment's pause and then Margaret said in a voice so broken that Jean knew she was crying:

"I cannot quite believe it . . . a letter from . . . Stephen . . . after all these years."

It was then that the operator intervened and said briskly:

"Will you finish this call, please?"

"I will send the letter tomorrow," Jean said quietly. "Good-bye."

"Good-bye, Jean . . . and thank you! . . . Thank you!"

The line was silent and Jean replaced the receiver. The incredulous gratitude in Margaret's voice was ringing in her ears. She went across to the fire and knelt down, holding out her hands to the flames.

"I have not been quite useless here," she thought. "They have helped me and now I have been able to help them."

The pronoun was in the plural but she knew that she was thinking of Tally. Margaret had not said how he was; in fact his name had not been mentioned. She had not expected it, but now she was bitterly disappointed.

There was hardly a moment when he was not in her thoughts and it seemed to her that the memory of him accompanied her whatever she did or wherever she went. Sometimes she would lie awake at nights, going over and over the conversations they had had during the times they had been together. There was nothing too trivial that she could not remember, no moment too light or unimportant that it would not come back to her mind in every detail.

Sometimes there was an aching pain in her heart which was almost unbearable. She wanted Tally so much. She wanted to see him, to hear his voice. Over and over again she thought of that moment when he had raised her fingers to his lips. Sometimes she dreamed wild, ridiculous dreams in which he held her in his arms and she knew the exquisite tenderness of his mouth.

It was all impossible, she knew that. Now that she had left St. Moritz it would be easy for Tally to reinstate himself with Melia. She could visualise them dancing together and ski-ing down the mountains. Once she dreamed that she saw them in the sunlight while she stood alone in a deep shadow. The dream haunted her because she knew how true it was. They were born for the sunlight, while she was not.

She was not always unhappy. There were moments of joy when she was grateful for having known Tally, when she told herself that even the pain was worth the fullness and richness of loving someone so wonderful as he. Sometimes she pretended, as she put Jim to bed, that he was her child and Tally's and she held him close not only for his own dearness but because even such a child- ish pretence seemed to bring Tally a little nearer to her.

Tally had taken her to the station the morning she left St. Moritz.

"I would come with you," he said, "but I think Mother needs me. I am afraid she might be upset if I left her here alone to look after Gerald."

"Of course you must stay with her," Jean said quickly.

"You will be all right, won't you?" Tally asked. "I have telephoned to the aerodrome and told the officials to give you every possible attention and I've arranged for a car to meet you at Croydon."

"I shall be all right," Jean assured him.

All the same, she had felt very small and lonely as the train steamed out of St. Moritz station and Tally van-

239

ished from her sight. She had only the memory of his words:

"It is wonderful of you to do this. We shall never be able to thank you enough."

They had comforted her as the train disappeared into a tunnel, the sudden darkness hiding the sunshine and the man she loved.

He had not written to her, but she had not expected it. Though she had written to him more than once, she had merely torn up the letters when they were written and thrown them into the fire. There were many things to occupy her and yet it seemed that there were long stretches of the days and nights when in her thoughts she was with Tally. She often wondered if for the rest of her life he would always be with her in such a way. It was like living with a ghost, she thought, and realised that that was what Margaret had done ever since Stephen Melton's death.

She took up the letter that Stephen had written to his wife and looked at it. The writing was small and full of character. Theirs was the way to love and to be loved, Jean thought; to find somebody who was part of one, never to let him go. She wondered if after reading this letter Margaret would find faith. If she believed that Stephen was waiting for her, she would not live in utter despair any longer. For her, then, was hope; for herself, Jean thought, there was none. Tally did not love her, would never love her and therefore they could not come together, would never be one.

The thought depressed her so much that she got to her feet and went upstairs to see if Jim was all right and asleep. She switched on the bedside lamp. He looked the picture of innocence in his small bed, his lashes dark against his cheeks, while a small fat hand lay over the bedclothes. Quite suddenly as she looked at the sleeping child Jean found the tears running down her face.

"I am overwrought," she thought, and knew it was the reaction of the afternoon. But it was more than that; it was the aching desire within her for happiness and love and for children. But she would never find a perfect

union as Margaret Melton had or the blissful content-
ment of marriage as Betty knew it.

Quite suddenly Jean dropped on her knees beside
Jim's bed.

"Oh God, dear God," she prayed. "Let me have
Tally. Let him love me. Let us be together if only for a
little time."

She was ashamed of herself even as the prayer was
said. Tally was not for her.

She got to her feet as the telephone rang shrilly
downstairs. Wiping her eyes, she hurried down to it. She
was told to hold on and then with a sudden constriction
of the heart she heard Tally's voice.

"Hullo! Is that you, Jean?"

"Yes."

"I say, what has happened? My mother has just come
and told me that you have found a letter of Stephen's.
She is so excited and so overwrought about the whole
thing that I rang you up in case there is some mistake
and she has misunderstood you."

"No, there is no mistake. I found a letter for her. It
was behind the photograph."

"What photograph?"

"The one in your mother's bedroom in Berkeley
Square."

"You found it? But what were you doing there?"

Shyly and not a little embarrassed she told him why
she had gone to Berkeley Square.

"This is the most amazing thing I have ever heard. Do
you mean you guessed the letter was there?"

"No . . . not exactly. I just felt there was something
the photograph was trying to tell me."

"But how could the photograph tell you? You mean
that you thought Stephen was trying to tell you something? Stephen himself?"

"Yes."

Jean's answer was simple and direct and for a moment Tally made no comment and then he said:

"I don't understand it, Jean."

"Nor do I, but I have got the letter for your mother."

241

"But . . . Oh, damn it! I wish I could see you. I want to talk about this. I am frightfully interested. If it is true, it is the most amazing thing that has ever happened."

"It is true enough. The letter is on the table in front of me."

"I cannot begin to think what this may mean to my mother. Of course, we don't know what is in the letter, but the mere fact of your having found it opens the door to so many possibilities, doesn't it?"

"I think it will make her happier."

"I am sure of that."

There was a moment's silence and then Tally said:

"Are you all right?"

"Yes, of course. I like looking after Jim. Tell Gerald he is always asking about him."

"Yes, I will tell him. And Betty?"

"She is very tired, but I think Lizzie is going to get well."

"Good! And Jean, there is something I want to ask you . . ."

But now maddeningly they were cut off and with a sudden click the line went dead. Anxiously Jean held on.

"Hullo! Hullo!"

But there was no answer. At last she replaced the receiver. She was not certain what the conversation had meant to her, for, excited and bewildered, she was not sure if she had actually spoken to Tally or if it had all been a dream. Only of one thing she was sure—that she loved him to the exclusion of all else. It was both joy and pain to have him speak to her.

She turned out the lights of the drawing-room and was preparing to go to bed when the telephone rang again. She sprang forward eagerly. Perhaps it was Tally to continue the cut-off conversation. This time it was Betty.

"Jean? Lizzie is worse."

"Oh, no!"

"I am afraid so. She seems to be sinking, the doctors are giving her a blood transfusion."

"But . . . but I thought she was better."

"She has had a relapse, nobody quite knows why. Oh, Jean, I think I shall go mad. She is in the operating room now. I had to talk to somebody. That is why I am telephoning you."

"Oh, Betty, what can I do? Isn't there anything I can do?"

"Nobody can do anything," Betty said, and it seemed to Jean that her voice held no tears, only a desperate unhappiness that was past expression.

"We can pray."

Jean was surprised at her answer. It was something which ordinarily she would have been too shy to say.

"Yes, we can pray," Betty said brokenly. "Pray for me, Jean. I think I am past doing it for myself."

She put down the receiver and Jean, shaken with sobs, got up from the writing table.

"What can I do?" she asked. Indeed what could she do?

She tried to pray, but the words would not come. She thought of Lizzie fighting for her life in the hospital and she was filled with an overwhelming compassion that was past formulating into words. She felt her whole being going out in silent prayer that Lizzie might live. She prayed—wordlessly, but with an intense concentration—which left her exhausted as if the effort had been almost superhuman.

Finally she went out to the landing. Should she go to bed or should she wait up in case Betty wanted her, she wondered. She decided that if anything happened, Betty might come straight home. It would be best not to undress. She would go down to the kitchen and make herself a cup of tea.

She went down the narrow stairs into the little hall and as she reached the ground floor she heard a taxi draw up and stop outside. She held her breath. Surely it could not be Betty already. She stood hesitantly and then a key was inserted in the lock and the door opened. Instinctively Jean raised her hands to quell the startled thumping of her heart and then she saw standing in the open doorway a tall young man in naval uniform. It was

243

not hard to recognise him from the photographs that were everywhere about the house.

It was John—John Wilding, arrived home at just the right moment when he was most needed.

Jean went forward.

"Don't let your taxi go!" she cried, not stopping to think that such a greeting might in itself be a surprise. John raised his eyebrows, yet wasted no time with questions but turned round and shouted through the doorway.

"Wait a minute, cabby, I may want you!"

He put down the big suitcase he was carrying on the floor and turned inquiringly to Jean.

"Betty has just rung up," she said quickly. "You must go to her at once at the hospital. Lizzie is worse."

"What is the address?"

The question was sharp and yet even in that tense moment Jean thought that she liked his voice, deep and sensible, the voice of a man used to authority. She told him, and before she could do or say anything more he was gone. The door slammed behind him and she heard the taxi drive off. She was left with only a suitcase at her feet to tell her that the brief encounter had not been a figment of her imagination.

Jean carried the suitcase upstairs to Betty's room, switched on the electric fire in the bedroom and turned back the bed. John Wilding might come back and if he did everything should be ready for him.

It was only when she had unpacked and put his things away, guessing where they were usually kept, that she suddenly felt incredibly fatigued as if she had gone through a deep test of endurance. But she knew sleep would be impossible and that she must listen all the time for a ring of the telephone. Finally she made herself a large cup of tea and sat down in the arm-chair in the kitchen.

She must have fallen asleep despite her resolution not to do so, for she dreamt of Tally and woke with a start with his name on her lips. She felt very cold; the fire had gone out and the clock on the mantelpiece told her it was three o'clock in the morning. Shivering a little, she got to her feet. She would do no good by sitting there. She had better go to bed.

She walked upstairs feeling colder and more miserable with every step she took and though she had a hot-water bottle she lay shivering in bed for a long time before finally she fell into a fitful slumber. She was awakened by the alarm clock, which she set every night, ringing to tell her it was half-past seven. She got up at once and found that Jim was awake, as she expected he would be.

"Good morning, Auntie Jean," he said cheerfully.

He was sitting up in bed with his toys round him: a golliwog, a broken engine and two woolly dogs which he loved beyond all else.

"Good morning, Jim. Are you hungry?"

"Very hungry."

"Well, I will go down and get breakfast ready. I should not get up yet because it is very cold. Wait until I come up to you."

"I'se not cold. I help you."

Knowing he was unlikely to stay in bed, Jean dressed him and took him downstairs with her. It was a dull, foggy morning and she felt the dreadful greyness of the atmosphere was echoed in her heart. What news would the morning bring? She listened for the telephone, yet dreaded to hear its ring; and then, just as she was giving Jim a second helping of porridge, she heard a key turn in the front door. She ran out into the hall and to her surprise and her first instinctive recoil of frightened anticipation she saw Betty. It rushed through her mind that it was all over, that Lizzie was dead and Betty had come home. Then with a sudden uplifting of her whole soul she saw that Betty was smiling.

"Oh, Jean, it is all right!"

"Thank God! Is it really?"

"Yes, she will pull through. She took the blood transfusion splendidly and when she came round John was there. She just looked up at him and said: 'Daddy come home to make Lizzie well.' It was just as if she

245

had expected him, and now she is sleeping peacefully. The doctor sent me home while John stays by her. He says I have got to rest."

Betty swayed even while she spoke and Jean saw that despite the quick, excitable note in her voice she was absolutely all in. It was only a question of seconds before she had her upstairs, undressed and into bed; then she ran downstairs to the kitchen to get some hot milk and tell Jim he could go up and kiss his mother good morning.

When she reached the bedroom with the milk, Jim was sitting on the bed beside Betty, his head resting against her shoulder. They made a very pretty picture, but just for a moment Jean felt a pang of envy. Yesterday morning Jim had clung to her and now Betty was back she was forgotten.

"Drink this," she said to Betty.

"I will try to," Betty answered, "but I feel it will choke me. Be careful, Jim, my love; have you been a good boy with Auntie Jean?"

"I'se always a good boy," Jim said with dignity. "When is Daddy coming home?"

"Later. Perhaps he will be back for tea. We will see."

"He will have Lizzie now. Lizzie got everything," Jim said sullenly. "Lizzie had all Mummy and now she has all Daddy."

"Bless me, he's jealous," Betty laughed.

Jean, taking away the empty glass, thought to herself that Betty was the one who had everything—all John, all Jim and all Lizzie. She smiled a little wryly to herself at the thought. What was the point of being jealous? If Betty had less, she wouldn't have more. Besides, Betty was a lovely person and deserved all the happiness in the world. She put the glass down in the kitchen and went upstairs to fetch Jim.

Betty's eyelids were already dropping. She was nearly asleep.

"Thank you, Jean," she said softly, "You are an angel . . . but you know that, don't you?"

She was asleep before she said the last word and Jean,

246

carrying Jim in her arms, went out of the room and shut the door.

"You have got to play very quietly," she said, "because Mummy mustn't be wakened up."

As they went down the stairs, Jim's arms tightened round her neck and he asked:

"Will you play with me?"

Jean nodded.

"Of course I will."

"I love you, Auntie Jean," he said, and with this declaration Jean was comforted.

15

Tally was restless! He did not know why, but somehow even ski-ing seemed to pall on him and he found himself speeding back to the hotel long before the sun sank behind the mountains. He told himself that he missed Gerald's companionship. It was very pleasant when he went up to Gerald's bedroom to find him talking cheerfully while Margaret sat beside his bed, sometimes talking, sometimes lying back in her chair silent, but definitely not so withdrawn into herself as she had been in the past.

The moment Tally entered the room he seemed to bring what was almost an atmosphere of electricity with him. Gerald would turn to him eagerly and even Margaret would become quite animated as they talked over the events of the day and his plans for the morrow. Yet, Tally was not entirely satisfied.

He should have been, because since Jean had gone home it was quite obvious that Melia was kinder and more encouraging in her attitude towards him. In the evenings she would often come unasked and have coffee with Margaret when dinner was over; and on one occasion she openly invited Tally to dance with her, saying in a provocative manner:

"Everyone in the hotel is betting whether we will or will not . . . so let us give them a treat."

They had gone together into the bar, but they danced in silence and when the dance ended Melia led the way back to the lounge and sat herself down by Margaret. Tally made no effort to stop her; he had the idea that all this was premeditated and that Melia was acting according to plan. Worried over Gerald, he had after the accident made no effort to see Melia alone and had contented himself with waving to her when he passed through the lounge or smiling across the dining-room in her direction.

He was wise enough a day or so later to understand that he could have done nothing which would have intrigued Melia more, especially as he was certain in his own mind that she thought Jean's sudden return to England had been made entirely on her account. Tally forbore to disillusion her, not because he wished to encourage such ideas in Melia, but merely because he was too lazy to enter into an argument. He disliked rows and scenes, and Melia's anger on the two occasions he had seen it really roused had made him unwilling to inflame her for no particular reason; but as the days passed, he began to think that perhaps Melia's attitude towards him had changed very considerably.

And Tally was right. Melia's attitude had changed. To begin with, the Prime Minister was not yet dead. Every day bulletins were issued from Downing Street saying that he was critically ill and that the doctors feared there was no hope of saving his life. But he did not die; and though Ernest Danks was still prominent in most people's thoughts in the political world, he was without confirmation of his highest hopes.

Melia therefore had to be content with waiting, an activity in which she had never excelled; and in the crisp, elevating air and amidst the beauty of the mountain scenery, Downing Street, far away, seemed foggy, dark and rather dull.

The impression, too, that Ernest Danks had made on her had begun to fade. He also, far away, seemed dark and somewhat dull. In the meantime there, before her eyes, was Tally—incredibly good-looking, virile, vital, and a person it was not easy to forget even if he were not, as he was at this moment, in the foreground of her attention.

Melia had with her usual skill collected every presentable young man in the hotel around her; but they were not a particularly prepossessing lot; most of them were callow youths enjoying their holidays from the university or rich young business men of doubtful antecedents who thought that Switzerland was a good place to further their social interests. Tally was in a class by himself, and Melia began to regret that she had been so hasty in being "off with the old love" before she was quite certain that she could be "on with the new". Ernest Danks wrote her long letters which she received by air mail practically every day, but the interest of them had begun to pall. For one thing, he wrote almost exclusively about himself and his plans for the future. This, of course, included her, but Ernest Danks was not particularly good at making love either in person or on paper and Melia was used to very voluble love letters.

After she had yawned her way through four pages of Ernest Danks' latest effusions about his political future, she put down the rest of the letter unread and came to the conclusion it was time she did something about Tally. Accordingly that evening she made it very plain that their quarrel, if it had been a quarrel, was over and that she would appreciate his company the following day. Tally was amused at this change in the atmosphere and then chided himself for not being more elated. What was wrong with him? Surely this was what he had been waiting for and like a good general he could smell victory before he pulled off the final coup.

Now he thought of Melia's smile, the touch of her hand as it had pressed on his as they said "good night," and he knew with absolute certainty that it was only a question of days, perhaps hours, before he could take her in his arms again. He thought of that lovely head lying against his shoulders, of her dark eyes raised to his and the softly parted lips of her red mouth. He deliberately imagined her yielding softly . . . he would bend his mouth to hers . . . he would smell the fragrance of her perfume mingled with the flower-like scent which always seemed to emanate from her hair . . . he would hold her close, so close that she would be a little breathless, and then . . .

Tally pulled up his contemplations with a jerk; his thoughts did not seem to be leading quite where he expected, for somehow the idea gave him none of the satisfaction that he had anticipated. His pulses were not roused, he did not even feel eager and ardent, as he had felt before when he had known that some lovely woman whom he had pursued and desired was his for the taking.

"What the devil is the matter with me?" he asked himself out loud, and walking from his own bedroom into his mother's he found her standing in the centre of the room with tears streaming down her face and a look almost of ecstasy in her eyes.

"Mother! What has happened?" he asked.

She held out both her hands to him and he took them in his.

"Something wonderful, Tally," she said at last. "Something so wonderful that I can hardly believe it is true."

"What is it?" he asked.

"Jean has just telephoned me," she said, and then as he looked incredulous that such an explanation should have such an effect on her, she explained what Jean had said. She was so bewildered and so incoherent about it all that Tally left her and went to the telephone himself to speak to Jean. They were cut off before the conversation was finished and in a fury he told the operator to get a re-connection.

"I am sorry, but there is some trouble on the line between here and Zürich," he was told. "There will now be over three hours' delay, perhaps more."

Tally slammed down the receiver. It was infuriating. He had not learned half he wanted to know, and yet he had heard enough to understand that this was something inexpressible, something he had never encountered before in his whole life. If it were true, how much that letter would mean to his mother! He wondered what Stephen could have said. The whole thing was too strange to be either accepted or rejected until the whole of the facts were known.

Tally attributed his restlessness next day and the day after to the change in his mother. She was tense with anticipation, watching every mail with an eagerness that was so pathetic that at times Tally felt terrified that Jean should have raised such high hopes. Supposing the letter was not from Stephen; supposing it contained nothing of any importance. He remembered only too vividly how near his mother had come to losing her mind when Stephen had been killed. She was better now than he had seen her for years and not only was he frightened at the thought that anything might cast her back into the Slough of Despond from which she had emerged so slowly, but the very possibility of it made him extremely angry.

"I will murder Jean if this is all false and untrue," he said to himself out loud, and remembered the frightened look in her eyes when he had been angry with her for going to see Melia, her trembling hands and the little pulse which had beaten so quickly in her white throat.

It was easy to frighten her and yet she had a pride and resilience which came from some inner strength which was unassailable. What a strange contradiction she was in many ways, Tally thought, and he found himself remembering with delight the way her face would light up with pleasure, the dimples at the corner of her mouth, the shining brilliance of her eyes when she was happy.

"She is a nice child," he said, and knew it was not so easy for him to dismiss her from his mind.

She was often there beside him and he told himself it was because he was worrying about her future. He had swept her out of the life to which she belonged and now it would be impossible to put her back and forget about her.

"I feel rather responsible for Jean," he said to his

253

mother and thought that she looked at him rather strangely.

"I am sure you do, dear," was all she said, and there was no condemnation in her tone, rather an acceptance of his statement as if it were a natural one.

"What am I to do about her?" he asked.

"That is for you to decide," Margaret answered, and then added breathlessly, "Do go and ask if there is another post in."

The letter came at tea-time. The concierge handed it across the desk to Margaret as though it was quite an ordinary letter. She took it from him, saw Jean's writing and turned very pale. Tally thought she was going to faint and went up to her, but she moved away from his supporting arm.

"No, no," she said, "I want to be alone."

She turned and sped away through the lounge like a girl running to meet someone she loved.

Tally went and sat down on the sofa where they usually had tea. When the waiter came up for the order, he waved him away. It was no use. He could not behave ordinarily either. Something tremendous was happening and he could not sit calmly drinking tea and eating rich cakes when his mother's future happiness was at stake.

He felt on edge and ready to curse Jean for interfering. But Margaret had undoubtedly seemed better and more human in many ways since Jean had come into their lives. All the same, was this intensity wise or good for her?

He got to his feet on a sudden resolution and went upstairs to Gerald's room. Gerald's tea had been brought to him by the attractive young Swiss nurse who was looking after him. They were laughing together as Tally entered and somehow their lightheartedness annoyed him. Gerald hailed him gaily, but he made the excuse that he was looking for his mother and left the room.

He walked up and down the passage. How long must he wait before he inquired what the letter held? How long must he be kept on tenterhooks before he was able to tell by one look at Margaret's face whether the news was good or bad? He forced himself to go walking up and down for over a quarter of an hour and then at last he knocked on his mother's door. There was no answer and Tally felt his heart drop. She must be too despondent to reply. He knocked again and as there was still no answer, he opened the door.

Every sort of fear was besetting him now. He remembered the sharp drop outside the window. He remembered how desperate Margaret had been; recalled that after the news of Stephen's death they had had to nail down her windows in case she attempted to take her life.

He went into the room as a man might go into action, ready for any emergency, ready to face anything, however terrible. Margaret was sitting in the arm-chair, her eyes wide and tearless, staring straight ahead of her as though she was looking at something outside the room. Her lips were smiling and it seemed to Tally that she looked younger and happier than he had ever seen her before. She had no idea he was there until his voice reached her consciousness.

"Mother!" he said urgently. "Mother!"

She turned to him then, and it was as if she came back to earth from a long, long distance.

"Tally," she said softly, and her voice was faintly surprised as though she hardly expected to see him. Then he saw that she held against her breast with both hands . . . a letter.

"It is all right then?" he asked.

She nodded.

"Is it a letter from Stephen?" he insisted.

"Of course! A letter to me! Oh, Tally, it is so wonderful. Thank God I have got it! Thank God it has found me!"

She moved her hands and looked down at the sheets of paper. There was so much tenderness and so much beauty in her expression that Tally suddenly felt his eyes grow misty. This was his mother as he remembered her when she had been so happy. Gone was the vagueness, the air of withdrawal, the tired unapproachability of the

255

past few years. This was Margaret glowing with happiness, alive and lovely as she had been when Stephen loved her and all her being had been his.

Tally crossed the room. He had intended to sit down on the arm of her chair, but suddenly he found himself kneeling at his mother's knees, his arms around her shoulder and his cheek against hers.

"Tell me about it, darling," he said.

"I can hardly realise it myself as yet," Margaret whispered. "Oh, Tally, this letter explains everything. It casts away all the fears that have haunted me ever since Stephen left. You see, darling," she went on, her tone gathering strength, "I was never quite certain what I believed happened when people died, and stupidly enough Stephen and I never discussed it. I wonder why we didn't and he explains to me here in this letter that it was because he felt shy of mentioning death when your father had died . . . and he knew how much he had loved me. But Stephen really believed in his heart that love is greater than all things and that where love is there can be no death, no dividing. He wrote this letter when he knew he was going East, and in it he says:

'I hope and pray, darling, that you will never receive it and that I shall come back and be able to tear it up. But in case anything happens to me, I want you to know that I shall always be near you, always be waiting until the moment when we are re-united again. It won't be for long because time is unimportant and does not exist in the vast scheme of the Universe. It is a limitation imposed by man; and so if you have to wait years without seeing me, do not think that I shall not be there, because I shall be—always.'

Margaret's eyes, wide and starry, looked into Tally's.

"You see, darling, I was so afraid that I had lost him for ever."

"I never thought you could do that," Tally said simply.

"How wrong I have been! How stupid!" Margaret said. "I have wasted so much time crying when I might
256

have been trying to get in touch with him, feeling him, being convinced that he was near me."

"I wonder why you couldn't?" Tally asked. "Why should he make himself known to a complete stranger like Jean?"

"I have asked myself that question, too," Margaret said, "and Jean gave me the answer."

"What did she say?" Tally asked.

"It was when she was trying to explain to me what she had felt about the photograph the first time she went to Berkeley Square. She told me how vivid and real Stephen seemed to her, as if he was trying to speak, and she said that when she was a child she sometimes had strange feelings, moments of being 'fey' as her old nurse used to call it; but when she was so unhappy she could never experience them. She said she thought unhappiness deadens one's inner self and blankets it with a kind of fog."

"She said that, did she?" Tally asked.

"Yes," Margaret answered. "She was explaining herself, of course, but even as she said it I saw what I had done. I had blanketed with unhappiness my perception, my awareness by which I could know that Stephen was there. It would be impossible for him to get to me through the darkness with which I had covered myself. Oh, Tally, I see it all so clearly now. This letter has released me, swept away everything which has made my life miserable. There are many, many more things in it, of course, wonderful things such as only Stephen could say to me. I feel a changed person; I feel like someone who has been born again. I am alive and Stephen is alive, and very soon we shall be together."

Tally held his mother close. He had no words in which to express his own feelings, but he knew that she understood. She pressed her cheek against his and he thought that he could almost feel the happiness throbbing through her. They were together, mother and son, united by a sympathy and understanding deeper than anything they had ever known before in the whole of their lives.

At last they drew apart. Tally got to his feet, and Margaret still holding her precious letter, walked across the room and stood looking down at Stephen's photograph by her bed.

"What a fool I have been!" she said, and yet her tone, which was light and joyous, belied the statement. She turned round: "How can I ever thank Jean, Tally? What can we do for her, this child who has done so much for us?"

"It is strange, isn't it?" Tally said. "It was the luckiest thing I ever did when I found her crying in my office."

"Quite the luckiest, Tally," his mother agreed.

It was some time later that Tally went to Gerald's room and told him what had happened. Gerald was as excited as Tally had known he would be.

"It is amazing!" he kept saying. "I can hardly believe it is true, can you, old boy?"

"I have been so frightened that it would not be true," Tally said, "while I have waited for the letter to arrive; but I am still keeping my fingers crossed in case it is all a dream."

"I am so glad for Mrs. Melton," Gerald said. "Do you know. Jean said something to me the first day we went to Berkeley Square . . . Of course, now I come to think of it, it was immediately after she had seen the photograph."

"What did she say?" Tally asked curiously.

"I can't exactly remember the conversation," Gerald replied, "but I think she asked who Stephen was and I was telling her about your mother and how unhappy she was, when Jean said: 'She can't be a very religious woman.' It struck me at the time that Jean herself must have a pretty strong faith. I have the feeling that Jean could always be trusted in her judgment of people. Betty is like that. It is a sort of simplicity in them; they go right to the depths of a person while we are still groping about on the surface."

Tally was quiet for a moment and then very surprisingly he said to Gerald:

"You don't like Melia, do you, Gerald?"

258

Gerald hesitated and then told the truth.

"No, Tally."

"Why?"

The question was sharp and Gerald looked embarrassed.

"Look, old boy, I am a great friend of yours and very fond of you. I don't want to start an argument and I am not in a position to hit you back if you hit me."

"I am not going to hit you, you clown, but I would like you to answer that question."

Gerald hesitated.

"I may be quite wrong," he said at length, "but I have a feeling that she is the very opposite of what we have been saying about Jean. She is superficial . . . now, don't be angry," he added hastily, "you made me tell you."

"Yes, I know," Tally said in an unusually serious tone of voice.

There was no time to say more, for at that moment the Swiss nurse came into the room.

"Miss Melchester asks if she can enter, Captain Fairfax?"

The two men looked at each other and laughed.

"Talk of the devil," Tally said.

Gerald pretended to look shocked.

"Really, I thought we were speaking of Melia!"

The nurse straightened the pillows behind Gerald's head, took up the tea-tray and said:

"I ask her to come in, yes?"

"Yes, of course," Gerald replied.

Melia entered the room a moment later. She had changed from her ski-ing suit into a dress of ruby-red wool which she wore with a short coat trimmed with sable. She looked exquisitely lovely and she gave first Gerald and then Tally one of her slow, inimitable smiles which were calculated to make any man who received them feel extremely fortunate.

"How are you, Gerald dear?" she asked. "I have been thinking of you so often and feeling so terribly sorry for you, cooped up here while we are outside in the sunshine."

259

"Oh, but I get the sun too," Gerald said. "They move my bed up to the window. I can even watch you skating elegantly on the ice."

"Can you?" Melia asked. "I shall remember to wave to you tomorrow."

"That will be nice of you," Gerald replied.

Melia looked at Tally who was standing on the other side of the room.

"Will you take me to a dance in St. Moritz tonight?" she asked Tally. "I have promised to join up with a party of friends at Chesa Veglia."

It seemed to her that Tally hesitated for just a second and then she thought she had imagined it as he answered:

"But of course I will."

Somehow Tally was not surprised when they reached Chesa Veglia late in the evening to find that the party had not materialised and he and Melia were alone. An old Swiss inn with all its characteristics left unchanged, Chesa Veglia had an atmosphere all its own. Upstairs was a big dance-hall with tiny tables covered with gay cloths, a balcony from where one could watch the dancers, and every form of gaiety and amusement.

Downstairs there was a long, low-ceilinged room divided by wooden screens with a small dance-floor in the centre and a pianist whose melodies haunted the air and who played exclusively for lovers. Here the lights were low, the atmosphere seductive, and Melia preceded Tally to a quiet, shadowy corner where they sat with a little check-covered table in front of them.

They talked very little, but Tally knew that there was an invitation in Melia's eyes. Her voice was very low and sweet and there was no sharpness on her tongue. They rose to dance and he felt her slim and lissom in his arms. Her cheek was very near to his and her mouth provocatively close. The pianist played old melodies which brought back old memories. Melia told the waiter to take him over a glass of champagne and then asked for one or two favourite tunes to which she and Tally had danced in London.

"Do you remember?" she asked, and Tally knew that she was doing all this for his benefit. He should have felt glad, but something within him drew back with resentment. He liked to do his own hunting; he liked to be the chaser and not the chased. He uncomfortably felt that Melia was playing with him; that he was only a puppet dancing to the strings she pulled.

He was too masterful and had too strong a nature not to enjoy fighting against opposition and he was always faintly dissatisfied when he was the conqueror. He had not expected to feel like this about Melia, but suddenly it seemed to be a very tame ending to his quest. She had not yet capitulated, but the moment was very near when he need have no further anxiety. But instead of being glad and thrilled he found himself withdrawing a little, staring down his wineglass instead of into Melia's eyes, and ignoring the hand she had laid enticingly near to his own on the sofa on which they were both sitting.

Once again they rose to dance and this time Melia, throwing back her head, looked up at him and asked:

"Are you happy, Tally?"

"Are you?" he parried.

"Very," she answered, and added softly. "Sometimes I am a very silly person, Tally. I do things impulsively. You will have to bear with me and try to be understanding."

It was both an apology and an invitation, Tally knew that; but something strange within him made him say almost brutally:

"What do you mean by that?"

Melia's eyes widened.

"What do you want it to mean?"

Tally looked away from her.

"I am not very good at fencing."

Melia laughed.

"You are trying to punish me, aren't you, Tally?"

"Am I?"

He was deliberately being obtuse, deliberately avoiding every lead she gave him.

"We have known each other so long," Melia said. "I

261

think it would be very silly if we had to put everything into words. Shall I say something which I think you will understand?"

She paused.

"Yes?" Tally asked.

"Sometimes one makes mistakes," she whispered.

"But not you?" Tally said, "surely not the infallible Melia?"

"You are teasing me," Melia pouted, "and I am trying to be very, very nice to you."

"After being very, very nasty." Tally answered.

"Do you mind so very much?" Melia inquired.

Tally laughed.

"Didn't I look miserable?"

"You behaved very badly," Melia retorted, but there was nothing disagreeable in her voice.

She moved a little closer to him as they danced.

"But I forgive you," she murmured.

"Thank you!"

"And now we can be happy again, can't we?" Melia asked.

"Would you like to tell me exactly what you are driving at?"

Melia sighed.

"You are being rather difficult tonight, Tally. I think you know what I mean."

"Do I? I used to think I did a long time ago, and then I realised I was entirely mistaken. Now I am being cautious, exceptionally cautious."

"Oh dear," she said, pouting a little, but he saw that she was not annoyed. She was so sure of herself.

The music came to an end and they went back to their table. It seemed to Tally that they were isolated and alone. The room was now full of people, yet he and Melia might have been together on a high mountain. There was something they had to face together, a decision that had to be made. Everything faded and paled in comparison with the fundamental issue at stake.

Tally ordered more drinks from the waiter and then leaned back and looked at Melia. She was wearing white tonight and there was a string of perfect pearls around her neck. There were also pearls in her ears and a white camellia in her dark hair. She was lovely enough to make any man's heart beat quickly, and once again Tally asked himself what was the matter with his.

This was the girl he had always wanted for his wife. This was the girl he had imagined bearing his name. Lady Brora! He had imagined her at the head of the long table when it was laden with the gold and silver ornaments that were heirlooms and which would one day be inherited by his son. He had imagined her standing under the chandeliers in Berkeley Square, receiving their guests, the Brora diamonds glittering in her dark hair. He could imagine her at Greystones . . . No, by God, he couldn't!

He tried to think of her going round the estate as his mother had done; tried to see her entering the cottages, giving away the prizes at school, knowing the children on the estate by name, visiting their mothers when they were sick. It was no use; he could not see Melia doing any of these things any more than he could see her sitting on the other side of the fireplace during the long winter evenings.

Tally had a sudden vision of Greystones as it must be at this moment. Grey against the wintry sky, the snow on the lawns and icicles hanging from the bridge over the lake. Perhaps there would be a glint of sunshine which would be reflected on the many windows, and perhaps the pigeons would wheel in sudden flight around the flagpost on the top of the house.

How he loved the place! How he loved Bredon Hill standing like a sentinel behind it! He knew then what he wanted . . . only as the knowledge came to him was he aware that Melia was looking at him, waiting for him to speak. He had no idea what she had said or what he was expected to answer; instead he called to the waiter and asked for his bill.

It was moonlight outside and the car was waiting to take them back to the hotel. Wrapped in her fur coat, Melia snuggled down into the rugs.

"How cold it is!" she said softly, and as the chauffeur shut the door and climbed into the front she looked up at Tally and moved a little closer to him. He knew what was expected of him. They were alone together in the scented darkness, and in the light of the moon he could see the lovely oval of Melia's face and the invitation on her lips. He hesitated, and then to be absolutely sure, to convince himself, he bent forward.

"What are you trying to tell me, Melia?" he asked, and his mouth was very near to hers.

"I am not trying to tell you anything," she answered, her eyelashes flickering.

"Aren't you?"

"Perhaps I am."

Her mouth was very near now, and suddenly Melia reached up her arm and drew his head down to hers.

"I have missed you, Tally," she whispered, and kissed him.

For a moment he held her closely, a moment when he told himself that his own coldness, his own lack of response was only imagination. Then he knew the truth.

He took his arm away from her and raised his head.

"It is no use, Melia," he said quietly. "It is too late!"

She stared at him in bewilderment. It was the first time in the whole of her life that anyone had kissed Melia Melchester and let her go.

"What do you mean?" she asked.

"I mean, Melia, that once I should have been in the seventh heaven if you had been as kind to me as you have been tonight, but now I am only sorry."

"Sorry!" Melia said sharply. "For whom?"

"Perhaps for us both," Tally said gently, "because we have wasted so much time."

"I don't understand!" Melia cried.

"I think you do," Tally said. "Some things, Melia dear, are best not put into words. I will only say one thing and I mean this in all sincerity: I hope that you will find great happiness in your life. I would like to think of you being as happy as my mother was with Stephen, as

Betty is with John Wilding, and I hope one day to find that sort of happiness myself."

For once Melia was completely bereft of speech, bereft of words in which to express herself. Her mouth opened a little in surprise; she stared at Tally as if he had gone mad; and then, before there was a chance to say anything more, the car drew up at the hotel and the porter was opening the door.

It was still quite early and there were people sitting in the lounge and coming away from the bar. Tally stopped at the lift.

"Good night, Melia."

"But, Tally . . . we can't part like this. There is so much I want to say to you."

"I don't think there is," Tally answered.

Melia looked up at him. She knew by Tally's expression that he was finished, knew that once he had made up his mind nothing would change him. Angrily she turned away her head.

"Very well then, if you want to say 'good-bye.' "

"Good-bye," Tally repeated, and he would have moved away but she put out her hand to stop him.

"Tally, what are you going to do?"

"I am not quite certain," he answered gravely, "but I think I am going to London."

16

"How are we going to thank you, Jean?" John Wilding asked.

"For what?" Jean asked absently, bending across the table to pull Jim's plate nearer to him and arrange the napkin tucked round his neck, so that an overflow from a too-full spoon would fall on it and not on his blue jersey.

"You know quite well what I mean," John answered, and Jean smiled at him.

"I don't want to be thanked," she replied; "I can't tell you how happy it has made me to be able to help Betty."

"Betty was talking about it last night," John said, "and we felt we ought to do something really wonderful for you, but we just don't know what."

"You have done something wonderful for me already," Jean replied. "At least Betty has in letting me be her friend and in allowing me to look after your quite adorable son."

Jim looked up and said with his mouth full:

"That's me!"

Both Jean and John burst out laughing.

"We must be careful what we say in front of him," John said, trying to speak seriously. "He is getting much too pleased with himself and it is about time I came home."

"I believe Betty has been feeling that for a long time," Jean answered: "but I still think it was a miracle that you arrived when you did."

"As a matter of fact it took me quite a bit of wangling," John answered, and the satisfied expression on his face was so absurdly like Jim's when he was pleased with himself that Jean found herself beginning to laugh again.

"What's the joke?" John asked suspiciously.

"I shan't tell you," Jean replied. "I think Betty would appreciate it, but go on with what you were saying."

"Well, when I got Betty's letter telling me about Lizzie, I seemed to sense that things were a good deal worse than she was making out," John told her. "She has always tried to prevent me from being anxious about the children when I am away, but this time I read between the lines. So I went to see the old man—that's the Captain—and asked him if I could have compassionate leave. I had done him a pretty good turn during the war and I knew he was not likely to refuse me."

"What good turn did you do him?" Jean asked.

"Well, as a matter of fact I saved his life," John answered, "but that's another story."

"Did he thank you?" Jim asked with interest.

"Yes," his father replied.

"Did he give you a present?"

"The present he gave me was letting me fly home to see Lizzie."

Jean sighed.

"I shall never forget how glad I was to see you. It really seemed as if you appeared as an answer to prayer. I was utterly desperate and didn't know what to do. Betty had just rung me up and I could not go to her as it would have meant leaving Jim alone; then I heard your key in the door . . ."

"And you gave me orders as if you were the old man himself. If I had had time to think of anything, I should have been overcome by your efficiency."

Jean smiled.

"You are making me sound terrible, but I don't mind. Betty said that if you hadn't got to Lizzie just then, anything might have happened."

"Betty was just about all in herself," John agreed.

"Well, after this I am going to take the whole family away for a holiday. I don't care what it costs. They need a change and, incidentally, I want to see a bit of them. Jim and I are almost strangers to each other, aren't we, old boy?"

"No, you are my Daddy," Jim said scornfully and looked surprised at the laughter which followed.

"Where will you go?" Jean asked.

"I have not really decided yet," John replied, "I should like to take them to Switzerland."

"Oh, they would love it!" Jean exclaimed. "I can just see Jim on skis. Even smaller children than he go ski-ing and what is so humiliating is that they are so much better than I shall ever be."

"You enjoyed St. Moritz, didn't you?" John asked.

"It was wonderful," Jean answered. "I shall never forget the mountains, and the sunshine on the snow was almost too beautiful to be believed."

"And yet you left it to come back here and help us?"

"Now, don't start that again," Jean admonished. "More pudding, Jim?"

"No, thank you, Auntie Jean. Can I get down?"

"Yes, darling. Say your grace."

Jean got up to take his napkin off, wipe his mouth and pull back his chair. John watched her and as Jim scampered to the corner of the room where until luncheon was ready he had been absorbed in a game of soldiers, he said:

"Tally is a jolly lucky fellow, but I suppose everybody has told him that."

Jean was still for a moment, then she turned away towards the mantelpiece so that John might not see her face.

"When are you going to get married?" he continued.

"I don't know," Jean answered.

There was something in her voice which told John that she did not wish to continue this conversation. He got up from the table and took a cigarette out of the silver box on the sideboard. There was a little pause during which they were both thinking of something to say. Jean turned round:

"I must wash up and take Jim for his walk. Are you going to the hospital?"

"Yes, I am relieving Betty at three o'clock. I expect she will come back here and have tea with you, but she ought to get a breath of air first."

"Yes, of course," Jean agreed.

"I will take Jim for a walk," John said. "I would rather enjoy it."

"Yes, do," Jean said enthusiastically. "You would love that, wouldn't you, Jim?"

"Go now?" Jim asked hopefully, jumping up from the floor.

"In two or three minutes, old man. Let me finish my cigarette first," John replied.

"I will go and get my coat," Jim said, and they heard him patter across the hall and start slowly to climb the stairs.

"He is very independent," Jean explained. "It is splendid to see all the things that he can do for himself."

"You know I am leaving the Navy, don't you?" John asked.

"Betty did mention it," Jean replied.

"I have not told Betty yet, but I have got the offer of a pretty good job. It is with a firm of engineers and the best thing about it is that we can live out of London. They have got a factory at St. Albans and I know Betty will be thrilled when I tell her that we can move to the country."

"How wonderful!" Jean exclaimed.

"Yes, we shall all be together at last," John said. "I have dreamt about this for years."

There was a smile at the corner of his lips; a tender smile, and Jean thought of Betty's joy and excitement when she heard his news. There was a little choke in her throat as she took up the dishes and carried them into the kitchen. She wondered if she would ever see an expression like that on Tally's face. Would he ever look tenderly and lovingly at his wife, utterly content because he and she could be together alone with their children? A tear dropped from her eyes into the basin of washing-up water.

"What a fool I am," Jean said aloud, "crying for the moon!"

At that moment she heard the telephone ringing and wiping her hands, she hurried to answer it. It was Betty.

"Oh, Jean, are you all right? Lizzie has just dropped off to sleep after eating quite a good lunch and I had to ring up to see how you all are."

"We are all right," Jean answered; "Jim has had two helpings of everything, likewise John, so I don't think you need worry about either of them."

"I'm not worrying about either of them," Betty answered. "I'm only frightened that you will spoil them so much that they won't want me back."

"I don't think you need worry about that," Jean answered. "When are you coming back?"

"That is one of the reasons why I rang up," Betty said. "I wanted to tell you that I am coming home tonight. The doctor thinks Lizzie will be all right now with a night nurse and if she goes on as well as she is doing, he will let her come home at the end of the week."

"How marvellous!" Jean exclaimed.

"Yes, isn't it?" Betty said; "when the surgeon saw her this morning he was delighted with her."

"What did the doctor say about you?" Jean asked.

"Oh, he was ridiculous. Said I must rest and all the usual things. He need not worry about that now that John is home. I shall recover as quickly as Lizzie. John is the only tonic I want, you know that."

"Yes, I do know that," Jean agreed. "Shall I call him now and you can tell him your news?"

"Yes, do; and Jean, be an angel and iron my best nightgown for me. You will find it in the top drawer of the chest of drawers in the bedroom. I have been keeping it for over a year until John should come home. I washed it the other day because it looked tired of waiting, but I never had time to iron it."

271

"I will do it for you."

"Thank you, darling."

Jean put the receiver on the table and went to call John. He was sitting in the arm-chair in the dining-room where she had left him.

"Betty is on the telephone," she said.

She saw the light in his eyes and the quick eager way in which he sprang to his feet. She went back to the kitchen so that she could not overhear anything that was said.

She finished the washing up, took off her apron and rolled down the sleeves of her jumper; then she got the ironing board ready and went upstairs to fetch Betty's nightgown.

Jim was in his bedroom slowly buttoning up his over-coat.

"I'se all ready, Auntie Jean," he said, " 'cept I can't tie the laces of my shoes."

"I will do that for you," Jean said, kneeling down beside him. "Have you got your gloves?"

He pulled them out of the pocket of his coat.

"You are a very clever boy," she said. "Now tell Daddy you are ready."

"I'se been helpful, hasn't I?" Jim asked. "Mummy said I'se to be helpful."

"You have been very helpful," Jean replied. "Give me a kiss."

He put his lips against her cheek and then started to pound down the stairs, shouting "Daddy!" as he went. A few minutes later Jean heard the front door slam and knew they were gone.

She went into Betty's bedroom and took the nightgown from the top drawer and then stood for a few minutes looking round her. It was a pretty bedroom. The walls were in a soft shade of peach, and the curtains were a gay chintz of coloured flowers on a peach background. There was a big bed which Betty had told her had been her father's wedding present to them.

"He did not approve of the modern habit of twin beds," she said, "and John and I agreed with him. We like our big bed even though it does take up so much room."

There certainly was not much space for a lot of furniture. The dressing-table with its chintz covers caught the light from the window and there was just room for a chest of drawers by the door. But it was a happy room, Jean thought, and she decided that she would buy some flowers when she went out and put them on the dressing-table for Betty.

It was then for the first time that she felt herself unwanted. John and Betty would wish to be alone this evening. It would be the first moment since he returned that they would have had the chance of talking and being together without anxiety hanging over them, without their fear for Lizzie clouding everything they said or did.

Jean put her hand in her pocket and drew out a letter which had reached her that morning. It had come to her air mail from St. Moritz and for one moment she had thought that it was from Tally, but when she looked at the writing she knew she was mistaken and guessed it was from her mother.

It was a long letter and a sad one. Patience Plowden was doing her best to reach out her arms to the child she had deserted so many years earlier, but the years of separation could not be bridged so easily.

I know you are engaged to be married, dear, she wrote, *and your plans for the future are made; but if at any time you want to come to me, there is always a room waiting for you here and I want you to be certain that I shall be very pleased to see you. We hardly know each other, but somehow I feel that we could be real friends. I would like to know you better, little Jean; so remember that if you need a friend you can always count on your mother.*

Jean read the letter through twice and then she folded the pages together and put them back in the envelope. She thought of her mother, thought of her as they first met, remembered that thrilling voice holding spellbound the crowds of people in the big ballroom.

Had they much in common? Could they be friends?

She was not sure of the answer. It was difficult to understand her own feelings. Her mother had meant so little in her life until she had found the letter and the newspaper cuttings in her aunt's bureau; and then she had been filled with bitterness and an almost fanatical hatred for the woman who not only had left her when she was only a baby, but who was almost directly responsible for the suffering and misery she had experienced in her aunt's house. She had thought of her then as someone of whom she must be ashamed, of a shadow, dark and sinister, clouding and despoiling her childhood. It was difficult to readjust herself to the thought of Patience Plowden—brilliant, intelligent, and very charming.

Something within Jean shrank instinctively from taking advantage of the proffered kindness. It was easy, she thought bitterly, for Patience Plowden to be friendly to a daughter whom she believed was making an important marriage. Would she be just as gracious and equally welcoming to an impoverished girl without a penny to her name and no background of any sort?

There was in the question a cynicism which Jean knew was unworthy of her even while she asked it; and remembering her mother's gallant war record, she was ashamed of herself. At the same time she found it difficult to respond whole-heartedly to such belated kindness.

What then did the future hold for her? Could she ask Betty to look after her? If she told Betty she wanted a job, it would mean revealing Tally's secret to yet another person without his permission. But need she worry about that? At this moment Tally was very likely re-engaged to Melia and it was only a question of days, perhaps hours, before the whole world would know that her own engagement to Tally had been nothing more than a flash in the pan. With a sigh Jean left the bedroom, shutting the door behind her, and went downstairs.

She ironed Betty's nightgown, tidied the dining-room,

274

made up the fire in the drawing-room and was on the point of going upstairs to put on her outdoor things when the telephone rang again. She hurried to answer it and this time it was a telegram and it was for herself. She wrote it down to the dictation of the operator:

Flying over tomorrow. Dine with me tomorrow night. Tally.

That was all! It was so typical of him that she smiled. He had forgotten, of course, that she was not Melia and therefore would not have a crowd of young men pressing her to dine with them. He had to make sure that she was free simply because all his life he was used to women who must be dated at least twenty-four hours ahead, otherwise they would have another engagement. Jean smiled and then her heart, which had begun to beat quickly, gave a sickening thud. Tally had asked her to dinner. She knew only too well why he was coming.

It was, of course, to tell her about Melia. Why else should he fly over? What was the hurry unless plans were afoot which would brook no delay?

It was then she knew with absolute certainty that this was the one thing she could not face. She could not bear his voice, calm and impersonal, thanking her for her services and saying good-bye. He would offer to help her, of course, perhaps in money. She would be discharged like a servant who was no longer any use. He would touch her hand, he would smile at her and she would look up into his eyes, those eyes in which she had seen every sort of expression at one time or another. This time they would be kindly and friendly, and Jean knew that she simply could not bear it. If only she could stir some sort of emotion in him, even of anger, rather than that he should just say good-bye pleasantly and in the tone of voice one would use to an acquaintance who had made herself very pleasant.

"I cannot bear it, I cannot!" she said out loud, and the intensity of her feelings shook her so that she realised she was trembling and her hands were clenched.

She looked wildly round her. Suddenly Betty's house had become a prison in which she must wait until Tally

275

came to offer her not escape, but merely a living death because she would know him no longer. She knew now that without him the world would always be grey, the sunshine would be dimmed and there would be no happiness for her.

"I am like Margaret Melton," she told herself, "I can love one man and one man only in my life." Yes, that was true! She was as sure of it as if she had been told so by someone older and wiser than herself. She was the faithful type. A person who would love with all her heart and soul to the exclusion of all else. But what did that matter? That was her problem to face in the future, while immediately before her was the horror and the agony of Tally saying good-bye.

"I cannot bear it, I cannot!" she said again and at that moment she decided what she must do.

She sat down first of all at Betty's desk in the drawing-room and wrote a letter. It was not a long letter. In it she told Betty that she had had to go away unexpectedly and hoped she would understand. She thanked her for all the happiness she had found in her house and for the kindness she had shown her.

There were tears in Jean's eyes as she gave her love to Jim and to Lizzie, and then at the bottom she wrote:

I believe Tally is coming over tomorrow. Will you, please, give him the suitcase which I have left in my bedroom and also a letter which I am leaving here with yours?

She folded her letter to Betty, slipped it into an envelope, and then took another sheet of paper. Her letter to Tally consisted of only three lines, but it took her a long time to write. When at last it was finished, she jumped up from the writing-table and went downstairs.

She made some cakes for tea and a pie for supper; then she cleaned and prepared the vegetables, putting them ready in their saucepans. When that was done, she laid the tea and afterwards went upstairs to her bedroom. She packed quickly. She realised that she had not got much time before Betty would be arriving, but her clothes were soon stowed away into the suitcase and she left the house wearing the blue dress and coat that she had worn that first evening when she had gone down to Greystones. She carried a small cardboard box which she had taken from Betty's store-cupboard.

When the door of the house slammed behind her, she looked both ways as if deciding which way to go and then walked straight ahead until she came to the bus stop. She took a bus which deposited her not far from Tally's flat. She went up to the big block which she had only visited once and having entered the building rang for the lift attendant.

"Is there anyone in Lord Brora's flat?" she inquired.

"I think his manservant is away," he said sourly.

"I wonder if you can help me," she said. "I am Lord Brora's fiancée, Miss MacLeod . . ."

His attitude changed.

"Good afternoon, Miss," he said, and touched his cap.

"What I want," Jean went on, "is a suitcase that I left in the flat before Lord Brora and I left for Switzerland. Do you think you could get it for me?"

"Certainly, Miss. You say a suitcase?"

"Yes. A black one."

The man nodded and went up in the lift while Jean waited. She moved restlessly about the hall until the lift came down again and the attendant stepped out carrying the suitcase she had purchased in Glendale when she had first intended coming to London.

"Is this the one you mean, Miss?"

"Thank you."

Jean tipped him and turned towards the door.

"Will you be wanting a taxi, Miss, or have you got a car?"

"No. I will walk, thank you. I have not got far to go."

He looked at her in surprise and Jean realised that Tally's friends as a rule did not walk away from the building carrying heavy suitcases.

She hurried off and only when she was round a corner

and out of sight did she set the suitcase down and wonder where she should go. The first thing was to find a lodging for the night, the second to look for work.

She had made up her mind now that she had got to escape not only from Tally, but from the life into which he had introduced her. She told herself that her only hope of facing the future was to dismiss all this as if it had been a wonderful dream. She had got to start again and forget the Jean MacLeod who had worn Michael Sorrel's clothes, who had been on equal terms with such people as Margaret Melton and Gerald Fairfax. She must go back into obscurity. She must become what she had been before—a quiet, unobtrusive typist whom no one would notice in the great pulsating crowds of London.

She picked up her suitcase again. Better try one of the suburbs for a lodging; but before she did this, she must change her appearance. She went to a public lavatory in Oxford Street. Here she took off her dress and coat and put on the old, ill-fitting tweed coat and skirt that she had worn when she first came to London. Either she had forgotten how terrible it was or else her eye had become used to the cut and finish of the expensive clothes she had been wearing. Anyway, she was quite horrified at her appearance when she looked at herself in the mirror.

She put her hands up to her hair to pull it away from her cheeks and twist it into the old familiar bun she had worn at the nape of her neck, but somehow she could not bring herself to do that. The coat and skirt had changed her appearance enough, and she contented herself with putting on the unattractive brown hat which matched it, stowing away in her suitcase the little feather cap which had framed her face like a halo. Once again Jean looked at herself in the glass. For a moment her eyes swam with tears and then she said to herself sharply:

"Come along, Jean MacLeod, pull yourself together and stop being sentimental. You've had a good time, but it is over and the sooner you face facts the better."

Her voice reminded her of her aunt's. That was the way she would have spoken. Jean tried to laugh at the imitation, but failed because her voice broke on a sob.

She picked up her suitcase, left the lavatory and got on to the first bus she saw. She bought a fourpenny ticket without asking where it would take her. Half an hour later she found herself in Streatham. It had been raining a little when she got into the bus, but by the time she got out it was almost a downpour. There was a wind, too, which seemed to cut into her as she staggered along laden with her suitcase and the cardboard box, looking up at every house as she passed in the hope of seeing "Apartments to Let." Finally, when her arm was aching and she was wet and bedraggled, she asked a policeman.

"Can you tell me, Officer, where I could get a lodging for the night?"

He looked her up and down and Jean knew he was deciding what she could afford to pay.

"Difficult to know what to advise," he said after a moment. "You might try Arcadia Road. There's two or three houses down there that lets lodgings."

"Oh, thank you," Jean said. "Which way do I go?"

"First turning on the right and the second on the left."

It was some distance and Jean was soaked through by the time she reached Arcadia Road. At the first two houses she was told they had no accommodation to offer her, but at the third the landlady hesitated.

"Oh, please take me in," Jean said desperately. "It is such an awful night and I don't know where else to try if you can't help me."

"Well, I really don't let temporarily."

"If I like it, I would like to stay."

"That's different, then."

The woman looked thin and harassed. She led Jean up a long flight of dingy stairs and showed her a small, inadequately furnished room on the third floor.

"This is really a double room," she said sharply, as if expecting to be contradicted, "so I couldn't take less than 35s. a week for it. It is two guineas with breakfast, and other meals are extra. Baths are extra too, of course."

"I will take it," Jean said wearily.

It would be more than she could afford, she was certain of that, but at the moment she was so desperately tired and so wet that she would willingly have paid double.

"You will be wanting supper?" the woman asked.

"No, thank you," Jean answered.

She felt she never wanted to eat anything again. She just wanted to be alone.

The landlady shut the door behind her. Jean put down her suitcase and as she did so caught sight of herself in the mirror over the dressing-table. For a long moment she stared at the stranger she saw there; at the ill-fitting, ugly clothes; at the fair hair lank and wet against a white face pinched with cold and tragic with unhappiness. This was a stranger in appearance, and yet the aching misery in her heart and the pain within her breasts were all too familiar. Jean sank down in a chair and hid her face in her hands.

17

Tally was humming to himself as he finished dressing and fixed a red carnation into the button-hole of his dinner jacket. He was looking forward to an enjoyable evening and had in fact been anticipating this moment ever since he left St. Moritz before dawn.

As he flew in the aeroplane high above the clouds, he had thought of Jean and realised that he was starting off on what was in reality a quest. He was about to make a discovery—what it was he was not quite sure—but he was certain that it was of importance and something he had desired for a long time.

He felt in himself that strange sense of urgency and of excitement which was always the prelude to adventure. The curtain was rising on another episode in his life, and for once he was not certain of his goal. There was to him something attractive and at the same time enticing about this uncertainty, and at the back of his mind was the belief that here at last was what he had been seeking and waiting for all his life.

In argument and in debate Tally had often propounded the theory that Don Juan was not a great lover but merely an idealist who had never discovered the perfect woman. In his own adventures he had always felt that he was looking for something greater and better than the small triumphs which inevitably were his after a hard-fought fight. There had been an inevitability about them which in itself was disappointing, and far more often than he cared to admit, the glittering prize when it was finally won seemed dull and unexciting and he was left with a feeling of bathos.

What did he want of Jean? He could not for the moment even formulate that within himself. He only knew that she attracted him because of her unexpectedness. His thoughts had begun to centre round her for longer than he realised; and now in this last amazing development, when entirely on her own initiative she had brought happiness and comfort to his mother, he had realised that she was indeed very different from any other girl he had ever known.

Tally was also honest enough with himself to know that his lack of interest in Melia was not unconnected with Jean. But it was not entirely a question of being off with the old love and on with the new. He had begun to question if Melia had ever meant more to him than something that was difficult to attain. He knew now that he had never loved her. He had admired her beauty; he had wanted to possess it even as a man might wish to possess a beautiful vase or a picture which, while giving him pleasure, could neither change nor in any great degree enrich his life.

He had wakened up to the fact that to hold a lovely woman in one's arms was not enough in itself. It might satisfy the body, but the mind and the spirit would be crying out for something more. It was, he told himself, this new knowledge which urged him to return to London and to see Jean.

It seemed to Tally that she had become greatly enhanced in his estimation since he had last spoken to her. Then she had been a pretty, attractive girl who had done him good service. He had liked her; he had enjoyed giving her pleasure because she was so natural, unspoilt and spontaneous. But she had not seemed to him in any way extraordinary; she had not awakened in him a desire to know her better, or incited a sense of spiritual hunger which must be satisfied because its demands were so peremptory.

"Maybe I am exaggerating the whole thing," Tally

said to himself in the aeroplane and wondered, as he had already wondered a dozen times, why his mother had been so reticent at his abrupt departure. Neither she nor Gerald had questioned him when he announced lightly that he was returning to London for a few days.

"I am coming back, of course," he explained, and added to Gerald, "We ought to be able to take you home in about a week, old boy."

He waited for their comments and had the impression, though only a vague one, that they were deliberately silent.

"I hope you won't have too bad a journey," his mother said quietly. "The newspapers say there is fog over the Channel."

"Oh, I shall be all right," Tally answered, and was puzzled as to why they did not ask him the reason for his journey.

When he went into his mother's bedroom to say good-bye, because he would be leaving long before she was awake in the morning, he said:

"You will be all right, Mother, won't you?"

"Of course, darling!"

She gave him a radiant smile and he had the feeling that she would always be all right now wherever she was.

"If I see Jean, shall I give her your love?" he asked.

"Of course! I wrote to her today to try and thank her; not that one could do that in words. Tell her I hope to see her very soon."

"She had better come down to Greystones when you get back," Tally suggested.

"I think that would be a very good idea."

Margaret said nothing more and Tally somehow felt that she was deliberately refraining from making any comment.

"Well," he said at last, rather lamely, "I shall be able to tell her how different you are. You won't mind my saying that?"

"To Jean?" his mother questioned. "No, of course not. She . . . she understands."

283

Tally had wanted to ask her why Jean should understand—why this young girl, a stranger of whom they knew nothing, should have crept into their lives and should have been capable of affecting, inspiring and changing them. But the question could not pass his lips. Instead he kissed his mother good night and went to his own room.

He lay awake for the greater part of the night—a very unusual occurrence where he was concerned—and yet he felt extraordinarily alive and fresh as the car took him away in the darkness to the station for the first part of his journey. They were held up for a few hours by the fog and on his arrival in London Tally only had time to go to his flat to have a bath and change before he was due to pick up Jean.

His flat was all ready for him; the fire was lit in the grate and his evening clothes were laid out. It was only ten minutes to eight as he came out of his bedroom into the hall. His man was waiting for him, his evening coat over his arm.

"The car is downstairs, m'lord."

"Good," Tally said and held out his arm for the coat.

"I don't know whether you knew, m'lord, but the lift man tells me that Miss MacLeod called for her suitcase. I was not here at the time, so I thought I ought to mention it."

"Which suitcase?" Tally asked.

"The one you left here before you went to Switzerland, m'lord; a little black one. You said something about it not being wanted again; but it was full, so I left it in the hall pending your instructions."

"Yes, of course! I remember now."

Tally recalled both the suitcase and the fact that it was the one which contained Jean's discarded clothes. Why had she fetched it? he wondered. He gave himself various explanations as the car, driven by a chauffeur, took him towards Betty's house; but he was still wondering a little at Jean's action when finally without waiting for the chauffeur to open the car door he jumped out to ring the bell.

John opened the door.

"Good heavens—Tally!" he exclaimed. "I was not expecting to see you!"

"Nor I you," Tally answered. "How are you, John?"

"On top of the wave . . . at the moment."

"When did you get back?" Tally asked, walking into the small hall. "I thought you were in the East."

"I flew home; compassionate leave."

Tally stopped suddenly.

"Is Lizzie all right?"

"She is now," John smiled, "but it has been touch and go."

"I thought she was better."

"She had a relapse," John answered and explained briefly what had happened.

"Poor Betty! I had no idea. I telephoned Jean several nights ago and she said she was better."

"I think it must have happened after that," John said. "Anyway, why are we standing here? Come in and talk to Betty."

Betty was in the drawing room. She was sitting on the sofa with her feet up and was darning a very large hole in a small white sock.

"Tally!" she exclaimed. "Why didn't you let us know you were coming?"

Tally looked surprised.

"Surely Jean told you."

Betty opened her eyes.

"She left a letter for you, but she didn't say you were coming here tonight."

"A letter for me?" Tally echoed. "She is not here then?"

"No."

Betty looked troubled.

"Oh, Tally! Both John and I have been very worried about her. She went away yesterday evening."

"Where to?"

Tally's voice was sharp.

"We have not the slightest idea," Betty replied. "She

just said she had to go. We thought you might know; in fact I started to write to you today."

"What about this letter Jean left me?" Tally inquired.

"It's over there on the desk."

He walked across to it and behind his back John and Betty exchanged anxious glances. John moved on to the hearthrug, his back to the fire.

"I have told Betty not to fuss," he said conversationally. "She has been imagining all sorts of things, but I expect there is some very ordinary explanation. Anyway, you will doubtless be able to explain everything when you have read your letter."

Tally said nothing. He slit open the envelope and stood reading it. After a moment he raised his head.

"You have no idea where she has gone?" he asked, and there was a note in his voice that Betty had not heard there before.

"None," Betty answered. "In fact I was astonished when I came here from the hospital at tea-time, to find that Jean had left. There was a letter for me—you will find it on the desk—in which she says she 'has to go' and asks me to give you your letter and her suitcase."

"What suitcase?" Tally asked.

"The one she came here with," Betty answered. "Its upstairs, and . . . Tally . . . all her clothes are in it."

Her voice broke. John moved to the sofa, bent down and took her hand.

"You are not to worry, darling. She has been through quite enough, Tally, without this. She keeps thinking Jean has committed suicide or something absurd. Knowing Jean, you will realise that such an idea is ridiculous."

"But why should she go away?" Betty asked. "She was happy here with us. She kept saying so."

"Of course she was happy," John answered.

Tally stood still and silent in the centre of the room; very slowly his fingers closed over Jean's letter and then he thrust it deep into the pocket of his dinner-jacket. Still he did not speak and at last Betty cried out once again:

286

"Tally, why should she have gone away?"

"Because she did not want to see me," Tally answered.

Betty gave an exclamation of surprise, but it was obvious that his words were a relief.

"But why? Why shouldn't she want to see you? She loves you, Tally."

"How do you know that?"

Tally almost shot the words at her.

"But of course she does; No one could deceive me, Tally—not where love is concerned. I have loved John too long myself not to know all the symptoms. Jean loves you desperately. I have watched her face when I have talked about you; I have seen the expression in her eyes . . . the way her mouth grew soft and tender at the very mention of your name. Of course she loves you! Now Melia was different. She was never a scrap in love with you. I knew that. She was far too much in love with herself. Jean felt about you as I feel about John. She would have died for you at any moment if you had wanted it . . . as I would for John!"

She looked up at John as she spoke, and he bent down and laid his cheek for a moment against her hair.

"Silly darling," he said, and there was a wealth of tenderness in his voice.

"So she loves me." Tally said very quietly.

He moved from the centre of the room and walked to the fire to lay his arms upon the mantelpiece and stand looking down at the flames.

"But of course she does," Betty answered. "That is why I have been so happy about you, Tally. We have always been a bit afraid—Gerald and I—that you would be married for your title or your money, or just because you are so ridiculously good-looking and so much publicised; but Jean loves you . . . the real you, even as we love you, only much, much more."

Betty's voice died away and then she said in an almost frightened whisper:

"But you should have known all this. What has happened, Tally?"

"I have been a damned fool," he said, without turning round.

"Oh, Tally, you haven't quarrelled with her?"

"No, I have not quarrelled with her," Tally said, straightening his back. "It is a long story, Betty, and I don't want to wait and tell it to you now. What I have got to do is to find Jean. Now, where do you think she has gone?"

"Where could she go?" Betty asked. "Has she any relations?"

Tally shook his head.

"No, none. Neither here nor in Scotland, at any rate."

He did not mention Patience Plowden, for he knew that this would sidetrack the issue. He wanted to concentrate on immediate action.

"This suitcase," he said at last. "You say it is full of her clothes? What, then, has she taken with her?"

"That is what has upset me so much," Betty said. "I was so worried that I looked into it. I knew most of the clothes she brought here, and Tally . . . she has taken nothing with her except the blue dress and coat that she was wearing when she arrived here from St. Moritz."

"I remember it," Tally said, and his heart sank lower, for he understood now why Jean had fetched the suitcase from his flat.

"But why has she . . . ?" Betty began.

"John," Tally interrupted, and his voice was desperate, "how does one start to find a girl who has disappeared; someone who is hiding and wants to remain hidden?"

"I honestly don't know," John answered. "There's the police, I suppose."

Tally's lips twisted bitterly.

"Can you imagine the publicity? . . . *"Lord Brora loses his fiancée"*—*"Search for the missing bride"* . . . No, John, we have got to do without the police or the newspapers."

"You say she has got no relations?" John asked. "What about friends?"

"If she has any, I don't know who they are."

288

Betty looked frightened.

"Oh, Tally, what can we do? We must do something. Has Jean got any money?"

Tally put his hand up to his forehead.

"That's the question I have been asking myself," he said. "Betty, if any man deserves to be shot, I do."

There was so much contrition in his voice that Betty held out her hand to him.

"Don't, Tally, darling. It will come all right. I somehow feel it will. I only wish I had known before that you and Jean were not as happy together as you might have been. I thought sometimes that she looked sad, and once or twice I suspected that she had been crying. I was so taken up with my own troubles, so worried about Lizzie, that I am afraid I was rather selfish."

"There is nothing for you to reproach yourself with," Tally said sharply. "It is all my fault, Betty. I didn't understand. I didn't know. It is only now I am beginning to see things more clearly, and I am half afraid it is too late."

There was a depth in Tally's voice that neither John nor Betty had heard there before. He had changed from the gay, light-hearted young man to someone immeasurably older, someone stronger and finer, who was facing big issues. There seemed to be nothing they could say to him.

"I am going back to my flat," Tally said. "I am going to get hold of one or two chaps I know and ask them to get busy. I will keep in touch with you, Betty, and if there is anything you can do or anything that you can remember that might help, you will let me know, won't you?"

"Of course I will, Tally and I hope you will find her soon."

"So do I," Tally said, and the very simplicity of his reply was somehow infinitely moving.

Driving back to his flat, Tally faced the truth. He knew now what he told himself he might have realised very much sooner if he had not been half-witted. He loved Jean. He had loved her for some time. She had

289

crept into his life and into his heart, and was there even while superficially he was unaware of it. Now, in the shock of her disappearance, he was aware of an aching sense of loss which told him all too clearly the truth. He loved her.

Now he understood why Melia had seemed unattractive and uninteresting. Now he understood what had brought him hurrying home to England, unable to wait even another few days until his mother and Gerald could come, too. He had wanted Jean; wanted her even while his brain had fought against the idea, trying to remain detached, ready up to the very last moment to produce excuses to explain his actions.

Yes, he wanted her! He thought of her little face turned to his; of her eyes, so expressive both when she was happy and when she was frightened; of her lips, which trembled when she was angry and which parted ecstatically with delight. Lord, what a fool he had been! What an idiot, dense and self-satisfied, not to have realised from the very moment of their meeting that here was the one person worth fighting for! He thought of the time he had wasted pursuing Melia, and of the tears he had caused Jean to shed, and he felt inclined to do himself a violence for being so stupid and so obtuse.

The car drew up at his flat and he told his man to wait. He went up the stairs three at a time, because he could not bear to wait for the lift. Once in the sitting-room, he went straight to the desk and, opening his telephone book, rang up Miss Ames at her private number.

"Is that you, Miss Ames?" he asked, when a voice answered at the other end.

"Oh, it's you, Lord Brora. I didn't know you were back."

"I got back this evening," Tally said. "Now listen, I want two or three of our men to do a job for me. They have got to find someone. Someone who is lost. They have got to be discreet, and at the same time they have got to be intelligent. Whom can we get hold of, and at once?"

Miss Ames thought for a moment.

"There's Robinson," she said. "He is on the telephone; and Minny, you remember him?"

"Yes, of course. He's slow but thorough."

"And let me see . . . what about Yates? I can contact him; he lives near here."

"Good. Can you get the three of them round here within an hour?"

"To your flat?"

"Yes. I can send my car for them, if that would be any help."

"Well, better not send to their houses," Miss Ames said. "The neighbours might talk. Now, let me think. If the car could pick up Robinson and Minny at Hammersmith Broadway it would save time. This part of London is too far off for Yates to connect with them, and he had better find his own way to you."

"Tell the other two that the car will be outside the Tube station, and tell Yates to take a taxi, if necessary," Tally said, and put back the receiver.

He rang down to the porter, asked him to fetch his chauffeur to the house telephone, and gave him his instructions. Then he rang for his servant. When Boles answered the bell he found Tally pacing the room, having forgotten why he rang.

"Would you like something to eat, m'lord . . . as you are not going out to dinner?"

Tally looked at him vaguely, as if for a moment he could not understand what he was saying.

"No, I don't want anything," he said, and then added, "Better bring some beer. I am expecting three of the men here at any moment."

His servant, who had also been a Commando, fetched the beer and four silver tankards, setting them down on the table. Then he said hesitantly:

"Let me help, m'lord."

"Help?" Tally questioned.

"There's a job on, isn't there? I would like to be in on it, m'lord. Things don't happen very often these days, and—"

Tally gave a short laugh without humour in it.

291

"They do to me," he said. "All right, Boles, you are in. I will explain what is wanted when the others arrive."

The man's face lit up.

"Thank you, m'lord," he said gratefully.

Two hours later they all sat round the fire while Tally explained.

"No police, no newspapers," he said. "That is the first consideration. You will have to make inquiries discreetly. I am almost certain that Miss MacLeod will try to find work, either in a typing office or perhaps in a shop. Anyway, she will have to lodge somewhere. It is going to be difficult, but you chaps know how to make inquiries in the neighbourhood. She may be hard up . . . and there is just a chance that she may . . . go to a pawnbroker."

He paused for a moment, as if the subject was embarrassing to him, and then he added, with his voice purposely hard and impersonal:

"The most likely thing she might pawn would be a blue dress and coat made at Michael Sorrel's. It is trimmed with beaver which would have a certain value. You have seen her in it, Boles. Do you remember it?"

"Yes, m'lord," the manservant answered.

"Very well, then, you concentrate on the pawnbrokers."

"Any idea which neighbourhood she might fancy, Guv'nor?" Minny asked.

"None at all," Tally answered, "except that she is certain to avoid Putney. She has been there before."

"Do you think she will have changed her name?"

Minny was a quiet, thin little man, but with a wiriness and strength which had proved a surprise to the enemy on more than one occasion.

"I have thought of that," Tally said, "but I have a feeling that she won't. It is against her nature to lie or prevaricate it she can possibly help it."

He saw Minny nod as though he understood, and suddenly deep within himself he felt his whole being cry out.

"Oh, Jean . . . Jean, how can you do this to me!"

He was brusque and business-like in all he said and did, and yet he had the feeling that all four men to whom he was talking were desperately sorry for him. They understood; and he knew there was no need for them to express in words their faithfulness and devotion.

Only when they had left him, having each promised to go ahead right away and do everything in his power to find Jean, did he feel an utter sense of despair and a feeling of loneliness which was beyond expression. It was a feeling which was to become intensified day by day as the search went on and nothing materialised.

Two days passed, three, four, and finally when Tally spoke to his mother on the telephone he was obliged to confess the truth that he had not seen Jean, and that she had disappeared.

"Disappeared?"

He could not bear the horror in Margaret's voice.

"I am trying to find her," Tally said. "I am doing everything I can, but so far it has been hopeless."

"But, Tally, she must be living somewhere, and she had very little money!"

"How much has she got?" Tally asked.

"I gave her twenty-five pounds," Margaret answered; "but she spent several pounds of it on some flowers for me, and I only discovered a few days ago that she gave one hundred and fifty francs to the chambermaid here for her niece. The girl told me how kind Jean had been to her. Of course, she thought she was rich, and she went to her with some hard-luck story about her niece, who was ill. She asked her to lend her the money, and Jean gave it to her."

"Lord!" Tally exclaimed, "that leaves her practically nothing, because Betty said that she bought Jim several presents when she was with them, and also paid for some coal which the man refused to leave unless he was paid. That means that she could not have had more than two or three pounds with her. This makes things even worse."

"What are you going to do?" Margaret asked.

293

"I suppose we shall have to go to the police," Tally said. "I can't lose her like this."

"Have you any idea why she has disappeared?" Margaret inquired.

"Yes," Tally replied.

His mother asked no more, keeping silent as if she understood that some things were past expression.

"Gerald and I thought of returning next Monday," Margaret went on. "We will manage alone. You are not to come over to us."

"I must have news by then," Tally said.

"I hope you will," Margaret answered. "Take care of yourself, my darling."

She spoke as though she guessed how little he was doing such a thing. He could not sleep, and he spent a great part of the night thinking out new schemes, planning out new ideas, thinking of fresh places where they might make inquiries, of other avenues of investigation.

In the day he worked as hard as his four Commandos. He knocked at the door of hundreds of apartment houses. He visited typing bureaux in the suburbs and in the centre of London, went to employment agencies, asking to see the lists of typists they had on their books, and leaving them bewildered and surprised when he seemed more interested in the applicants' names and addresses than in their qualifications.

Miss Ames was working, too. Tally had felt obliged to tell her what had happened. She had accepted his story quietly and without comment and set to work in her own way, telephoning, inquiring and investigating, keeping a methodical memorandum of everything that was said or done.

By Saturday, Tally was almost desperate. Every day the search went on. Every day he felt more and more discouraged and more and more oppressed by his own impatience. How could he find one girl amongst the millions teeming through the London streets? Besides, Jean might not even be in London. She was not in Glendale. Inquiries had been made there, and one of Tally's men had been sent up to find out anything he could.

Of only one thing was Tally certain, and that was that unless he found Jean he would never know happiness again. All through the long sleepless nights and the busy, energetic days, he had learned in every passing minute how much she meant to him. He cursed himself until his anger died away and left only a dull, aching misery. He knew now that he had had within his grasp the most precious thing that can happen in any man's life, and he had let it go because he had been blind, and because he had not understood its value.

He saw how shallow his personal life had been up to this moment, and he told himself that this was a just punishment for having failed to put the more important things of life in their right perspective. He had not really understood what Margaret meant when she had talked of love, when she had told him what a person must feel who really loves and really needs another. Now he understood. Now the lesson had come to him with a full force that was dynamic. Now he knew that without Jean his life would be a hollow mockery. He realised at last just how much his mother had suffered when she lost Stephen.

The whole world seemed dark and empty because without Jean the sunshine had gone from it. He needed her. She had crept into his heart and possessed it utterly. He kept remembering things she had said, things so simple that he had not understood at the time the wisdom and even the greatness that lay behind them. More than once he found himself quoting: "Unless you become like a little child . . ."

Jean's innocence and her simplicity had been child-like, and yet for Tally his whole kingdom of Heaven lay with her. She was the completion of himself. He knew that now. She was all the things that he was not. United, they would become one, and could strive together towards the nearest thing to perfection that mankind can attain.

It was on the fifth night of the search that Tally finally broke down the last fortress within himself and sank on his knees. He prayed as he had not prayed since

295

he was a child, and with a passion and a fervour which swept away all restrictions and inherent repressions.

He prayed for Jean, for her safety and welfare, and in all humbleness that he might find her and give her happiness. That was what he wanted, to make her happy; and he knew then that, if he could devote his whole life to her, the years, however long, would not be enough.

Every evening about six o'clock the men brought him their reports for the day. They talked over new plans, then they went out again during the evening. Two of them were in jobs, but they worked first thing in the morning, during their lunch hour, and far into the night. They brought their expense accounts, which were not inconsiderable, but Tally paid them without question, and knew that, because they were devoted to him, not one of these men would cheat him of even a halfpenny.

Robinson was the first to arrive on Saturday evening.

"No luck, Guv'nor," he said. "I tried down at the wharfs today. Old Charlie at the King's Arms usually knows if there is anyone new in the district."

Minny had the same story to tell; and Yates, who had been in South London the night before, was merely despondent.

"Thought I was on the track of something," he said, "but it turned out to be a French girl. She had dyed her hair and you never saw such a sight. I says to the chap who had sent me to her, 'Call that a blonde. If that's one, then I'm a Pekinese.' "

Tally turned away impatiently.

"I am afraid, boys," he said, "there is only one thing for it. I shall have to call in the police. I hate to think we have been beaten."

"We will go on trying, Guv'nor," Robinson said.

"I am beginning to think it is not much use—" Tally began, when the door burst open. It was Boles, so excited that he was still wearing his cap.

"I think I have found her, m'lord."

"What?"

Tally stepped forward as the other three men jumped to their feet.

"It was the dress and coat, m'lord. I saw it down in a pawnbroker's in Streatham. I was just coming home, and near as anything I would have missed it. In fact, I was just going to jump on a bus when I saw it out of the corner of my eye, so to speak. I ran back, and there it was hanging up on a stand. I went in. Had a bit of trouble with the man at first; he seemed to think that I must be after stolen goods. It cost me a fiver to get the address out of him, but he gave it to me in the end. He knew the woman who had pawned it. She's a lodging-house keeper."

"Yes, yes, go on," Tally said, as Boles paused both for breath and for effect.

"Well, I went down to the house, 79 Arcadia Road, and when the woman opened the door I asked her if a Miss MacLeod lived there. 'Are you a friend of hers?' she says. 'Not exactly,' I replies, 'but I heard as how she might be interested in a job as a typist.' I didn't want to frighten her, you see, in case she hopped off again before I got to her."

"Quite right," Tally approved. "What did she say?"

"She said Miss MacLeod was ill. 'But she is getting better,' she says, 'and you may be sure she will be glad to have the job. She needs the money,' 'Well, don't say anything to her,' I says, 'in case it raises her hopes unnecessarily. I will get the particulars and be back as soon as I can.'"

Boles was still talking, but Tally was through the door and into the hall.

"What did you say the number was?" he shouted.

"Seventy-nine Arcadia Road, Streatham," Boles replied, and then there was the sound of the flat door slamming sharply.

18

Jean, struggling up for the first time, felt as though her legs were made of cotton-wool as she crept downstairs to sit in front of the fire in Mrs. Lawson's own sitting-room.

The landlady's relations with her newest boarder had undergone many changes since Jean's arrival a week earlier. First, when Jean woke on her first morning in Arcadia Road with a high temperature and a throat so dry that she could only speak in a croaking whisper, Mrs. Lawson had been annoyed.

"You can't be ill here," she said sharply; "I am short-handed as it is, and if you want food in your bedroom you will have to come and fetch it."

"I don't want anything," Jean murmured. "I shall be all right by tomorrow. Please don't worry about me."

Mrs. Lawson, who had come up to Jean's room to find out why she had not appeared at breakfast, stamped out, muttering furiously to herself.

"I've only got one pair of hands," she declared, to no one in particular, "and people that's ill should go to hospitals."

She made no effort to go near Jean for the rest of the day; but by the evening either her curiosity or her heart prevailed upon her to climb the stairs. Jean was lying very still, with her eyes closed and her skin hot and dry. There was a bright, unnatural colour in her cheeks, and it was obvious to the most casual observer that she was running a temperature.

"Look here," Mrs. Lawson said, "it's against my principles to wait on anyone, especially those on the top floors, but I will bring you up a glass of hot milk when I come to bed, and a couple of aspirins."

Jean thanked her weakly. She felt so ill that she was past caring what happened or what was said to her. The next day she was no better, and though it was obviously a struggle with her conscience, against what had, until now, been a strictly kept rule, Mrs. Lawson came to see her twice during the day, bringing her on the second occasion some tea and buttered toast.

Jean was grateful for the tea, but the toast stuck in her throat and she could not swallow it. By the end of the day her breathing was laboured, and she had a sharp pain in her side which hurt her every time she drew a breath.

"If you are not better in the morning I shall have to send for a doctor," Mrs. Lawson said grudgingly. "I don't know what's wrong with you."

"It is only a bad chill," Jean gasped. "I got so dreadfully wet the night I came here."

"Where did you come from?" Mrs. Lawson asked curiously, but she was not much wiser when Jean told her it was "near Oxford Street."

The doctor came the following morning, fetched by a worried Mrs. Lawson. Jean's appearance as she looked in on her way down to breakfast had really horrified her, and she was agitated by the idea that a death among her lodgers would bring the house ill-luck.

"It is nothing serious," the doctor reassured her, after he had examined Jean. "Nothing, in fact, that careful nursing and regular doses of M. and B. won't cure. I hate to mention the word pleurisy, but we have got to watch out for it."

"I can't nurse her here, doctor," Mrs. Lawson said. "You know that, as well as I do. I have got the house full, and only a girl of fifteen to help me, and the lord knows she's more trouble than she's worth."

"Well, I can't get Miss MacLeod into hospital," the doctor replied. "We are absolutely packed out and just as short-staffed as you are. Be a sport, Mrs. Lawson, and do your best. She is a pretty little thing, and if you don't get your reward in this life, you will get it in Heaven."

Mrs. Lawson sniffed, but she was mollified enough by the doctor's banter to allow a faint smile to twist the corner of her lips.

"Heaven's about the only place where I will get rewarded," she said tartly. "I know her sort; no more than a week's wages on them, and the only capital they have is their health and strength."

The doctor laughed.

"If I hadn't known you for a great number of years, Mrs. Lawson, I would believe you were a hard woman; but as it is, I know you are the last person to turn that child into the street."

"Then you know too much," Mrs. Lawson retorted, "and none of it to my advantage."

All the same, she toiled upstairs after he had gone, tidied Jean's room in a haphazard manner, and saw to it that she took the tablets four-hourly as the doctor had prescribed.

"I'm so terribly sorry to be a nuisance," Jean said miserably.

"I am not going to say it isn't a trouble," Mrs. Lawson said. "There's the old lady in the first floor front room down with rheumatism, ringing her bell as though I had a staff of footmen to wait on her; and there's Miss Moffat, on the ground floor, that has been ordered a special diet! 'A special diet'!—I ask you; where am I to find the time to fiddle about with fancy dishes—I can't abide invalids, and that's a fact."

"I will help you as soon as I am better," Jean promised her, and there was something so sincere and honest in her voice that Mrs. Lawson softened.

"You will be all right in a day or two, dear. Nobody can help getting knocked up occasionally. My husband was just the same when he was alive. He would come over queer all sudden-like. Bright as a cricket one moment, and then so weak the next that you could have knocked him down with a feather."

"There is one thing I was going to ask you," Jean said, and now her voice was timid and faltering.

"What is it?" Mrs. Lawson asked, and added ominously, "I can't stop long; I put the supper on before I came upstairs, and that girl will let it burn under her nose. She never notices when anything is wrong."

"It is about money . . ." Jean whispered, and then hesitantly, not daring to look at the darkening expression on Mrs. Lawson's face, she went on. "There will be the doctor to pay, and I owe you for food and the medicines he ordered me. Do you think you could possibly pawn or sell something for me?"

"What is it?" Mrs. Lawson asked.

"It's a dress and coat," Jean replied.

Mrs. Lawson's eyes turned towards Jean's tweed coat and skirt which were hanging on a hook behind the door.

"No, it's not like that," Jean said quickly, before she could speak. "It's a *Michael Sorrel* model, and it is trimmed with real beaver. I think it ought to be worth quite a lot."

"Let's have a look at it," Mrs. Lawson suggested, without much hope in her voice.

"It is in my suitcase," Jean told her.

Mrs. Lawson drew the suitcase from under the bed, threw back the lid, and took out the blue dress and fur-trimmed coat. Against the background of the dingy, ugly-patterned linoleum and the general sordid poverty of the room, it looked strangely out of place and beautiful. Mrs. Lawson's lips were pursed together as if she might have whistled.

"Where on earth did you get this?" she asked.

"It was given me," Jean replied.

Mrs. Lawson shot her a quick glance from under narrowed eyelids. Jean knew what she was thinking. She flushed a little, but decided that explanations might make things even worse that they appeared already.

"There is a hat to match," she said.

Mrs. Lawson found it in the case and held it up.

302

"Well, it is certainly very tasty," she approved. "Must have cost a pretty penny, too, when it was new."

She looked at the label, embroidered flamboyantly with Michael Sorrel's signature, on the back of the coat.

"You ought to get enough for this to carry you on for a week or two, at any rate."

"If you would take it to a . . . a pawnbroker for me, I would be . . . very . . . very grateful," Jean stammered.

"I don't see as how I can do anything else, seeing as what you owe me."

Mrs. Lawson picked up the dress and coat, putting them over her arm, and having slammed down the case, gave it a kick so that it slid along the linoleum and was hidden under the bed.

"I will take these tomorrow morning when I go shopping," she promised. "Good night, and don't forget to take your tablets last thing."

"No, I won't," Jean answered, "and thank you so much."

"Don't thank me until we hear how much you are in hand on this lot," Mrs. Lawson retorted, and she shut the door sharply behind her.

Jean closed her eyes. It hurt her strangely to see her blue dress and coat going away in Mrs. Lawson's arms. They were her last link with Tally. Now they were gone, she felt absolutely abandoned and alone. Nothing remained of the past, except her memories and her love for him. Those, indeed, were, if anything, intensified. She had thought in St. Moritz that her love had reached a climax in which all her being yearned for him, and was so utterly possessed by the thought of him that it was not possible to care more deeply; yet now in her loneliness and isolation she knew that being cut off not only from the sight and sound of Tally himself, but also from those people who had known him, could wound her afresh, so that her thoughts and imaginations were even more agonising in their empty longing.

More than once she asked herself whether she had been right to go away, whether it would not have been

303

wiser to wait until Tally arrived; but even when she felt so ill that she thought she must die, even when she was so unhappy that her whole body was shaken with the violence of her tears, she knew the pain was as nothing compared with what she would have felt had she been obliged to listen to Tally saying "Good-bye."

No, she had done the right thing, not only from her own point of view, but from his, too. It would have been an uncomfortable moment for him, although he had no idea that she loved him. Even when he was most ruthless, Jean knew that Tally had moments of tenderness, moments when he hated to hurt people or to be unkind. Anything that was weak and fragile could command his compassion; that was why he loved children and animals, and it was also, perhaps, Jean thought whimsically, the reason why he had been so kind to her.

Once he had said to her half-jokingly: "I only fight people of my own size," and she had understood from that that he counted Melia as his equal. She was not in that category, and she knew it was not only because of her small, and what she considered her insignificant appearance, but because in many ways Tally treated her as though she were a child.

He would have been sorry for me, she thought now, and decided that his pity would have been too humiliating to be contemplated. No, things were better as they were, even though at times she cried out in the darkness. She tried to tell herself that her utter depression was due, in a large part, to her being ill, but even so it was difficult to decide where the bodily and mental pains divided themselves. At times it seemed to Jean that she was just one large aching agony for which there could never be any cure.

On his third visit the doctor, unaware that he was treating a broken heart, pronounced that she was better, and the best thing she could do would be to make an effort to get up. Accordingly Jean dragged herself downstairs, wishing as she went that she could shut her eyes and die, rather than attempt to live and feel so ill. Mrs. Lawson was unexpectedly kind.

"Now, sit down by the fire, dear, and here is a rug to put over your knees. This is my own sitting-room, and nobody will disturb you. I had to have one hole and corner which I could call my own, though if the lodgers had their way they would take this from me, too. Many is the time they have asked if they could have this as a Bridge room, but my answer has always been the same: 'Whiles I own this house,' I says, 'I will have this bit of privacy, and they that don't want that can go elsewhere.' Don't you think I'm right?"

"I'm sure you are," Jean answered, leaning back in the armchair and thankful that she must force her legs to go no farther.

"Now, dear, you may get a glint of sun later in the afternoon," Mrs. Lawson went on. "I would have liked a room which faced south; but there it is, the lodgers have to have the best. Not that they are grateful for it. I will bring you a cup of tea a bit later on, and if you have your supper down here, it will save me bringing it upstairs to you. The doctor said I was to feed you up, and I promised him I would do my best."

"You are much too kind to me," Jean said. "I am ashamed of being such a nuisance to you."

Mrs. Lawson knelt down and poked the fire.

"To tell you the truth," she said, in a surprisingly soft voice, "you remind me of my daughter. She was ten when she died, knocked down by a lorry in the main High Street, but I suppose she would have been about your age now. It is not often that I thinks of her, but there is something in the way you speak and the way you turn your head. She was a pretty child, and I was that cut up at the time I thought I would never get over it."

"It must have been a terrible shock," Jean said sympathetically.

"It was, that," Mrs. Lawson replied briefly. "I told myself after that I would never be sentimental again about anything or anybody, but . . . there's no fool like an old fool."

She got to her feet and slammed the poker down on the hearth.

"I can't stay here talking to you. I have got too much to do."

She hurried from the room, but not before Jean had seen a suspicion of tears in her eyes. Jean gave a little sigh.

What a lot of unhappiness there was in the world, and yet people were amazingly kind! She knew what a burden and trouble she had been to Mrs. Lawson since she came here. Thank goodness she could afford to pay for everything. Mrs. Lawson had managed to get eight pounds for the dress, coat and hat—a sum which was laughable when one thought of the prices Michael Sorrel charged his customers. But eight pounds from a second-hand clothes shop in Streatham seemed to be a fortune, and Mrs. Lawson had been suitably impressed.

"At least it spares me any anxiety for the moment," Jean thought, "and next week I must start looking for a job."

She wondered how long she must go on hiding from Tally, and if he would really make an effort to get in touch with her. Somehow she felt that he would accept her desire to be left alone, and after a few perfunctory inquiries would forget her very existence. That, she told herself severely, would be the sensible thing for him to do; and yet she could not help wishing, perhaps hoping, that he would be more concerned.

He would want to give her a present, that would be like his generosity. He might leave instructions with Miss Ames and anyone else with whom she was likely to come in contact that if she would communicate with him she would hear something to her advantage. Oh, well, if the worst came to the worst, and she was really starving, she supposed she could write to Tally and ask him for his assistance for old times' sake. If this happened in ten years' time or more, he would be married, and perhaps have a number of children. It was not difficult to imagine him at Greystones, with his son running after him through the park, and a daughter waiting for him at the top of the big staircase.

Tally would be very sweet with his children. There

306

was no doubt that Jim and Lizzie loved him, and it was not only because he had brought them big and expensive toys. There was something about him which captured their imagination . . . "even as he has captured mine," Jean said to herself.

On the wall beside her was a small oval-framed mirror. She glanced into it and wondered what Tally would think if he could see her now. Her face had grown very thin during her illness. There was almost a look of transparency about her. Her eyes seemed abnormally large, and the only colour about her was the burnished gold of her hair, falling to her shoulders. She had an old white woollen shawl of Mrs. Lawson's round her shoulders, and the whole effect was one of a pitiful waif who needed both love and care.

Jean gave a deep sigh.

"I wish I had died," she said suddenly out loud.

What was there to look forward to? What, indeed, did the future hold for her? She thought how often she had considered the future when she had been enjoying the present. She had always known that this moment would come when she would be alone, and everything she cared for was in the past, and there was only a grey blankness ahead.

She closed her eyes, as if she would shut out the horizons stretching before her. She must have fallen asleep, for when she awoke the room was in darkness and the fire was sinking. The glint of sunshine which Mrs. Lawson had promised her must have come and gone, and the night had fallen. Jean could hear the soft patter of the rain against the window panes. After some minutes the door opened, and Mrs. Lawson came in.

"Oh, you are all in the dark," she exclaimed, switching on the light. "I told that girl to come and pull the blinds, and don't tell me she didn't bring you any tea?"

"I didn't want any," Jean said quickly. "I have been asleep."

"I will murder her one day, that I will," Mrs. Lawson said viciously, pulling the curtains across the dark windows with a jingle of rings. "I had to go out, that is why

I didn't come myself. I said to her: 'Take Miss MacLeod her tea, make up the fire, and pull the curtains.' But I don't suppose she listened to a word. I would just as soon have a lunatic in the kitchen, I would, really."

Mrs. Lawson put some coal on the fire.

"Supper is just coming in," she went on. "I have got some hot supper for you, and it's fish tonight. Cod, of course, but I have done it in a pie. I'm sure you will fancy a bit."

"Thank you," Jean answered.

But the supper, when it came, was tasteless, and although Jean made an effort to eat, she could only force a few mouthfuls down her throat. Mrs. Lawson came and fetched away her tray.

"There, now," she said, "you haven't eaten enough to keep a sparrow alive. Would you like a cup of tea? I am going to have one."

"It would be nice," Jean said, "and after that I think I had better be getting back to bed."

"Are you feeling bad again?" Mrs. Lawson asked.

"No," Jean answered; "but I don't want to be in your way. I know you sit here in the evening and like to be alone."

"You needn't move for me," Mrs. Lawson said decidedly. "I'm glad to have you here, and as it happens I have got quite a lot to do this evening. The second floor back left this afternoon, and I have go to get the room tidied up. There is a new lodger arriving first thing tomorrow morning. Coming down from the North, and if the train is punctual he will be here at half-past eight."

"What a bother for you to do it tonight," Jean said.

Mrs. Lawson shrugged her shoulders.

"Beggars can't be choosers," she said. "You have to learn to take things as they come."

Jean thought there was a lot of truth in that. She had got to learn to take things as they came. It would be no use her complaining or finding fault with the vagaries of Fate.

She sipped the strong, lukewarm tea which Mrs.

Lawson brought her, and tried not to think of tea as it had been served to her last week. It was no use making comparisons; she had got to get herself into the frame of mind when life could become an adventure again. She had felt it was that when she came south from Glendale. She had sat in the railway carriage, gazing out of the window, feeling that every milestone brought her nearer to something exciting, to a new world in which anything might happen. Well, things had happened to her, and now she was complaining.

"I am ashamed of myself," Jean said out loud.

There was so much for which she might be grateful. For Tally, first of all; for the love and affection she had felt for Betty and for Margaret Melton. She was grateful, too, that the heavy burden of secrecy had slipped from her shoulders when she met her mother and realised that there was no bad blood in her.

One day, not yet, when she was brave enough to face Tally and Tally's friends, she would write to her mother and ask if she might see her. She might even swear her to secrecy so that she could go out to Switzerland to her, and yet Tally might never know. At the present time too much was involved; there would be too many explanations; and besides, Tally might ask Patience Plowden to help him in finding her daughter.

Jean remembered the expression that "time heals everything." In time even her unhappiness and loneliness might heal, and then she would be glad to see her mother again, and talk to her and perhaps find a real friend in the woman who had suffered and who was soon to die.

Yes, she had a great deal to be grateful for, a great deal for which to thank God.

"I must never, never have any regrets," Jean whispered to herself.

At that moment the door opened. Mrs. Lawson was standing there.

"There's a gentleman to see you, dear," she said; and even as she spoke someone pushed past her and came into the room.

He stood there looking at her, and it seemed to Jean that he was bigger and better-looking than she had remembered, or perhaps it was just in contrast to the smallness and shabbiness of the room. She heard the door close behind Mrs. Lawson, and they were alone. But she could say nothing, nor make any movement, save that her hands crept tremblingly upwards to cross themselves over the white shawl.

At last Tally spoke, and his voice was hoarse.

"You have been ill?"

"Yes."

She could only whisper the word.

"Why didn't you let me know? Why did you go away?"

Jean thought that there was a strange note in his voice as he asked the question. It was not the imperative tone which she remembered so well, it was rather as if he pleaded with her for an explanation, and yet there was something more . . . something emotional, something which made her whole being vibrate, pulsating.

She had no words in which to answer his questions. It was too difficult to know what to say. The blood was pounding in her ears, and she felt a strange excitement creeping over her . . . an excitement so seductive, so sweet, that she must fight for a stern control over herself.

He came nearer to her, crossing the room until he stood by her chair, looking down at her.

"You have been ill," he repeated, as if he spoke to himself.

"I am better," Jean answered.

"You have driven me nearly mad," Tally said. "I have searched all London for you."

"Why?" Jean's eyes widened as she looked up at him.

"Do you want to know the answer to that?" he inquired.

She looked away quickly. There was something strange in his eyes, something she had never seen there before; something which startled and disconcerted her.

310

"I am sorry if I have been a nuisance," she said quiveringly. "I thought it was best."

"For whom?" Tally asked. "For you or for me?"

"For you, of course," Jean answered quickly. "I knew that you didn't want me any more; my job was finished, and——"

"Who said I didn't want you any more?" he interrupted.

With an effort Jean forced herself to look at him.

"I thought . . ." she faltered, "that . . . you . . . and . . . Miss Melchester . . ."

"Melia has nothing to do with it," Tally said.

"Oh, then she won't——"

"Melia is going to marry Ernest Danks," Tally said quickly and impatiently, as if it was all very unimportant, "we may expect the announcement of the engagement very shortly. I expect you saw that the Prime Minister died three days ago."

"No, I didn't see it," Jean murmured.

"But before that," Tally went on, "before I left St. Moritz I had learned something which you and my mother were wise enough to see very clearly; that Melia didn't love me, and I didn't love Melia."

"But I thought you did!" Jean gasped.

"I didn't know very much about love then," Tally said, and quite unexpectedly he knelt down beside Jean's chair.

She gave a little convulsive sound, half astonishment and half fear, and then she was very still, as though she were frightened to move, frightened that this was only a dream, and she might wake up. Tally did not touch her; he just knelt there looking at her, his face on a level with hers.

"I want to ask you a question," he said softly.

Jean was trembling, but her eyes were on his face.

"Yes?"

"I want you to tell me the truth," Tally said. "No . . . I needn't ask that . . . somehow I think you always tell the truth. It is one of the amazing things about you. This is very important, and because it is so important I know you won't lie to me."

"No, I won't lie," Jean repeated.

"Then tell me," Tally said, and his voice deepened, "do you love me, Jean?"

Her face went deadly pale and then a deep crimson flush spread over it, flooding slowly and painfully until it reached her eyes, which suddenly filled with tears. But because of some fierce pride within herself she would not flinch or turn away. Tally's eyes held hers and softly, in an almost inarticulate whisper, she answered him.

"Yes . . . I do."

"But why? In God's name, why . . . when I have behaved so badly to you?"

"I can't help it," Jean said brokenly. "I just love you . . . terribly."

"Oh, Jean!" Tally cried, and his voice was vibrant, "now at last I know what I ought to have known ages ago. We belong to each other."

She looked at him wonderingly, but still she did not understand. He saw her bewilderment and bending forward, he put his arms about her and drew her close.

"I love you," he said gently, "I love you completely and absolutely as you were meant to be loved. You are mine, and you cannot escape from me any longer. I have wanted many things in my life, Jean, but never anything as much as I want you now."

He held her closely, and at last the amazement which had seemed to hold her spellbound seemed to break, and she could speak.

"Oh, Tally!"

Her head was against his shoulder and her face up-turned to his. For a moment he looked down into the darkness of her eyes, at the tears which lay glittering on her cheeks, and at her mouth, which was trembling.

"Oh, my darling," he said, and then his lips were on hers.

For a moment Jean felt as though she must faint; then suddenly the sheer ecstasy of it crept over her like a burning flame. His kiss seemed to draw her very soul from her body. She was joined to him, united to him, They were one as they had been together only in her dreams.

Tenderly Tally drew her to her feet, holding her closely in his arms and lifting her until she lay against his heart.

"You are mine," he said, and he kissed her again. His lips touched first her mouth, then her eyelids, and lastly the pulse beating wildly in the whiteness of her throat.

"I love you! I love you!" he repeated, and there was something more than tenderness in his tone. "Oh, Jean, how mad I was not to have known it sooner, not to have realised from the first moment I saw you that you were my woman . . . mine for all time!"

It was then that Jean realised that she was awake, and this was no dream. She hid her face against his shoulder. She felt the strength of his arms, the fierce possessiveness of his lips, and yet she was not afraid. This was the man she loved, and she knew that together they would find happiness, because in their love they were one and indivisible.

She was quivering, every nerve in her body alive with delight and wonder. Tally put his hand under her chin and turned her face up to his.

"You are not to look away from me," he said masterfully. "What are you thinking about?"

"You."

"Do you still love me?"

"You know the answer to that."

"But I want to hear you say it."

Now she was shy. Shy, not because of her love for him, but because of his for her.

"Tell me," Tally commanded.

He took his arms from her suddenly, so that she almost fell, and she had to reach out her hand to support herself against the back of a chair. Wrapped in the white shawl, she was very small and pathetic looking; and then suddenly she felt afraid, insecure . . . this must, after all, be just a dream . . . a figment of her delirious imagination.

"Tally!"

There was a desperate appeal in her cry, and he understood.

"But I want to look at you," he said, "you are so small, and yet you hold in your hands all my happiness, and all the things I shall ever want of life. Oh, Jean, be kind to me and help me. Only through your love shall I understand what is worth while, and seek that which is highest and best."

It was a cry of utter sincerity, and as she heard it Jean's fear left her. She held out both her hands.

"Tally, my darling, of course I will help you . . . if you want me."

"If I want you," he repeated, and she was in his arms again. "Look at me," he commanded.

She threw back her head to meet his eyes, and then at last she understood all that would be demanded of her. She saw deep down in his eyes the burning soul of a man who would demand much but in return would give much. Their way would not always be easy, but love would bridge every torrent and provide a shelter against every hurricane.

For a long, exquisite moment they looked at each other, and they saw the spiritual needs one of the other, and knew that in that moment they came very near to heaven.

Then human nature broke under the strain. Once again Tally took Jean up in his arms; his kisses became more possessing, more demanding. They bruised her mouth, and yet she gloried in it. This was love—passionate, burning and demanding. She could not offer less than absolute surrender in this moment of victory.

"I love you," she heard Tally say, and her own voice, faint and shy, yet triumphant, echoed his:

"I love you, Tally."

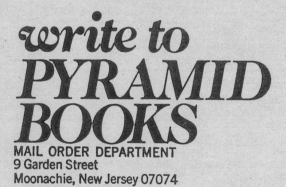